ELEMENTS OF ROYALTY
BOOK ONE

PRINCESS OF AIR

NATALIE CAMMARATTA

PRINCESS OF AIR

ELEMENTS OF ROYALTY BOOK ONE

NATALIE CAMMARATTA

Cover by Seventhstar Art

Edited by Gray Plume Editing and The Fiction Fix

1st Edition 2024

https://www.nataliewritesthebooks.com

For anyone who isn't sure which crown to don.
Wear the one that makes you shine.

Chapter One

Thin cushions of air catch my feet as I creep down the hall. My shoes don't hit the floor, and I make no sound. Creating the buffers beneath each footfall takes little effort. The air around me practically anticipates my wishes like a well-trained pet. Mother says it's because I don't force it, that being friendly with elements makes them more cooperative.

Noises ring through the palace as servants clear breakfast trays and clean every already-pristine surface. They'll be busier than usual today. Even the small family celebration of the prince's birthday is a special occasion. After all, this is the precursor to the coronation to officially mark him as the heir—the very reason I float toward his chamber now. Past paintings in gilded frames and ancient tapestries, I approach my target in silence. A flick of my hand slides a wall of wind under the door, encasing the entryway. I open the door and close it behind myself.

Prince Rylan sits at his desk facing the window. He's likely engrossed by some report or something, confident in his belief that no one can sneak up on him. It's adorable.

Wind chimes tinkle delicately over my head—a rather useless alarm from within my shield. *You'll have to do better than that to catch me.*

I still the air around them and drop the shield. My lips press together as the anticipation reaches its peak.

"Happy birthday!" The air works with me to amplify my voice.

Rylan jumps up, throwing the chair halfway across the room. The entire palace shudders with his shock; his green eyes are like saucers when he wheels on me. "Gods, Ara! We've talked about this!"

I collapse onto a featherbed of air in a fit of laughter.

"It's not amusing."

Between chortles, I say, "Oh, but it is. Your face..." Wall hangings continue to sway slightly from the quake. If I weren't already tearing up, I'd cry from sheer pride.

The door swings open, and two figures appear. "What happened?" Marcus demands.

"Arabella happened."

"Arabella can't *shake* the palace." Nina sighs and glances at the wind chime. "When did she figure out how to get past your alarm?"

Rylan crosses his arms and glowers at me. "I was about to ask her that."

Another fit of giggles totters my shoulders until a shock of cold water hits my face. I gasp and jump to my feet. "Marcus, that was completely unnecessary!"

"Everything *you* do is unnecessary. Perhaps I'm learning from your example."

Ry rights his chair and sinks onto it. "Of all of us, *Arabella* is the sibling you want to emulate?"

I pull a warm gust to dry my face and run my hands through my damp locks, blowing heated air through the strands to evaporate the water. "Silly Marcus, there's only one among us worth modeling yourself after, and he is your future king."

Rylan rolls his eyes. "What do you want, Ara?"

"To bring you a gift, *of course*. It is your birthday, and I am your favorite sister."

"No, you aren't."

"Well, at least I'm Nina's favorite sister."

"Having no other options will do that." Nina smooths her yellow dress as she sits by the vacant hearth. A fire springs to life without wood or kindling.

"Nina." Rylan's voice takes on an annoyed sense of authority. "It's too warm for that."

"Ara?"

The request is understood without her voicing it. I cool the room so we can all be content. As much as my brothers and sister complain of the turmoil I cause, I'm always the one to clear the air between us.

We fall into a routine without any cues: Marcus fills the kettle with a snap of his fingers, I float it over Nina's fire, and Rylan pulls some leaves from one of the many plants in his sitting room.

"Aside from a heart attack," Ry says as they wither and dry in his palm, "what *is* my birthday gift? Shall I don armor before receiving it?"

I waft the dried leaves into cups on the table near the fireplace. "Armor would be about as useful against me as your ridiculous wind chimes. Here." I flick my fingers toward him, forming an airy halo atop his head.

"What is this?" He pats his hands along it gingerly.

"A cushion for your new crown. I wouldn't want it flattening your lovely curls or straining your princely neck."

"Despite the irritating way you present it, this is actually a nice gift. The weight of the crown will be less when I have my second favorite sister around."

"Not only when I'm around. It will maintain itself even if I'm away from it."

All eyes fall on me. My siblings can't leave their elements to follow orders from a distance. It did take quite a bit of work to keep it stable.

I shrug innocently. "You all think I play with my power for fun, but it's called practice."

Fire dances in Nina's eyes. "Does Mother have any control over air anymore?"

"This isn't about me. It's Rylan's birthday—"

"Answer!"

I sigh. "No. It's all mine."

Each of us is leaching our mother's powers. We have been our entire lives. As Rylan's ability to control earth strengthens, Mother's weakens. The same with the twins' water and fire. They shouldn't be jealous of me. We all know air was Mother's weakest ability. She never had a knack for it like I do. It's an effort for her to grow a tree now while Rylan can raise a forest. Nina and

Marcus are improving every day. They'll transfer all their power soon enough.

"That's wonderful, Ara." Rylan's smile is tight.

Guilt pools in my chest. I really hadn't meant to take his spotlight. "Enough about that." I grab the kettle by hand and pour boiling water into the cups. Now would be a bad time to flaunt my magic. "What does a soon-to-be-crowned heir do for fun?"

"Seek revenge against his mischievous little sister?" His head tilts as though he's plotting.

I grin and blow the balcony door open, content to leave the tea and this conversation behind. "Only if you can catch me." A strong gust carries me out into the warm spring day.

Free to tumble through the air is how I'm meant to live, like a leaf going anywhere the wind takes me. But a princess cannot live that way. It's almost a shame our magic is bound to the right to rule. The people who have control of the elements should be free to live amongst them. Instead, we're revered and set on thrones in a palace. Although, when I twirl about to look back at it, there are worse places to live.

Vines climb higher along the tower toward Rylan's balcony, forming a grand living staircase which he descends with more courtliness than the occasion merits. Meanwhile, the river flowing past the palace shoots upward, giving the twins a slide of water on which to get outside. Much more appropriate for the mood.

Mirador Palace is a reflection of the magic that passes through our family, keeping the elements close and allowing them to flow through it. It's a portrait of our kingdom as well. Alchos is as beautiful as the graceful slopes of the palace's domed roofs. Our people are as colorful as the city that stretches out before the palace, with minds as open and accepting as Mirador is to nature.

Alchos has my heart completely. I'd do anything for this kingdom. Except it hadn't occurred to me that the thing it would need me to do is leave.

I sigh and shake off the premature mourning. More than half a year has passed since that decision was made, and we still don't have a date for it. It may be quite a while, and regardless, I want to enjoy it here while I can. Landing in the soft grass far behind the palace, I wait for my siblings. I will either make sure they miss me terribly after I move away or make them eager to be rid of me. Either way, I'm in the mood for some fun.

Chapter Two

The dinner is much like any other. We all dress a little finer, and the decor is heightened, floral garlands and thick greenery bedecking the room for the Prince of Earth. An artistic assortment of leafy plants serpentines down the center of the table. Ry, Mother, and Grandfather almost certainly know each species of flora, but the rest of us seated here can probably only identify them as plants.

Both sets of grandparents are here to celebrate Ry with us. And it does feel like a celebratory day again now that my siblings and I had time to relax and blow off steam. Of course, even that came with some turmoil. It wouldn't be us without that.

Across the table, Nina twists to thank the servant who fills her wine glass. The scrape on her shoulder is covered by a swath of fabric, so we can avoid that reprimand. During our afternoon out, I did catch her in a net of air, but not before she got a little banged up. Somehow, she was less upset with Ry for dropping the ground out from beneath our feet than she was at the fact that I didn't fall at all. Then Marcus accused me of showing off by catching Nina when he had created a perfectly acceptable spring for her to fall into.

This is exactly why I hadn't told them I came into my full power. The sooner they all take theirs, the better.

While my ridiculous siblings grumble about having slightly *less* power than me, half the table has no such ability. No one without magic complains at all, yet those who do squabble over how much. Well, Mother's father may not complain, but not having magic is the reason he's always so grumpy. He waves a servant over to refill his glass. Amber liquor swirls around as he brings it to his lips, then a discontented sigh escapes him after he takes a sip. Before he has the chance to ask for it, another servant rushes to him with a glass of ice cubes.

To the staff, it's an eccentric preference of the former king, but it's one of the many things he can no longer do himself. Grandfather has been without magic for over two decades, but the loss of it still lingers. I'm not sure if anyone else notices these little things like I do. So many little disappointments when he starts to do something but realizes he can't. Magic departing slowly seems like it would make it easier, but I understand. My magic is so deeply ingrained in me that I can't imagine the hollowness it will leave behind when it passes to my own child someday.

Air braids through my fingers without me making a conscious effort—a little reminder of my magic which only I can sense. Are the scraps of power Mother still holds enough to keep her from feeling the same listlessness as Grandfather?

Her smile is natural and warm as she chats and laughs with the family over the remnants of our final course. It doesn't appear to bother her. Not that I should be surprised—nothing rattles the Queen of Alchos. Her beauty is renowned, though most of the kingdom never gets to see her relaxed. It's times like these when she's most stunning. These times also remind me that I'm the only one who doesn't bear much resemblance to her. Her dark hair has its variations through my siblings: rich brown on Rylan, Nina's with hints of red, and Marcus' hair is so black it's nearly blue. My golden locks leave me standing out in a way I've never much enjoyed. Less so tonight with our father's parents here. I take after the Valnora side of the family.

"You let them forget their places," Grandfather grumbles. I can only relegate such conversations to background noise for so long before some things get through. Boring though they may be. "The ministry are only higher-ranking servants to the crown. Do not let them think they have their own power."

Mother's bright countenance remains in place. "Father, I cannot hope to manage the entire kingdom myself. The purpose of having trusted people in the ministry is to alleviate the burden on me, and they can't do anything helpful if they don't have some power." The appointed members of the ministry give a voice to Alchosians outside the aristocracy. It's still a bold concept to our former king.

"Illiam," Grand Mama says, "you forget that you too had well-trusted advisors during your rule." She makes a graceful gesture between herself and Grand Papa, bracelets clinking against each other delicately. Silvery gray blends in with her golden locks enough to mask her age. That'll be a helpful side effect of inheriting my hair color from Father's family.

Grandfather takes another sip of his drink. "You're family. That's different."

"They weren't at the time, dear." Only Grandmother can correct someone who had been a sovereign without making him prickly. She carries the elegance and charm of someone born to be a queen in her gentle manners and unshakable confidence. One could easily forget she had married into it.

I don't know if I can be like her.

"Is it the ministry giving you trouble?" Rylan asks. While I try to block out such conversations, he's been badgering Mother about court business more and more.

"We can discuss that after cake," Father says.

Finally. I had been pulling a breeze from that direction, hoping the sweet smell of chocolate would entice someone to initiate dessert.

"Yes, please." Nina lights the tapers on the cake from across the room without so much as glancing at it, possibly attempting to bolster her self-esteem.

"Why can't we discuss it over cake?" Of course, Ry won't be so easily distracted. He'll be in these ministry meetings soon enough, so I don't understand the rush. Once he's the official crowned heir, he'll have to be present for all of it. If it were me, I'd stay away from all such business until it was required.

Mother sighs. "It isn't exactly dessert conversation, dear."

Well, *that's* a good way to pique everyone's interest.

"What happened?" Marcus asks.

Loving—albeit worried—gazes scan us. Grandfather shoots a pointed glare at Mother, then Mother and Father look at each other. "It's only slightly sooner than we'd planned," he says.

Mother frowns as she looks about the room then rolls her shoulders back. What's about to come isn't from our mother—it's from the Queen of Alchos. "There has been a growing sense of unease throughout the kingdom. Anti-magic sentiments are bleeding in through our border with Penum. People are finding it more difficult to trust us."

Nina rolls her eyes. "Doesn't King Kirnon feel at all embarrassed by his obvious jealousy?"

The thin, snake-like shape of Penum slithering up the west coast always seemed fitting. Tucked as they are between mountains and ocean, one would think they wouldn't be so irksome, but this nuisance still manages to prod us. The concern wasn't one I'd thought about much until I learned it was enough to put me in my current situation.

"That's why you divided your magic." Rylan's voice edges on angry with a deep timbre. "People are afraid of one person with too much power, so you spread it amongst us." *Instead of giving it all to me* goes unsaid. Traditionally he would have received it all, as Mother did from Grandfather, and he from his father before him. The rest of us would have no magic at all—or more likely, not exist. It's been several generations since an Exos had more than one child. Resentment from a younger sibling with no magic was avoided this way.

Instead, our family enjoys resentment dripping down from the eldest. Rylan accepts it for the good of the kingdom (and because he can't do anything about it), but if taking away three-quarters of the power he could have had is for nothing, I have no doubt his bitterness will fester.

"That was the purpose," Father says, rubbing small circles on Mother's wrist with his thumb. "However, some people believe four people of magical ability are more dangerous."

"Four people each with a quarter of the power *I'm* supposed to have!"

And there we have it.

A scorching heatwave hits from Nina's direction, and I throw up a shield to contain it. "Stop it, Arabella! If he wants my power, he should be able to handle the heat."

"That's not what I meant," Rylan says.

"Isn't it, though?"

"Enough," Mother says. "Both of you."

I take a sip of wine. "I told you I'm your favorite sister."

Ry only glares at me.

"What do they want then?" Marcus asks. "Are you meant to have another child with no powers to be the heir?"

"*I* am the heir," Ry sneers.

"Plus," I say, "a fifth would make you the proper middle child, Marcus, and I don't think you're ready to take my mantle as troublemaker." Rather than being entertained by my wit, my siblings' faces drop into exasperated expressions. Father suppresses a smile, though.

"Don't you ever know when to stop?" Nina snaps.

"Not at all." I flash her a smile. "It's something I rather pride myself on."

"This is serious."

"No it isn't. Rylan is about to be crowned as heir. Pomp and ceremony are a fantastic way to regain popularity. Then it won't be long before we march through a parade of our royal weddings, followed by Ry's coronation as king. We put on some good shows, and people forget all about us *monsters* up here in the palace."

Rylan sighs. "You're absurd."

"I'm correct. Pop some gold and gemstones on that head of yours, and people will bask in the glory of your seismic power."

"It isn't only the fear of our powers." Mother rubs her temples. "Rylan, darling, I know you think I took power from you, but it wasn't my intention." She takes his hand in hers. "It's true that the four of you are more powerful than your grandfather or I ever were." Grandfather scowls at that. "Having four minds and hearts to control the elements makes you formidable as a unit. But..."

"What?" The veins in Ry's neck strain against his skin.

Father interjects. "Some wonder, if one person doesn't control the magic, who's to say which of those who *do* should rule the kingdom."

Wine shudders in the glasses, and I tense for worse. People are questioning Ry's claim to the throne?

"As far as I know," Rylan says in a low voice, "being first-born is sufficient for every other title and court. How is it that a queen's first-born son, who can, in fact, move mountains, is possibly *not enough*?"

"Our court has never been like any other," Mother says. "Power to rule came with magic. With the magic split,"—she lets out a slow breath—"it's agreed that each of the four of you have equal claim to the throne."

Oh, no. A tremor rattles the palace. Wine glasses go toppling over. I hold out one hand to raise them into the air, righting them before they spill. The other, I wave toward the cake to keep it from toppling, blowing the candles out while I'm at it. I don't suppose Rylan will be quite in the mood.

"Hasn't enough of my birthright been taken?" As the words are bellowed, I wrap the room in a shield to keep this conversation private. His outburst would be heard on the other end of the palace. "We can't have *four* rulers!"

"We won't." Mother folds her hands together. "All four of you will have the opportunity to prove yourselves. There will be a series of trials, and the winner—whoever passes and is deemed most worthy—will be the next ruler of Alchos."

Chapter Three

My hands drop, but everything remains suspended in mid-air. She didn't just say... We're not...

"I have to *compete* for *my* crown?" Rylan springs to his feet. "This is outrageous! I've been preparing for this my entire life!"

A cool waft brushes my face of its own accord, focusing me. This is so unfair. Rylan...

"You shouldn't be worried then." Marcus tries to grab a wine-glass from the air, and I let everything settle back into place. "You have the advantage over us, so what's to fear?" He looks at our older brother over his glass as he takes a sip.

"I'm not *worried*. The whole thing is degrading."

Nina scoffs. "Sorry to drag you down to our level."

The four of us have always bickered and bantered, but this is different. I don't want us set against each other. "Mother, don't you see what this will do to us? How can you allow this?"

"My loves, it's the only way—"

"No," I say. "It can be whatever way you say. You're the *queen*."

Grandmother offers me a slight smile. "Arabella, you'll soon learn that being queen doesn't mean the world bends to your will."

"I'm only to be a consort. Mother is sovereign." Saying *only* a consort to Grandmother sounds unkind, but she knows what I mean.

Nina cocks her head. "What happens if Ara wins?"

"She *won't*," Ry growls.

"Would she still marry Prince Jamys?" Nina continues as if Rylan hadn't spoken. "Could she be queen of both kingdoms?"

My betrothal contract certainly couldn't have taken this ridiculous turn of events into account. The heir has freestanding choice over his or her marriage, but since I'm already locked in...

My heart races. Surely no one could expect me to—

"Her betrothal would remain intact." Father's eyes find mine, and a tremor rattles me from within, worse than any of Rylan's quakes. "If you win, you would be Sovereign of Alchos and Queen-Consort of Ceraun."

The thought of multiple crowns makes my shoulders buckle. If I didn't know better, I'd think Marcus was trying to drown me. I've only recently come to terms with my betrothal. It's not what I'd have chosen, but shoring up our alliance with Ceraun is vital when Penum's simmering animosity toward us is always threatening to boil over. Whether or not I want Jamys is irrelevant; I want to protect my family and kingdom. My task in that effort has already been assigned. It would be wildly unjust to drop the responsibility of both kingdoms and the alliance on me. I'm not capable of it all.

Pressure builds behind my eyes. "No, I—"

"Is that what the ministry wants?" Rylan wrings his hands and paces the length of the large table. "To join Alchos and Ceraun as one under Arabella and Jamys?"

"They would still be individual kingdoms," Marcus says. "Right, Mother?"

"Yes."

Rylan tries again. "It would certainly strengthen our relations, though."

"Some think that would be beneficial," Mother says. "However, plenty of them believe it would be a conflict of interest to have the King of Ceraun as consort here."

To think of my future marriage being a matter of debate in ministry meetings turns my stomach. It's difficult enough to picture Jamys and me side by side as King and Queen in Ceraun, and I've sat with that idea for the better part of a year. It'll take a massive transformation for me to fit into Cerauno society. There's no way for me to be Alchosian and Cerauno. Our kingdoms are too different. I've accepted I'll have to suppress my style, outspokenness, and my overall personality to make my future there work. I can't do all that *and* be Alchosian enough to rule here.

I push away from the table. "Would you all stop speaking about me as if I'm not here? This is my *life* you're talking about, not strategy in some game. None of it matters. I won't do it. I'm not participating." As I rush out of the room, I add, "If the three of you want to tear each other's throats out for the crown, be my guest. I'll not have anything to do with it."

The transparent shield I'd soundproofed the room with shatters as I walk through it.

So flustered am I that I stomp up the winding stairs rather than shooting up through the middle. I need the feel of stone under my feet, the strain in my legs, to remind myself I'm not dreaming.

The kingdom comes first. It must. Magic isn't a gift given to us to play with—it's a tool we must use to aid and guide Alchos. The well-being of our people is the primary driving force of my heart, but if it shreds our family, what good can we be to them? That's all this will do. Marcus was already being an ass, poking at Rylan's confidence. Nina's first priority will always be Nina. Her perpetual desire for anything she can't have—from toys as a little girl to wine as an adolescent—never strayed to the crown, because that was obviously not possible. Now that it is, I have no doubt she'll do anything to get it simply because it wasn't supposed to be hers.

It's sad how little it takes to unravel us.

Well, I suppose this isn't a little thing.

Lucy is waiting in my chambers when I enter and drops to a low curtsy. "Good evening, my lady. It's earlier than I expected you. May I help you out of your gown?" She's being too formal. News must be spreading through the back halls of the friction at dinner. Some things are no match even for my magic.

"No, thank you. I can manage." Plus, I don't suppose I'll be left alone, so there's no point in getting undressed yet. "I won't need anything else tonight."

"All right." She dips her chin. "Goodnight."

"Goodnight."

I sprawl out on my chaise lounge and immediately regret not asking for wine or taking some of that cake with me. That would have really done it: *Sorry, Ry, you may not get your crown*, and *I'm taking your birthday cake.* After some time brooding with my swirling thoughts, I reach around to the side table and pull out a sheet of paper and a quill. As I finish scrawling a note, the door opens. I glance up to see Rylan peeking his head through.

"Come in."

As I sign it, Ry says, "Can't you float the quill to write?" His hands are held conspicuously behind his back.

A warm breath of air dries the ink. "I've never tried. I don't suppose my handwriting would be very good."

"It wouldn't actually be *hand*-writing at that point."

I almost grin. He seems to have calmed down at least. "What's behind your back?"

Rylan presents a large serving of cake and sits next to me.

My note floats out of the open window on a determined breeze. "You know, regardless of where I rank against Nina, you are my favorite brother."

"You *are* my favorite sister... now."

At that, I grin around a forkful of cake. The minty filling between layers of chocolate sponge is divine. "Your birthday was rather ruined."

"Your gifts were the highlight."

I wouldn't think the cushion for a crown he may not wear would bring him much joy at this point unless he's so confident in winning.

"Your refusal meant a lot to me."

Oh, that gift. "Of course. We've all always known the throne would be yours. This entire mess is absurd."

"Absurd indeed, but it's going to happen. And you do have to participate."

"Rylan, I *don't* want it. I don't want the pressure of uniting the kingdoms; I don't want the anxiety *against* the idea of uniting the kingdoms; I don't want to take the crown from you."

"Thank you, but if you don't participate, there will always be discord over whether you would have won. Also, Marcus and Nina will no doubt team up against me. I could use your help."

I shake my head as I shovel more cake into my mouth. "Can I help by reasoning with them?" I swallow my cake after that glorious example of why I should be no one's queen. "If we have to go along with this, perhaps the three of us can just let you win."

"I do not need you to let me win."

"Well, I don't like the idea of waging a war against the twins."

He sighs and leans an elbow on the back of the sofa. "You may want to wait a while before negotiating a peace treaty. Things got a little… heated after you left."

Rylan tells me the story as I eat my cake. Nina's questions took the turn of assuming she'd win which aggravated Ry beyond the limits of his grounded patience. The vision of garlands ensnaring Nina as our parents and grandparents tried to stop their fight is much too funny for me to keep being solemn. I almost wish I had stayed for that part.

"When she torched the branchlets, which I admittedly should not have shackled her with, the tablecloth caught fire," Ry says. "Marcus dowsed the flames. The dining room is a bit of a disaster."

"But you saved the cake." Laughter rocks my shoulders. Of course, Nina would never be angry enough to destroy the cake.

"You're welcome."

Laughing with Ry after all that is as surprising as the announcement was. The outlook for the two of us may be all right, but the trials—and getting past the twins—are far from over.

I wonder if my note has arrived. That'll give me something to look forward to in the morning.

Chapter Four

Glittery dewdrops outline spiderwebs in the sunshine. The world smells new this time of year—fresh and damp and floral. I could go to the cabin we keep out here, but being outside is so much more calming. On a nearby hilltop, Mirador Palace overlooks these meadows and forests. From here, the entire capital city of Mirador defines regal serenity. No one would imagine the turmoil buzzing within the elegant main keep. I had to get out and clear my head before dealing with it all.

My horse whinnies as hoofbeats thud toward us. A brown mare stops where mine is tied to a tree before the rider dismounts. As he secures the horse, I say, "I was beginning to wonder if you'd come."

"Who am I to disregard a summons from the Princess?" Tomas gives me an exaggerated bow, his dark hair falling across his brow.

I return his greeting with a graceful curtsy. "Your loyalty to the crown is a testament to your house, my lord."

He approaches me with slow, measured steps, his gaze never straying from my face. "You look lovely with your hair loose, Your Grace."

"I like to feel the breeze blow through it."

"You could have a breeze blow through it whenever you like."

I squeeze my hands together to keep from fidgeting with the ends of my long curls. Or worse—reaching out for him. "It's different when it's natural. I like to let the wind be free."

"Oh, you don't always need to be in control?"

Flutters low in my stomach threaten to make me squirm, but I hold still. "Giving up control in some situations can be rather... liberating."

He stands near enough for me to see every shade of blue in his eyes. Holding his eye contact is more sensual than it deserves to be, and pinpricks tickle every inch of my skin in a wave from my neck to my toes.

"I'm sure the wind relishes the freedom to caress you as it pleases."

Warmth blooms in my cheeks. "What would you do with such freedom?"

"If I were the wind, I'd brush along the most delicate areas of your skin to get your attention. You'd be attending court, and I'd slip under your skirt then slowly coil up your leg to see if I can crack that regal facade while some aging regent makes small talk with you." His words trace that imagined path up my leg, winding me up like a spring. "And if you should manage to continue speaking, when I got to the top—"

My mouth covers his. Silky hair slides between my fingers as I tug at the roots. His hands press into my back as our bodies mold against each other. The way his tongue caresses mine gives me the distinct impression he's showing me the end of that sentence.

I can't believe he did it again. Every time I tell myself *next time* I'll hold out. I tell myself I'll keep my hands and everything else to myself until he touches me. But that has yet to happen. He leaves no doubt of his desire, but it's always me who has to close the gap. My anger over it fades as he eagerly makes up for every moment his skin wasn't on mine. I keep expecting it to feel less exciting than the first time, but that hasn't happened either.

Last summer on the coast was different from all the years before. What had been a family tradition became an annual escape for our generation when we were deemed old enough. The Valnora estate—Father's seat—is a perfect spot for it, only a couple days' ride from the capital and settled on a stretch of glittering shore. For one week we got to relax, away from the scrutinizing eyes of our parents and the expectations that come with our ranks, to have fun with our siblings and friends.

This time, though, Tomas didn't feel like he was simply Rylan's friend or my friend's brother. The months spent in Lambridge with his mother's family did him good. He appeared to have grown up. And he certainly didn't look at me like the irritating sister figure he'd always known. The group dynamic remained, but I'd feel his eyes trailing me whenever I walked away. At night, he wouldn't retire to his chamber in Etherlee House until after I did, and I was sure he was trying to get me alone. The thought of it was dangerous and intoxicating.

Ry probably wouldn't approve, and I could imagine Josslyn's mock-disgust at me finding her brother attractive. It was impossible to ignore, though. I'd had stolen kisses before—all meaningless.

Those already seemed trivial compared to whatever was brewing, and nothing had even happened.

I found myself watching Tomas too. Had his chest and shoulders broadened since last I saw him? Was his jaw always so defined? The sweep of stubble across it wasn't new, but the urge to brush my hand over it was.

One morning when I took my daily tonic, gratefulness for Mother's insistence sprang up in me. She'd put me on it years ago, and somehow, it made me want to avoid sexual intimacy rather than giving me the freedom to explore. Perhaps because it felt like she would *know*. Regardless, contraception had never seemed necessary, and it couldn't be necessary now. I was getting well ahead of myself.

On the last night of our stay, I waited up as everyone else trickled off to bed. When Tomas and I were alone at last, the glaring issue of me having no idea what I was doing hit me like a sudden storm. My stomach tumbled. "I'm going for a walk."

"Do you think it safe to walk along the shore alone at night?"

The prior year, I'd have rolled my eyes at such a suggestion. Here and at home, my siblings and I had been freed from watchful guards when we got old enough and had ample control over our magic to defend ourselves. Granted, we were within very secure borders in both places. Tomas knew that as well as I did. Which was why, rather than annoy me, his question bolstered my belief that he wanted to be near me.

A smile tugged at the corners of my mouth. "It's perfectly safe for me. I can't guarantee the same for whoever might follow me."

"What if it's someone you know?" His voice vibrated through my bones now. Everything with Tomas felt new, even without anything occurring.

I shrugged and turned on my heel. It worked; he followed me out past the tall grasses of the sand dunes and toward the southern edge of the property, away from the ocean view bedrooms. When I walked straight to the water's edge, he said, "I thought you were going for a walk, not a swim."

A wall of air pressed ahead of me, holding back the water as I stepped onto the seafloor. When I was far enough for the water level to reach my shoulders, I turned to enjoy the impressed look on Tomas' face. "I thought you were escorting me?"

He walked down the aisle I left in my wake. I pulled the wall in behind him, encircling us in water, and continued farther. When the water was above both our heads, I stopped. Tomas eyed my work then let his gaze rest on me. "I didn't know you could do all this with air."

"It can't be seen, so it's underestimated. Like me."

"You can certainly be seen."

I quirked a brow. "Yet, I'm underestimated."

"You shouldn't be." He gestured to the water held up around us. "This is impressive."

"I am quite talented."

His grin sent a shiver down my spine. "What other talents do you have?" He closed most of the distance between us. Those few steps transcended years of playful camaraderie. We were somewhere new, and the slightest move now would make it impossible for us to go back to how we'd been before.

I didn't want to go back.

The walls of air twitched as my heart raced. I tipped my face up to look at him—our lips dangerously close. "Shall I tell you?"

"Show me."

His invitation formed as a demand heated my blood. There weren't a lot of opportunities to truly misbehave in my life. As royalty, we had to be mindful of our reputations and cautious of anyone who may want to misuse us. For unnamable reasons, this always seemed more pressing for me. Because I was the first second child in our family in so many generations? Because my element was seen as breezy and gentle, so I had to be as well? Whatever it was, I was the good girl. And Tomas seemed to feel my desire to relinquish that. Letting me incite it, choose this little rebellion, was exactly what I hadn't realized I'd wanted.

I pressed my lips to his, and the world ceased to exist. Though my heart was racing, everything seemed to slow down. Minutes stretched as his lips moved with mine in deep, slow waves. The stubble I had been dying to touch was rough under my hand in stark contrast to the softness of his mouth. His hands pressed into my lower back, and my concentration was broken enough that my wall dissipated.

There was a delay, like even if I couldn't save the moment, the world wanted us to have it. But inevitably, the sea crashed in on us.

Now, as we lie in the warm grass, I think about that wave crashing into us and how it feels that way still. Every time.

Tomas' finger brushes up and down my spine. "Bell, are you telling me I may have just bedded the next Queen of Alchos?"

"For so many reasons, no. Not the least of which being that there is no bed in sight."

Laughing on the ground, he's even more alluring than the smooth, confident persona he tortures me with. That all gets shed with his clothes. When we're dressed only in sunlight, he stops trying to impress me. He doesn't need to.

"How did Ry take it?"

"Minor earthquake, almost strangled Nina with a plant, but he offered me cake."

He snorts. "That isn't how he typically treats adversaries."

"I'm not his adversary. I'm going to help him hold off Nina and Marcus so he can win."

The news came as a shock, of course. Reclined and panting in post-coital bliss was probably a more jarring time to hear *Rylan may not be crowned heir after all* than our dinner was. With the help of some tactile distractions, Tomas had just calmed down, but now he sits up with a start. "No you're not."

"Yes I am."

"You're too competitive for that."

I prop myself up on my elbows and cover my face with my hands as I sigh. Having this conversation naked feels like a worse idea by the second. "This is quite different from my... *motivation* to master my magic." That wasn't a competitive issue at all. It was more a matter of completing myself. Then, there were other reasons to... But that doesn't matter. "I do not want this crown. It's meant to be Rylan's."

Tomas' eyes darken. His disapproval is so subtle I shouldn't notice it. But without clothing to shield him, the same tightness in his jaw is visible in the extra definition of his broad chest and muscled arms. "And you're getting your own."

"And I'm getting my own." I hold his gaze, silently daring him to say more about my betrothal. He won't, though. He never has. Somehow, the topic always feels like a fight we aren't putting into words. My nerves simmer before frustration with myself for getting more heated about this than he does takes the place of the argumentative tension.

"What would happen if you won?"

"They'd expect me to wear two crowns, which sounds like a disaster for my hair." This time, he ignores my banter. Perhaps I'm losing my touch. I sit up and turn to grab my dress. If I'm not looking at him, I can imagine he looks disappointed that this is not an opportunity to get out of my betrothal. Not that he should—we're merely a physical and temporary dalliance.

A sigh pulls my shoulders down along with my spirits. As I dress, I say, "They'll likely be waiting for me to delve into further details about this inanity. Hopefully everyone has calmed down by now."

"You're already eerily calm about the matter." Tomas' voice is tighter as the ruffling of fabric tells me his trousers are back on.

I turn back to face him again. "That's because I'm the only one with nothing to lose."

Chapter Five

A stable hand drops his shoulders in relief when I come into view. "Your Grace, you're wanted in the Queen's study."

"Thank you." I hop down without taking his offered hand.

"Miss, I..." His face reddens as he takes the reins.

"What is it?"

"The stable master was... displeased I had readied a horse for you and not told him. When asked if you had left, he didn't know, and—"

"Oh my. You won't be in any trouble, I assure you. My movements should not be reported at all times, and frankly, I don't need a horse to leave the palace grounds, so it's beyond anyone to know where I am. I'll take care of it."

He nods hastily. "Thank you, Your Grace. I'm sorry to be a bother."

"None at all." I hurry into the palace, making one last sweep over myself to ensure there's no grass on my dress, and checking the laces that cinch the outer layer around my waist. When I enter Mother's study, everyone's attention snaps to me.

Nina puffs out a breath with as much drama as possible. "How nice of you to join us."

"I went for a ride."

"Didn't you think we had some things to discuss?"

"I was hoping to avoid the part where Marcus has to extinguish an inferno." I sweep my skirt forward as I sit. "Have you already gone through all that?"

Father gives me a reproachful look, but it's half-hearted. He appreciates my wit more than anyone else, though he doesn't always approve of my timing.

Mother clears her throat. "If you're quite done..."

"By all means, Mother." Tomas' crossness over my stance on the trials has me feeling cheeky, so I don't stop when I should. "Please, do tell how any of us could possibly hope to deserve your throne."

She ignores my impudence and gets to business. "Firstly, we must tell the kingdom what we'll be doing. At what would have been Rylan's coronation, we will make the announcement."

"Do we still get to have the ball afterwards?" I ask.

Marcus groans. "Arabella, honestly."

"The dress I've had made for it is truly spectacular. It would be a shame to waste it."

"Why are you even here?" Nina asks.

I shrug a shoulder. "I have no idea. It didn't seem optional."

"Yes, we will have the ball," Mother says. "This is all meant to be a good thing. We are progressing, changing, adapting, and we will celebrate as such."

Surprising though it is, this could all be seen as a continuation of what Mother has done for her entire reign. She divided magic among us then divided power with the ministry. This is another shift from all power going to the assumed recipient.

"Afterwards," she continues, "there will be one month for preparations, then the trials will begin."

"Is the royal family of Ceraun still coming for the ceremony-turned-announcement?" *I do so look forward to seeing my betrothed.* Goodness, I can't even turn the sarcasm off in my head.

"Yes, they are," Father says. "And they'll be invited to stay through the trials."

An entire month or more with Jamys here? We haven't spent any time together since our betrothal was agreed upon. I can't imagine what it'll be like to be around him. And with Tomas present so often as well... My stomach rolls.

"What will the trials consist of?" Rylan asks, much more to the point. "How will we be preparing?"

"The content of the trials will not be revealed until they begin. Each trial will test the qualities Alchos needs in a ruler as well as your magic. After the first trial, one of you will be eliminated. There will be another break of a few weeks, then a second trial, after which another will be eliminated. The trial for the final two will culminate in the crowning of our heir. Are there any questions?"

Questions? Of course not. *We'll surprise you with a challenge; good luck,* seems a thorough explanation.

"How are we meant to prepare," Nina says, "if we don't know what's coming?"

Father leans into his armrest. "The time is for us to prepare the trials, not for you to prepare for them."

"Everything you'd need to win," Mother says, "you already have. Tighten your control over your magic, focus, and be prepared for anything. Everything that truly tests a ruler is a surprise, and how you handle the unexpected says more about you than when you have time to plan."

Marcus shifts in his chair. "Who will determine the results?"

"The Queen," Mother says with a coy smile.

I rise from my chair. "I think this could have been left as a note."

"Arabella, I need you to take this seriously. We are trying to preserve our monarchy and our kingdom."

"Mother, you know I'll always do what's best for the kingdom." Even marry Jamys. I'm a regular martyr.

"I expect you all to compete fairly"—she gives Marcus and Nina a pointed look—"and to the best of your ability." Now, her gaze falls on me.

"Of course, Mother."

Her eyes scrutinize me, but it's Father who says something. "Arabella, would you join me in the garden a moment?"

What a state we must be in for Father to be sent in to manage me.

The palace gardens remain lush year-round thanks to Mother and Rylan, but there is something about spring that makes it all look more vibrant. And of course, I never tire of how the air is cleaner around plants.

"You were scarcely walking when we realized you didn't simply *control* air."

I tuck my arm through Father's. I've heard this story countless times, but it never grows old. The story might, a little, but the way he tells it—all pride and awe—makes me an enthralled audience every time.

"You stumbled and fell, but you didn't hit the ground," he says. "The air caught you. It held you for a moment, then set you down gently. I looked to your mother, but she hadn't done it. I asked if you could have managed that already, and she didn't believe so. You were much too young to manage that sort of manipulation over your element, and even with time and practice, it would be exceedingly challenging to do it so quickly.

"No, you didn't *make* the air catch you—it simply wanted to. It recognized you as its friend and counterpart. Your relationship with your element has always astounded even your mother. We've long known that your power is something quite exceptional."

I drop my gaze. "Are you saying I'm the most powerful, and hence I should rule?"

"Not at all. Having greater mastery of your ability would not make you a more suitable ruler than your siblings, but the way in which you achieved it bespeaks the qualities of a ruler that come so naturally to you. The very *air* feels compelled to follow you anywhere, protect you, do your bidding—if people rallied around you as such... what a reign that would be."

"Father." A weight presses down on me, and I can't float it off. "Isn't it enough to be Queen of Ceraun? To unite our kingdoms, make sure Penum doesn't lure them to join against us, be Rylan's ally, and..." *Live for duty and kingdom.* How can that not be enough? I may jest about everything and play the difficult one, but when it comes to it, I do everything they want. I don't want to leave for a stuffy kingdom with antiquated views and constricting etiquette, but I'm doing as they asked. Will they never stop wanting things from me?

He rubs his forehead. "You weren't born into a simple life. I'm sorry for that sometimes, but even without the magic and your royal bloodline, I doubt you could ever lead a quiet life."

"Because I'm troublesome?" I bat my eyelashes, earning a smile from him.

"Perhaps when you want to be." He pats my arm with his free hand. "Mostly, I'd call you... vivacious."

"That's the loving version of troublesome."

He shrugs. "Sometimes the world needs trouble."

Chapter Six

A target bursts into flames. Then another farther back in the yard. And another.

Marcus stands at Nina's side, forming an orb of water in his hands. He thrusts his hands forward, and the water shoots to extinguish the first target. From nowhere, water rains down on the next. Marcus presses his lips together and closes his eyes. The ground rumbles, and I look for Rylan, but he isn't here. Water shoots up from the ground to drown the last target.

"New trick?" I ask as I approach the twins.

Marcus looks at me with a self-assured smirk. "You can't be the only one coming up with new ways to use magic."

"Especially when you're trying to take a crown from your brother."

Flames flicker around Nina's arms, but the sleeves of her tunic are unharmed. "You're really going to sit back and let Rylan win?"

"It's not *letting* him win. He'll need to prove himself, but he has been preparing for this crown his entire life. It's not unreasonable for him to get it."

"It's not unreasonable for any of us to get it." Nina keeps her eyes on me, but fire springs about behind her like a rabbit. The control without her full attention is very good, but I wonder if she could really be as ruthless as she thinks she is.

"So, if it comes down to the two of you," I say, "you'd go after each other full tilt?"

"Yes."

Sadly, Nina might actually mean that. Her twin is her favorite and has always been on her side for everything. Their united front has been a problem for Rylan and me on numerous occasions. While tiny Ry and Ara shouted our excuses and pointed fingers when a curtain panel from the sitting room went missing, Nina and Marcus calmly presented their alibis which supported each other. I'm still convinced she burnt it to ash. So, working *against* Marcus would be a big change for her and may soften the way she competes, but I have no doubt she'd justify it if Marcus took a stance against her.

Marcus remains silent on the matter. He couldn't compete whole-heartedly against her. He would put her before the crown, so I should hope he understands my choice to do the same for Rylan.

"I don't suppose there is any way for me to convince you otherwise?" It's worth an attempt. "I'm sure Jamys has a palace somewhere they aren't using that I could give you."

"You're going to be quite the wife," Marcus says. "Already giving away your husband's palaces?"

"If I give Ceraun a magical heir, I don't imagine there is anything I couldn't have." If they want to buy me, they'll pay handsomely.

Sparks flash along Nina's fingertips, but she says nothing. She isn't betrothed yet, and I already pity whoever gets saddled with her. A vision of an arbor ablaze with Nina storming away in a smoldering gown flashes through my mind. Is this why she wants to win?

I'm about to ask when Marcus looks past me and smiles. "Hello, Jo."

I whip around to see Josslyn coming toward us. "Jo, darling!" I rush to embrace her. "What a lovely surprise."

"I simply *had* to come see you." Blue eyes—so much like Tomas'—bore into me. Well that was quick.

"Let's go chat then." Over my shoulder, I say to Marcus and Nina, "Good work. Keep it up," and stroll off arm-in-arm with Josslyn. "He told you then."

"Of course he did, and I must say, I'm disappointed he knew first."

"I was going to come to you next. I was strung up about it, and you can't quite relax me the way he does."

She groans quietly as we enter the palace and go toward my chambers. "Gods, Ara, he is my *brother*. I don't need to hear about this."

"You aren't hearing *anything*. Do you have any idea how painful it is to keep the details from my dearest friend?" Jo is the only person who knows about Tomas and me, though only in the most general way. Regardless of how open-minded Alchosians are, an affair during a betrothal would be a scandal for anyone. People think of Jamys and me as a couple, romanticizing our "love story" into something far from reality. Jo understands, though, and has been my secret keeper. Still, she wouldn't appreciate hearing that

I can't possibly worry about matters such as the future of the kingdom when Tomas' touch leaves me a mere puddle of myself.

We drop onto the chaise in my sitting room, and Jo takes my hands. "Are you all right?"

"Yes, I'm fine. Mostly annoyed."

Her head tilts. "Not distraught? Hysterical? None of that?"

"No?"

"Then you've lost your mind, because you don't have any of those excuses for your absurd idea to let Rylan win." She leans back with a dramatic huff, crossing her arms over her chest.

Dead gods take me if Rylan hears people saying I'd *let* him win. "Might anyone consider that I don't wish to be sovereign because it would make the King of Ceraun our consort and that seems precarious?"

"That is *not* why."

"It is true, though. Alchos and Ceraun are far too different to be one kingdom, but once our heir were sovereign of both, how long would they remain separate?" I tilt my head toward her and blink expectantly. "We don't want their stuffy customs down here anymore than they want our far more fun and relaxed way of life up there."

She shrugs. "Well then, they're rather foolish."

"Exactly."

"Why did we agree to move there?" Jo will be in my court—my bit of home and comfort to take with me.

"Because we are also idiots," I deadpan.

There's a knock on the door, and a maid peeks in. "Tea, Your Grace?"

"Yes, please."

Two maids walk in with trays, setting out sandwiches, sweets, and tea for us. I ask them about their families as they work and thank them on their way out. Then I pour tea while Jo's glares attempt to skewer me.

"You're serious then?"

"About these cakes? Absolutely." I pop one into my mouth. This is Jo, so I don't have to bother with ladylike nibbles. "I cannot have this conversation again. Isn't there anything else we can talk about?"

She sighs and takes a cake. "Fine. On a selfish note, will this affect our week at Etherlee?"

"I hadn't thought of that. I don't know." The mention of it shocks me as much as nearly drowning did last time I was there.

Too rattled by the rush of water, or the kiss, or both, I couldn't manage to push the water away from us again, so we swam and trudged out, laughing all the way. My dress hung heavily on me. If it weren't so ridiculously funny, I'd have been mortified.

"It would appear I have some talents too." Tomas pushed his hand through his sodden locks.

"Such as?"

One eyebrow cocked up. "Distracting you."

"For now, perhaps. I haven't come into my full power yet. There will come a time when it will take much more than one kiss to break my magic."

A mischievous grin sent me reeling. "Is that a challenge?"

Had he always been so smug? I pushed air up under his feet to elevate him off the ground, and he wobbled as he looked at me wide-eyed. "Are you mad?" It was only a step up, but it was enough to crack his confidence. Somehow, that was even more attractive.

"Do you think you can do it again?" I raised myself to level with him. "It was only the surprise of something new, Tomas. Don't flatter yourself into thinking you could have more power over me than I do over air."

"I wouldn't dare underestimate your power." It was sincere—not sarcastic or challenging at all.

Even more than being underestimated, having him believe in me was inspiration to prove myself. With the sand dunes concealing us from the house, I draped my arms around his neck and kissed him again—to prove myself, and because he believed in me, and because I wanted to feel his lips on mine again. He squeezed my hips, and when our mouths opened and his tongue brushed mine... we fell.

"Damn!" Hands still behind his neck, I dropped my chin to avoid seeing his victorious expression. "I need more practice."

"With which part?" He lifted my face back to his and kissed me.

This time I didn't have anything else to think about. No shields to keep up. No power to maintain. I let myself enjoy it. I melted into his arms and memorized the taste of him. My body pressed against his, and controlling the air around me was out of the question—I could hardly breathe.

Then I shuddered with cold, and he leaned back, rubbing his hands up and down my arms. "You need to get out of that wet dress."

"And you'll want to change out of your wet clothes." My eyes skimmed down his torso, taking in the way his tunic clung to his body and had become transparent before I ripped my gaze away to go back inside.

My heart raced as we walked back into the house in silence. I tapped my teeth together, trying to determine what exactly we were doing. When we got to my door, I hesitated with my hand on the knob.

"Do... you need help with that?" Tomas gestured to my damp dress.

"No, I can manage."

"Right. Of course. Goodnight then." Disappointment flashed through his eyes, and I realized I'd answered too quickly. It was a reflexive response—refusing assistance. To have him help me out of my dress... *I shouldn't, though.*

"Goodnight." I turned and entered my chambers as he walked away. Inside, I leaned against the door a moment, pondering what just happened. What would we be like around each other now? Would it happen again? I wanted it to. I reached back to unlace my dress, but suede and water are not a good combination, and pulling the laces out proved difficult. I'd have gone to bed dressed if I wasn't freezing, but as it was, I went to wake Jo for assistance.

However, when I stepped into the hall, I jumped back in surprise at the sight of a figure just next to my door. Tomas started as well.

"Gods, I'm sorry. I hadn't gone yet. I'm going now. I'm—wait, what are you doing?"

"I was going to wake Jo. As it turns out, I do need help with this." Now it was my turn to gesture to the sopping dress. It occurred to me I didn't have a plan for how to explain this to his sister.

"You needn't wake her."

I took a deep breath. "Well, since you're here. Come in." I turned and walked back in with quick steps. The sound of the door closing behind me sent a shiver down my spine that had nothing to do with the cold. I pulled my damp braid over one shoulder so it was out of the way, and he began pulling the laces through the back of my dress. His fingertips brushed the skin of my back, and I focused all my energy on not squirming.

This was a bad idea. A terrible idea, really.

But when he'd finished, I turned around—still too close to him. "Thank you."

"Of course." He started to step back, but I leaned forward and kissed him again. He kissed me back more forcefully that time. The feel of his hands on my back where the dress was open broke me. I dropped my arms, letting the weight of the wet dress help it fall.

Tomas paused a moment, breathing rapidly as he looked me over. I was sure I'd burst into flames—the cold from our impromptu swim thoroughly negated by the heat of his gaze on my bare skin. Then he flung his tunic off, and my mind ceased functioning. His bare chest and stomach were so beautiful to behold. This had to be a new development. How could I have gone so long without knowing how devastatingly gorgeous he was? But looking at him was nothing in comparison to being pressed against him.

Skin on skin, we crashed into each other again.

"... don't see that being a problem, though. Unless you make it one. I swear, Ara, if you go sneaking off with Tomas and make it uncomfortable..."

I blink back into the present conversation. "What?"

"At Etherlee. Were you listening at all?" Jo shakes her head and takes a sip of tea.

"In a sense, yes, I was listening. I was thinking about Etherlee." Which is what she was speaking of, so that qualifies. I nab a sandwich as if roast beef and horseradish sauce can keep my mind on the here and now.

"It would certainly be different this year. Even if all of you survive the trials, you're bound to be impossible to be around."

"Aren't the four of us always impossible to be around?"

"Yes, which is why I dread thinking of it being *worse*."

I offer a coy smile. "At least we aren't boring."

If it were possible for anyone to be bored by us, Jo would be. She's always been as good as family—all the Coyles are. Highbluff has always been close with the royal family, both in proximity and affection. The vineyard-lined seaside estate is like a second home to us. With Tomas only a year older than Rylan and Josslyn my age, it was only natural for us to grow up together. Jo is as much my sister as Nina—sometimes more. She's been right alongside us as our powers developed, so it's all rather commonplace to her.

"So, what happens next?" she asks with the exasperated tone of someone whose plans are constantly shifting.

"Rylan's coronation becomes the big announcement, the ball still happens, and in a month, we see what happens when four magical siblings face off."

"Sounds delightful. Are the Cerauno royals still coming?"

"Yes, the Merricks will be here tomorrow, and possibly through the trials." I rub my temples.

She lays a hand on my knee. "It would be nice for you to get to know Jamys better."

"I know, but it's going to feel real then. Like time is hurrying toward our wedding, and I'm not ready to say goodbye."

Her eyes twinkle as she cocks her head. "To whom?"

Oh. I didn't mean to add the goodbye part. "To everyone and everything I know. My life here. Our kingdom." Because I certainly can't mean I'm not ready to part ways with Tomas. We had an agreement. We knew our time was limited.

"Not *everyone*. Thank you very much."

That draws a smile from me. "You'll be the best part of life in Ceraun." I don't know how I could bear it without her. Even if I know her eyes will always remind me of Tomas.

I have thoroughly sabotaged myself, haven't I?

Chapter Seven

Even in my most conservative dress, I'll be considerably more exposed than our Cerauno guests, but at least I made the attempt. Nina did no such thing. All that connects the ethereal skirt to the swatches of fabric covering her breasts are intricately braided and knotted strands. It's stunning, and I must borrow it sometime, but it will be shocking to our esteemed guests.

A footman informs us they are nearly here, and we go out to the front steps to greet our northern neighbors. The sunshine and breeze on my skin remind me of how much of it is showing, but at least I've got one shoulder and arm covered. Most of my body is as well, though under the elaborate flourishes, it is rather sheer and form fitting. I've never minded such a thing, but waiting to see Jamys, I feel like a wrapped gift. *Here is your prize.*

It shouldn't matter. Jamys should find me attractive. It is, I believe, preferable in a marriage. But I'd like to temper his expectations. Our marriage shall be a matter of state. I don't intend to make any attempt to attract him, and I don't know how we'll be around each other now that we're betrothed. Our trip to Ceraun in the winter was cancelled, so I haven't seen him since it was first arranged.

Banners appear at the end of the promenade—purple and teal—billowing in the wake of a parade of carriages. Riders lead the one with the royal family in it, and I keep my gaze there, ready to be as convivial a bride-to-be as I can. It isn't until one of the riders starts up the steps that I realize I know him. Fair-haired and clean cut, if not slightly disheveled from riding, the man I'm to marry arrives.

We'd met plenty of times growing up, and Jamys was always the definition of cordiality. Hence last year, when my mother opened a conversation with, "Jamys is a lovely young man, isn't he?" I answered honestly that he was. By the time I realized where she was going with that, I didn't want to try to take it back and was nowhere near prepared to tell her Tomas made it a problem for me.

Then she was so earnest about our need to secure our relations with Ceraun, how she feared the vile king in the west would try to marry his daughter to Jamys to outnumber us. Not only did I want to help, but I was somewhat honored that she trusted me with it. As a spare heir, the expectations on me weren't all that pressing when compared to Rylan, and I enjoyed that freedom from responsibility. Still, to be needed by my kingdom sparked something that compared to the flame lit within me by Tomas.

Jamys greets my parents with a bow, and they dip their heads accordingly. "Welcome back to Alchos, Prince Jamys."

"It's an honor. Thank you." He continues down the receiving line, paying his respects to my grandparents and Rylan before getting to me. "Your Grace." He bows as I curtsy.

"I thought we were done with such courtesies, *Your Highness*." My lips turn up in a smile. He holds my eye contact, his gaze not wavering to my body in the slightest. I can't decide if I'm relieved or offended.

Doubt shadows his features before a confident smile vanquishes it. "Perhaps next time, Princess." He takes my hand and brushes a kiss on my knuckles. Sunlight reflects off the gold and stones wrapped around my wrist to project spots of rainbows across his brow. Then he moves on to Marcus and Nina.

The King and Queen of Ceraun step out of the carriage, followed by Princess Lillian. Pleasantries are exchanged down the line again, and eventually, our gaggle of royals retreats into the palace, led by Mother on the arm of King Urian and Father with Queen Anilla.

The worst is over—the anticipation. He's here, and it's fine. I had worked myself up for nothing. Jamys is a perfect gentleman, just as he's always been. If anything is uncomfortable, it's going to be my own fault.

"I'm still not very good at this." I tap my jaw as I look at the joko board.

"You've improved."

I look up to find Jamys grinning tightly. "You're only being nice." Ever the gentleman not to tease or challenge me. It was years ago, during one of his visits here, that Tomas was teasing me about being terrible at the game, and Jamys offered to help me with it.

"Do you see that, Tomas?" I gave him an impertinent look. "You merely mock me, while Jamys tries to help. He's a gentleman."

Tomas rolled his eyes. "A gentleman who doesn't know you well enough to know you don't like anyone to help you with anything."

He knew me well then, and far, *far* more now. My perfect gentleman may not know me yet, but there's time.

Jamys shrugs. "It's true. You have improved... slightly."

"There we are—much more honest."

He is a pleasant person to be around. Soothing and comforting even when the unexpected arises. He took the news of our plan for the coronation tomorrow in stride. He didn't seem concerned about the possibility of my status changing, nor did he seem eager to have me crowned. All very matter-of-fact in confirming the details. Again, a welcome change from how my own family took the news.

"You can be honest with me in other things as well," I say.

He looks at me wide-eyed. "Oh, and what do you suppose I haven't been honest about?"

"You can't have so little a reaction to the possibility of me becoming my mother's heir." Despite my low volume, Nina perks up and turns ever so slightly toward us. The need for privacy in this family is one of the reasons I've gotten so much practice with my magic.

"My opinion doesn't matter." He continues placing his stones in an even rhythm with me. "What will be, will be."

"But you must have some preference."

"I'm not sure that I do. There would be benefits and difficulties to your being crowned. We would cross that bridge if we came to it."

Now I utilize my ability to keep the conversation from being overheard by curious bystanders. "What if I were to tell you I don't want it?" He follows rules, so I don't think he'd appreciate me intentionally losing, but perhaps I can share my feelings on it.

"Why wouldn't you want it?" The question carries no weight of accusation, simply the desire to know.

Why is it that him making it easy for me makes me uneasy? This conversation has been a fight with everyone else. Relaxing out my readiness for that is strange. "Two crowns seem like too great a responsibility. Also, while the alliance between Alchos and Ceraun is wonderful, I don't see how it wouldn't eventually lead to their merging into one kingdom."

"Would that be such a bad thing?"

"Not *bad*. It just seems like they aren't meant to. They're so different." Ceraunos always seem so solemn and serious—an odd response to being slighted by the gods so many centuries ago, in my opinion.

"We aren't all that different," Jamys says. I glance up and down at his stiff, layered suit and cock an eyebrow when I get back to his face. "Fashion aside."

"Fashion is the least of it." Though it is one facet I am, perhaps ridiculously, concerned with for myself. "Do you really believe the gods still live?" They don't. The gods of Earth, Fire, Water, and Air gave their powers to the first Queen of Alchos. They relinquished their immortality and united Alchos under one banner from its many small, unorganized states.

"I believe death isn't as final as what we can see from here," Jamys says. "Especially for gods."

Tap, tap, tap go the stones. The gods are gone enough not to care that Ceraunos worship them reverently. It would be rude to say, though. "Well then, fashion and religion aside, Alchos has always been a kingdom with magic, and Ceraun without."

"That's going to change anyways."

Right. With our little magical heir. What a lovely picture we will paint. We're already the type of story to inspire songs—a perfect match by all accounts. The fair prince with the honey-colored hair and the magical princess, strengthening the alliance and making beautiful little blond heirs. To be king and queen of both king-doms would wrap it all up rather nicely. The world at our finger-tips. It's what any girl would want. It's what I *should* want. Sitting here with Jamys, I'm certain I'd be perfectly content with that life.

I shrug. "I suppose so."

"Whatever happens, we'll manage."

Jamys would be the perfect person to have by my side for it—grounded and calm and experienced in preparing to inherit a kingdom. Not that it matters. He might understand my concerns over having so much responsibility thrust upon me, but I can't tell him how I'd be tortured by having to rule here and sit across from the next Lord of Highbluff in meetings.

I swallow back the discomfort from even thinking about it.

No, tomorrow's announcement will not be the start of my rise to queen.

Chapter Eight

Wind bounces between my palms like a ball under my steepled fingers. To the outside observer, I appear to be standing bolt upright, but if it were possible to lie down vertically, that's what I'm doing. A hardened but pliant wall of air conforms to my back so I can relax against it. Rylan pretends to read a book on the other side of the sitting room, though he hasn't turned a page in a while, and the twins sit opposite each other on a settee, waiting for today's events to commence.

Jamys comes in and greets me with a smile. "Your people are in for quite the surprise today."

"We like to keep things exciting in Alchos." Even with my hands hovering near the brown leather straps where my gown cinches below my breasts, his gaze never slips to the exposed skin down the middle of my chest. He is either the definition of self-control, or more uncomfortable with the differences between our kingdoms than he lets on.

Or he prefers men. Wouldn't that be a delightful twist in our marriage.

His mother very thoughtfully gifted me quite a few Cerauno gowns. To maneuver between appreciating them and rejecting the idea of wearing one today was a skillful dance. *Oh, I wish I could, but I must look Alchosian whilst telling the kingdom I may be the next queen.* I'll have to wear them for our dinners during their extended visit, though.

The season is going to feel like an eternity. Perhaps if I'm disqualified from the trials early, they'll leave.

"People will look at you differently when they know you may be queen," Jamys says, much too kindly for someone whose departure I just fantasized about. "They'll watch you more closely. Not that you ever step out of line, but I wanted to warn you: being the heir has a different kind of pressure about it."

I press my lips together in a tight smile. "You do a wonderful job of it. You'd be an invaluable support to me if I become my mother's heir." It's true. But his assumption that I'm perfect anyway twists my stomach.

"It would be an honor to help you in any way I can." He kisses my hand before departing to take his place with his family.

Rylan puts down the book and crosses his arms. "Is he lusting over Father's throne?"

"He isn't acting too eager in front of me. Are you ready to act like you aren't furious about all this?"

"I've come to terms with it. The people will love me more for having earned the crown. And perhaps these trials will be fun."

Nina and Marcus share an annoyed look, and I tilt my head. "Are we certain Ossana doesn't have some magical ability? Getting you to settle down is far more impressive than anything I can do."

Ry rolls his eyes, but his cheeks flush slightly. His disappearance yesterday did not go unnoticed.

"Is the cabin still standing, by the way?" I cannot resist the opportunity to embarrass him. "Releasing that level of stress must have come with a decent earthquake."

He narrows his eyes. "Nina is my favorite sister again."

"It's just that I had a nice pair of boots there."

"Go to hell, Ara."

"I love you, too."

Mother enters and clears her throat. "Shall we?"

She leads the way onto the veranda, arm-in-arm with Father, making the promenade erupt in applause. My siblings and I follow in age order—Rylan, me, Marcus, then Nina—and line up as planned. When the roar settles, I push Mother's voice out to amplify her, marking the first time she hasn't done it herself.

"Good people of Alchos, you honor us by coming to celebrate the crowning of my heir. This day will be remembered for years to come. However, this crown"—she lifts the ring of gold and gems—"will not be laid upon my son's head today." Murmurs rise from the crowd. "As each of my children possess magic, each of my children have been deemed eligible to rule. In the spirit of what is best for the kingdom and our people, we have devised a process to determine which of them would be best suited to rule this magnificent land."

The entire length of the promenade is full of people here to witness Rylan's coronation, and more line the terraces of the bordering buildings. Anywhere a person might possibly have a vantage point to see us is taken as she goes on to explain the trials. The love of our people is a palpable thing, and I can't imagine the venom our enemies spew taking hold here.

If I could freeze everything just like this, with the towers of Mirador Palace behind us and troves of adoring subjects before us, I would. But seeing the King and Queen of Ceraun—my future family—in a place of honor reminds me this is far from permanent. Jamys smiles at me next to his sister. On the other side of our grandparents are the Coyles. Josslyn's face gives away nothing of what she may be thinking, but Tomas is in a rage. I hope Rylan thinks it's on his behalf.

"Ruling Alchos is the greatest honor for our family, and we look forward to building the best possible future for our kingdom." The masses eat up Mother's words. Whoever this scheme is appeasing, it seems the kingdom would go right along with whatever she said. I can't imagine them being any less excited if she had just crowned Rylan today, but that's not an option anymore. Not as she gestures to the four of us, and we step forward together. "Rylan, Prince of Earth." He bows his head and raises it. "Arabella, Princess of Air." I give a slight curtsy. Marcus and Nina follow in turn. "Marcus, Prince of Water. Nina, Princess of Fire. One of which will be the next ruler of Alchos."

Gauzy skirts in a rainbow of colors brush the marble floor of the ballroom. Perfumes and colognes blanket the air in a heady, spicy scent, but the collected crowd is quiet as Mother and Father open the ball. The song begins softly while the Queen and King step into the middle of the dance floor. Then the violin virtuoso jumps into the piece, and they dance as though their feet are singing the lyrics poured forth by the strings.

Every step they take is in perfect sync as she turns with practiced grace. Their eye contact is coy, even as their expressions remain poised and regal. When she arches back, his hand is there to support her, though she holds herself up with ease. That's the way it always is—he's ready and willing to catch her, but I've never seen her fall. They are a perfect love story of childhood friends becoming more. It's a rare and beautiful thing at their station—something I envy.

When the second song begins, we join them on the dance floor: Rylan with Jamys' sister, Princess Lillian, Marcus with Josslyn, Nina with Tomas, and Jamys leads me out, our hands folded together.

Jamys and I have been friends, too. Not to the same extent—seeing each other infrequently due to distance and circumstance. Our first meeting was so long ago, it has the blurry edges of a dream. I had to be about ten years old. My family had all gone to Ceraun, and I remember tumbling through tall grasses and wildflowers. Lillian and the twins would have been eight, but Lillian remained in the shade, sitting quietly and observing rather than playing with us. Jamys seemed content to keep her that way—safe and still. He looked on as well while my siblings and I bounded around like wild beasts. Jamys and Lillian were regal at a much younger age than any of us were. Then again, how regal did any of us really become?

We're all the picture of perfect nobility now, gliding across the floor in all our finery. The phantasmal quality of this song keeps me feeling like I'm in a memory or dream. Or watching someone else.

I squeeze Jamys' hand to ground myself in reality. He's decorated in full regalia, with gold accents reflecting light off his epaulettes. His suit seems like it might not be comfortable to wear, but the sharp lines do the job of making this already-handsome man look majestic.

Jamys tells me about the summer palace in Ceraun—how lovely it is and how he hopes I'll enjoy it. It's in the mountains, a cool, comfortable escape from the heat. I smile and nod but scarcely listen. I like Etherlee House in the summer. It represents an entirely different kind of heat for me now—a heat I crave in any season. This year may be the last time I go for that tradition. That is, if the trials don't cancel our plans.

It's terribly sad to think last year may have been the last time. It ended brilliantly for Tomas and me, but that all crumbled as soon as I got back. Two surprises in jarringly rapid succession. First the thrill of what Tomas could be to me, then the shock of Jamys taking that place.

Now, Jamys' hand rests on my waist, and I wonder how much time will pass before I feel settled about it. As our dance comes to an end, Jo catches my eye, and we approach her as Marcus excuses himself.

She curtsies, her raven curls spilling over her shoulder. "Your Highness."

"Lady Josslyn, it's a pleasure." Jamys bows his head. "I was just telling Princess Arabella about our summer palace. I'm certain you'll both find yourselves right at home there."

"That's wonderful. I look forward to exploring Ceraun."

He reaches out a hand. "Shall I tell you about it as we dance?"

"Yes, please." Jo smiles as she takes it.

They sweep off together—a beautiful, graceful sight. Josslyn has always been a better dancer than I am. It's the power that comes naturally to her, while mine is manipulation of air.

"Do you know why she's a better dancer than you are?" Tomas appears at my shoulder, the slightest of grins touching his lips.

I smile back at him. "Because despite my wishes, I cannot be the best at *everything*?"

His grin twists up a bit at my quip, and my heart sputters. I can practically hear him say, *You're the best at quite a lot.* "It's because you don't follow well. In anything."

"Don't go pointing that out to Jamys. He might not consider it to be an ideal quality in a wife."

Tomas doesn't say anything for a moment. I'd feel guilty for bringing up my betrothal, but it's only ever bothered me.

He was the first person I told all those months ago. As soon as I got away from my parents and their *happy* news, I was on my way to him without ever consciously deciding it.

The ride to Highbluff Castle blurred by. My mind too muddled for me to decide what I was going to say. So, when I found myself stepping into Tomas' chambers, I was quite certain I was going to make a fool of myself. There hadn't even been time to consider how my freedom to move about Highbluff to visit with Jo could have been very convenient if Tomas and I continued to…

He entered from his bedroom, hair still wet from a bath. The neck of his tunic was open to reveal a column of skin down the middle of his chest, and my panic was tempered by a twinge of longing as my fingers twitched against my shaky will to *not* touch that skin.

I was undoubtedly going to make a fool of myself.

"Oh, hello, Bell. To what do I owe the honor?" Did I imagine the glint in his eye? Maybe it was my nerves. I was as wound up as I'd been a few nights before when we'd first kissed. This time it wasn't in a warm, expectant way. Now I was shivering from the cold and dread in my bones.

"Tomas, I… My parents have informed me…"

"Are you all right?" He guided me to sit, and his hand on my lower back sent a chill up my spine. "Would you like me to call for tea?"

"No, I'm fine. Thank you. I…" I took a deep breath and stared at the floor. "When I arrived home, I learned my parents are arranging for my betrothal,"—I looked up at Tomas' eyes—"to Prince Jamys."

"Oh." His dark eyebrows furrowed. "Are you happy about it?"

I swallowed hard. "Why shouldn't I be?" *Give me a reason to fight them on it. Tell me it should be you instead.* That was too much to think about after one encounter. I'd look ridiculous asking what he thought of that possibility.

He stood and walked to the window. With his back to me, he said, "You should be. I mean, I hope you are… happy." His shoulders rolled back before he turned to face me again. "Congratulations."

My stomach tumbled. "Thank you. I should go. I only thought you should know so you weren't surprised when it's announced. After..." It felt as if a hand wrapped around my throat.

"Bell, you needn't worry about me telling anyone."

And he didn't.

I keep my eyes on the swirling sea of people—none of them aware of the biggest secret in the room, of the pulsing tension between the two of us.

The news of the potential shift in the line of succession would be enough to distract them anyway, but I don't think they care what they're celebrating, so long as the music is good and wine flows. The civilian members of the ministry are dazzled by the luxury of it all, plus they already knew this was coming. High lords and ladies whisper with mischievous grins, probably more interested in the excitement than the politics. Or maybe it's all in my head and this is how they always are at events.

The attention Marcus and Nina are getting is both typical and new. They are always popular targets for anyone trying to make gainful connections. This time, however, the twins appear pleased by it. Marcus is always cordial, so his warm smile at the young woman who keeps touching his shoulder as they talk is not surprising. But Nina? She's been known to burn potential suitors with her words just as thoroughly as she can with fire. Now, though, she chats animatedly in a circle of men and women, as if their interest is proof she might win the trials.

At least being betrothed means there's less reason for people to pay attention to me—a pleasant result from a less-than-pleasant situation.

The only person from whom I want that kind of attention is already at my side, perhaps as aware of the small distance between us as I am.

Tomas offers me his hand. "May I have this dance?"

Chapter Nine

I look at Tomas' offered hand as if it might burn me.

It has before. As it turns out, I quite enjoy that burning. Too much to turn it down now, regardless of how stupid it may be.

Turning him down would be infinitely more suspicious than dancing with him, I tell myself as I reach out to accept. We step onto the dance floor, and having his hands on me, even in this most innocent of ways, twists my stomach. Perhaps it's Jamys' presence—an unnecessary reminder of the fact that this will be the only way Tomas and I can interact soon enough. As we flow along with the music, a terrible thought pops into my head: *Will we dance at my wedding?* Could I stand to have his hand on my waist, knowing it will never touch the skin there again? It will be unbearable to want him and know I can't be sated. The logical thing to do with that knowledge is to start pulling back now. Instead, I create a bubble around us. Not completely sealing us off from the room, but the sounds around us are muffled.

Tomas cocks an eyebrow at me. "Whatever is that for?"

"I enjoy my privacy."

"To say what?"

I turn under our joined hands. "That you don't seem to mind if I'm not good at following."

"I've never had a problem following you, Bell."

"Anywhere?"

"What, are you running away?" His expression remains vaguely disinterested as he looks past me at the room full of people.

"I wouldn't do that."

"I know."

I want to ask him to follow me to my chambers, to a rooftop, to the back stairs—anywhere to feel his skin on mine. But I also want him to suggest it. Like a terrible wretch, I want him to be jealous having seen me on Jamys' arm.

"Now you're showing off," Tomas says with a grin.

"How so?"

"Keeping the shield up for no reason at all."

I bat my eyes—the picture of innocence. "I am supposed to be preparing for the trials."

"Is this very good practice?"

Practice. An unlikely word to excite every nerve in my body, but I've had a unique training regimen.

I watched from the bridge as the Cerauno banners disappeared in the distance.

It was done. The contract was signed. I was officially betrothed. Days after having the memory of Tomas' body branded into my mind, I was planning to give mine to someone else.

The cave which this bridge from the west tower led to had always called to me. I needed its comfort then, the shadows near its entrance guarding me from this reality.

My future husband was on his way back to my future home. How could I live in a place I couldn't even picture? The entire thing was abstract—something happening to someone else. I could see someone who looked like me being happy at Jamys' side, but I didn't know the feeling myself. *There's time. It'll come.*

"Is this still your preferred hiding spot?" Tomas was halfway across the bridge before I noticed him. Now he came to my side.

"What do I have to hide from?"

"I can't begin to imagine what the most powerful of Queen Elea's children would need to hide from." It sounded like it was meant to be playful, but a dark edge tinged his voice.

"I'm not the most powerful."

"I think you are."

"You are mistaken. I can't even keep myself a couple of inches off the ground when I'm kissed." I couldn't say things like that now. But when those memories took up all the space in my mind, what other words could I conjure?

"Perhaps that speaks less to your weakness and more to the quality of the kiss."

My jaw clenched as I put all my focus on not biting my lip or pressing my lips together as they yearned to feel his again. I kept my eyes trained on the horizon where my future husband had just gone out of sight.

"I'm sorry," Tomas said. "I've overstepped. I shouldn't—"

"No." I turned to face him. "It's quite all right. I don't want you to tread carefully around me." My gaze dropped to his lips then snapped back up to his eyes, a blush warming my cheeks. "I don't want you treating me differently at all. We've always teased each other, and I don't want that to go away. After all, you may be right. It was a lovely kiss. But I should be able to hold my power all the same."

"I'm sure that would come with practice."

My resolve to keep my lips still melted. I rolled them in and ran my tongue over them, remembering Tomas' tongue doing the same. Slowly, I backed toward the cave. "I'm sure it would. And I am expected to master my power."

"An important responsibility." He followed me step for step.

"It is."

"Well, as is my duty, I am at your service for whatever you need, Princess."

We were blanketed by the cave's darkness now. My heart was going to rupture. "Your commitment is without comparison."

His chin dropped, and his eyes sparkled. "I should hope so."

I couldn't hold back anymore, not with that mischievous look on his face. I kissed away his coy smile—his lips were so much better suited for this. Kissing him was consuming. It was all there was in the world: no betrothal, no responsibility or rules. Just him and me.

His lips grazed my jaw, and my core melted. When he reached my ear, he whispered, "Weren't you supposed to be practicing something?" His breath on that sensitive area made my toes curl.

A sound, half-laugh, half-sigh, escaped me, and I pressed the air up underneath us. This time, Tomas remained steady. "Better?"

His mouth crushed mine again, and to the air, I thought, *Please, stay this way. I have other things I'd rather think about.* Though all I could think of was Tomas, it did.

Kissing him was somehow more than I could have ever hoped for, yet not enough at the same time. A feast but only a taste. And I was starved.

I pulled back, and his lips traced a path of kisses down my neck. I swallowed past the lump in my throat to whisper shaky words to him. "It would appear this is too easy a test."

He looked in my eyes, searching for answers, approval. I answered with a small smile before pulling his tunic off.

"Bell..."

"It's all just a political contract." I skimmed my fingers down his chest.

"I know..."

"They didn't ask if I was what they'd consider tainted."

He huffed a short laugh. "Wise move. I can't imagine Elea would have responded well to that."

"She wouldn't have. She told me it is neither their business nor hers."

Mother did add that it might be considered poor taste to have such relations now that I was betrothed, though, and I had to agree. Since a betrothal is romantic for most people, it wouldn't be understood that I'd only be living normally until a contract—that's all this marriage would be—changed my circumstances. Ceraun's opinion would be harshest. Probably not enough to break our betrothal, but pride and self-righteousness have made people do stupider things. It would be complicated here—not a situation I wished to put any of us in. Tomas could assume that easily enough, though, and I wasn't of any mind to give us reasons not to be together in that moment.

"It's not as if I'm married already." My words were a faint breeze.

"And once you are married?"

I dropped my forehead onto his bare shoulder. *Married.* The thought should have thrilled me, but it felt as if I was careening toward a cliff. "Once I'm married, we go back to what we were a week ago. Friends."

That's how I turned lust into training. Sex into practice. The game was to see if I could keep us shielded or afloat through the throes of passion. It turned out the challenge wasn't my concentration; rather, any shield I created was so thoroughly a part of me that they'd tremble, melt, shatter when I did. I had to learn to separate my power from myself. Keep it as a dear friend but with boundaries.

It took a lot of practice.

It took the rest of summer, autumn, winter, and now into spring. It's a wicked excuse but actually helpful, as he seems to be my only weakness. We both know keeping a little sound barrier around us while dancing and flirting is no test of my powers. And so, the tease begins.

"This isn't much of a challenge, but every little bit helps." I send a wisp of warm air to brush his ear and down his neck.

"That's quite unfair. You can be in plain sight and do whatever you like to me, while I'm helpless against you."

"I can't do *anything* I'd like." This vague mention of it in the middle of a room full of people is a thrill all its own.

"Is torturing me not your favorite pastime then?"

My lips curl up at the corners. "It's a close second."

"A princess should always have her first choice of everything."

Ha. If only. We continue dancing in silence, the warm scent of him enveloping me in the discreet enclosed space. It tugs at my core and distracts me enough that I miss a step. "Perhaps you could help me in learning to follow."

His blue eyes glimmer. We understand each other so well when it comes to this. Fortunately, he doesn't see past my lust to the feelings I am not supposed to have. "I have been meaning to check the wine cellar. Not that I don't trust the staff to keep track, but I'd be remiss if we ever let the palace run dry."

And I shall follow him there. "Your service to the crown is admirable."

"It's always my goal to anticipate your needs."

The song ends, and I hide my blush with a curtsy as he bows his head to me. "Thank you, Lord Tomas."

"Your Grace." He strides off through the throng of people, and I watch from the corner of my eye as he slips out of the ballroom.

I take my time, getting a glass of wine and telling curious courtiers how honored I am for the opportunity to be crowned heir. Responses to the outcome not affecting my betrothal range from tight concern to sparkling excitement. Only one of the disappointed replies gives me the feeling that my hand not becoming available again is the real problem. Alas, that's a response I'd have preferred from the next Lord of Highbluff, not Donehan. Still, foolishly, it's Tomas I'm on my way to.

After enough time has passed, I go out a different way, sneaking into a back hallway and down the stairs to the cellar. The shield of air goes up as the door closes. I don't even give Tomas the chance to continue the devilish dance we've mastered. He doesn't get a word in before my lips meet his with starved passion.

Chapter Ten

"Go ahead." I slide a pin into my hair, using the distorted reflection in a wine bottle as a mirror. "I'll leave enough of a gap between your return and mine."

Tomas leans against a large oak cask. "You're the one who will be missed if you're gone too long."

It's true under any circumstance, except now it makes me think of Jamys' warning that people will pay more attention to me since I could be the heir. This entire escape from the ball was probably ill-advised, but we've gotten away with it for so long. Jamys being here highlights the fact that we are almost out of time. I'm not ready for it to be over.

I sigh and turn to face him. "How do I look?"

His blue eyes scan me for evidence of our escapade. "Perfect."

I school my face into a serene smile. "Enjoy the rest of the evening then." I turn away and retrace my path in reverse back to the ball.

The festivities roll on, dancing and drinking and flirting hopefully stopping anyone from noticing my absence. Grandmother catches me in her sights and prowls toward me. The two things I have been most masterful of since my betrothal are hiding my affair and avoiding my grandmother. As a former queen-consort, she wants to offer me guidance, but I don't want to face that future yet. I scan the room and spot Jamys and Josslyn. Ironically, the very future I don't want to discuss with Grandmother is the escape.

"How are we enjoying the party?" I loop my arm through Jo's with a smile.

She inspects me more meticulously than her brother did, and I wonder if she can tell. "It's lovely, of course. Are you being badgered more than usual now?"

I shrug. "A few hours into my new role, I can't say it feels particularly different."

Her lips tug up on one side in a thoughtful way. "I've got to make my rounds as well. If you'll excuse me." She dips her chin and drifts away.

My gaze meets Jamys', and avoiding Grandmother seems like a terrible mistake. Being alone with him when a familiar soreness still lingers between my legs turns my stomach to lead. I can't continue like this with Jamys around.

"Are you feeling well?" Jamys asks.

"Yes, I…" I glance around, searching for an excuse. "I need some fresh air." My smile comes more naturally now. "It's more important to me than most."

"I'd be happy to escort you outside. Unless you want to be alone." The last part is added hastily with a self-conscious undertone. I don't doubt he means it, but I'd feel even more guilty to leave him behind now.

I hook my hand in the crook of his elbow. "Thank you."

Outside, an unbidden breeze caresses my face, reminding me this was no mere excuse. I *do* need to get out into the fresh air often. My relaxing makes the disparity between us evident. Jamys is rigid and unnaturally still except for his legs carrying him forward. I hope it's not because of me.

"Are celebrations in Alchos quite different from what you're used to?" He furrows his brow at my question. "You seem tense. I don't want you to be uncomfortable here or with me."

His cheek pinches in where he bites it. "Arabella, my only discomfort is in guessing that you didn't expect your marriage to go this way."

"Jamys, I'm a princess. I had no reason to believe it would be any different." Except for the part where I had just bedded another man. "I consider myself lucky it's someone I know and like." The words are true but hollow. My betrothal could have been so much worse. Of course, my parents wouldn't force me into something I was adamantly against, but it would have to be abominable for me to fight them on it. Arguing against such a thing would require profound motivation.

"I'm glad to hear that." Jamys' smile is uneasy.

I don't deserve gallantry from him, but I want to loosen his nerves for his own sake. So, I go with my typical contingency—sarcasm. "You, on the other hand, have the dreadful luck of being stuck with me."

That turns his smile warm. "That's not it at all. I just don't want you to be disappointed."

"You're a prince and heir to a throne. It isn't as if I'm settling."

"But you're a *magical* princess—the Angel of Alchos."

"I hate that moniker." Even before my affair made it more ridiculous, that was true. It was no miracle for Mother to have a second child—she simply chose to break with tradition. "And the only magical princes are my brothers, so again, it's a brilliant match for me." Standing here with him, it does feel like a brilliant match. Everything I said is absolutely true.

"You didn't seem happy when our betrothal was negotiated and agreed upon," he says.

"Neither did you." We were both silent and preoccupied during the entire process as far as I could tell.

He tilts his head, and I get the distinct impression he isn't spoken to this way very often. "The entire thing was so dreadfully unromantic and sterile. It was rather miserable."

"That's what we were born into."

He nods absently and reaches toward a blue daisy before stopping short to look at me. "May I?"

"They grow back quickly enough," I say with a smile.

The blossom comes away smoothly and rests in the palm of his hand. "It may be what we were born into, but now that we're living it, we can improve upon the situation. Don't you think?"

Classifying this as a political contract makes some things so much easier for me. In the long term, what he's insinuating should be my greatest desire—for us to truly be a couple, not just business partners. If my brain could convince my heart that the other option it entertains is not an option at all, I'd jump at this possibility.

Not if. *When.*

I *will* get over the infatuation with Tomas, and marrying some-one so open to forging a strong relationship with me will be won-derful. "Yes, I think we can."

His fingers brush against mine as he hands me the flower. "I know you're uneasy about the matter of the crown, but I can't help think we're lucky to be able to spend so much more time together before we're bound for life."

"Yes, I suppose we are." We may have been placed into this situation, but we can make of it whatever we wish. Someday, we'll probably be happy together—once I get the blue-eyed obstruction between us out of my system.

Chapter Eleven

A fireball hurdles toward Marcus but turns to steam when water fans out before him. Across the courtyard, another appears in Nina's palm until she jerks her hand back and shakes off droplets from Marcus' defensive maneuver. Flames appear on her other hand. They jump to her shoulder as she pulls her hand away, water splashing onto the ground. Like a lightning-fast dance, fires bounce and swirl around her. Water hits her or misses just as quickly as she moves. Flames coil around her arms en route to her hands, and she rolls them together between her palms before launching the glowing orb toward the sibling who is somehow both most like her and her opposite.

He blocks it again, and the beginning of a cocky smile appears on his face before he notices a ring of fire surrounding him, growing to wall him in. His smile warms as he nods to Nina. "Well played." A quick wave shoots around him, dousing the flames.

She shakes water off as they both walk toward me. "Not bad, but not enough to ever thwart you for long."

Marcus shrugs.

"If only we could all be so confident as to not require any practice at all." Nina drops her chin as she shoots me an accusatory look.

"Perhaps I am practicing, and you just can't see it." I blow a cool gust at her, and she rolls her eyes. Though, of course she's right. I'm not practicing for this nonsense. Not because I'm so confident—I simply don't care enough to. Rylan would be furious with me if I lost in the first round and left him to be outnumbered by the twins in the second, but to be done with it is tempting. Losing would soothe so many of my anxieties. There would be no more concern over what would happen if I won, and my staunch opposition to winning would be one less lie to keep up. And though part of me is warming to the idea of getting to know Jamys, the knowledge that he'd leave once I'm out does offer a guilty kind of solace. The Cerauno royals don't appear overly interested in my potential change of status, however Ceraun's future queen-consort becoming sovereign of Alchos would be quite different than what they agreed to with our betrothal. Any other result is of no consequence to them, so once I'm out, they needn't stay for the result.

Jamys' presence is a reminder not only of the impending end of my affair, but of the fact that he is someone I should be thrilled to be with. I could be happy about our betrothal, except I'm not ready to let go of... everything I'll be losing.

I leave the twins to it, setting off to snatch some food from the kitchens rather than taking a formal lunch. The back hallways are quiet, but the kitchen is bustling. I don't want to get in the way—or get caught—but asparagus and goat's cheese tartlets are calling to me. When the nearby cook is occupied at the stove, I pull air up underneath one where it sits on the cooling rack. It rises and makes its way to the doorway where I wait until a hand snatches it from midair. The body attached to said hand comes around from the corner, its face pinched with aggravation.

"Hello, Mary."

"Do you realize you do not actually have to *steal* food from your own palace?"

I smile widely. "It's so much more fun this way, though."

"I have told you to stay out of my kitchens."

"And I have. I did not step foot—"

"Oh, off with you!" She shoves the tartlet into my hands with a huff.

"You'll miss me when I move away."

"I'll have to go to Ceraun to warn the staff about you." She marches back into the kitchen.

It's not a bad idea, really. They can't possibly realize what's coming. I take a bite of the tartlet, and though the center burns the roof of my mouth, it is absolutely worthwhile. "This is divine, Mary. Perhaps instead of simply warning them, you could stay and work in Ceraun."

She lets out an incredulous laugh, and I take my leave. A new staff who hasn't known me my entire life is another drawback I hadn't considered. I've got this one accustomed to my jumping out of windows, floating around, and sneaking into the kitchens. It'll be an entire undertaking to start over.

When I emerge from the back hallway to head out to the gardens, Lillian is coming from the opposite direction. I float the tartlet behind my back before she sees it. Jamys' sister probably doesn't even know where her own kitchen is located, since a princess has no reason to seek out snacks for herself. Her polished perfection is the kind that must be bone deep. Having never seen the slightest slip from it, I'm certain she is just as well comported in private as she is in public settings.

"Hello, Arabella." Her tender smile is portrait ready, as always. "Are you done training for the day?"

"Perhaps. I'm taking a break, at least."

"Well deserved, I'm sure. I'm sorry to miss you, but Jamys is still out there. I'm going in for a little rest."

"Enjoy that." I slide the tartlet around and continue down the hall while she might still see me. Before I can divert from my course, Jamys appears in my path. His clothing is less stiff and ornamented than last night, but the rich purple waistcoat and gold cravat are a jarring contrast to my leggings and tunic.

"Hello, there." His eyes brighten to see me despite my casual appearance.

It should be easier to avoid people in a place so big. The tartlet is like a moon orbiting around me for all the ways I have to hide it. "Good afternoon. I'm surprised to see you about. It seemed rather dreadful to arrive after long travels and have a full itinerary of festivities the very next day."

"A busy schedule is nothing out of the ordinary. Are you taking a break from yours?"

"Honestly, I don't feel as if there's anything I particularly need to be doing anyway."

He tilts his head. "I thought you were preparing for the trials?"

"Without knowing what they'll consist of, I don't really see any way to prepare, so I thought I'd go sit in the garden for a while."

"In that case, may I join you?" His green eyes are so open and inviting, I'd feel terrible to sound like I'm avoiding him. He's trying to get us on a better track than the sterile one provided to us, and I should want the same.

"I was actually just about to have a bite to eat."

"In the garden?"

Of course when I'm being honest, it sounds like an excuse. "Yes." I pull my filched tartlet from behind my back. "I vex the staff terribly by not always taking proper meals."

His face strains, lips pressed together, as if to contain laughter.

"I know, I'm—"

"Delightful. You're delightful." He gestures toward the door he'd just come in through, and I lead us out.

I wouldn't think the Prince of Ceraun would appreciate such a thing. I've got to be everything he and Lillian were always taught not to be. King Urian has always struck me as the kind of person who could sniff out indecorum from a mile away and would assemble an army to snuff it out. I don't suppose he's missed my unsuitableness. Having magic to pass on to an heir probably forgives all my faults.

"Our cook might argue with your assessment, but regardless, I could never be half as delightful as this tartlet." We make our way to a stone bench behind a bushy tree covered with white blossoms. "Would you like to try it?"

He looks confused for a moment, as if he can't even imagine how he *could* try it without polished silverware and fine dishes.

"Just take a bite." I hold it up to him, and he leans in to do as I say. His lip brushes my fingertip, sending contradicting messages through my body. Part of me likes the intimacy and wants to lean into it, but a noisy, stupid part shouts that those aren't the lips I want to touch.

"That's delicious."

I swallow back the whirlwind of feelings. "Of course it is. And now we're both eating a stolen tartlet in the garden like a pair of uncouth thieves."

"I suppose we are."

"Was this what you had in mind when you thought we might do something together?" I take a bite, enjoying his unsteadiness almost as much as the treat.

"Not at all."

"Whatever shall we do then?" I ask.

"I'm realizing anything I might think of would probably be terribly boring to you."

"No, I'm easily entertained."

"How fortunate for me."

Jamys' self-deprecating tone is the kind of thing that usually makes me more comfortable with a person. On him, though, it's a touch mysterious. He was born to be a king. He's known that as long as he's known his own name. Why wouldn't he think more highly of himself? He seems worried about not being enough for me, but where does that come from? I try to be interested in him, or at least to appear to be. It's not even all false. He's a lovely person and, in moments like this, intriguing.

"Jamys, what do you do for fun?"

His eyebrows pull together as if I've just asked the most ridiculous question. "We're royals, Ara. When does it ever matter what we *enjoy* doing?"

"If we're to be married, then it matters to me."

Being the spare has probably spoiled me with free time. He undoubtedly has greater demands as heir, and we'll both be busier as king and queen someday. I should still know these things about him, though. Maybe I'll even find ways to slip moments of fun into his schedule.

He looks at me as if my motives and intentions might be written deep in my eyes. "All right," he says finally. "I'll show you."

Chapter Twelve

The way Jamys got so nervous about *showing me* whatever it is he's going to show me—his disappearance into his rooms, his insistence that we go somewhere private—equates in my mind to him having some horribly scandalous fetish. Whether I will come to regret asking him about it or find it amusing or alluring, is yet to be seen as we cross the bridge from the west tower to the cave adjacent the palace.

His immaculate posture is more rigid than usual, like he's bracing for battle. Perhaps he's a murderer. He couldn't possibly kill *me*, though, so why drag me out here?

"I'll admit, I am intrigued," I say as we approach the cave.

We get inside, and his expression drops. "Oh. It's much louder here than I expected." Case in point—he very nearly has to yell the sentiment to me.

"There's a waterfall on the other side of it." With a swirl of my hand, I pull a soundproof bubble around us. "Is that better?"

He looks around and runs his fingers down the shield. "I don't think I'll ever get used to this."

"You have ample time to find it perfectly normal, if not dull."

This sprawling room has countless tunnels branching off it. I've gotten lost in here more times than I can recall, though my parents were always more concerned about those incidents than I was. Despite all my wandering through it, I still haven't explored the entire cave.

"I thought this used to be a temple?" Jamys asks.

"That was centuries ago. Part of it was destroyed."

"And you don't have any temples at all now." It's not a question, but I answer it anyway.

"The dead can be remembered and honored, but they do not need to be worshipped."

Omaliya, the First Queen, did not care for religion, and as she was the one the gods gave their power to, she was a dependable authority on how we should proceed with it. It's enough to use the magic gifted to us to maintain peace in our kingdom. Our actions are the greatest thanks we can offer the gods. Of course, only ever mentioning them as a method of swearing is probably blasphemous to Jamys.

His lips quirk, but he says nothing.

"What is it?"

He brushes the shield again. "I suppose it's easier to think that way when the gods left you a parting gift."

It isn't as if the gods made every citizen of Alchos magical. That would certainly incite jealousy from the other kingdoms. But to assign one family as the keepers of magic doesn't amount to choosing a kingdom to favor. Alchos wasn't even a kingdom when the Lord of Mirador found Omaliya washed up on his shore. She didn't remember where she'd come from, but she seemed to be blessed, as her presence ended a drought and made the land more fruitful. It was because she used that blessing to help those around her that Alchos united under their rule, and the gods saw fit to leave the power in her hands. With their magic went their immortality, and so they died, trusting Omaliya and her descendants to rule over the elements and the land. Worship didn't get us anything—it was the virtuous actions of our ancestors.

I sigh at Jamys' discontent. "Do you think your devotion to them will result in magic being shared with you?"

"Isn't it?"

My face heats. *No, Jamys. The gods aren't giving Ceraun magic. You're getting me, but that may be more of a curse than a blessing.* I take a deep breath and get back to the purpose of our little excursion. "Why are we out here?"

He presses his lips together before he reaches into his pocket and pulls out a pipe of some sort. I look down at it, up to him, and back again. "It's an instrument?"

"Yes." The word is drawn out and tips up in pitch at the end.

I slap my hand over my mouth and bite my lips together for good measure. The laugh I contain threatens to spill into my eyes as tears, though.

"It's ridiculous. I know." Jamys' face reddens, and he begins to put it away.

"No! No. I'm so sorry. It's not at all. I was just..." I cover my mouth again as I swallow back a chuckle. "All the secrecy. I was really expecting it to be something horrible or scandalous."

"Like what?"

"I don't know!" I put my hand on his shoulder to steady myself into some semblance of maturity. "I'm sorry. I'm fine now. It is beautiful. May I have a closer look?"

He raises one eyebrow but hands it to me. It's polished to such a luster, I wouldn't think it was ever a tree. Masterful flourishes are carved into the length of it, with brilliant stars around the holes.

"Did you make this?"

He shakes his head. "Goodness, no."

"But you play it?"

"Yes." This time, the word is a little more confident, though still nervous.

"Will you play it for me?"

He scrapes his lip with his teeth. "I suppose that's why we came here, though I am rather regretting the idea."

"Oh, please don't. We can't have such secrets… once we're married." The end is tacked on in a flurry as I consider a secret I keep that is considerably more pertinent.

"All right."

He folds one leg over the other as we sit on the cave floor. Then he puts his lips to the pipe, and a beautiful sound whispers forth from it. The tune is gentle, subdued, like it's unsure of what it's trying to be. Light but dark. The space between twilight and darkness. It's haunting. Watching Jamys play it, I'm torn between gratitude and guilt. He's a real person when he's sitting here on a cave floor with me. Usually, he's just a plan for the future, far away where I don't have to think about him yet. I knew I'd get to know him better while he was here, and that's a good thing—it has to be. Still, knowing him too well feels like a violation of us both. This is a gift I don't deserve from him. It's too beautiful for the woman who lies with another man knowing she'll marry him.

When the song is over, he looks up at me, waiting.

"Jamys, you make magic with air, too. Even I can't do *that*. It was beautiful."

"Well, it's not something generally considered practical for a crown prince to do."

"Beauty is rarely practical. That doesn't mean it isn't worthwhile."

Silence builds for a moment before he says, "You'll be good for Ceraun, Ara." His smile holds words he isn't saying, but I have no right to pry. Mine always do the same.

"I hope so."

CHAPTER THIRTEEN

The warm feelings growing for Jamys and Ceraun are tempered by my first go at Cerauno fashion.

"Are you certain that's where it goes?"

Lucy strings a ribbon through a loop at my waist. "I don't see where else it could go. Could you put your finger here, please?" She guides my hand back to hold something in place while she ties something else.

"Do they require an entire *team* to dress a lady in Ceraun?" Cerauno fashion is known as "classical," which is kinder to say than antiquated. They claim to have remained true to the time of the gods. If that's the case, the gods' choice to submit to death is no surprise.

"It would explain why the royal family brought so many attendants," Lucy says.

"Their gowns don't *appear* to be this complicated."

Lucy sighs. "That's because there's another layer to go atop all this."

I drag my hand down my face. This is utterly ridiculous—all this effort and none of it will even be seen. Furthermore, it's already heavier than what I wear to go out into the snow! Fully assembled, this gown seems to have the purpose of anchoring me to the ground. In my case, that might actually be considered useful, but why on earth must anyone else be weighed down like this?

When the process is done, Lucy steps back.

"Thank you, Lucy. You should take a long break. That was quite a feat."

Her shoulders slump, and she tucks a stray lock of hair behind her ear. "Thank you. I hope it's easier to take off."

"Oh, if it's too difficult, I'll have Nina burn it off me."

She smiles as she sends me off. Tonight, floating down the middle of the spiral staircase is not for fun—it is a necessity. Walking down these stairs wearing my weight in fabric can only lead to disaster. The combination of aggravation, pity, and awe for the women who propagate this is difficult to reconcile.

Lillian lights up when I enter the dining room—late, since getting dressed took infinitely longer than getting dressed ever should. "Arabella, you look stunning!"

"Thank you." I sweep the layers of skirts underneath myself as I sit to find it's more uncomfortable when seated. "I love it." It's not that it isn't pretty, there is just so much of it. If a dress is going to be so insistent on covering as much skin as possible, *why* doesn't it care about covering up my shape? It's as tight as tight can be to ensure *that* isn't lost under everything. A torso-length shackle has shoved my breasts up nearly to my chin, only for them to be covered up. Then it pinches in at my waist before ensuring my legs and hips are completely lost under a tent of a skirt. It couldn't be more opposite our fashion if it tried.

Queen Anilla bubbles with joy over my appreciation of her gift. Nina keeps quiet about it, but her coy, tight-lipped smile tells me she's compiling jests about it for later use.

I can scarcely eat for the lack of room allotted me by this ensemble, and if not for the power to control air, I might suffocate. Perhaps Lucy didn't put this on correctly. I'll have to ask Lillian about it in private. I survive dinner, though I'm still hungry by the end of it. Lucy can bring something to my chambers later. Although, the kitchens should be quiet, so I could just get something myself. Mary would never know.

All I want to do is get out of this dress, but I remain with the party into the parlor. I won't survive months of this. It's not possible. Jamys walks me in and asks if I'd like to play joko. I agree, and we sit down to it.

"You do look beautiful." An unspoken hesitation lingers after his words.

"Are you certain?"

"I am. However, as much as I anticipated seeing you in Cerauno fashion, I must admit, I preferred you this afternoon."

This afternoon—in a tunic and leggings, sitting on the floor of a cave. He is a surprising one at times. "That's what you prefer? Not my Alchosian dresses?"

He keeps his eyes down as he places the pouch of white stones before me. "Those are also... lovely." His cheeks color ever so slightly. Which of my dresses might he be picturing? They all reveal lengths of skin Cerauno *undergarments* probably keep covered.

"I wasn't sure if you ever actually noticed."

"I notice, Ara."

It stirs something in me to think of him admiring me that way, but I'm not sure if the stirring is pleasant or uncomfortable. My entire torso being squeezed isn't helping matters.

"Regardless,"—he places a stone on the board—"I did still prefer this afternoon."

I could explore the topic further. Perhaps I *should*. But getting to know Jamys better is a slippery slope. If we have a relationship before we're married, then a pre-wedding affair becomes something I'll feel horribly guilty for. Instead, I turn my attention to the game, or rather, to losing the game, as I so often do.

"The recommended strategy is to secure the borders first," Jamys says. "Then you can move into the center of the board."

"But there is more space to concur here."

"It's harder to do, though." He kindly doesn't tease me about my whiny tone. "You're more likely to win in small chunks."

"Well, there isn't anything I can do on that side now; you've got it all."

"You need to fortify that side so I can't expand my territory."

I tap my teeth together as I look over the board. It's a mosaic of black and white stones with plenty of options, but none seem useful.

A footman enters and goes to Mother. I miss what he says, but I pull the air to hear her say in a low voice, "Tell him to come in, please. He's as good as family."

The stream was broad enough for Jamys to hear as well, apparently, for he looks at me with a bemused smile. "You use your magic to eavesdrop?"

I shrug innocently. "It comes in handy every now and then."

"Who is as good as family?"

Behind Jamys, the person in question enters, and my dress isn't the only thing impeding my breathing anymore. "Tomas Coyle."

Three in a large crowd was one thing. Tomas, Jamys, and me in this smaller setting flushes my face and neck with heat.

Tomas' eyes meet mine in a solemn look before flittering down to my dress. Now he appears to be containing a smirk. I purse my lips and flick his neck with a burst of cold air. He continues toward Mother unfazed.

"Good evening," she says at normal volume. "To what do we owe the honor?"

"The honor is mine, as always. I'm sorry to interrupt your gathering, but a messenger has arrived at Highbluff from my uncle at Lambridge. They are requesting aid, and my father wanted your leave to send forces from Eglingen."

"Why are they in need of aid?" Mother asks.

"Odd occurrences in the west are being blamed on magic."

She rubs her wrist. "How could that be when all the magical people are here?"

"It's the easiest way to explain things they can't understand."

Being as close as they are to Penum, I suspect our hostile neighbor has something to do with people looking to blame magic for their misfortunes.

"Is there any violence?" I ask.

All eyes divert to me. "Not yet," Tomas says. "It's simmering, though, and they're afraid it will boil over."

"And sending soldiers will do what, exactly?"

"Dissuade people from becoming violent."

"For how long?" Somehow, it feels as though Tomas and I are alone in a close conversation, rather than across a full room from each other. "You can't keep them there forever, and it doesn't solve the problems they're upset about. If they think our magic is a bad thing, we should show them it isn't."

Mother looks at me openly. "What would you recommend?"

"Send us out there. This entire…"—*Don't say something negative. Scheme. Contrivance. Stratagem…*—"arrangement with the trials is about us earning our people's trust and love. We don't need to do that here. People around the capital already love us. We should go where it's a problem."

Mother's jaw ticks. "I'll consider it. Tomas, please tell your father to hold off for now."

"Perhaps both," Rylan offers. "The four of us could go *with* a contingent of the Eglingen army."

"That wouldn't exactly look like we're arriving to make peace."

He glowers at me. Fantastic—he's going to act as if I'm stepping on his toes. This isn't about the damned competition. I'm trying to secure *his* kingdom. Perhaps I shouldn't bother. It won't be my problem, anyway.

"I'll let you and Lord Coyle know in the morning." Mother stands and takes Tomas' arm. "Thank you for bringing us this news…" she begins as they leave the room.

Jamys grins at me once they're gone but says nothing.

I give us some invisible privacy. "Go ahead. No one can hear us now."

"Are you certain? I still hear them, though it's muffled."

"I control what goes in and out. I want some sound to come in, so I'm not caught completely off guard by someone speaking to me. But watch." I keep my eyes on him and smile convivially, but I raise my volume as I say, "Nina, your hair looks dreadful." There is, of course, no response besides Jamys pressing his lips together to hide his amusement. "See?"

"All right. Well, I wanted to point out that you aren't as bad at these games as you think." He gestures to the board between us where his impending victory is obvious. "Lambridge is near your border, correct?"

"Yes."

"You're fortifying your border, as I had said."

I quirk a brow. "Actually, I'm the one who suggested sending four magical royals to shake hands and kiss babies *instead* of sending an army."

"There are different ways to strengthen the area. I'll be interested to see how this option works out if your mother chooses to go with your idea."

"Would you go as well?"

He shrugs. "If you win the crown, I'll be king-consort someday. It seems fitting I see more of Alchos than just Mirador."

This time last week, I'd have been jumping at the opportunity to distance myself from Jamys, but now, I might appreciate this idea of his. I glance at his parents. Would they allow it? Would Jamys be quite different away from them? More like the musician playing a haunting melody in a cave than the perfect prince?

My smile isn't the one I rehearsed when I fretted over his arrival. It's real, now. "I suppose we'll find out tomorrow if that will be happening." And to my surprise, I think I want it to.

Chapter Fourteen

"Will you require any formalwear?" Lucy goes to the wardrobe that holds that collection.

I look at the piles of clothing already deemed necessary and sigh. "I suppose one or two dresses." At this rate, we're going to have to bring an army just to transport all our things.

"Both yours, or do want any of the new Cerauno gowns?"

"Goodness, no! I can't possibly burden horses with dragging those things around the kingdom."

She snickers as she picks out far lighter and more appropriate options. "You're certain you don't wish for me to come?"

"Yes. Royals traveling is so complicated for everyone. I'd like to simplify it as much as possible."

"Your sister is bringing Kristance."

Of course she's bringing her maid. Nina doesn't care how much of a burden she is on anyone. "I'm not my sister."

A day of preparations comes and goes. Our convoy is packed. We're all ready, and goodbyes are said.

Jamys and I walk out to the courtyard which is still hazy with morning mist. I turn to him with a smile. "I'm surprised your parents allowed you to traipse about a foreign kingdom with us."

"They're content to let me stay at your side."

Whether to secure their investment in me or for sentimentality, I don't know, but I don't let it worry me. Jamys' intentions are the only ones that matter, and he's transparent as a clear sky about wanting to get to know me and build a real relationship.

I come across Tomas checking a saddle. "Have you come to see us off?" I ask.

"I've come to escort you."

My jaw clenches. "What?"

"I'm going with you."

"Why?" The idea of being in such close company with Tomas and Jamys leaves a sour taste in my mouth. Never did I think I'd be so put off by being around him, but having Tomas nearby will make it impossible to feel comfortable around Jamys. He's my future, and any time I spend with Tomas will make it more difficult to move on. I want to take Jamys up on his offer to make our relationship real.

"My uncle asked *my family* for assistance. We can't decline without an explanation."

"People are being sent. *We* are going there."

He scoffs. "Highbluff can't very well take credit for sending the royal family."

"I can explain it."

"We have personal relations there, Bell. It'll come from me."

I rack my brain for any other excuse, though I know it won't matter. Tomas is stubborn. There's no use arguing with him. If he's determined to go, he's going to. It's so *nice* to see him sure of what he wants and being assertive about it. But it's never been me.

Could I have flown the distance to Lambridge? I've never tried to go anywhere *near* this far. I doubt it would go well. However, depending on how our time here goes, I may risk it for the return home. I couldn't keep the trajectory going with Jamys under Tomas' gaze. Even if he wouldn't be jealous, his lack of caring would only make me more upset. Not speaking to Tomas proved to be completely miserable, and by the third day, I had forgotten why I was angry with him. Or I realized it was nonsense. It didn't matter. At that point, it was a matter of pride to keep it going.

We are nearly there now, and a wave of relief rushes over me. Traveling can be its own separate incident, and this shall be a fresh start to our adventure. There is work to be done here—helping our people, showing them who we are. It should be more than enough for me to forget the web of personal dramatics I've spun for myself.

For our arrival in Lambridge, we don our finer riding clothes. None so fine as Nina, but that's because she is in a carriage. Before the city is even in sight, guards from Lambridge Castle meet us to escort us in.

"It isn't every day we see House Exos banners pass through," the captain says. "We want to make sure you aren't bothered."

"We appreciate the gesture," Rylan says.

Not that our people's attention should be a bother, but I hold my tongue on the topic. The sun is high in the sky when Lambridge comes into view. The town doesn't take up much space on a map. It's densely packed to keep this little outpost at the edge of the kingdom secure. We take a round-about route, skirting the edge of the city.

"Are we not to pass through the town?" I ask a guard flanking our party.

"A caravan of this size would have a difficult time getting through the streets, Your Grace."

"I see." I've never been to Lambridge and want to roam through it. There's time enough for it later, I suppose.

As we pass by the farms at the border, some fieldworkers huddle together, watching as we pass by. The distance is probably too great to notice, but I offer them a smile as we go. Disquietude prickles the back of my neck—a feeling that they are wary of us in a way I've not previously experienced. I wonder how much of our route has to do with traffic concerns, or if it's a matter of security.

Lambridge Castle comes into view in the rolling foothills before the sharp mountains which demarcate the border between Alchos and Penum. Such mountains seem like they should do a better job of keeping Penum and their hatred of our magic out of our lands. Alas, snakes can slither through the valleys to tell people they should be afraid of us.

We pass through the gates and are greeted by a retinue of nobles. Lord and Lady Altman are the first to welcome us. Horace shares his sister's dark hair and blue eyes which she passed on to Tomas and Josslyn. As we move on to their children and other family, Lady Kathlyn's daughter looks particularly excited, nearly bouncing on her heels as she curtsies. Ceanna is about my age. Her late father was Lord of Windamere, but when her mother married Horace, she came to live here, rather than remain at home with her brother as the new lord of the castle. Her eyes are bright with joy, which hits a new peak when we continue and Tomas reaches her. She squeals and throws her arms around his neck, her long red curls bouncing along her back as she lifts her feet, hanging off him.

The gods in their graves blessed Mother with the foresight not to give me fire, because I'd be an inferno right now.

"It's been almost a year. I didn't think you were going to stay away so long." She latches onto his arm, and I turn away before Tomas can make eye contact with me—if he even would.

We make our way into the castle, me on Jamys' arm, trying to ignore the voices behind us without putting myself in a bubble of silence and possibly missing something I actually need to hear. Practically at our heels, Ceanna prattles on to Tomas, and my stomach lurches as I piece it together. Last summer's stay at Etherlee was shortly after Tomas returned from almost a year here in Lambridge. That was when I first noticed a new gleam in his eyes, the confident swagger. I was a bundle of nerves when we finally came together, but he was perfect: gentle when necessary but forceful in the best ways.

Too good to not have known exactly what he was doing.

It hadn't occurred to me at the time. I suppose some part of me knew it wasn't his first time, and it really doesn't matter. Unless I have to be around someone else he's slept with. This is quite different than there being a hypothetical other person somewhere in the world. This one is right here, her hands on Tomas, and the resulting pressure in my chest builds to an explosive level.

Horace stops in the sprawling entrance hall. "Please, make yourselves at home. Rest and wash after your long journey. It will be our honor to catch up with all of you over dinner tonight."

We offer our thanks, and attendants guide us to our rooms. Tomas says he knows where he's going, but Ceanna seems intent to escort him up the opposite staircase from the one the rest of us are herded to. Excellent—a trip meant to help the kingdom, which then added a lovely opportunity for Jamys and I to spend some time together, has turned into a nauseating situation where I'll be thinking about Tomas fucking someone else under the same roof.

Chapter Fifteen

Alone in the well-appointed room given to me, I pull a sound-proof bubble around myself and let out a good, loud scream. My shoulders rise and fall with my heaving breaths. Of course, the only person I'm truly angry with is myself. I have no right to be jealous. He's certainly free to do whoev—*whatever* he wants. I have no claim on him. And anyway, I was starting to warm up to Jamys. To have my thoughts thrown back to Tomas is so ridiculous. It's as if every time I make any progress, I revert even further.

A knock sounds from the door, and I look at it accusatorially. If that is Tomas, I will undoubtedly regret how horribly I act toward him in this moment. Perhaps he's coming to apologize or explain. Would that be any better? Shouldn't I use this to sever whatever it was we were doing?

"Ara?"

What is a combination of relief and disappointment called? Whatever it is, that's the feeling when it's Jamys on the other side of the door. Relieved that I don't have to fight with Tomas. Disappointed that Tomas doesn't want to try to fight with me. I'm a fool.

I open the door and gesture for Jamys to come in. "Did you miss me already?"

He hesitates before entering—*propriety at all times*—and I close the door behind him. "Do you need anything? Are you well?" His brow furrows, his lips slightly pinched. It reminds me of his nervous tension when he revealed his musical hobby.

"I'm fine, thank you. A proper bath and bed are all I need."

"Good. I..." He takes a breath, and slight shifts in his face transform him into his typical confident persona. "There was no opportunity for a private conversation during the journey here, but you seemed cross."

"Oh." His concern for me lightens my mood considerably. "Traveling was exhausting. Nothing's the matter, I promise."

He nods. "Glad to hear it. Before we left, you and I... seemed to be getting on well, and I wanted to make sure I hadn't damaged anything by coming here with you."

"We are getting on, very well." I lead him to a sofa and sit close to him. "All this mess with the trials is really against my taste, but it's gotten us this time together, and for that, I'm grateful. Truly, I'm glad you're here." *It would be so very easy to love you.*

His shoulders relax. "I'm happy to hear that, and I'm grateful for this time together as well. Being that we have already travelled together, I wondered if perhaps you might like to go up to Haarton Castle with Lillian and me for the summer?"

The summer castle in the mountains he told me about. I thought I'd have more time—that there would be one last trip to Etherlee with our usual group of friends. That plan didn't include spending the entire spring with Jamys, though. I couldn't go off and have a holiday with Tomas now.

Still, my answer almost surprises me. "Thank you for inviting me. It sounds like a wonderful idea."

The smile that lights up his face confirms the choice. "Excellent. We'll work out particulars when we're back in Mirador, but I'm so glad you'll be able to see more of Ceraun."

"As am I."

"I'll let you get to your bath and bed." He stands and crosses to the door. "I'll see you later then."

"Yes. Please come collect me on your way down to dinner."

"All right." He slips out of the door, and it closes quietly.

I ring for a maid to draw a bath and sink back onto the sofa. This trip hasn't offered the opportunity to connect with Jamys as I'd intended, but summer in Ceraun would. It'll be good for us. And Tomas won't be able to ruin that.

A groan rumbles through me. Every thought leads back to the same thing. Why is it that when I'm with Jamys, I'm happy for it, but the moment I'm alone, I think of Tomas?

The thoughts can't be washed away in the bath. Actively trying not to think about someone is counterproductive and results in only thinking about him. By the time I need to go down, Jamys is a stranger to my thoughts. He takes my arm, and I have to start the process of establishing a comfort level with him all over again.

We enter the parlor where everyone has gathered prior to dinner. Tomas is in the far corner; his eyes meet mine and immediately divert away. With any luck, he won't stay for our entire visit. There's no reason for him to be here. Unless it's to reunite with Ceanna, of course. She keeps close, leaning toward him in such a way that even I can't help but look at her breasts.

"How have things been?" Rylan asks Horace.

I take a seat near them while Jamys gets wine for both of us.

"Strange times all around," Horace says. "A few people vanished into thin air, and there were reports of odd strangers passing through, though we cannot find any trace of them either."

"Air can do a great many things people don't consider,"—I take the glass offered to me by Jamys—"but people cannot vanish into it." *Unfortunately,* I think as I take a sip. It's something I'd be interested in doing right about now.

"It's inexplicable, though." Kathlyn folds her hands together in her lap. "Gone without a single clue. Our guards haven't been able to find anything at all."

"Are the missing people connected in any way?" Nina asks.

"They couldn't be more varied," Horace says. "An old man, a stable boy, and a... lady of the night." His voice drops for the last one as if prostitution is something princesses are unaware of.

Marcus smirks. "I can think of a couple possible connections."

Horace laughs openly. "Your station does not hinder your sense of humor."

"Well, don't let our mother know he said that out loud." Ry spares Marcus an exasperated look. "I don't see how any of that could connect to our magic even if we weren't on the other side of the kingdom, but we'll be happy to speak with the people in the area. Reassure them that we're doing everything possible to keep them safe and solve these mysteries."

"That would be wonderful," Kathlyn says with a smile.

"Indeed," Horace says. "But I'm not sure it's your magic they're afraid of. They think they are, because magic and the Exos name go hand in hand, but the whispers are about other dark magic lurking."

Nina scoffs. "All magic is possessed by our family."

"The magic is split now." He gestures to the four of us. "It leads people to think perhaps some split off elsewhere."

Rylan tenses. If he was looking for further evidence that he should have all our magic, here it is. This time he keeps such thoughts silent, though I'm sure all four of us are thinking it.

A sigh escapes me. "It shouldn't be difficult to show people we mean well, but how are we to convince people that nonexistent magic doesn't exist?"

"Don't fret over it," Horace says. "Being so far removed from civilization makes people superstitious."

"You were worried about it enough to ask for reinforcements," Ry says.

Horace's brows furrow. "I did no such thing."

Everyone's attention snaps to Horace. "You asked my father for a militia." Tomas' brow furrows. "It's why we're here."

"If I had asked for a militia, I should be confounded by an assembly of royals instead."

"That was Princess Arabella's doing." My full name sounds foreign from Tomas' mouth. Has he *ever* used it? He's never even called me Ara like everyone else does. Formal greetings are reserved for sarcasm and foreplay.

Horace laughs. "Another generation of surprising royals in the palace. Gods bless this kingdom."

"Only another generation of involved royals," I say.

"We always wish to have close relationships with our people," Rylan adds. "We wanted to ease the tension in the area. But if you didn't request forces, who did?"

"I haven't the slightest idea. When word came of your impending arrival, we were curious as to what we had done to earn the honor."

Tomas rolls his eyes. "You needn't flatter them, Uncle. They know it's an ordeal to have to host them."

Kathlyn gasps. "Tomas!"

"It's all right," Marcus says. "We're quite used to his impropriety."

If it wouldn't make the lady of the castle faint, there's no doubt Tomas would have a colorful rebuke.

"Difficult as we may be," Nina says with a pointed glare at Tomas, "we are here, so we may as well make the most of it."

"Of course," Rylan says. "I'm glad things aren't as pressing as we'd been led to believe, but how could a false message have been received at Highbluff?"

I swirl the wine around my glass. Another mishap to confuse matters when there's already so much disruption in the kingdom. "Perhaps it's that dark magic."

Chapter Sixteen

Sleep was not my friend last night. Between the missing people, the forged message, tension between my siblings, my jealousy over Ceanna, and guilt about Jamys, rest was simply not possible. It's fine, though. I take advantage of being awake before anyone else and slip out from my balcony. Once we're all together, everyone will notice us from any distance. Alone, I might be able to explore the town without countless eyes on me. People act differently around a princess. I'll get a more honest impression of the town, and perhaps their opinion of us, if my title doesn't precede me.

Outside in the fresh air, I can relax. My boots land softly on the ground. A stranger strolling in from the hills at this hour might be suspicious, but I can't be on the road near the gatehouse and risk being seen. The town seems to wake earlier than the castle—shops are opening; the smell of baking bread wafts from windows. A man walks out of an inn, and the aroma of bacon draws me to the door. I enter, and a barmaid briefly glances up as she welcomes me. Yes, this is perfect. I don't need her getting flustered and curtsying before me.

"Good morning," I say. "It smells absolutely delicious in here." And feels cozy, the large hearth adjacent the dark wood bar giving it a homey atmosphere. Only a couple of tables are occupied—one by a lone man, and the other by an older couple.

"It should. It's the best breakfast you'll find in town," the round woman says without looking at me.

"How lucky for me."

"Is it just you then?"

"Yes."

She shakes her head. "Not wise to be traveling through here on your own, miss. People have been going missing. A woman ought not to be about alone."

Her fear wrenches my heart as the concern for me warms it. "I had heard about that. Weren't two of the three people men, though? It seems like my chances are as good as anyone's." Better, actually. Much, much better.

"One was only a boy, but you're right. *No one* should be about alone. I'll get your breakfast. Would you like some tea?"

"That would be wonderful. Thank you very much."

She prepares me a large mug, and I wrap both hands around it as I take a seat. Steam wafts toward my face in aromatic tendrils. This place with its quaint warmth and charm could be an advertisement for a simpler life. To think, I could blow through towns like this without being fussed over... It would be delightful.

A small boy comes out from the kitchen and sits by the unlit hearth with some wooden figurines. He plays with them until my breakfast comes out, perking up and eyeing me then.

"Good morning, young sir. You know, there is far too much bacon here for me. Do you think anyone could help me with that?"

He lights up and scurries to my table. "I could help you." He rests his chin on the table, putting the toys down.

"Could you? That is so very lucky for me." I hold out a crispy slice, and he takes it happily. "What's your name?"

"Richard," he says, crunching on the bacon.

"It's a pleasure to meet you, Richard. Is that your mother who works here?" A spoonful of steaming porridge tastes like comfort and warm spices.

"Yes. I have to come with her now that Grandfather is gone."

"Oh, I'm so sorry to hear he's gone."

"It's all right." He licks his greasy fingertips. "I think he went somewhere more fun."

"I'm sure you're right."

"Mummy doesn't think so." Dead gods, what did she say about her father in front of the boy? "That's why she told you not to be about alone. She thinks something bad happened to the people who disappeared."

Oh! He didn't die; he's the old man who vanished. "Well, perhaps we'll find out where they went soon. In the meantime, it's quite all right for me to be alone. Would you like to know why?"

He nods fervently. The boy won't keep a secret long, I'm sure, but it'll be long enough for me to move on.

I put a thin sound shield around us before saying, "I have magic."

"Are you a witch?" Richard's eyes widen.

"No, witches aren't real."

"Yes they are," the boy says matter-of-factly. "People say that's who took my grandfather and the others."

"You just told me he went somewhere fun."

"I think witches could be fun."

Well, that's one spin on it. "If they existed, I quite like the idea of witches being fun. But the only magic is natural magic, and it's all kept in my family."

His face scrunches up. "Not your family. Only the princes and princesses have natural magic."

I lean in close to whisper to him. "I am a princess."

He looks me up and down. "Where is your crown?"

"I never wear it to breakfast."

One eye narrows in a skeptical look. This kind of fun is exactly what I wanted out of an anonymous visit to town.

"I can prove it to you. Would you like to see what I can do with your toys?"

"Not if you're the one who controls fire!"

My hand covers a less-than-ladylike laugh. There is no doubt of this being the best breakfast in town, regardless of the food. With a flick of my fingers for effect, I blow the toys off the table, catch them in a net of air, and float them before him.

Richard gasps and gapes at me. "You're the Princess of Air!"

"Shhh. I don't want anyone hearing." I let the toys back down onto the table.

"Why not?"

"People tend to fuss over princesses, and I don't need a fuss."

He taps his nose. "If I marry you, would I be a prince?"

That is the most forthright any potential suitor has ever been about his intentions, possibly ever. Not that he's the first to be motivated by that. "You would. Sadly, I'm going to marry someone else. But my sister is not yet betrothed, so I'll recommend you to her."

"Is she as nice as you?"

I squeeze my lips together, trying not to grin. "Not quite."

He frowns and considers for a moment. "Who are you going to marry?"

"A prince."

A pensive nod. "That makes sense."

"It does make very good sense." His honesty seems to have pulled the same from me. Though the logic behind my betrothal has stayed at the forefront of my mind—lest I forget why it must be—the sensibility of it seems to have increased as I consider my compatibility with Jamys. Still, I'm not completely ready to accept being sensible.

"Is he nice like you?" Richard asks.

"He's even nicer than I am."

Before the boy can ask more questions the door swings open, and a familiar form enters, scans the room, and locks eyes on me.

"Is that the—" Richard begins. "No, that's Lord Tomas."

I remove our sheet of privacy in time to hear the pounding of Tomas' footsteps. "Well, it certainly isn't the very nice prince I'm marrying." I smile at Tomas as he approaches with an annoyed scowl on his face. "Good morning."

"Bell, what do you think you're doing?"

"Having breakfast. I'd invite you to join me, but Richard and I were having a private conversation."

Tomas puffs out a breath and musses Richard's hair. "Go back to your mum."

He looks at me. "Do I have to?"

"Yes!" Tomas says.

"*She's* the Princess. I'll listen to her over you."

Tomas' glower must be concealing a rainbow of colorful language not appropriate for children.

"You're very clever, Richard," I say. "I certainly outrank Lord Tomas, but I do think it's time you went back to your mother."

"All right," he grumbles. He starts to walk away then gasps and turns back to bow.

"It was a pleasure to meet you, sir," I say with a dip of my chin.

He flashes a bright smile before disappearing into the kitchen. I wonder how long my identity will be our secret.

Tomas watches him leave and turns to glare at me. "I don't even know what to say to you."

"Then I don't know why you're here." I lean back into my chair with all the petulance of a teenager.

"I'm here to cover up the disappearance of an inconsiderate princess to avoid a full-scale panic." *Me* inconsiderate? After he inserted himself into this trip to explore the many ways he might make me miserable?

"I wanted to interact with people without the pretenses of my title."

"Excellent," he says. "Would it kill you to tell someone?"

"If I had *planned* it, I might have."

"You're not at home, Bell. You can't run around without anyone knowing where you are. Do you realize how close we are to Penum?"

It's an effort not to roll my eyes. He knows the extent of my powers better than anyone. This isn't a safety issue; this is him being a controlling ass, overstepping the role *he chose* in my life. "What could Penum possibly do to *me*?"

"I'd rather not find out! You aren't indestructible."

"Well..."

He slams some coins onto the table. "Let's go."

I cross my arms. "I'm not your responsibility."

"You don't even know the meaning of the word."

My teeth clench together as I jump to my feet. My blood boils. Close enough to see each hue of his eyes, words are beyond me. Any wisp of an idea implies he should have some responsibility *to* me, but that's nonsense.

"Tell me I'm wrong." His voice is unnervingly steady and low. "Tell me you actually think it's reasonable for you to vanish from Lambridge Castle without anyone knowing about it."

Of course I can't do that. I had only considered that I couldn't be under the same roof with Tomas, Ceanna, and Jamys anymore. It was suffocating, and I needed to get away. My silence condemns me, and facing him is too much to bear. I turn to walk around him, but he grabs my arm, forcing me to face him. Well, he can't make me look him in the eyes. I keep mine downcast and wonder how it's possible that this man who brings out my most confident and daring sides can also make me feel so meek.

"Do you know what you've done so far today that is the *most* typical of you?"

Being stubborn? Forgoing rational thinking because you're in the vicinity?

When I don't reply, Tomas answers his own question. "Endearing people to you."

I glance up at him to confirm he's past his fury. His demeanor has softened, and his gaze has warmed. All right then. I offer my own olive branch. "Richard wanted to marry me."

He chortles. "Exactly. Now, come on."

"Back to the castle?"

"Not yet." He leads me out and turns the opposite direction. We continue down the road I'd been on, venturing farther into town. More people are out and about now, and several passersby smile and nod to Tomas in recognition. "I love seeing you like that, Bell, but you need to do it in a way that doesn't trigger a kingdom-wide emergency."

"I didn't mean to worry anyone."

"Fortunately, I discovered you missing before anyone else did. I left word that the two of us went to town."

In these narrow roads and alleys, it feels as if we could get lost in the best way—sink into the crowd and be nameless faces without expectations of kingdoms hanging on us. We make a turn toward the edge of town.

"How did you notice me gone so early?"

Tomas' jaw ticks before he answers. "Things have been tense between us since we left Mirador. I couldn't allow us to remain that way indefinitely."

"I don't enjoy that either." Before we can get into the particulars of our silent standoff, Tomas knocks on a door.

"What are we here for?"

"You happened upon people involved with one disappearance. Here's another."

A boy of about seventeen opens the door of the modest farmhouse and blinks a few times before bowing to us. "Good morning, Lord Tomas. I didn't know you were back."

"Hello, Orson. I just arrived yesterday. My friend and I wondered if you could tell us anything about your brother."

His expression drops, and he comes out to join us in the yard. "George couldn't have gotten far on his own. He could hardly get around at all."

"Still that bad?" Concern paints Tomas' face.

"Why is that?" I ask.

"His knee was shattered the winter before last," Orson says. "He was kicked by a horse."

"Oh, that's horrible."

He leans on a fencepost, overlooking open fields. "Yes. It was difficult to keep up with the work without him, but some workers happened upon us, willing to work for half the usual wage. He was finally getting around, if slowly, but now who knows if I'll ever see him again. The investigators from Mirador seemed more interested in the woman who had recently passed through town than finding George."

Tomas and I look at each other then back to Orson. "What investigators?" I ask at the same time Tomas asks, "What woman?"

A sigh blows out of me. "I'm sorry. Investigators came to speak to you?"

"Yes, just the other day. I thought it amazing that the Queen cared enough, but as I said, they didn't seem terribly interested in finding him."

More importantly, they weren't sent by the Queen.

"Because there was a woman they were trying to track down?" Tomas sounds as lost as I feel.

Orson nods. "An old crone, no more agile than George. Perhaps they disappeared together, because I didn't see her again after I saw her speaking with George. It was the night he went missing. She wasn't from here. It was assumed she just continued on her way."

One of the strange people passing through. What connection does someone else see between that and the missing stableboy, though?

I nod along as Tomas inquires after the boy's mother and such, but my mind is on these supposed royal investigators and who really sent them.

Chapter Seventeen

"Those investigators were not sent by Mother."

Tomas clicks his tongue as we walk away from the stables. "Thank you, Bell. I hadn't figured that out on my own."

"Well, who did send them?"

He shakes his head. "I don't know."

"Where are we going now?"

"To see if anyone else was interviewed by these *investigators*."

Good. My chest tightens as I realize I'm now more interested in these frauds than our missing people—no better than the frauds themselves who cared only for the mysterious old woman. Still, they might know something we don't, so finding them will get us closer to discovering what happened to those who've gone missing. Hopefully.

We wind our way through a different part of town which seems a little quieter at this hour and sports an aroma of old wine and ale. "You're quite well known around town, by the way."

"I spent nearly a year out here."

The memory of who *else* he seemed to get to know well here draws my hands into fists. This is not the time, though. Tomas stops and knocks on a door. There's some muffled complaining about it being too early on the other side. I look around to decipher what this place is, but as I'm about to ask, the door opens. A woman wearing the smudged remnants of last night's makeup and a sheer robe which leaves *nothing* to the imagination answers.

Right. The other missing person was an escort.

The woman's face lights up in recognition. "Good morning, Lord Tomas. So good to see you back in town."

I can't imagine what my face looks like as I turn by degrees to glare at Tomas. He doesn't take any notice, responding to the woman instead. "Thank you. We've just arrived yesterday."

"Oh, you must be exhausted from traveling. Come in, then, come in." She leads us into a dark sitting room and gestures for us to sit on one of the burgundy velvet sofas. I do so reluctantly, not certain I want to be sitting on any surface here. "Well, sir, it's a little unusual to bring a girl with you, but I'll wake someone who will be great fun for the both of you."

Blood drains from my face, and I dig my nails into Tomas' knee.

"That won't be necessary," he says. "We've come to ask about Emblen. She went missing, didn't she?"

The woman frowns and shakes her head. "Yes. It's very good of you to care. I didn't think anyone would, but then some people did come asking after her, trying to find out what happened."

The urge to storm out of here is a physical force pushing me away, and I tense my entire body to resist it. The effort keeps my jaw clenched, so I won't be adding anything to this conversation, but it's safer this way. If I open my mouth, there's no telling what I'll say.

"Who was it that came asking?" That he can sit here conversing while I'm considering ways to kill him is rather impressive. How many women in this establishment are familiar with him?

"Some people from the capital. Wouldn't think anyone in Mirador would care for the likes of Emblen, but they did come asking."

"Of course they care." I unlock my lips to at least say that much. "The Queen cares for all of her subjects." Even if those people weren't ours.

"Yes, sweet thing, you keep on believing that."

I don't want to embarrass the woman, but I have half a mind to inform her that she's patronizing the Princess.

"It's true," Tomas says. "Queen Elea is a good and caring ruler, but you'll recall she has an entire kingdom to look after. I'm sure you can excuse her not knowing the name of every person in Alchos."

She bows her head, perhaps remembering she's speaking to the heir of a high house. "Of course. And I suppose it shows by sending people out here about the incidents."

"That and more. She's sent her sons and daughters as well. They travelled here with me."

Her face stretches into an impressed expression. "Imagine that. Shall I expect to see the princes about these parts at night?"

"I believe it's the elder princess who's the wild one in the bunch." A hardened ball of air hurls into Tomas' stomach. He only hunches slightly and tenses to steady himself.

The woman cackles. "Right! The Angel of Alchos will be in the debauchery of this neighborhood. You're too much, Lord Tomas."

His answering smile is tight, possibly due to the injury he recently sustained. "Did the investigators ask about an old woman who had passed through town?"

"Yes, but I told them I didn't know of any such person. They did ask for a description of the last client Emblen had before she disappeared."

"I'll take that as well, please."

She provides it and a description of the investigators, royal crests on their uniforms and all. I manage to keep up appearances until we leave then hurry away as Tomas thanks the woman and closes the door. When he catches up to me, he says, "That hit was completely un—"

I throw a soundproof wall around him.

He stops in his tracks, but I keep walking. He catches up to me again—walks alongside me speaking very animatedly, but alas... "I'm sorry, I can't hear you." I point to my ear and shrug. No doubt plenty of what he's saying is completely inappropriate to say to any lady, much less a princess, so it's probably for the best.

We continue this way the entire walk to the castle. How he has this much to say, I have no idea. But from the corner of my eye, I see he manages to talk the entire time. The guards look at each other with furrowed brows as they let us in and Tomas remains silent despite his actions.

"He's fine," I assure them. I take the express option to my rooms, flying up to my balcony before evaporating the bubble I kept Tomas in. He's loud enough for me to *just* hear him start to shout before I slam the door shut.

Chapter Eighteen

My room at Lambridge Castle is terribly crowded. Three grumpy royals speak over each other, which is helpful, as I'm unconcerned with anything they're talking about. This way I have a valid reason not to know what they say. Rylan seems to wish I'd brought him along with me, while Nina thinks we're both wretched to try to wriggle our way into people's affection this way. Marcus agrees with Nina—*of course*.

I lean my head on my hand and sip wine. The wine is good but not quite worth the alarm bells it set off about my return. It was when I rang for wine that my siblings discovered I was back and descended upon me like a pack of angry wolves.

"Well, I suppose everyone thinks Arabella is the sweetest person in the royal family now." Nina's snide smile slides right by me—I can't be bothered.

"Actually, I didn't tell anyone who I was."

Marcus arches an eyebrow. "Really?"

"Well,"—I take another sip—"I told a little boy. Nina, he might be interested in marrying you."

"I'm surprised you didn't tell him I'm horrible."

"He asked if you're as nice as I am, and I told him no."

Ry's shoulders rise with a silent laugh.

"He might not have been deterred," I add. "But more importantly, I spoke with some individuals connected to those who've gone missing. It appears people came through inquiring about the situation, claiming to be investigators sent by Mirador."

"We didn't send anyone." Rylan's words make me realize why Tomas was annoyed when I said it.

"Right, so I'd like to find out who is parading around claiming to work for us."

Ry agrees. "Yes, that should take top priority."

Marcus nods as well. "We'll need to get our own actual people on it. We need to warm this region to us before we go back for the first trial."

"Yes, I'll write to Mother," Rylan says.

He and Marcus leave, but Nina stays behind. Once we're alone, she leans toward me. "So, you spoke to people connected to those who went missing?"

"Yes. That's what I said."

"One was a..." A sly grin creeps up her lips as she waits for me to confirm this juiciest bit of information.

"Yes. I went to a brothel."

Her eyes light up as she covers her mouth. Nina is more openly adventurous than me, but even she wouldn't go to a brothel with as many eyes as she always has on her. "What I wouldn't give to have seen you in a brothel. What was it like?"

"Dark, and warm, and..."—*the matron thought Tomas and I were there for pleasures involving three people at once*—"uncomfortable."

"That's fantastic." Tears well up in her eyes from the laughter she scarcely contains.

"Get out."

"I'll see you for dinner." She rises, looking no less giddy about my discomfort.

"I think I'll take my meal in here. I'm tired from an early morning." And I will be sick if I have to face Tomas.

"Fine then. Rest up. Tomorrow is our *sanctioned* visit into town."

"I can't wait."

She leaves, and it's finally just the wine and me as it was meant to be. The situation in this town is confounding, and the back and forth with Tomas is exhausting. The combination weighs on me enough to drop my eyelids, if only for a moment.

A knock on the door.

I hit the sofa and gasp. It takes a moment for me to place myself as I sit up and heave a couple of deep breaths.

The knock sounds again.

"Come in."

The door eases open, and Jamys steps through. "Hello, Ara." He closes the door behind himself without looking like he's sneaking cakes from his mother's tea this time. "How are you?"

"Well, I had fallen asleep, and I fell when I woke."

"I believe everyone has those dreams of falling." He leans back against the wall, and I almost feel bad that I'm about to pull the rug out from under him now that he's regained his confidence.

"Mine are real. I sometimes float in my sleep if I'm not comfortable."

He nods, unable to respond to such an odd thing. It's kind of adorable, so I choose not to feel bad about it. "Well, I heard you were going to take your supper in your rooms and wondered if I might join you."

"That would be lovely."

"Good." He comes to sit beside me. "I already asked the maid for it."

"Confident in my answer, were you?" It's a good look on him. That confidence comes naturally to him in his role of prince, and I rather like seeing it in personal matters.

"Hopeful." His smile offers everything warm and sincere.

"I think you always are—hopeful."

"Is that a good thing?" The question is more loaded than he realizes. I suppose one of us should be hopeful about our relationship, even if his hope ignites my remorse.

"Yes, I think so."

"How was your excursion into town?" He refills my glass and offers it to me.

"No, thank you. I'll wait until I have some food before me. You enjoy it." I wave it off, and he takes a sip of wine before setting it down. "It was interesting. The town is lovely. I enjoyed conversations with a few people without them knowing who I am which was pleasant."

"That's certainly a unique opportunity."

I nod. "It was. Oh, I should inform you—I received an offer of marriage from a boy in town."

Jamys' chin pulls back. "Really, now?"

"Yes, he was quite smitten with me. If he were fifteen years older, you really might have had some competition on your hands."

Jamys' laugh reminds me of his music—bright but somewhat shy. "I'd have liked to witness that."

A calm settles over me, and I realize I'd have liked for him to be there. Jamys' presence is a welcome warmth in the usual tempest of my life—something steady and grounding. This business with Tomas makes it desirable to drop from the billowing winds and tether myself down.

Chapter Nineteen

After a lovely evening together, Jamys returns to his rooms, and I go out to my balcony before washing up for bed. Clouds cover any glimpse of stars or moon. In the distance, lightning flashes through them. There's still some time before they reach us, and the warm smell of rain entices me to drop down to the ground.

Alone feels okay but somewhat dangerous. I should probably stick to Jamys' side as much as possible. When I am, I'm happy with him, but I need more for it to sink in. I know I can fall in love with Jamys. I should, even. I'm not there yet, though. It feels too fragile, like a seed trying to take root that needs tender loving care. It's so easy for it to be forgotten under the soil while on the surface, Tomas' heat keeps snagging my attention.

My eyes remain on the ground as I think of it. All that lies beneath. How does it feel to have the power Rylan possesses? Can he feel deep down into the earth? It seems rather... heavy. But my attention is pulled upward by two people on a balcony—Tomas and Ceanna.

Pressure builds in my ears at the sight. He leans back against the stone railing, and she stands close enough to lean in for a kiss. I can imagine the cunning look in his eyes, the one he's given me so many times before as he leans so casually. He's probably acting like he's disinterested while hissing words that make her want to devour him like he always does to me. Perhaps part of me thought it was an act, his way of being alluring. I didn't think we were as casual as we claimed. But apparently, I was wrong.

She takes a step closer to him, and without giving it any real thought, I slam a barrier down between them and push him back over the rail.

Her scream as he falls is drowned out only by the thundering of my heart. Of course, I blow the air up under him to slow him down. Not as much as I could, but he should consider the rough landing on his feet to be a gift. He steadies himself, and I march toward him.

"Why did you even come here?" I demand as he says, "Thank you."

He also calls up, "I'm fine," to the hysterical Ceanna up above us.

My jaw drops. "Thank you? Did you just *thank me*? I just pushed you off a tower. It wasn't as a favor to you!"

"It was a favor all the same." He brushes himself off. "She doesn't know how to take a hint."

"Perhaps"—I shove his shoulder—"your *hints*"—and again—"are misleading!"

He takes my rage like a stone wall. Unflinching. Unmoved. His eyes only narrow when he says, "You are going to draw the attention of every person in this castle."

"I don't care!"

"Don't you?"

He growls the words, and I look down, remembering Jamys and how much I *do* need to care about making a scene with Tomas. A grunt rumbles in the back of my throat. I fling a bubble around us both and throw us across a pond and up over the outer wall. It dissolves while we're still moving into a thick patch of forest, and I use the momentum as I stomp off deeper into the woods.

"Is she why you insisted on coming here?" His steps sound behind me, but I have to keep moving or I'll explode. "Because honestly, right in front of me!"

"Are you insane?" Tomas' voice is close. Close enough to make his frustration clear. Good. I'm glad I'm not the only one pissed off. "I forgot she was here!" He grabs my shoulder, stopping me, and spins me toward him. "How can you possibly be jealous of someone from my *past* when..." His mouth sets into a hard line, and he takes two steps back. The rise and fall of his shoulders are exaggerated. His eyes bore into me, accusation sharp in his stare, as if I'm the one who wronged *him*.

"Is she from your past?" Neither of us will mistake my quietness for calmness, but I fake it anyway. "She seems to have flitted right into the present."

"Again, she can't take a hint. Or a direct explanation. I haven't been with anyone but you since our first time." He says it like I should know, like it's obvious. Wide-eyed and silently pleading for me to understand when he hasn't given me any certainty that I understand anything.

My eyes prickle as my chest continues to heave. It isn't infor-mation I'd known I wanted, but it lets something take root in me—the thought that we are more than a physical affair for him too. That idea is more dangerously forbidden than his body ever could be. "At the time, it didn't occur to me you had been with other women before me. It seems obvious now. You clearly knew what you were doing."

In a flash of lighting, his demeanor shifts to the confident one I've grown so familiar with—broad shoulders back and a lopsided grin so faint, I have to stare at his lips to be certain it's there. "I always thought you benefited from me knowing what I'm doing."

It's all I can do not to squirm. "I did, but I didn't know."

"Why does it matter?"

"Because I didn't know what I was doing." Gods, I can't believe I'm admitting this. "And I was probably awkward and dreadful, and—"

"Bell. You know that was not the case." He moves toward me, and I have sense enough to back up, but a tree stops my retreat. I've never been more grateful to be thwarted. "For starters, you know it was incredible." He braces one hand on the trunk above my head, looming over me. My desire and the heat radiating off him cage me in. Somehow, I think he knows I couldn't possibly move away. "Also, if it were bad, it wouldn't have continued for as long as it did."

I flinch at the use of past tense. We are through, aren't we? We should be. I can't let this continue. This man is my past, not my future. But with him so close, all I want is to close the gap between us. Desire to feel the rough stubble along his jaw is still powerful, though I know the feeling so well now. The need to see his body consumes me, as if I don't already have the image preserved in my mind. It'll all fade. I'll lose it if enough time passes, and that's too terrible to conceive.

Wedged between Tomas and the tree, the rumbling of thunder sounds closer. It doesn't take much to open the floodgates, not when our attraction makes the very air between us tremble. I brush my fingers through the hair behind his ear and let my hand settle on his neck. He leans into it gently—a grounding weight in my palm.

"Am I part of your past?" My voice is no more than a whisper. Any louder and it would crack.

His face sinks toward mine so slightly, but my fingers press into his neck the way they would if he'd moved all the way in to kiss me. "That has always been up to you."

Has it? It's never felt as if I have any control over this. He always gives me every opportunity to pull away, to end this, yet I never can. Odd it was he whom I'm powerless against who first said I was the most powerful of Mother's children. Magic can't help me make the good, sensible choice. Our affair carries me on its own momentum, and no power in the world could allow me to stop it.

I lick my lips. "One last time?"

His throat bobs, and he nods so slightly, I feel it against my hand more than see it. I pull him toward me gently, and his lips come to meet mine as if I had jerked him forward. I can't hold him tight enough, can't kiss him hard enough as he presses me back against the tree, every rough line and edge scraping me through my blouse. I could provide myself a comfortable barrier, but I want to feel everything about this moment. My clothing may get shredded. I'll certainly have bruises. And none of that dampens my frenzy.

He spins me around, and I press my palms against the rough bark. Good. I may cry, and I don't need him to see that. Tomas wraps his arms about me and nestles his face into the side of my neck. The scratching of his jaw against my skin slows time down. Contentment in feeling like this *one last time* could last forever settles into me.

"I didn't mean to deceive you about having previous experience." His lips are close enough to suck my earlobe between them. "But the most important things... I learned from you."

I shake my head and pull in a shaky breath. "Don't patronize me. I know you—"

"It's true." He kisses the soft spot behind my ear, and my core melts. "I know you like that, because your toes curl when I do it." And they have. I stretch and flex my feet within my boots, as if that would disprove him.

"I know this pleases you..." His fingers graze down my collarbone, under my tunic, and to my breast. I take a sharp breath when he rolls my nipple between two fingers. "Because you gasp, and Bell, that is one of my favorite sounds."

A fingertip sweeps down the center of my body, and even with a layer of fabric in between, my skin tightens. "I know you love this..." His hand slides under my leggings. "Because I find you wet." A finger slides through the inevitable moisture, and my knees turn to water.

His other hand slides onto my stomach as he massages and explores me with his fingertips. "Without words, you tell me you like this..."—two fingers thrust into me, and my back arches, pushing my ass against the evidence of his own desire—"with every one of those little movements you just made." His fingers slide out and in, curling inside to press against the front of me. "The way the muscles in your stomach clench." His hand presses there to bring it to my attention before sliding it down to grasp my thigh. He pulls my leg back, spreading me open. "The way your hips circle and press against me."

They are. An instinctive movement to try to get more of him. Under my clothes, his palm molds to my body, and I reach back to grip his hip, fingers digging in as he pulls me higher and higher toward the precipice of pleasure. Rain begins to fall, plastering my hair to my face, but I don't care enough to block the water. He sways and rocks with me as the world tilts and spirals then it doesn't exist at all. My shoulders contract forward, and I cry out the name of the only person still with me in the abyss.

He holds me through it and rests a hand over my thundering heart. "I know how to pleasure you because of my experience with *you*." His tongue traces the rim of my ear, and I suck my lips in against each other. "Fortunately, I have a good amount of experience with that."

I turn around to face him. His hair and skin are soaked in rain, and I've never thirsted for anything more. I lick a trail up his neck to his ear, the rain diluting his taste while giving me enough to make me feral. I'd be happy to lick every last drop off him. The continuing downpour would make it a perpetual task I'm all too eager to accept.

"Allow me to show you what experience has taught me."

Chapter Twenty

The town square bursts with excitement and happiness, but I'm content to sit at a table outside the pub and observe from the outskirts. Strong black tea spreads its warmth through me. It'll take a lot of it to sharpen the haze of my exhaustion.

"This was a good idea." Marcus watches as Nina amuses some children with flames darting around her arms and waist.

People are much more excited to be against something if it's something they never have to face. It isn't difficult to win them over. Showing our faces, having conversations with them, making ourselves real people instead of theoretical figureheads somewhere does the trick.

"All of my ideas are good." Except ideas involving Tomas. Those are idiotic. Enjoyable, but very bad as ideas go. "You should go participate."

He sighs and begrudgingly sets off to mingle with the people of Lambridge.

Across the square, Tomas and Rylan speak with the woman from the inn—the one whose father disappeared. It's offensive, really, how Tomas can look so perfectly *awake* and put together.

We were both left with the same *very few* hours to sleep. How was it enough for him, but I'm a sleepy mess?

Our interpretation of *one last time* came to mean one last *night*, which became an impossibly long night with many last times packed into it. I was utterly drunk on him, and all the aftereffects—soreness, fatigue, sluggishness—are assaulting me now. How can he look fresh as a spring flower? The sun was beginning to rise by the time he left me.

I sip more tea as if it can reverse how pathetically I clung to him last night. Any excuse to keep him touching me, I took. *You'll need to help me wash this mess out of my hair* led to washing other things, which led to getting messy again, which led to my bed...

A sigh escapes me as I brush a fingertip across my forehead. At least knowing it was the last time meant we took full advantage. It's probably easier than if we hadn't been aware when it was over.

Jamys appears at my side. Rather than being wretched as seeing him today should make me, confusion and concern swirl through me at the sight of him. Even when I'm warming to him, there's never a flaming desire to be on top of him.

"Are you sure you're feeling well?" he asks.

"The tea has woken me right up." I pop up to my feet as sprightly as I can manage. "Would you like me to introduce you to the person who might try to steal me away from you?" I regret the words the instant they leave my lips. The circumstances with the little boy are funny and sweet, but it seems as if someone else should be trying to steal me away. He won't, though—not in any way that matters.

So Jamys offers me his arm, confident in his hold on me. "Yes, please."

We make our way across the square, and Richard spots me in the crowd. "You look more like a princess today."

"Because I'm wearing a dress?" He nods. "I suppose I do. Have you met my sister?"

"I did, and she's perfectly nice."

You don't know her very well. "This man here wanted to meet you."

Jamys gets down on one knee to level with the boy. "I understand you wanted to marry Princess Arabella."

"Only so I could be a prince."

I gape and lay a hand dramatically on my chest. "You wound me, Richard."

Jamys laughs. "Being a prince is overrated, except in being matched with a lovely princess."

"She said you were nicer than her."

Jamys smiles up at me. "Arabella is surprisingly modest for a princess. I think she's *very* nice."

As they chat, I suppress the guilt threatening to consume me. I haven't deserved such praise from Jamys, but from now on, I will.

Lord Horace's invitation to make ourselves at home in his castle has been accepted wholeheartedly.

Nina sinks onto a chaise and tugs her soft knit sleeves farther over her hands. "Thank you for suggesting this, Ara. It's really lovely to experience other parts of the kingdom."

"Did everyone hear that? Nina thanked me. Such words shall never be uttered again, so please, commit it to memory."

She rearranges her fingers into a rude gesture around her wineglass as she takes a sip.

"Being in town was fun," Marcus says. "And now we look like we're having a preview of this summer's visit to Etherlee."

Lounging about the sitting room in our most casual garb does bring on that feeling. Jamys is stiff and uneasy about daring to be comfortable in front of anyone, but not so uneasy as I am at the mention of returning for our annual stay at the shore.

I make every effort to keep my voice casual. "Glad to have this experience then, because I don't believe I'll be going to Etherlee this summer."

My siblings all frown, but Tomas doesn't direct his attention to me. He understands.

"Why not?" Ry asks.

"Jamys has invited me to spend the summer up in Ceraun." I return the smile he flashes at me at the mention of it.

Nina clicks her tongue. "Will you be married by then?"

"There's been too much excitement with the trials to set a date." Jamys crosses his ankle over his knee, the forced attempt at looking relaxed comical. "I'm certain we'll have it planned soon, though."

"Well, you're quite welcome to join us at Etherlee if you so choose," Marcus offers Jamys.

"Thank you."

I shake my head. "Of course, but I don't think we'll go."

"Can I go?" Ceanna bats her eyes at Marcus.

"Perhaps." His smile is tight.

The idiot shouldn't have mentioned it in front of her. Apparently, Ceanna has moved on from Tomas, much to Marcus' chagrin. All I know is that he calmed her fears when Tomas "fell" off the balcony.

"Can we get back to the present, rather than planning our summer holiday?" Rylan rakes his fingers through his hair. "Where do we start on finding the people impersonating royal guards?"

"I'm not sure if anyone gave them information that would have guided their search," Tomas says. "The proprietor of the establishment where the missing woman worked said they didn't seem to find her information helpful."

Rylan chuckles. "That's quite the description of her when we all know you're on a first name basis with the *madam* of the brothel."

Tomas rolls his eyes and leans his arm on the back of the sofa. "Let's not get into a match over who has participated in the most raucous behavior."

I groan. "Do spare us." *Please. Please. Please.*

"It's relevant to the business at hand," Nina says with a mischievous grin. "Didn't you know the woman who vanished, Tomas?"

My shoulders tense, and I try to will it away. It doesn't matter.

"Yes," Tomas huffs out. "However, I met her outside of her... place of business."

"Saved a little coin, did you?"

He throws a pillow at Nina, and I pop a shield in front of her.

Tomas turns to me, exasperated. "She did not deserve your help."

"I didn't want her to spill the wine on the furniture. Be a more thoughtful guest." I'll miss this part of our holidays together—the teasing and rivalries. Perhaps in time, I can enjoy these things with Tomas without thinking about everything else we've been.

"Anyway," he says, "we became *friends.*"

Nina looks skeptical, but it's Rylan who unknowingly prods at *me.* "There are worse ways to start a friendship than by—"

"I would *really* love it if you could wait until after I'm married to make it so glaringly obvious to Jamys that I grew up with a pack of miscreants." In case I wasn't already wretched enough, I'm now using Jamys as an excuse to spare myself from finding out uncomfortable things about Tomas' past. Things that wouldn't matter even if Tomas were an option for me and *cannot* matter since he isn't.

"I'm almost certain you used to be fun." Nina sets down her wineglass.

"Terribly sorry to disappoint you." I stand and further the point of me not being fun anymore. "I'm going to bed. Yes, I know it's early. No, I don't care. Good night."

As I clear the doorway, a thud sounds, followed by Nina's screech. "You ass!"

"It was a debt owed which your sister prevented before," Tomas says.

Even as I'm laughing about it, I imagine Jamys really does think us a ridiculous bunch. I get up to my rooms, but a voice stops me before I enter.

"Ara," Jamys says as he rounds the corner, "you got up here very quickly."

I shrug. "Flying will do that."

"Yes, well, I hope you sleep better tonight."

"Thank you." No doubt I will.

"I hope your sleep wasn't disturbed by... It wasn't exactly proper for us to spend the evening alone together the way we did."

The idea of him thinking what *we did*—a private meal in my rooms—was improper is mortifying when I know the truth of it. "Not at all. Last night was wonderful." My stomach turns to lead at the realization that the words are accurate for two very different segments of the night.

"Oh, good. I don't want to rush you into anything or put any pressure on you. However you'd like our betrothal to be is fine for me."

"You haven't, but thank you. I meant it, you know... when I told the boy you were nicer than I am."

He smiles, takes my hand, and lays a soft kiss on my knuckles. "Good night, Ara."

"Good night, Jamys."

Inside, I lean my head back against the door. I never want to lie to him again.

CHAPTER TWENTY-ONE

Green sprouts dot the soil in neat rows across the field. Several people are working in it, but Breda, the mother of the missing boy, is off to the side with us. Even without full finery, our group of royals is discordant with the scenery. My siblings, Jamys, and I managed to get out on our own today. It's only unusual for Jamys, but he's taking our peculiarities in stride.

"I'm sorry we couldn't be in town yesterday," Breda says. "We had only recently received the new fertilizer and had to treat the fields right away as we're already into spring."

"No apologies necessary," Ry says. "We didn't come to disrupt your lives or work."

"That's very kind of you, Your Grace."

"I spoke with Orson briefly upon our arrival," I say.

His mother goes wide-eyed. "He didn't mention meeting the princess."

"He wouldn't have. I didn't announce my name. Far more important than etiquette is your younger son's disappearance."

She blinks away a glassiness from her eyes. "You're very kind to care."

"It's the barest minimum, I think. We should be able to get answers for you." I'd like to say we will get her son back, but having so little information, it doesn't seem like a hope I can offer. "We will continue trying."

"Thank you." Her voice is no more than a whisper. "It's difficult, but even in the shadow of George's absence, work must go on." She gestures to the field.

"What is this new fertilizer you're using?" Rylan looks out over the land, and a wave of growth ripples across it. "I'd help further, but don't want to spoil the timing of the crops with the weather."

"This head start is incredible, Your Grace. A man came peddling this treatment, said it has been working well up in Windamere and gave us some to try free of charge. Expects it to increase our yield enough that we'll buy it next season."

"I hope it works out."

"Is this it?" Nina reaches into a barrel of green granules and runs her fingers through it.

Marcus swats her hand away. "Don't touch it."

She turns her head toward him, opening her mouth, but remains silent.

"His Grace is probably right," Breda says. "It's a chemical you won't want on your skin."

Nina brushes her hands off against each other. A spark pops off her palms and drifts into the barrel with the slow grace of a feather.

Her eyes widen, and her lips part in a gasp. Before she can say a word, a scorching blast throws us all clear off our feet and away from a green inferno.

It's too fast for me to catch anyone. The air softens my landing by its own accord as everyone else hits the ground in a chorus of thuds and groans. I fling a shield up to block the searing temperature, but panic and fury keep things just as heated on this side.

A piercing chord claws at my ears. I see Rylan shout at Nina, and her and Marcus yelling back at him, but the sound is drowned out by the ringing. I shake it out of my head in time to hear Jamys.

"Are you hurt?" He's on his knee, hovering over me, sweat glistening on his flushed face.

"I'm fine. Tend to Breda." I swing my legs under myself to get up to my feet.

"Put it out then!" Rylan commands, pointing to the blazing barrel.

Nina's eyes narrow in concentration, but her expression shifts to frustration, confusion, and finally, dread. She rushes toward it and slams her hand into the massive fire like one might pinch the burning wick of a candle to snuff it out. A sharp yelp pops out of her as she removes her hand as quickly as she put it in.

"Nina!" Marcus grabs her by the shoulders and yanks her away.

She stares at her angry red hand as if it betrayed her. "I can't put it out."

Marcus takes the injured hand in his own, and a cast of water swirls around it between their palms. The bright green flames crackle fiercely, and Marcus' free hand waves toward them, though his focus is on our sister. A splash of water hits the fire, but it only flares up higher, making sparks fly.

In the blink of an eye, the ground has caught. Flames sprint and multiply across the freshly treated field. Warnings and expletives are screamed all around me. I reach out with my magic to get a blockade in front of it, but the green light beats me in the race across the field. Those working in the distance only have time to turn away before they're besieged.

Breda screeches behind me over the roar of the fire. The massive blaze is so bright, my vision is veiled in a green glare. I swipe my hands away from each other, and a wall of air races around the perimeter of the burning field from both sides, meeting with an impact that pushes the breath from my lungs. Simultaneously, I reinforce the barrier around the fire and try to reach in to pull the people from the field. Any form of air I can muster burns up in the raging inferno. I can't even see the people out there, but I make futile attempts again and again. *Oh gods.*

Water pours down on the fire again, only to anger it further, explosions of sparks rearing out where liquid attempts to smother it. They bounce off my containment wall with quick stabs I feel as if it were my palms holding it all in.

"Would you stop that?!" Rylan shoves Marcus and kneels, pressing his hands to the ground. The earth shudders beneath my feet, and the center of the fire begins to collapse. Smoldering land crumbles in on itself as a crater forms, the glowing green pit a peek into hell itself. Unnatural glowing fingers stretch and writhe within the trap containing it.

Soil falls in, and the fire wanes slightly. I pull the walls of air down to cover and suffocate it. It's slow going, but the blaze shrinks beneath acrid smoke as I stare at it, panting and horrified. A hand lands on my shoulder, pulling me from my shocked stupor.

"Are you all right?"

I look up at Jamys' crumpled expression and back to the destruction. "No."

"My son!"

Breda's wails scrape through my chest like icy claws. We came because she already lost a son. Now we've played a part in the death of the other.

Nina's lip trembles as she approaches the hysterical woman. "I'm so sor—"

"Go!" Breda snaps. "Just leave us be." Her shoulders sink forward as she sobs into her hands. Nina backs away to find solace in Marcus' embrace. People from town arrive and flock around Breda. People she trusts. People who will grieve with her in the wake of the disaster we've wrought.

Chapter Twenty-Two

By our fifth day in Lambridge, we know nothing more of our missing subjects or the imposters seeking them out. All the headway we had made with gaining the trust of our people here turned to ash with the strange fire.

Nina and Marcus have quietly insisted there is something off about the granular chemicals they were using. A fire Nina couldn't control and water couldn't put out was no natural matter. Guilt for their parts in the atrocity must weigh heavily on them, though, for they aren't as adamant about shifting the blame as I'd expect. Regardless of fault, half a dozen people died in a fire that sparked from Nina's hand and expanded due to Marcus' attempt to stop it.

If the people here weren't suspicious of us before, they are now. Guilt crushes my chest. *This was my idea.*

"You realize they have staff who could do this for you?" Nina sits on my bed, knees tucked up under her chin and arms wrapped around her legs, shaking her head at me as I pack my things.

"What else do I have to do?"

"Anything. Packing is horribly dull, and we'll have plenty of opportunity for *horribly dull* as we travel to Brasport."

Our next stop has been added due to other strange occurrences. The general consensus is that it'll be good to visit another area, since we have time before the first trial. Personally, I feel we should go home and not spread terror over anymore of our kingdom. Far from preventing an increased military presence in Lambridge, Eglingen is now moving forces here. There are questions about who brought in that incendiary treatment, the false investigators, the disappearances, and, thanks to us, the people here are terrified of the magical royals who started the fire which killed their people and destroyed their land.

Since my last idea was so epically awful, my opinion doesn't matter much now.

A breeze whips through the open balcony door, and Nina groans. "Enough with the damned wind already."

"I didn't do that." I go outside where a strong wind pushes into me. A prickling sensation scurries up my neck, and under the rush of air brushing my ear, another noise is buried.

Nina comes out behind me. "Is a storm coming in so quickly?"

"Shh." I drop my gaze and focus only on sound. "Did you hear that?"

"Hear what?"

"Someone's out there. I hear voices on the breeze."

"Don't be ridiculous."

I push air up underneath both of us and send us into the wind.

"Excuse me!" Nina cries. "I do not wish to"—I wrap a sound-proof shield around us—"float around out here chasing ghosts."

There's no one around. We get to the outer wall, and I raise us high enough to see over it. The scenery should be familiar to me, but I didn't pay much attention to it when Tomas and I were out here. Moonbeams reflecting off falling raindrops gave it a glittery veil that night, but all I could see was him.

Now, three men stand near the wall conversing as another emerges from the woods, all wearing our royal seal on their uniforms. Nina gasps and covers her mouth.

I remove our sound barrier.

"The markings are on the leaves," a man says. "Time pulled here."

Another groans. "Are we sure the royal brats haven't found some way to expand their magic?"

A ball of fire appears in Nina's hand, but she puts it out when I give her a cross look.

"She's convinced it's someone else, and lucky for us."

"This wild goose chase does not feel lucky."

Nina swishes her hand in a circle and points to her mouth.

I give us a shield. "Go ahead."

"What do we do?"

"Alert Lord Horace. They won't claim to work for us if one of us seizes them."

She nods. "Let's go then."

"You go. I'll keep watch over them."

"All right." I lower her to the ground below me.

"Could this person have infiltrated the castle?" one of the men asks. A chill runs down my spine.

"If the person can change form like she believes, they can infiltrate anything."

The old woman they were searching for?

"We can't very well check the castle, though, can we?" This one sounds put out, as if he's quite done with the entire thing.

"No, we cannot, and being near the elementals is a risk we can't keep up."

I purse my lips at the use of the archaic term. Our magic isn't even referred to as elemental anymore, much less the holders of it being *elementals.* They argue amongst themselves a bit longer before a tree sprouts up next to me, bringing Rylan, Marcus, Nina, and Jamys.

I ensure our privacy and gape at Jamys. "What are you doing?"

"If you're here, I'm here."

I squeeze his hand in appreciation. Rylan focuses beyond the wall, and I peek over to see a gradual thickening of the trees blocking off their retreat. "What have they been saying?" he asks.

"Nothing that makes any sense." I pull the shield down just as they speak about returning home. Now if only they'd say where that is.

"You there!" a voice calls from the direction of the gates.

The intruders lurch toward the wood, only to find it impassable, thick branches having filled in the spaces they'd have come through. "They're here," one whispers.

Marcus' sly grin looks like he is all too pleased to be spoken of as if we are malicious spirits haunting these men. They look along the clearing by the wall but stand their ground rather than attempting a chase around the castle.

Lord Horace, Tomas, and a retinue of guards come into view. "Who goes there?"

The men look back and forth between each other, and one rolls his shoulders back. "We are looking for someone who has been prowling your lands, my lord."

"I see several people prowling my lands," Horace replies.

"We are sent by Queen Elea," the one who has taken the mantle of leader says.

Tomas scoffs. "You can't possibly think that will work here. I travelled here from Mirador on the Queen's orders. She sent her sons and daughters, not you."

"The princes and princesses might not have been made aware. The Queen does not tell them everything."

Heat rolls off Nina as flames dance over her shoulders.

"You are aware," Horace says, "there is no escape for you. Let us make this simple. Put down your weapons and come with us so you can tell a more accurate story indoors."

After a pause, they unsheathe their swords and drop them to the ground. A couple of them reach for other weapons, then, quick as lightning, two daggers dart through the air toward Tomas and Horace. Terror slows it down. I see the blade on a direct path to Tomas' neck as clear as day. That skin where I've possessively felt his pulse under my lips would split open and coat his perfect chest in crimson.

No.

A shield materializes before them. The daggers strike it and fall.

Before I know what I'm doing, I'm over the wall. The barrier that protected Tomas and Horace thrusts toward the attackers, sending them sprawling to the ground. It curls over them like an animal attacking until a hardened bubble of air surrounds the imposters. I compress it to throw them against each other. The space shrinks by degrees as I hover there. Every nerve in my body tingles, and though there's a faint background of shouting, all I hear is blood pounding through me.

Until one word gets through.

"Bell."

It isn't the loudest voice. It's firm but quiet.

I glance back at Tomas, who fixes me with an understanding stare. "Stop."

It pulls me back to the reality of the situation. I look at our enemies as they're crushed together. A snapping bone reverberates through the shield I've trapped them in, and I close my eyes for a breath. *Stop.* Tomas' directive isn't for the sake of those men—it's for me. The force pushing in on them dissolves as I lower to the ground. They collapse in a cacophony of groans. Every nerve in me trembles, but I'm otherwise still until a warm weight settles onto my shoulders.

"Let's go in." Tomas guides me to turn back toward the gate.

I walk along with him as if sleepwalking, looking at nothing, feeling nothing but his arm around me. I keep an indifferent expression on my face, or so I hope. As if it costs me nothing to defend my people this way. Like I would do it again in a heartbeat.

The fact of the matter is, regardless of the cost, I would.

Chapter Twenty-Three

A footman takes the trunk from my room, and I scan the space for anything I may have missed.

"There's no hurry," Jamys says. "After last night's excitement, I think it's perfectly reasonable to take a day of rest."

"I do not need to rest. I'm quite well to travel." Plus, I can't stand to be here a moment longer. I wrap my cloak around my shoulders, and the image of Tomas' arm around me appears in my mind. Everyone else stayed to deal with the intruders, thank the gods, because I'd never needed to be alone with him more.

As soon as we were through this door, I collapsed into him and cried against his chest. He swept me into his arms to put me to bed. Who knows how long he sat with me while I kept my knees tucked up, shuddering? I never thought I could be near a bed with him without wanting to tear his clothes off, but the soft kiss on my forehead when he laid me down was everything I needed.

I shake off the memory. "I'm ready to leave."

"We don't need to go to Brasport then. We can return to Mirador." Jamys can see there's something wrong with me, but I don't think he knows what it is. Frankly, I'm not entirely sure what it is either. Bless him for trying.

"There is no reason to alter our plans."

He frowns. "Is there any reason to go there, though? With those imposters dead, there aren't even any clues to follow."

In the end, it didn't matter that I didn't kill those men. They had some quick way to poison themselves, apparently. Everyone was furious about losing the ability to interrogate them. Tomas was only relieved it wasn't my doing—a fact he repeated to me countless times last night after the news was brought up to us.

"You did not kill those people."

"I could have, though. I was going to."

"But you didn't."

I swallow hard and focus on the present. "We don't even know if the events in Brasport are related to whatever those men were looking for here." Even as I say it, I don't believe it. For these things to be isolated would be absurd.

Jamys doesn't appear to believe it either.

"Or perhaps we'll find something they didn't," I try instead. Also a flimsy idea. "Either way, we should show up when there are issues in our kingdom." As much as I didn't want to go to Brasport before, now, I'll take any distraction. An unfamiliar place with nothing to remind me of my murderous response to Tomas' peril will be a welcome change.

"As long as you're ready for it."

"I am. You may not be ready, though. It will be rather hot on the southern coast."

His gentle smile tells me he'll accept my shift to a lighter mood. "I'm getting used to the Alchosian heat."

Outside, everyone is about ready for our departure. I thank Lord and Lady Altman for their hospitality. They apologize *again* for not discovering the imposters before we did. I excuse them—*again*—and walk into the courtyard. Tomas watches me intently, looking to see if I'm cracking, even if he won't ask it out loud. Approaching him for a goodbye is as confusing as it is distressing. Even if I was coming to terms with him relinquishing his role as my lover, last night proved him to have another place in my life equally as intimate.

"Safe travels." His eyes beg the question, *Are you certain I can leave you?*

"You as well." I snap a little shield around us, the act like a stab to the chest as I recall the last use of my power. "Thank you... for hiding my breakdown last night. I'm fine now, really."

Unspoken thoughts whisper across his face in minute shifts of his brow, lips, eyes—things I shouldn't notice, but I know too well. The shield dissolves. I can't remain in enclosed spaces with him.

"I'll see you when you return to Mirador."

I nod. "Send my love to Jo and my parents." *You take all of it with you anyways. No! Stop thinking like that.* I turn and step into the carriage.

"What are you doing? You always ride horseback." Nina bristles as she smooths her already perfect dress.

"Today, I want to ride in a carriage." Letting my element flow around me outside is the last thing I need. I'd always thought it was the gentlest of the magics, but seeing it turn violent... Of course, I can't very well blame the air when I was the one controlling it. "Is that a problem?"

"If it's too crowded, I can ride horseback," Kristance offers. Nina's attendant is more friend than staff.

"I'm not bothered at all." More specifically, I'm not bothered by sitting three to a carriage. I'm bothered by ample other things, but I do my best not to think about any of them as we set off.

On the second day of our trip, Nina and Kristance put on their riding clothes and forego the carriage. Apparently, my company was not desirable, and I couldn't care less. As I make my way to it, Jamys asks if he might join me in their place. Rolling along, out of the hills and toward the southern plains, it's stuffy in the enclosed space.

"You have no obligation to keep me company. It's not particularly comfortable in here."

Jamys adjusts his collar but makes no complaint. "Isn't it? Well, if you're uncomfortable, I'm certain you could do something about that."

The idea is only somewhat less repulsive than the thought of explaining it, so I pull a cool breeze through the carriage. It sweeps over my face—a soothing embrace. Still, my heartbeat picks up.

"I must admit, that is better." Jamys turns to face into it. "I'm surprised you weren't already doing this."

Even though he isn't posing it as a question, I feel him trying to understand. But how could he understand suddenly being afraid of part of himself? I've always thought my power was lovely—comforting, fun, useful—but I'd never used it in a dangerous way. That I so naturally wielded it as a weapon has rattled my understanding of the magic. And perhaps myself.

"Do you know," he says when I don't respond, "I've probably seen more of Alchos than Ceraun now?"

My gaze falls to the face of this man who seems to genuinely want to connect with me. It isn't required—we could easily be strangers who appear beside each other at engagements and share a bed to breed heirs. He could be polite and impassive toward me, and it would be a fair match. Instead, he's actually interested in me, and apparently, he wants me to know him.

All indications say I should want to know him completely. The problem is that if I come to care about Jamys, how could I stand to leave him stuck with a wretch who sneaks around and becomes murderous in the face of a threat to a man who isn't him?

"That's a shame," I say. "Not seeing Alchos—of course, I think it's beautiful. But why haven't you seen more of your own kingdom?"

"When we travel around Ceraun, it's usually directly from one castle to another. I don't get to explore towns as we've done here."

"I'm surprised your parents allowed you to come on this adventure with us if that's how they prefer to keep you."

"Apparently, the rules can be bent to accommodate time for you and me to be together."

A smile comes unbidden to my face despite a prickling in my eyes. "Well then, perhaps after we're married you can take your new wife on a tour of the kingdom so we can both explore it."

"You wouldn't mind me using you as an excuse that way?"

"Not at all." His ways of using me are perfectly innocent compared to his father's designs in securing me. Not that Urian wants a magical heir for Ceraun for any nefarious purposes. Still, my future child being an asset to be sought is nauseating. "It sounds like fun, doesn't it? Wandering about the kingdom for leisure."

It paints a lovely picture, just as the future with Jamys always does. I can see us laughing, drinking, even falling into bed together. One hand sliding up under my dress, the other in my hair. I can see it all, but it's like watching it happen to someone else. I can't imagine the feeling. Can't think of it really being me.

Jamys' mild smile and distant gaze tell me he can see it too. "You floating around like a leaf in autumn, and me playing music to bring you back down to earth?"

"Was I so obviously enamored by that?"

His cheeks flush as he jostles slightly with the carriage's bounces. "It was a thrill to bring you any happiness or pleasure."

"Would you play for me now?"

He sucks his lip in against his teeth and glances out of the window.

"I can make it so the sound won't escape."

"Do you think me foolish for being so nervous about anyone hearing?"

"No. I rather enjoy the idea of it being just for me."

He pulls the beautiful pipe out, and I snap a barrier around us. This time, the song is mystical. It ebbs and flows in a way that begs the body to dance. My muscles tense and move me in the slightest ways—the shadow of how I would dance to it if space and situation allowed. Within my shoes, my feet twitch with the intent of the steps and turns I'd take.

It really is remarkable what he can do with air. It's reprehensible that I'd bask in it being for me when so much of what should be exclusively for him isn't at all. My heart sinks into my stomach. Gods, he deserves a good wife. Tomas and I are over now, though. By the time Jamys and I marry, it will be as if it never happened. All that should be Jamys' will be. He's not my husband yet, so there's no reason to feel guilty for things that transpired before our union. I've even cut it off early.

The attempt to bolster my dignity is flimsy, but it's all that's available to me. Just as Tomas' past shouldn't matter to me, my own shouldn't hold me back. There is only forward, and I'll go forth with Jamys.

Chapter Twenty-Four

Lord and Lady Kinrade are welcoming as can be, but without the close connections our party had to Lambridge, we aren't quite so casual in Brasport. In our manners, anyway. Even without summer's official arrival, the heat down here keeps us casually dressed. I keep a breeze on our faces as we ride into town, physical discomfort taking precedence over my unease with magic. Wispy panels of skirts blow behind Nina, Lady Cara, and me. Thin linen shirts on the men blow open at their chests. Jamys looks good in his lighter, newly-acquired regional wardrobe, and the glimpses of his skin, bronze from days in the sun, are rather alluring.

Going south as temperatures rise must be madness to him. Haarton Castle, where he summers—where I will too—is in the far north, as far as we could possibly get from here. Within the next few months, I'll have toured the whole continent. Aside from Penum's strip up the coastline, of course.

"I've already assured the woman of our financial support," Cara says. "She says she can manage the care herself."

Rylan shakes his head. "How can anyone be prepared to care for three infants without any notice?"

"She lost a baby at birth recently. Very sad, but she was producing milk, so it worked out well enough. I think she's grateful to have a baby."

"*Three*, though." Nina sounds incredulous.

Three newborn babes found without any sign as to where they came from. When did Alchos become the land of bizarre events? We lose people, find people, have nameless enemies impersonating royal staff. Why Rylan and Nina are so desperate to rule over it all, I don't know.

We reach the home where the mysterious infants now reside—a modest but charming dwelling. It's painted in pale colors with a shaded porch stretching across the front. A woman opens the door for us and curtsies. "Your Graces. My lady. It's an honor."

"The honor is ours," Rylan says. "You're doing a great service by caring for these children."

"Not at all. Please, come in." She leads us into a sitting room which opens to the kitchen. "May I get you anything to drink?"

"No, thank you," Marcus says. "Please, sit and rest."

She tucks her hair behind her ear and smooths her simple brown dress before sitting. That she would bother trying to keep up appearances, exhausted as she must be, is astonishing. I step over to a large bassinet where three little faces peek out from thin, wrapped blankets.

"How are they doing?" Cara asks.

"Very well, my lady. All strong and sweet as can be."

"What have you called them?" I keep my eyes on the two little dark-haired heads and one golden one.

"Gavan, Dollin, and Tessa."

"Two boys and a girl, then?"

"Yes. The blonde is my sweet girl."

I brush a finger over a golden curl, and a weight hangs on me. Perhaps it's Jamys' gaze. It's easy enough to think of there being a baby in our future when it's hypothetical, but standing here together, over one who could be what ours will look like—babies all look the same—solidifies the idea. It's a reality I tell myself I'm ready for, but if he's watching me with a baby right now and getting warm flutters in his stomach, I'm not sure how I feel about it. It shouldn't be uncomfortable, but I'm not ready.

Tosha continues to deny offers of assistance, as if admitting she needs sleep makes her unfit. One starts to fuss, and that disturbs the others. She rushes to them and lifts two, bouncing and rocking them in her arms.

I gesture to the baby boy still in the bassinet. "May I?"

"Only if you wish to, Your Grace."

"I do." I pick up Gavan or Dollin, whoever he is, and cradle him in my arms. My swaying quiets his cries. "You're doing a wonderful job. Would it be too much to ask to borrow the little ones for the afternoon? We haven't yet taken Prince Jamys to see the shore, and I've heard the salty breeze is good for babies."

Nina looks at me like I grew four heads, and Tosha goes wide-eyed, looking like she can't decide if she can reach out and grasp the assistance I've offered.

"It would be such a kindness if you allow us to take them as well." I turn to fix a look at Jamys. "Wouldn't it?"

"Yes, of course."

I tilt my head toward Tosha, keeping eye contact with Jamys. He takes the hint and asks to hold one of the infants. Tessa looks even smaller against him. His hesitant tenderness is adorable. Damn it, now I'm the one looking on with warm flutters.

Rylan rolls his shoulders back as if preparing for battle and takes the last baby from the tired woman. She looks frightened and sad, but it isn't as if she can continue like this. "If it's what Your Graces wish, of course. I only hope they aren't troublesome for you."

"Not at all. We're delighted to do it."

After some preparations, we take the babies on a little outing.

I thought I invented the idea, but the sea breeze does indeed seem to soothe the little ones. I breathe in the salty air, Dollin rising and falling against my chest. Well, who wouldn't be soothed by such a thing?

"If you wanted to act out your fantasy future with Jamys," Nina says, "you could have found a way that didn't involve all of us."

I glance over to where Cara corrects the way Jamys holds Tessa as waves lap up on the dark sand and my bare feet. Even if it wasn't my purpose, is Nina right about what I'm doing?

"It was to give that poor woman a break." The glimpse of my future husband as he might be with our child is either an added benefit or a curse, I can't tell yet.

Nina purses her lips. "If you say so."

Marcus glances back and forth between Jamys and me with a confounded look. Is family life really so confusing to him? It's coming for all of us soon enough, and it could be just this lovely.

Over the course of the few days allotted to us, I stop in at Tosha's as often as possible, letting her bathe, eat, and sleep in peace. Jamys comes along with me, and I wouldn't have ever thought having regurgitated milk wiped off me would be endearing, but laughing at our state together while he does it warms me.

As we go back to the castle for our last night here, he turns to me. "Are you happy to be going home tomorrow?"

"Yes, though I hope Tosha lets others help her. And it was nice being away. Being in different places allowed us to… live in different circumstances. Don't you think?" Perhaps that sounds horrible, that I need to remove myself from my real life to feel a connection with Jamys.

He nods, though. "Being back at Mirador will come with different expectations. I understand that. Do you think… Have we made things too serious between us? Being around infants and all that? I don't mean to—"

My laughter cuts him off. "Jamys, our marriage is already planned. We've known for some time that would be our future. How much more serious can we be than that?"

"I just don't want you to think I expect us to jump into that part of our life so quickly. I know it's expected of us, but it's for us to decide when."

Quite the opposite of his intention to make me feel more relaxed, this assertion is so sweet it makes me feel as though I'm careening toward something very serious indeed. "Oh, do you not think I'm ready to be a mother?" Of course, I deflect it with sarcasm.

"No, you looked…" His throat bobs. "It was wonderful to see you like that. Many in high stations hand over their young as soon as they're born to nannies and the sort. My mother didn't take to that method. She was more involved than perhaps was appropriate, but I like to think Lillian and I benefited from it. It appears you might have similar ideals regarding mothering."

Deflection failed. Instead of lightening the conversation, I maneuvered it to confirm the warm feelings he got seeing me with babies. This should be a good thing—I had the same feelings. I want us to fall in love with each other, but every sign of that happening terrifies me.

Chapter Twenty-Five

Mirador comes into view, and I realize how much I missed it. The graceful slopes, the way it blends into its natural surroundings—all easier to appreciate when I haven't seen it in weeks. My focus pulls to the cave connected to the palace's left side by the bridge. For some reason, I feel I've missed that in particular.

We all speed our horses up in anticipation. My bouncing isn't only due to the trot—it's me. "Will anyone hate me if I go ahead?"

Nina rolls her eyes. "No more than we already do."

I blow her a kiss. "Jamys? Do you mind?"

"Go ahead." He takes my reins, and I jump up to stand on the saddle before lifting myself into the air.

Is it being home that makes me feel lighter? Or has enough time passed since the incident with the false investigators? Either way, my power feels like a natural, happy part of me again after my brief stint of avoiding it. Flying over the grand promenade refreshes me. My home beckons me toward it—a safe haven where the worst of my mistakes never involved death or destruction.

Mother, Father, and Josslyn step out of the front doors, and my heart soars higher than my body. I hadn't realized how much I missed them until now. So much has happened since I last saw them, and I can't decide if I want to fall back into life as if none if it ever happened, or if I'm eager to catch them up.

My feet touch down in front of the palace, and Josslyn practically pushes my parents out of the way to embrace me. A restless part of my soul settles now that I'm reunited with her. Father is the next one to greet me, followed by Mother.

She holds me out at arm's length and smooths my hair. "How far back did you abandon everyone?"

"Practically at the gates. They'll be here momentarily."

"Tomas told us about what happened at Lambridge." Father squeezes my hand. "Are you all right?"

"Yes." A deep breath almost convinces me that's true. "The fire was awful, and we all feel wretched about it. The run-in with the imposters posing as royal investigators was startling but not particularly difficult to handle." No need to delve into how the ease with which I fell into that dangerously protective stance made me feel about myself. Regardless, it's unfair for that event to distract from the other problems in Lambridge.

"We're glad to have you home." Josslyn loops her arm through mine and pulls me inside. "I missed you."

"I missed you too. If I had known ahead of time that Tomas was coming, I'd have insisted you come as well."

She snickers and shakes her head. "No, thank you. Being around the two of you is difficult enough. I don't know if it would be better or worse with you fighting, but I'm glad I wasn't there. I don't want to be in the middle of *that* mess."

"There isn't any mess." I let out a long breath. "Not anymore."

"That's for the best."

I suck my lips in as I nod. We reach the staircase which leads to my rooms, but I still feel pulled elsewhere. "Jo, you go ahead. I'll meet you up there shortly."

"What are you doing?"

"Just going to get a little something from the kitchen." I don't even know why I'm lying. My real intention isn't anything that needs to be hidden. It's just hard to explain when I don't understand it myself.

"They hate when you do that. Ask a maid to get you something."

I smile as I pull away from her. "Oh, Mary must have missed me."

"I doubt it!" Jo calls behind me and starts up the stairs with a huff.

Rather than slipping into the back hallway, I pop up the staircase to the bridge. There might as well be a rope tied round my chest for the way I'm drawn out there. The rest of my party arrives at the front of the palace as I cross the bridge. When I step into the noisy cave, the rushing sound of water on the other side of its walls filling the space, calm washes over me.

My eyes shut, and my shoulders rise and fall with a deep breath. I'm where I'm meant to be, even if I'm not sure why.

"Bell?"

My calm shatters as I turn to see Tomas sitting against a wall, his arms crossed and resting on his knees. "What are you doing here?" I ask too sharply.

"It's as good a place to be as any."

"Yes, equally as comfortable as the sitting room and lounge." I drop to the ground next to him—not so far as to look like I'm *trying* to put distance between us, but not close enough to be intimate.

He focuses his gaze forward, away from me. "How are you?"

"Fine."

We're usually good at being quiet in each other's presence, but this silence makes my fingers rap on my ankle.

"How was Brasport?" he asks eventually.

"Lovely, actually."

"Good." His gaze drops to his feet. "Did you enjoy your time with Jamys?"

"I did." That simple fact, which I was so pleased by, now makes my stomach sink. I shouldn't feel guilty about time spent with Jamys. On the contrary, it's my memories with Tomas that are problematic. Now, the closeness with Jamys rings like betrayal.

"Was that why you were upset I went to Lambridge with you?" Tomas keeps his focus away from me. "Because you wanted the time with him?"

"I suppose it was." We've known I'd be with Jamys after the wedding, but something about admitting I could have any kind of relationship with him before that feels like infidelity. Marrying him without much say in the matter was one thing, but if I develop feelings for him now...

"I'm sorry. I didn't mean to get in the way of that."

Didn't you? I keep the thought to myself. There isn't an answer that would be good for either of us. "It turned out to be a good thing you were there." *Not because of the sex.* "Although, I suppose if there hadn't been an attempt on your life, I wouldn't have nearly killed anyone." I shrug at my own circular argument.

His eyes meet mine and sparkle with unspoken thoughts. The urge to reach out and brush my fingers through his hair is agonizing. *I would kill for you. There is no safety for anyone who would hurt you.* Isn't that what the events of that night proved? I'd have defended anyone, but my violent reaction was based on it being Tomas. He must know that as well as I do.

His throat bobs, then his lips turn up in a coy grin. "I suppose it was good practice for the trials, though."

Who would have thought the trials would become the easy subject to discuss? "I don't plan to come anywhere near killing any of my siblings."

"Probably for the best."

"Speaking of siblings,"—I stand and smooth my tunic—"I've got yours waiting for me. Are you staying here?"

"For a bit."

"Suit yourself."

"Rest up for the trial, Bell. The twins won't hold back."

I practically snort. "Of course they won't. I'll be the one holding them back."

He drops his head to look up at the ceiling, and his exposed throat makes my heart drop at the memory of a blade flying toward it. "Watching that is going to be horrible." For a moment, I think he's narrating my thoughts, but we're still talking about the trials.

He's fine. He's safe.

"No. It'll be fun." I walk backwards toward the bridge. "Stop worrying so much."

"I have to worry for the both of us, apparently."

Chapter Twenty-Six

Lemon and blueberry swirl together in the perfect balance of tartness and sweetness. The shortbread crust melts in my mouth just as easily as the jammy filling. *Heavenly.* Actually, if this is what heaven is like, the gods stayed here much longer than I would choose to.

Rylan clicks his tongue in response to my satisfied sigh. "If Mary knew you left the palace for treats…"

"She'd be relieved I'm not in her kitchen." This treat came from a city bakery that *doesn't* shove me out of their doors.

"Shall we test that theory?"

"Don't you dare!" The only thing worse than me stealing food from our kitchens would be preferring the food elsewhere. Not that I *prefer* this—our food is just as delectable. It's the experience more than anything: strolling down the promenade on a beautiful day, slipping into a bakery, enjoying the scenery and the people coming and going.

The palace being tucked into the capital gives us the opportunity to live in a community rather than in isolation, something we should and do take advantage of. Though the residents here are quite used to seeing us around, these days we are met with more interest and attention. People smile excitedly at us, wish us luck with the upcoming trials, and ask if we know anything about what they'll entail.

Ry assures them we are in the dark and waiting as eagerly as they are to find out.

Alone on our walk, he asks, "Do you think you're ready for the first trial?" His tone is casual in contrast to his stringent posture, hands clasped behind his back.

"They said we couldn't do much to prepare, so I don't see how any of us could be truly ready or unready."

"Exhaustion from traveling wouldn't help."

I sigh. "Traveling isn't the primary cause of my exhaustion."

Ry tilts his head and gives me a patronizing look then lifts a finger to his lips. The volume of surrounding noises drops when I wrap us in a shield. "Ara, you can't blame yourself for the misfortunes in Lambridge. There is a lot going on there that none of us can understand. Nina told us they mentioned marks on the leaves, time pulling, our magic expanding. The plants did have a strange energy about them, like they had been frozen and thawed without any damage. It doesn't make sense, and I don't know what it signified to those men."

"We might have found out if they'd survived."

"You didn't kill them, so that isn't your problem."

I take a deep breath then a bite of the lemon bar to cleanse myself of the thought.

"You're still planning to help me against the twins, right?" His voice is strained; whether because asking for help is uncomfortable or because he's been waiting to ask, I'm not sure.

"Yes, Ry." My exasperation comes through despite my—well, the effort was minimal, actually.

He relaxes somewhat. "Thank you. You've been handling this better than any of us."

"That's because I'm the only one who feels no pressure to succeed. I know this is stressful for you."

"Perhaps it's good practice. Securing the crown can't be half as stressful as ruling the kingdom."

"Yes, but even that you don't have to do alone. You'll have support and assistance as king."

He nods absentmindedly.

"You'll be an excellent king, Ry."

"That's not my concern."

The effort not to roll my eyes is stronger. I'm willing to bolster him when he's feeling downcast, but I don't need to fan his ego if it's still so strong.

"It's that I can't imagine what I could do or be if I'm not king. This has always been the only plan for me, the only future. Without it..."

"It's still your future." This is a worry I can sympathize with. He had a defined plan, and the potential erasure of it would be unnerving for anyone. I mostly lacked a plan when my life suddenly took on one I didn't expect, and that was jarring enough. "The path to it is just different than you anticipated." I pat his arm, and he responds with a slight grin. "Shall I assume you won't be around tomorrow in *preparation* for the trial?"

He narrows his eyes at me. "I will want to make sure I'm well rested."

"I doubt you and Ossana will be resting much, but have no fear—I'll cover for you if anyone asks." I flash him a cheeky smile, which he only counters with a shrug.

"You'll understand someday."

I take a bite of the tartlet, certain any flushing on my part will look like I'm embarrassed to talk about me having sex *someday*. Really though, I don't know that part of it. To be relieved and relaxed afterwards is a foreign concept to me. Or at least fleeting. Those feelings are quickly replaced by sadness over the impermanence of it, knowing it'll be taken away from me.

Not anymore, though. Soon, the act of making love will fortify the stable bond between my husband and me. I'll be able to count on him always being there. Life will be easier and happier like that.

Until then, I'll have to get my relaxation by lounging about, like the angel I'm meant to be.

Chapter Twenty-Seven

It's quieter in the holding room under the stands than it has any right to be. Above, thousands crowd in to watch the first trial as my sister and I have our last private moments before the spectacle begins.

Nina stretches her legs, her black leather leggings like oil over her skin. "Ara, I can't believe you."

"I am proved right with every passing moment. Every word from my mouth should be regarded as prophecy." I lie on the stone floor next to her, not doing much of anything.

"I haven't the faintest idea what you're talking about."

"Wasn't it me who said if we put on some good shows, no one would remember anything other than how much they adore us?" I drop the permeable shield to let the full volume of sound hit us. "I'll admit, this is a rather different show than I had anticipated, but the theory is still correct. Weddings and coronations shall be boring now, I suppose."

My fiery sister hops up to her feet and tightens the leather strip around the end of her long, dark braid. She smooths her burgundy tunic and bounces on the balls of her feet. "Your nonchalance is unsettling."

"Your own worrying is what's unsettling you." Tomas was silly for thinking he had to do my worrying for me. Everyone is doing plenty of it.

Mother and Father enter, flanked by Rylan and Marcus, and Mother glances at me. Before she asks, I shield us from the cacophony above.

"Thank you," she says.

Nina offers me a hand to help me up, her palm hot enough to sear my skin. As I tug down my alabaster tunic, I fan her with a cool breeze, and a small smile offers me her silent thanks.

"The four of you are doing an incredible thing for Alchos," Father says. "This has sparked great excitement for people from every walk of life. We know you will make us proud."

Mother nods. "Enjoy the freedom to flaunt your powers. We live so much of our time restrained—have some fun. *Do not* maim or kill each other, however." She grins, but I wonder if such a rule might actually be necessary. "Best of luck, my loves."

The shield dissipates to let the Queen and King out to start the event. Marcus and Nina are the only ones to make eye contact as tension ripples through the air.

Rylan addresses us, cutting through the silence. "You should all know I do not resent you for making me work for the crown. This should not come between us. We are still brothers and sisters, regardless of what happens in this arena."

"Well, of course we are." I press Ry's hand and smile at the twins. "And I promise not to be terribly demanding of you all when I'm queen."

Marcus rolls his eyes. "Assuming this ever begins. Ara, aren't you forgetting something?"

"Oh, gods!" I run off after Mother and Father.

Their opening speech won't be particularly moving if no one can hear it.

The crowd feasts upon Mother's words—now that they're properly amplified. It's sad to think this is all about finding her replacement. I'm not sure any of us are truly up to the task of stepping up to her place. From the shadows of the tunnel, I close my eyes and let myself feel the air I breathe work through me to the tips of my fingers and toes.

"Almost show time," Nina says.

"... The Princes and Princesses of Alchos."

The crowd roars at Mother's crescendo, and I allow the full force of the noise to wash over me as the four of us step into the sunlight. Indistinguishable faces crowd the seating which surrounds and towers above us. My gaze follows Mother and Father to the box where Jamys and his family await. Jamys dips his head to me, and I give him a slight smile. Next to them are both sets of our grandparents. The Highbluff box is the next one over. A breeze brushes around Tomas' neck, and I gasp, not having intentionally done it. The gesture earns me a cocked eyebrow and an incredulous look.

I didn't mean to tease him, but the air pulls back so I can breathe in his warm scent. It soothes me as I take in the monolith in the center of the arena. Narrow steps wind around the stone tower, banners of four colors streaming from various places along it—forest green, azure, maroon, and white, matching our tunics. At its top sits a spire, sporting the banner of our house—a ring made of the four elements on a stormy gray background. One could almost think it's only three-quarters of a ring, the pale wind blowing through its quarter subtly.

Mother's voice booms again. "As rulers must strategize how to gather their resources, each contestant must collect all five banners of their respective colors. Their competitors will challenge them and drive their motivation, and the magic of the elements shall be set against each other in a way no one has ever seen."

The cheers are renewed with greater vigor.

"All five banners must be collected prior to a contestant retrieving the banner at the apex of the tower," Mother says in conclusion of the rules.

Marcus smiles and speaks through his teeth to hide it. "Which means you can't simply fly to the top to take the prize."

"Oh, Marcus. Don't you know I'm above all this?"

"Begin!"

The crowd erupts again at the Queen's command, and I do fly to the top. Not to the spire, but to the highest of the colored banners as Rylan, Nina, and Marcus dash toward the tower. The other banners seem easy enough to snatch off their perch, but the white one is tied on. *Clever, Mother.* This way, I can't simply blow them off to myself. I take the fifth white banner and begin the descent, collecting them in reverse, going fast enough to look like I'm trying, but not as effective as I'd be if I wanted to win. A delicate balance.

As I round the tower stairs, Rylan is rising to the first banner on an out-cropping of rock until a wall of water sends him tumbling back down to the ground. I pad his landing—it's unnoticeable, but it'll save him some bruises. He searches and finds me up above. He winks at me, and I nod as I continue down.

These reflexive utilizations of my magic are fine. It's defending and protecting, the way I'm used to my magic working.

Nina and Marcus tuck the first red and blue banners into their respective belts below me as I nab my fourth—or second, as it were. Rylan runs up to his first flag and leaps off the steps onto a rapidly growing tree. It takes him up to the third set of banners where we meet.

"Well, this is fun," he says.

"Consider yourself fortunate it wasn't Nina who attacked you."

He smiles and nods. "Thank you for catching me."

"Any time."

As we tuck the banners into our belts, a fireball explodes into the wall next to us. I shield Rylan and myself just in time to avoid being battered by rock.

"Nina!" Ry shouts.

She isn't the first one to come into our line of sight, though. Marcus rounds the bend, and I throw a shield up in time for him to pummel it with a wave. It isn't enough—Rylan and I remain dry, but the pressure of a towering waterfall presses against my barrier. My feet slide back on the step as I try to hold against it. Ry supports me from the back of my shoulders.

"No, just go!"

"Ara, I can't—"

"Go!"

He races up the steps behind me, and my arms tremble with the effort of holding Marcus off. My feet slide back, back, back, until the left one goes past the edge, then I'm easily toppled over. The endless current pushing me down keeps me from flying, so I wrap myself in a shell of air like an egg to protect myself from slamming onto the ground. Except the impact doesn't come. Instead, I sink through a newly-formed body of water. The waterfall pushes me down into the depths of a narrow sinkhole.

All right, Marcus, but you can't keep this up for long if you intend to keep going.

At the bottom, I pull my bubble up to enclose only my head. I press up against the current and find I can rise through the murky water now. There isn't enough air to propel me, so I swim up to the surface, pulling bubbles of air from the water around me for a comfortable supply.

When I breach the surface, Nina is nearing the fifth banner. A boulder lands in front of her to block her way before Rylan slides down the steps on a drift of water.

I've had about enough of my little brother. Marcus stands at the top of the plummeting river, focused more on stopping Ry than getting his own banners. I knew he was only going to help Nina. I sweep him off the side of the tower with a strong gust and wrap him in a bubble. My lip-reading skills aren't terribly sharp, but I believe he says some things unbecoming of a prince as I float him toward me.

"There now, you stay here." I turn to go back to the tower, but a wave sends me sprawling to the ground. *All the dead gods.*

I roll over and focus my energy on the bubble around Marcus. It takes more concentration than I've ever required to contain not only his body but his power. His angry countenance becomes confused then outright furious. Layers of impenetrable air wrap over each other around him. The entire thing pulses with my heartbeat. The memory of the imposters being crushed in a weaker shield sends a shiver down my spine, but Marcus has plenty of room. I feel jabs against it when he tries again and again to control water outside of the space I've given him.

Heat blasts me from behind and thunderous crashes bellow out. But I remain focused on Marcus. He looks around himself, fists clenched. Then his face melts into a calm, coy expression as he meets my gaze with a confident sneer.

And water begins to fill the bubble around him.

CHAPTER TWENTY-EIGHT

"What *are* you doing?"

Marcus can't hear me, but he gestures around himself and shrugs. Water rises quickly—to his waist, his chest...

"Can you even drown?"

Fire doesn't burn Nina, except that strange green one, and Marcus wouldn't really risk his own life like this. No, I'm certain he can't drown.

His hair floats around him like a dark halo, fully submerged. Large bubbles spill from his mouth when he pushes out the air from his lungs.

He can't drown. He wouldn't... But he needs air.

His lips quiver. The instinct to breathe can't be suppressed forever.

I shatter the bubble as he makes to gasp, and he drops to the ground with a splash, coughing out some water as I drop to my knees in front of him. "Marcus, are you all right?"

He nods, panting. "That took you longer than I expected."

I shove his shoulder. "You could have *killed* yourself, you imbecile!"

"I knew you wouldn't let me die, Ara!"

The ground underneath us rumbles, and both of us snap our attention to the tower.

"Nina!" Marcus shouts.

She's nearly at the top of the tower. Arms out, she steadies herself from the jolt then glares down to the ground where Rylan stands, covered in soot with a sleeve half burnt off. The ground shakes again, and the tower sways before crumbling to the ground.

I gasp and reach out a hand as wind pushes up under Nina. The tower drops from beneath her feet, but she remains suspended in the air. She shouts as I float her toward us, and when she gets close enough, I realize it isn't curses at Rylan. Her fury is directed at *me*.

"Ara! Let me go! He's going to get the—"

Cheers burst forth from the arena. My gaze snaps to where Rylan stands atop the pile of rubble with our family standard.

"Damnit, Ara! Mind your own bloody business!" Nina stalks out with Marcus on her heels.

I rise from the ground careworn, drenched, and irritated as Ry descends from the monument to his destruction and comes to me.

"Congratulations then."

He lays a hand on my shoulder and squeezes gently. "Thank you."

Not for my congratulations—for helping. Though I'm not certain I did much to help him. Mostly, I survived the twins. "You might be on your own for the other two. How many banners did our beastly little siblings retrieve?" I look at the three in my belt.

"I think Marcus got three before foolishly going head-to-head with you. Nina got all five."

"Did you get all five?"

"I would have, but Nina reduced my last two to ash. That can't possibly count, though. Vindictive little shit."

I suppress a chuckle as Mother, Father, Marcus, and the *vindictive little shit* approach us from the tunnel underneath the stands. It is quite like Nina to decide if she may not win, no one will.

"Are you both all right?" Mother asks.

"Yes," Ry says as I say, "Fine."

"Good. Line up." We shuffle into position, a web of glares tangling between us before Mother looks at me. "Arabella?"

Exhaustion is settling into me, but I nod and push the air to amplify her voice. How is this going to work when I live in Ceraun?

"Good people of Alchos, we thank you for joining us today. We are thrilled to be closer to finding the next ruler of our great kingdom. Three of my children shall continue to compete for the highest honor in the land. Eliminated from the trials is... Prince Marcus."

Marcus and Nina share a charged look, but he bows and steps back gracefully. Nina's chest heaves, her hand shaking at her side. I slip mine around it and give it a light squeeze. Her gaze meets mine and she lets out a slow breath, relaxing her shoulders.

"The winner of today's trial is Prince Rylan," Mother continues. The wave of cheering is so loud, I'd like to block some of the noise, but I can scarcely maintain amplification for Mother at the moment.

Ry steps forward and thrusts our banner into the air. He waves and smiles valiantly—a hero returned from victory on a battlefield. I suppose this was the point— to make the people love him. It sounds as though it's working.

"Gods bless you all. We look forward to seeing you at the next trial."

We follow in our parents' wake. When they stop in a holding room, I lean against the wall, struggling to remain on my feet.

"I collected just as many banners as Ara, *and* I bested her power multiple times!"

Mother is unimpressed by Marcus' outburst, glaring at him with stone-cold fury. "*You*, my son, came the closest to breaking the 'don't kill anyone' rule."

"The rule was we couldn't kill each other. You didn't say anything about ourselves!"

"You nearly killed my son!" Sparks dance across Mother's fingertips, even though she holds a mere thread of that power. "And for what? To use Arabella's love for you as a weapon against her?" Marcus drops his gaze. "Someone loving you is not a weakness to exploit, Marcus. It isn't a weakness at all. Arabella showed that she is not only the stronger of the two of you but also the more compassionate. *That* is why she could still be crowned as heir, and you are done." Her rapid steps echo back to us as she storms away.

Father is at my side. "Sweetheart, are you sure you're all right?"

Before I can answer, Jamys approaches, asking the same thing.

"I'm fine. Exhausted but fine."

Jamys doesn't look convinced. "Do you need assistance?"

"No." I take a deep breath and push off from the wall. My knees wobble, and Jamys wraps an arm around my waist to support me. The instinct to insist it's unnecessary is there, but instead, I offer him a small smile. "Thank you."

"It would be simpler if I..."

A little *yip* comes out of me as he scoops me up into his arms. Pressed against his chest this way, it's the closest we've ever been. He's solid, warm, and secure. The connection of our gazes is palpable, pulling warmth up to my cheeks.

"Is this all right?" His words reverberate through me.

My throat is too tight to push the word through, so I nod and allow him to carry me to a carriage which will take me back to the palace. During the short walk, I find my voice. "I suppose if you had ever pictured something like this, you'd expect me to look more elegant." The image of this perfect prince sweeping the half-drowned mess I am off my feet must be absurd.

He shakes his head with a bemused smile. "When have you ever conformed to expectations?"

CHAPTER TWENTY-NINE

Jo follows the maids in when they bring my lunch. It's set up at my bedside because I haven't mustered the motivation to move quite yet. Perhaps I should have trained for yesterday's trial after all.

"Are you certain you're well?" Jo sits near the foot of my bed. "It's midday, and you still can't get up."

"I wouldn't say *can't* so much as *won't*. The ordeal did take a lot out of me, but I may be using that as an excuse at this point."

"You've done bolder things with your power with the ease of strolling through the garden." She takes a strawberry from my tray and bites the fruit off its leaves.

You don't know half the bold things I've done. I've come quite a long way from Tomas' kiss stopping me from keeping us airborne. I clear my throat in an attempt to clear my mind and stay focused on this conversation.

"It wasn't so much the expulsion of power," I say. "Containing Marcus' power was a challenge unlike anything I've tried before. Blocking water itself isn't a problem, but I could feel him trying to reach through my shield with his power. Where our powers clashed, it felt... I don't know... strange."

"Well, you were brilliant. I was beside myself when Marcus threw you to the bottom of that pond. Tomas"—she shudders—"was troubled, to say the least. It's impossible to be around him when there's anything going on with you."

Tomas did say he'd worry about me, but anyone would be agitated by the scene which probably looked like my brother was killing me. His attention to the matter shouldn't excite me. We've always been close, and any reaction of his couldn't have matched mine when he was in danger.

"Of course," Jo continues, "he assured me it was nothing you couldn't handle."

"He was right. I can survive under water."

Once, while *practicing* my magic with Tomas, I broke the forcefield myself so we wouldn't lose the excuse. Though we never said as much, it was certainly an excuse—one I was all too happy to use. Whenever it started to get easier for me, Tomas would find new ways to wreck me, and I savored every moment. As months passed, my powers got stronger until finally, it seemed as though nothing could break me. I was content to let Tomas continue to try, but apparently, his pride was wounded by the issue. So, one day, he took me to a lake. By then, it was beginning to warm up, but winter hadn't released us from her grasp entirely.

"You've never tried your first failed trick again," Tomas said.

Our first kiss ending when a wall of water crashed into us wasn't a complete failure, though. It led to all these months of fun together. "Summer was a much more pleasant time to go for a surprise swim."

"Don't you think you can do it now?" The challenge shone in his eyes.

"You're dreadful."

"I won't think any less of you if you admit there is something you can't do."

"No, of course." I flung a bubble around us and sent it off into the frigid water. "Why shouldn't I be able to keep a water-tight shield around us and warm the air in it, all while you have your way with me?" The water rose around us, but I did keep the air warm as I traced my finger down his chest and stomach. "Or while I have my way with you."

My tongue danced over his as he freed me from my coat, and I fumbled with his trousers. Clothing dropped off our bodies like heavy rain, but we remained dry in our underwater sanctuary. He kissed down my neck to my breast and dropped to a knee to continue down my stomach. When he kissed my navel, the bubble shuddered.

"Do you have a death wish?" The words came out as sigh. The water was cold enough for this to be a complete disaster.

He looked up, the stubble on his chin scraping the lowest plains of my abdomen. "Am I not to kneel before my princess?" Then he dropped his face, and even my lungs had trouble keeping air in them, yet somehow, the bubble held. My knees threatened to give way underneath me, so I melted into a semi-reclined position, supported by a cushion of air I barely spared a thought for. My fingers tangled into his hair. Reality twisted and spun, and when my body exploded with pleasure, the bubble remained.

Suspended as if gravity had no claim on me, I was no more than a puddle. Tomas brushed his hand through my hair. "It would appear you have no use for me anymore."

"Oh, I can think of something."

As I made love to him, I tried to focus only on that, but there was something I couldn't ignore.

I was quite certain I had just taken the last scraps of my power.

Jo snaps me back to the present. "Do I want to know why he was confident in your ability to survive under water?" At least she looks amused.

"Not at all." Thinking of it is dangerous enough for me. I can't keep coming back to these memories.

"I'm glad you weren't hurt. The whole thing was terrifying to watch."

I almost roll my eyes. "You've seen us go at it before."

"Never like that." She snags another berry from my lunch and pops it into her mouth. "And don't think we didn't realize you could have ended it sooner."

"None of us *know* that. Nina and Marcus are a lot to handle. I didn't drop to the bottom of that sinkhole by choice."

Her lips twist to the side. "Still. You weren't trying."

I'm *trying* to get through this. I'm trying to think of an explanation for the debacles sweeping across the kingdom, and I'm trying to forget the dark side of my magic. All I want is for it to be over—to get back to normal life. Or as things stand, my new normal life. One where Jamys is taking up residence in my heart. The line of succession's potential shift would have been enough excitement, but with everything being fluid, it's a natural opportunity to let my feelings change too.

Isn't that enough of an effort? How many upheavals could I handle at one time?

CHAPTER THIRTY

Swords clash as Rylan and Tomas train in the courtyard. I've never understood my brothers' insistence on mastering swordplay. In what circumstance would they possibly prefer swords to magic? It's all to put on airs. For Tomas, it's at least logical—not that he isn't also showing off. Showing off his strength, stamina. The graceful way he moves is mesmerizing even if I weren't mentally equating it all to my more intimate knowledge of how his body moves.

I pull a cool gust to my face. How long after our last time will these errant thoughts continue to haunt me?

Marcus appears at my shoulder. "Ara." This is a suitable distraction.

"Hello, Marcus."

"I believe I owe you an apology." It's about time.

"Go ahead then."

He blinks a few times. "That was it."

"That wasn't an apology. All you did was say you *need* to apologize."

"Fine. I apologize."

I press my hands over my eyes as I consider throwing him across the yard. "You're terrible at this."

He sighs and shakes his head. "I wanted to help Nina. I know you understand that." He motions toward Rylan with his chin.

"How would it have helped her for you to drown?"

"You can't make this easy, can you?"

"You're one to talk! Do you know how terrifying that was?" Even if he didn't think I was shaken by my similar situation in Lambridge, he must know I'd be horrified by his possible death. And to have been a part of it!

"I am sorry."

I take his hand in mine. "I care for you more than this absurd competition. You are more important to me than a crown."

"I know. I'm sorry I used that against you."

"Thank you." I sigh as I consider the incident again. "Marcus, did you feel anything odd about our powers clashing that way?"

"It was certainly frustrating to be thwarted." His tight smile isn't as casual as he thinks. "Why?"

"No reason."

His mouth scrunches to one side, as if he's considering asking me something. "Right, then. I'll just…" Or that's all I'll get.

As he walks away, I call out, "You're as bad at ending a conversation as you are at apologizing."

He only turns and shrugs before continuing toward Ry and Tomas. "Can the defeated contender still compete in this?"

"Here." Tomas tosses his sword, blade aimed at the clouds, which Marcus catches on its descent. "I need a break." He comes to my side, wiping his brow with his sleeve. "Since when do you enjoy watching this?"

"I don't, but what other entertainment is available to me?" He only shakes his head. "What's got you out of sorts?"

"I was angry with Rylan for abandoning you yesterday against Marcus. New information tells me you're to blame, though."

"Why is me telling him to continue anything to be upset about?"

"Because I can't believe you're really not trying."

"I tried enough to not be eliminated." And I will try my best not to have this conversation with every member of the Coyle family. Why is it the two people I'm closest with who feel the need to scrutinize me?

"If you had actually tried, you'd have won without anyone almost dying or the tower coming down."

"What on earth would we have done with that tower? It couldn't have been meant to stay there forever."

"It's not a joke!"

My gaze snaps up to Rylan and Marcus, but they aren't paying attention, despite Tomas raising his voice. It's a heartbeat before I realize there's a shield up. *I didn't even...*

"First of all, you could have been hurt."

I cross my arms. "Tomas, you know I can protect myself."

"Of course I do, but do you think that made it easy to see you thrown off the tower?"

Again, I remind myself it shouldn't surprise or excite me that he cares enough to not want to see me killed. He's always cared about me that much—all of us, actually. Still, I'm stupid enough to crave these possible signs of attachment. He's always been my obvious weakness—part of me wants to be his. Not that it does any good. Why should I want him to be as entangled in this as I am? So his heart can break along with mine?

"I don't know what you want me to say. It was under control, but if it's so difficult to watch, don't go to the next one."

"Potential injuries aren't nearly as difficult to watch as you stepping back to let someone else win."

This isn't going to end quickly, so I lead him toward the stables and continue with a soundproof barrier floating around us. "From what misguided place does this desire to see me become Queen of Alchos come from?"

"If you *can* win, then you are the best option the kingdom has. When did you stop caring for the well-being of *your* kingdom?"

Heat explodes through me. "Rylan is not a *bad* option! You act as if I'd allow an enemy to rule. Alchos will be in good hands, and I'll have another kingdom to worry about."

From the corner of my eye, I see his jaw clench. It's not something I want to throw in his face, but if he's going to push me, I'll push back.

"What?"

His gaze drops. "This place won't be the same without you, Bell. If you were our queen, you'd be here more."

Another reason not to win—I don't want to see Tomas once I'm married. If my wedding is the last time I ever see him, it would be a mercy. The more time I've spent with Jamys and with both of them together the more I realize I can't simply choose to not be drawn to Tomas anymore. Attraction to Jamys happens, but not when Tomas' presence overwhelms my every thought. I need distance from him to have any chance of clearing my head.

Half a continent might be enough.

"Perhaps it's for the best if I'm not around." My throat tightens, hating the words even if they're true. "This has always been easier for you, but I..."

"What do you think is easy for me?" He scans the area before we step behind the stable.

Do you want me to lay my heart out on a platter? I expand my soundproofing to give myself more air that doesn't smell like him. Being enclosed with him is torture. His heat radiates, his magnetism consuming.

"This was my idea. I said we could be friends after everything, but now I don't see how that could work. It's terribly unfair to you, and I'm sorry, but..." I stop too close to him, my face near his neck without any contact. "It's so difficult for me to be around you without touching you." I grasp fistfuls of my skirt to keep my hands to myself.

"I'll ask you again." His voice is crunching gravel. "What do you suppose is easy for me?"

"Restraint." The word blows out of me, raising bumps on his neck close enough for me to lick. I can only whisper the rest of the embarrassing truth. "Sometimes, I wonder if you even want me or if you're only placating me."

"That's ridiculous." His words are clipped. His collar bones become more defined by the strain of his chest.

"You never touch me until I touch you." This isn't where our conversation was supposed to go. Perhaps this is my surrender;

being aggravated by it for months is finally over because we are. Now, I can admit he won the game he may not have realized we were playing. "Even now, this close, you're still as stone."

His stoniness may be experiencing a quake for the tremble hiding under his grave tone. "We said it was over."

"I know."

"We said last time was *the last* time."

"Well, we said that several times, didn't we!" My face feels like it's on fire. I wasn't trying to start things with Tomas again, but it's impossible to be around him without giving in to this magnetic attraction.

He lets out a slow breath. "Bell, you are betrothed to another."

I step back to regain use of my mind. "Am I his property then?"

"Can I not retain any scrap of honor? I'm already constantly seeking out the man's future wife. Can I at least pretend I'm not instigating the entire thing?"

"You never did! And whether it's honorable or not never seemed to matter much when you were fucking me!"

Tomas' eyes narrow. "Don't fight me for the sake of fighting me."

"You're right. There's no point in fighting with you. You don't fight for anything. You only stand there, the hypocrite"—I shove his shoulder with more force than I mean to—"expecting me to fight my own siblings for something I don't even want, when you..." *You didn't put up the slightest fight for me.*

When did I start crying? Tomas' hand moves toward my face as if to wipe away the tears, but I step back. "No. Don't mar your perfect record of keeping your hands to yourself."

All I want is to get away. I whip around, mortified by the ridiculous spectacle I put on—that I let Tomas see me this way. First my emotions, and now my damned powers betray me. I can't even push myself up and away from this catastrophe. Instead, I'm stuck stomping off like a child, each step like a stab to my gut.

Chapter Thirty-One

Pacing about my chamber, I don't even know why I'm angry at Tomas. His persistence about the trials is aggravating, but that's not the biggest problem. I want him to show that he wants me, but why? He's doing exactly what we'd agreed to. I'm the one trying to shift our dynamic, though we have no future. Losing what we did have is already torturous. What kind of masochist am I for wanting more? It's only more to lose. And wanting him to suffer it too... I'm a wretch.

I stopped a breath away from accusing him of not fighting for what he wants. It was close enough to make the meaning clear anyway. But perhaps he never wanted anything more with me. If he has any sense, he shouldn't. One of us might as well be sensible.

My maid comes in to draw my bath—how the day has nearly passed already, I don't know. "Dinner will be in the great hall tonight. In addition to the Cerauno royal family, the Coyles will be in attendance."

"Thank you, Lucy."

Slowly, I slip into the hot water. I roll my neck back and forth, willing the heat to permeate through me. Knowing water wasn't my problem doesn't stop me from being curious. I scoop up a handful of water and wrap it in a bubble. The orb of water floats where I wish. "Containing you isn't so difficult."

And now I'm a lunatic speaking to water. To think, there are people who'd like me to be queen.

Being around Tomas with unspoken, unresolved tension between us is almost as uncomfortable as suppressing desire for him. I didn't see him early enough to apologize before dinner, so our argument this afternoon hangs over me, and I can't stand the uncertainty of it. I suppose I never really know where I stand with him, but at least he isn't usually angry with me. He avoids eye contact, which leads me to test my theory that while my Cerauno gowns may be too constricting to eat much, I can still drink plenty of wine. Jamys' parents had several barrels of wine brought down from Ceraun as a gift to us, so I'm only doing my part to look appreciative.

"Have you heard from Horace?" Mother asks Wymond.

Tomas' father sighs, looking too much like his son with his hard, stoic expression even when he's upset. "Lambridge is highly charged, but our forces have shored up the border, so they're confident we won't see any more spies from Penum slipping through."

Father stiffens. "Did they find proof to link those imposters to Penum?"

Another reason to keep the wine flowing.

"No, but they must have been," Wymond says. "So close to the border, and no one in Alchos would dare."

Mother's frown displays only the exasperation of a ruler who doesn't like things to be messy. There is more care and concern behind that facade than she lets on. "And the missing people?"

"Still nothing," Wymond says.

The broken families, the confusion and fear we only made worse... My throat tightens at the thought. But as with my too tight dress, wine still fits.

After dinner, our generation enjoys the lounge together while the kings, queens, lords, and ladies retire to the parlor.

Lillian remains close to me, chatting animatedly. "I'll be so grateful to have a sister."

"And I'll be so pleased to have a sister who will never try to set me on fire."

Nina smirks. "Sounds like life will be rather boring in Ceraun."

"I don't see how life anywhere could be as exciting as it is here, with magic running in everyone's veins." Lillian looks awed by the entire thing.

"Exciting may not be the word you'll use when your niece or nephew blows you over."

Thank you for that reminder, Nina. "There's plenty of time to prepare you, Lillian." I drain my wineglass. The idea of Jamys and I having children together was warm and cute when we were in Brasport, but here, with tensions rising again, it's a disquieting proposition. Or perhaps it's because I can never feel closure with Tomas present.

Jamys trades my empty glass for a full one and sits next to me. I thank him, wishing I could maintain my warm feelings for him around Tomas. He is so delightfully kind and thoughtful. I should adore him.

It'll come. Once we're married, it'll come.

Jamys has a smile girls must swoon over. "I'm glad to see you enjoy our wine so much. We're quite proud of this vintage."

"It was very kind of your family to bring it. I only fear it won't last terribly long."

"Not at the rate you're going tonight." Tomas' comment draws my gaze to where he eyes me from a card table. In a far corner of the room, a phantom gust knocks over a vase. The shatter attracts everyone's attention, but Tomas keeps his eyes on me to see me flip him off. He only shakes his head.

I take a mental note of which maid cleans up my mess so I can leave her something nice later. Actually—I blink a few times—I should write it down. Tomas' observation was somewhat accurate. The edges of my vision blur in a barely acceptable range.

"The wine is wonderful," Tomas says. "I'm surprised Arabella enjoys it so much, though. This isn't the style she typically prefers."

"How is that?" I ask.

"This is quite complex and subtle. Any time I've presented you with such wine, you *thoroughly* enjoy it, and yet, if you can't immediately identify the varietal, you act as if you're cheated."

He is not having this conversation like this. "I beg to differ. I've always been *the first* to sing praises of your wines." *As I'm always the first to do anything with us.* "Though I will say, this is a little sweeter, which I do enjoy."

"I've heard you don't name your wines for the grape," Jamys says. "Quite the interesting practice. In that way, we are more straightforward in Ceraun."

"How very refreshing. It is easier to manage expectations when one knows what they're getting." I stare at Tomas as I take another drink of the wine in question.

"If you like it," he says slowly, "why does it need to scream what it is at you?"

"I may not need to know what it is if I'm only going to have a glass—"

"You enjoy wine by the barrel."

My cheeks flame as I gape at him. "Well, I'd need to know what it is if I'm to purchase more."

"It doesn't matter if your parents won't let you buy it."

I suck in a breath to throw my response—

"I doubt you're ever denied anything you desire," Jamys says.

Gods, he's still here. I should be grateful; I almost said something very, *very* stupid. This conversation has blown caution out of the water and possibly logic. I'm not sure how much sense any of it makes anymore. Tomas' commentary certainly doesn't.

"Of course not," I say to Jamys. "Tomas forgets I'm grown now." *And a princess can have anything she wants...*

"Growing up together will do that," Jamys says. "Friends start to feel like additional siblings."

I nearly choke. "Well, this friend is correct about one thing—I have perhaps enjoyed your wine a bit too much tonight." I should go to bed. "I need some fresh air. Jamys, would you come for a walk with me?" Spite wins this round.

"Of course."

Tomas' eyes burn my back as I leave on Jamys' arm. If tonight has shown me anything, it's that I should have ended things with Tomas long ago. I'm going to marry Jamys. We'll sit side by side on thrones someday. I can't keep putting off the idea of being with him romantically.

The outside air does revitalize my nerves and soothe the buzzing in my veins.

"Your parents seem very happy together," Jamys says.

"They are."

"That's wonderful. I don't know that mine are bonded in quite that way, but I'd hope to experience it someday."

I think I have. "As would I."

"I want to love you, Arabella." His voice is soft, his gaze warm as he looks down past his shoulder at me.

"I'm glad you don't yet." I cover my mouth with a hand. "Gods, that sounded awful! What I mean is, we should know each other better for either of us to be in love."

He laughs under his breath. "Have no fear. I'd like to properly fall in love. I'd like for you to fall in love with me."

"I'd like that, too. The challenge is"—I jump up onto a stone bench—"I'm quite incapable of falling." I walk to the other end, step off, and stand suspended in the air.

A smile spreads over his face as he takes me in. "You are spectacular."

I lower to the ground slowly. "Thank you."

"Do you think you'll return with us to Ceraun after the trials?"

This dress would be more comfortable in the cooler climate. My fingers trace whorls on the skirt as I consider it. "I suppose I will." Summer in the mountains... Can a change of scenery inspire a change of heart?

"I have a theory," Jamys says.

"Do tell."

"If you win the crown, I think we'll marry here."

It makes sense. If I were to be queen, with Alchos being the stronger power, I suppose we would marry here instead of Ceraun. "Can you imagine if we travel to Ceraun this summer as husband and wife?"

A short laugh bubbles from him. "I didn't necessarily mean that soon. Though, it *would* give us much more to explore than the kingdom."

My attention snaps to him so quickly, my hair slaps my face. "Prince Jamys, are you alluding to carnal relations?" *Did I say that out loud? Oh, I have had too much to drink.* Jamys is so very straight-laced, it's hilarious to hear.

He blushes, and I must admit, it's adorable.

"I'm sorry." I lean against his chest with less grace than I'd prefer. "I don't mean to tease. It's just surprising. I assumed you'd make no mention of it until we were bound before gods and men." My amusement is no doubt plastered on my face. I'm such an ass.

"Just because we can't act on it until then doesn't mean it doesn't cross my mind."

"Oh?" The idea of Jamys entertaining intimate thoughts about me is... exciting. I reach up to comb my fingers through his cornsilk waves. "What is on your mind now?" Intimacy with Jamys is an obvious way for him to slide into the space in my heart that Tomas has held. My state of intoxication helps, but I've always found Jamys attractive. Closing the gap between us feels good, and it's necessary.

He looks into my eyes, not with the self-assured confidence of a prince, but with the timid mildness he shows when his music comes up. "May I kiss you?"

It's all so sweet and lovely and innocent. "Yes, you may."

He presses his lips to mine, and yes, sweet is the right word. The golden prince is pure honey.

Jamys' lips pull back from mine with a light *pop*. And again. And again. Many little surface kisses, and when I try to slow one down, deepen it, he continues right on with the steady beat of kisses. *Pop, pop, pop*, like a pendulum. It isn't *bad*, it's just terribly boring. Some variety would really do wonders. We continue like that until I can't stand it anymore.

I pull back and drop my head forward. He kisses my forehead and wraps me in an embrace. Before he says something I won't be able to respond correctly to, I say, "It's getting late. I should be getting to bed."

"Of course." He releases me and offers me his arm—back to the straight-laced prince I'm used to as he escorts me to my staircase.

On the first step, I turn to face him. "Good night, Jamys."

"Good night, Arabella." He brushes a soft kiss on my hand, and we go our separate ways.

Damnit. I thought keeping Jamys at arm's length was keeping me from developing feelings for him. Apparently, breaking down those barriers doesn't help either. I drop face first onto my bed as disappointment spreads its coiling tendrils through me.

Do not hang it all on one mediocre kiss.

I fumble with the laces on the back of my dress with no success. A gust rings the bell for my maid, and I close my eyes while I wait.

Chapter Thirty-Two

Laces loosen. Fingers continue down my back as I lie on my stomach. I sigh and reach back to entangle my fingers with his. "Hello, love."

The hand pulls away quickly, accompanied by the sound of a sharp gasp. "Oh, Your Grace, I'm so sorry."

I jump to sit up and face Lucy, who is looking at the floor. "No, no. I'm sorry, Lucy! I didn't mean to fall asleep."

"I tried to wake you, but I figured you'd be more comfortable if the dress was at least undone."

"You were quite right. Thank you." I stand and turn my back to her. "I'm mortified. I'm truly sorry for that."

"You never need to be embarrassed around me, Miss."

She helps me out of my dress, and I slip into a nightgown. I shuffle to the vanity and drop into the chair with a plop. While she braids my hair, I notice a glowing light outside. "What is that?"

"A fire. I'm told there's nothing to be concerned about." She ties off the braid. "Shall I bring a tonic for your head?"

My head is propped on the vanity, face in my hands. "I suppose that's a good idea. Thank you."

I slide under my blankets while Lucy retrieves it from my wash-room. Tonic taken, I let the dark quiet sweep me off into uncon-sciousness.

When the sun comes into my room, I'm surprised to find that I don't have any trace of a headache. Either the tonic works very well, or Cerauno wines don't cause such effects. There's a metaphor in there, but I don't want to think about it.

As I dress, thoughts ricochet through my mind. Will Jamys think we kiss regularly now? I hope not. That's dreadful. How much did he drink last night? Maybe he was drunk. Perhaps he won't turn out to be such a bad kisser.

Outside, Tomas leans against the courtyard wall, watching Nina turn targets to ash. "Good morning." His voice is clipped.

"I believe we have multiple disagreements to settle."

"They don't matter."

Do the arguments not matter because he doesn't care, or because I made things even worse? "Are you angry with me for spending time alone with Jamys last night?"

"No."

"I half expected you to be in my chambers when I arrived. Based on your absurd display last night, I thought you might be jealous of that sort of thing." I had the best intentions of smoothing things over, but his nonchalance boils my blood. *This man* makes everything so unbearably difficult that I dig the hole deeper.

"Is that why you did it?"

"No."

He drops his chin conspiratorially. "Well, I might have been jealous, but it's *Jamys*. It's not as if anything would happen before you're married."

"We kissed." I'm absolutely pathetic. Why am I saying this?

"Really?" He cocks his head. "How was that?"

"Fantastic."

His mouth quirks up on one side. "Interesting. And yet you got to your chambers hoping to find me there?"

"I didn't say I was *hoping* to find you there, only that I thought you might be."

"Right, well I'm sorry I disappointed you—"

"I was not disappointed."

"But I had other things to deal with last night besides you snuggling up to your betrothed."

"Tomas!" Nina shouts. "Are you even paying attention?"

"No. You aren't doing anything remotely interesting."

She sneers and throws a fireball at him. It spreads and dissipates against a shield I create without a thought. "Nina, what is wrong with you?"

"I knew you'd shield him." She crosses her arms. "May I remind you, Tomas, that this is important?"

"What's important?" I ask them both.

"My training." A flame flickers around Nina's forearm.

I turn toward Tomas. "Why are you helping Nina train?"

"I want her to win the trials." Based on Tomas' tone, this is supposed to be obvious. Well, of course. Why not?

"Since when do you want *her* to win?"

Nina smiles at my confusion. "Since he realized I'd be the best ruler for Alchos, *obviously.* Marcus left for Etherlee with Grand Mama and Grand Papa this morning, so I'm left with him."

Tomas narrows his eyes at her. Neither seem happy to work together, so why do it?

I throw a soundproof bubble around Nina. She is no doubt cursing me as the remaining training dummies across the yard explode in flames.

"I thought you wanted me to win?" I say to Tomas.

"You don't want to win, so why is this a problem?"

My brows scrunch together. "Do you just want anyone *except* Rylan to win?"

"No."

"Did you have a falling out with him I'm not aware of?"

"No." Tomas crosses his arms. "I want Nina to be queen."

"That is absurd."

"It's not your problem if you're content to be Queen of Ceraun."

I see *red.* "I cannot believe you are helping her to spite me."

He laughs darkly. "This is *not* to spite you."

"To be honest, the details of our argument last night are fuzzy—"

"Not surprising."

"But I didn't think I'd offended you *this* much."

A long breath blows past his lips that seems to take the fight in him with it. His shoulders relax, and his gaze on me softens. "Bell, you didn't offend me. I shouldn't have brought any of it up."

"You can't actually *want* Nina to win."

"I do." He looks me squarely in the eyes. "I truly want Nina to win."

There's nothing I have any right to be upset about, but that doesn't stop me. If I had any reasonable level of self-control, I'd grab him by the front of his tunic and demand a better explanation. But if I lay a hand on him, it won't end well. Or rather, it won't end in a way my sister should see.

Damn him, I did want him to be there last night—a reminder of what a *passionate* kiss feels like...

"Fine then. I'll get out of your way." In a move both childish and spiteful, I give the bubble a tumble before dissolving it, dropping Nina in a heap.

"You conceited—"

"Throw me a ball."

She obliges with a devilish smirk. Flames dart forth from her hands, and I catch it in a bubble. It stays suspended between us.

"Fire requires air," I say. Her weapon consumes the air in its confined space, and the flames sputter and die. "So, a trick like Marcus' won't work for you."

"I have my own tricks, don't you worry."

I turn to Tomas. "Oh, you're helping her work around my magic?" Obviously, she can't use his methods, but does he know my power well enough to come up with other possibilities?

Nina's huff draws my attention from Tomas. Her fists clench so tightly, her arms tremble. She shakes her head then turns on her heel and dashes away.

"What is her problem?"

Tomas sighs. "Where can you even begin to answer that question with Nina?"

"Then why do you want her to be queen?"

"I don't have to like her to kneel to her."

Chapter Thirty-Three

Rylan believes I'm training with him because I want to help him. It's an easy enough ruse—he doesn't think of anything past his own goals. He wouldn't consider that it has anything to do with Tomas helping Nina. Or, if he did consider it, he might think I'm offended on his behalf. His own friend, betraying him this way. *A shame.* No, he wouldn't guess I'm being a vengeful lover, but Jo does. She watches us train with arms crossed, a stern frown pasted on her face.

She doesn't even flinch when Rylan throws a boulder my own size at me, though Jamys' jaw drops. I reach out to catch it in a net of air, toss it up, and set it down gently. Ry drops to a knee and presses a hand to the ground. I feel the rumble underfoot, and a smile creeps onto my face as I swipe a shield onto the grass. Pressure builds underneath it, and I sink invisible claws into the ground, holding it in place. Something bangs against it, and I look down as the ground shifts and crumbles beneath me—a tree tries to push up at the center. Rather than lifting me off the ground, it's crushed against the invisible barrier.

A tingling feeling creeps through me, and my magic moves and spreads along the ground, like a cat chasing a mouse. I can't feel where Rylan's power is trying to spring up, but it can. My body turns and moves with it, pulled by the power in my veins. If only following in a dance were so natural. Then it stops all together. "Are you done already?"

The rise and fall of his shoulders is more pronounced with exertion. Everything is still until a shriek sounds out behind me. I turn to see Josslyn cling to Jamys as the ground beneath their feet shakes and begins to crumble. *Honestly, Rylan!* A wave of my hand pushes them up and away from Ry's attack. The moment their feet touch the ground again, walls of earth shoot up around me, cutting off my view. They rise and come together to form a stone dome around me.

Well then.

I drop to the ground and sit cross legged, propping my chin on my hands as my elbows dig into my knees. No sound comes through to me, but I imagine Jo is expressing her displeasure to Ry in no uncertain terms. She has every right to—using her and Jamys to distract me was an unscrupulous move.

A wall of my prison cell parts and opens.

"See!" Rylan says. "She's fine."

"Of course she's fine! Ara is—" Jo bites her lip then purses them together, stiff from head to toe. Jamys stands to their side, probably ready to protect Josslyn, though at this point, I'd be more concerned for Rylan's safety.

I come out and lay a hand on her shoulder. "I'm sorry Rylan used you as part of our training exercises." I fix a pointed stare at him. "It won't ever happen again."

He rolls his eyes and his gaze lands on Jo. "You've been party to worse than that in all our—"

"Rylan!" I'm not going to stand here and listen to him make excuses.

"Of course it won't happen again." He drops his chin and grins at Jo. "You used to be more fun."

She kicks him in the shin and storms off. Jamys looks at me with rounded eyes, and I respond with a shrug. Our level of familiarity is something he's getting used to, but Jo's physical assault on the would-be heir is understandably shocking to an outsider.

Rylan rubs his shin and shakes his head. "That was excessive."

"You were excessive!"

"She knows I wouldn't have hurt her." He turns to Jamys. "I would not have hurt you."

"Glad to hear that." His unease is painted on his face.

I plant my hands on my hips. "That's quite enough for today."

Jamys walks away with me. He's maintained our typical boundaries, for which I am exceedingly grateful. I had been spiraling down thoughts of sex being as monotonous as that kiss. What is bad sex like? I can't imagine the act without being completely enraptured, desperate for more, fingernails dragging down his back as Tomas— *No! Not Tomas.* Well, it makes sense that I can only picture it with him. That's been my only experience. But Jamys might be even better. That's... certainly possible.

"Somehow, it still surprises me to see you out of a dress so often," Jamys says, and my eyebrows raise slightly. "I mean, in trousers—leggings, and a tunic *instead* of a dress."

His fumbling *is* endearing. "Well, when *I'm* training, there tend to be rogue winds, and I don't need my skirts blowing up and making a show of anything."

He blushes crimson. "Arabella, I... Should I apologize for the other night?"

My chin pulls back. "Why would you?"

"You'd had perhaps more than a bit to drink, and I'd hate to think I took advantage of you in any way."

Oh, sweet lamb. "Jamys, you asked me *very politely*, I answered, and I do not regret it." It saddens me a bit, but I don't regret it.

"You're sure I didn't cross a line?"

I don't think he can even see the line from where he is. "Not at all." I squeeze his hand. "It's very sweet of you to be concerned, though."

"I really don't know what I'm doing when it comes to you. It's rather unnerving."

"You needn't worry. We'll figure it out together." It's terribly unfair of me to judge our physical compatibility already. I'm certain Jamys will be eager to please me, and we'll build intimacy just like we have to build everything else: one piece at a time.

I excuse myself to my rooms for a bath, certain that some quiet time by myself will soothe away these concerns. But when I step inside, I'm not alone.

Chapter Thirty-Four

"What are you doing here?"

Tomas leans against the armrest of my sofa, his chin on his fist. His hair is mussed, making me wonder if he's been running his hands through it. The slight dishevelment extends to where his black sleeves are scrunched up to his elbows, exposing his forearms. He rarely comes to my chambers, and the scenario sets my pulse racing.

"I don't like leaving things in a bad place with you." His gaze pierces me, containing innumerable thoughts behind those blue eyes. "Even if it would make it easier."

"What would our fighting make easier?" I approach slowly, stopping behind another chair that faces him, as if such a barrier would keep us apart if we didn't want to be.

"Are you falling in love with Jamys?"

Dizziness sweeps through my head, like I'm not getting enough oxygen. I want to. It would make for a much happier life. "I think I could, someday."

"Someday," Tomas repeats, "but not yet?"

"Not yet."

The fact hangs between us like its importance is being weighed. Should that be the deciding factor in whether we continue down this path? Ending it early might give me room to fall in love with Jamys, but I'll have a lifetime of opportunity for that. I don't love him yet, and even if I did, he wouldn't fulfill the aching need gripping me now. Not until we're married. So why shouldn't I act on these needs?

"Tomas, our original plan... of my wedding marking the end of this... I think that was more reasonable." I can be the one to initiate—to say it out loud—if it'll ease his guilt.

"I thought things were progressing with Jamys. I don't want to make things more difficult for you." He means that; I'm sure of it. He doesn't want to cause my unhappiness, but we both become short-sighted when it comes to such things. What's tomorrow's misery compared to today's elation? Perhaps the world will end tomorrow, and it won't matter.

I slink around the chair to step toward him. "You're not the one making it difficult." Not that I haven't blamed him. It's unfair, though, to hold him responsible for his gravity. Neither of us seem to have any control over it as I close the space between us. I sit on his lap, straddling him without breaking eye contact, and my core tightens at the touch of him between my legs. His reaction presses against me through his trousers.

"My life is complicated," I say, "but when I'm with you, the rest of it ceases to exist. Being with you is the only thing that makes sense, and if that means it'll take longer to feel connected to my marriage, so be it. These moments we have together are worth it."

He slides a hand up my neck. "I'm sorry."

"For what?"

"That I can't simply walk away and leave you in peace."

All my problems with Tomas could come down to him trying to do just that. Even if it's for my sake, I fight against the aid like an animal that doesn't realize a person is trying to release it from a trap. This is a trap I'd walk into again and again.

"I don't want peace. I want you."

He pulls my face down to his, and our mouths come together, but not in the frenzied passion we so frequently find ourselves in. The kiss is tender even without being soft or gentle. A deep need runs through it. More than physical, this is the kind of pull I felt toward the cave when I returned home. A similar tether from my soul is drawn to him. Perhaps he was what drew me there then.

Between kisses, our clothing is shed, but how can it matter that he sees my naked body when I'm certain he can see my soul? His body filling mine can't be a betrayal to anyone if our joining completes me. We've had lusty sex, and I'd thought we'd made love, but this is more. In every panting breath, I resist the temptation to tell him I love him. In his moans, I hear the regret for our missed chance, mourning for everything we can't be.

His reasons for not fighting my betrothal were probably the same as mine. I wasn't brave enough to voice that I wanted him, so why have I been angry at him for not doing it either? He's shown me in every look and touch that he adores me too. My desperation for him was never anything to be embarrassed about because it matches his own for me. He knows me better than anyone—how reckless and selfish and impulsive I can be—and somehow, he still wants me.

Finally, I'm sure he wants us to be together. But we're too late for that.

We hold on, trying to make it last, as if it's our bodies that will see to our end, rather than fate and a collection of poor choices. But pleasure can't be held back between us. Tomas kisses me desperately as my core tightens around him. I moan against his lips as my body erupts, and clutch him against me when he follows shortly behind me.

This is all I need in this world, right here. Breathless and clammy, lying on his chest, I silently vow to myself to find a way for us to be together in every way, as we're meant to be.

His heart pounds under my hand, and I know it's mine. He's mine, and I'm his, and I will not give him up. Today, we lie in the bliss of being together.

Tomorrow, I'll devise a battle plan so we never have to give it up.

Chapter Thirty-Five

Only Tomas lying with me could make it more difficult to get out of bed. Even without him, this feels like a cocoon where I can dream we're together and everything is simple, but there is much to be done to make that happen. I roll onto my back and rake my fingers through my hair. Perhaps I should have spoken to Tomas about it yesterday. I'll need to, of course, but what if I fail? What if my only way out is to run away from my wedding and forgo my entire life? I might still do it. Even if I couldn't ask Tomas to do that, I can't imagine being anyone else's wife. Either way, I wasn't ready to discuss it with him—to potentially raise his hopes for something I can't accomplish.

There's only one way to find out, though. I pull myself out of bed and put on a day dress. Since I skipped dinner last night with the excuse of being too tired from training, I'll continue to ride that lie. Today's fight doesn't require such a uniform anyway.

I slip down to Mother's study and shut myself in. The locked cabinet must be the one with documents as important as my betrothal contract, so I kneel before it and push air into the keyhole. My eyes close as I focus on the intricacies of the air movement in the small space, poking and prodding for anything that can be moved. After a few attempts, the pins give way, and the lock opens.

Inside the cabinet, I find only a polished wood box. I place it in my lap and find a crown inside on a bed of blue velvet. It's larger than most crowns Mother ever wears, but there is an empty space in the front where a stone should be. Perhaps this is hidden away because it's damaged. I'm certain I've seen it before. Not on Mother... maybe in a portrait somewhere. That must be it. A previous monarch is probably immortalized wearing this somewhere in the palace.

Crown, box, and lock back in place, I move on. Absentmindedly, I brush a gust through the small wind chimes on the desk. They tinkle next to the plant, candle, and miniature fountain—all the little representations of the powers Mother knew so well but is losing. I sit in her chair to reach down to a drawer. The view of the study from this vantage point is unnerving. People think of royals on thrones, but how much strife does she deal with right here?

I shuffle through parchment rolls—regional censuses, family trees of high houses... Here. *Betrothal Contract.* Unrolling it farther, I see that it's not mine, though. It's the betrothal of Princess Elea Millicent Exos of Alchos...

My heart stops.

To Prince Kirnon Lawlor of Penum.

Mother could never have been meant to marry the King of Penum. She was always the heir to the throne. She'd have to have chosen that.

Adrenaline makes my eyes move too quickly over the page to read it. I need more time than what I can afford to spend snooping here in Mother's desk. I clutch it to my chest, tears springing to my eyes. A few deep breaths give me enough clarity to realize this could help me. Mother obviously got out of this betrothal. *Thank the gods.* Perhaps it can help me find a way out of mine. I continue digging until I find my own offending document and hurry to take them both back to my chambers.

The location of Mother's study on the main floor forces me to pass by common areas busy with staff, ministry members, and our resident guests, my heart in my throat and my trembling fist clenching the scrolls at my side. Unfortunately, as I stride through, King Urian stops me. "Princess, may I have a moment of your time?"

"Of course." The answer comes out as a reflex. I've never had a private conversation with Jamys' father, and this isn't an ideal time, but I'm too scatterbrained to think of an excuse.

He gestures to the sitting room, and I step inside. He closes the door and turns to me, a thin smile on his lips and ice in his eyes. I slide my hand back to move the contract behind my thigh. It's what's making him a prominent figure in my life, which sits even worse in my gut as he looks me over. "I heard you weren't feeling well last night."

"It was nothing. I'm only tired from training."

"Understandably so. And you're quite certain it isn't exacerbated by being with child?"

The air stills around us. Dust moats in the light cease moving. My neck and ears feel as if Nina is trying to set me ablaze. It's a feat to pull my voice past the tightness in my throat, but I go slowly, so as not to tremble. "It's not a possibility, of course. I don't know what you've come to think of Jamys and me spending time together, but we are quite content to wait for our nuptials."

"Yes, you're all too happy to wait, I'm certain. My concern comes from the idea that if a woman is foolish enough to have an affair while betrothed, she might be foolish enough to find herself pregnant."

Blood pounds through my ears, drowning out my ability to think, much less respond. Apparently, not asking about it when the betrothal agreement was made did not mean the Merricks had no interest in what I did with my body before Jamys and I marry.

"There are options," he continues, "if that should occur. I trust you'd at least give us the courtesy of correcting your mistakes."

A burning sensation rises in my chest. I think I'm going to be sick.

"I don't care if you whore your way through your entire kingdom and mine—it changes nothing in the betrothal agreement you signed. But you will arrive at your wedding with a vacant womb and produce an heir. The *Cerauno* royal family observes a certain level of decorum apparently unfamiliar here. Once you are a part of it, these"—he gestures to me—"scandalous Alchosian dresses will be a thing of the past, as will your illicit behavior. You will present yourself as a respectable princess, however far from the truth that may be."

He turns to open the door. His air of casualness after verbally shredding me chills my blood.

"And Princess? It should go without saying, but as your foolishness astounds, your affair with the lordling will cease. The Prince of Ceraun will not share his wife." He closes the door behind him, leaving me alone.

My eyes sting. He knows but won't break the betrothal. I knew my affair wouldn't guarantee a dissolution of it, and I never wanted to use that anyway. Still, if that doesn't help me... what will?

My lungs push out all their air like I've been holding in a sob. I crush the parchments in my fist. My chest heaves, but I'm suffocating. I pull in a deep breath and swipe a soundproof shield around myself before a scream rips out of me—inhuman, animalistic, as ill-bred as King Urian believes me to be. I drop to my knees and let the burning tears loose, too overwhelmed to decide what I'm most upset about.

Grief pours onto the heels of my hands, trickling down to my bracelets and making the metal uncomfortable against my skin.

The door bursts open and shuts again faster than should be possible. Or is it me, stuck in slow motion? How much time has passed?

"Bell, what happened? Are you all right?"

Tomas is at my side, hands on my shoulders, before I can even decipher if I've withdrawn my shield. His thumbs rub the tears from my cheeks, and I look up to see his brow furrowed over eyes a darker shade of blue than I'm used to.

My expression shifts to mirror it, though in confusion rather than concern. "Why are you here?"

"Your *blood curdling scream* suggested you might need help."

"How did you hear that? Was it audible?" Oh, no. If anyone else heard... If Urian heard...

"Should it not have been? I thought Nina was deaf not to have heard, but she looked at me like I was mad."

"I was shielded." I drop my face into my hands. "Perfect. My magic is also cracking. I needed something else to worry about."

"What were you already worrying about?"

I scrape my bottom lip with my teeth. Tomas might kill Urian for the things he said to me. I still might. We can't make an enemy of Ceraun, though. Penum would happily scoop them up as allies, then we'd be outnumbered and surrounded by hostile nations. "Everything. Pressure from all sides, expectations, looming changes. I suppose it's all catching up to me."

He wraps his arms around me, and I let myself slump into his chest as soothing strokes circle my back with precisely the right amount of pressure to slow my heart and calm my nerves. "Bell, I can't presume to understand what it's like to live under the weight of so much expectation."

"You're the next Lord of Highbluff. You aren't free of it."

"It's not the same. You've got two kingdoms looking to you, and if that weren't enough, you've got the most scrutinizing critic anyone could ever face analyzing everything you do."

I pull back to search his face.

"Yourself," he says.

"Oh."

"You're so hard on yourself, but Bell, all you've got to do is *exist* and you're the best person in the kingdom. Everything else is extra." My eyes water again, and I can't tell if the tears are happy, sad, or some combination. "And frankly,"—Tomas' head tilts—"you're making the rest of us look bad."

My heart lightens with his tone. "Stop making it so easy to make you look bad."

Chapter Thirty-Six

My calves ache from the endless pacing, but that focuses me. The betrothal agreements are stashed in my wardrobe for now. I glance that way but still can't settle enough to read them. Every time I try, my mind replays the scene with Urian, and I find my eyes have scanned paragraphs without me gaining anything from them.

"In the first place,"—talking to myself is an excellent sign—"King Urian has chosen to make an enemy of me, and he will live to regret it."

Urian's treatment of me—so bluntly showing that my only purpose is *magical heir breeder*—might be reason enough for Mother and Father to break the contract. He'd retaliate, though. The last kingdom meant to marry an Alchosian princess is now our enemy, after all.

I still can't believe Mother was going to marry Kirnon.

One thing at a time, though.

At the very least, Urian would reveal the truth about Tomas and me. I'm about willing to do that myself if Tomas would agree to it. However, I don't want to hurt Jamys. I cannot blame Jamys for the faults of his father. He can't know about any of it. Sweet as he may be, he wouldn't sit by and accept his bride-to-be *whoring around*, as Urian so elegantly put it.

I consider the betrothal contracts, and a groan rumbles through me. Even if those hold an answer for how to end it cleanly, Urian will make it messy. He'll know the real reason if I initiate the end of the betrothal. I need to make it as painless as possible for everyone involved.

All I have to do is exist. That's what Tomas said. What am I when I'm not trying? I roll my shoulders back as I contemplate it.

I'm... I'm the gods damned Princess of Air, and I am Alchosian to my core. Urian hates everything about that, apparently, so perhaps I can provoke him to show it. At the very least, it would be satisfying as hell to aggravate him.

I ring the bell and start searching through my wardrobe. The gowns gifted to me by Queen Anilla now appear to be cages rather than just stuffy, sad excuses for fashion. Perhaps Nina would like to play with them? I push those aside and admire my beautiful Alchosian options. *Don't worry, you shan't be replaced, my lovelies.* Delicate, silky fabrics feel like home.

There is a soft knock on the door before it opens. "You rang?"

"Yes, Lucy." I turn toward her, chosen dress in hand. "Would it be possible to remove this strap in time to wear the dress tonight?"

"Certainly, but without it—"

"I can manage. Thank you so much." I shove the dress into her arms, perhaps *too* enthusiastically, and send her on her way.

In the bath, I luxuriate in the spicy aroma of clove petals steeping in the water. Afterwards, Lucy weaves my hair into a dramatic array of braids, swirls, and fanciful flowers. Topped with a delicate diadem, it should sufficiently remind Urian that I am royalty myself and will not be disrespected. I give Lucy leave to be creative with my makeup, and the result is spectacular. Sweeping shades of gray and blue wash together seamlessly, and liquid kohl lining enlarges my eyes. Sliding into the dress feels positively sensual, and I wonder if I should really be this excited to enrage someone.

I take in the full view of myself in the mirror and can't help the mischievous grin which crawls up my face. Well, if the sight provokes him, he should have thought twice before arranging the marriage that would install me in his court.

Nina is making her way down the hall when I emerge from my chambers. She looks me up and down and dips her chin. "It would appear someone has remembered she isn't Cerauno yet."

"I'll never *be* Cerauno." I wouldn't have even if I was going to be their queen.

"Thank the gods." She loops her arm through mine, and we continue down the hall.

"Oh, let's not bother with the stairs." I push up the air underneath our feet, lifting us over the railing and down through the center of the spiral staircase.

"I think your magic makes you lazy."

"I think your magic makes you incendiary."

"Says the woman who is *clearly* trying to stoke a fire." She arches an eyebrow at me, though I know she approves of such behavior.

"I haven't the slightest idea what you're talking about."

She offers me a coy smile as we land and goes ahead of me into the lounge. Jamys approaches from the other side and goes wide-eyed. "Arabella. Good evening."

His discomfort is cuter than his father's will be. I feel sorry for his place in the middle of this feud. "Good evening."

"I heard you weren't feeling well today."

"I was only tired. I feel much better now."

"You do look... well." His face tints red.

"Thank you." I take his arm, and we walk into the lounge.

Urian appears to choke on his wine when he glances our way. My smile widens. His glare rakes up my body, and it's as if every inch of exposed skin adds to his rage. A well-placed gust displays how high the slit in the skirt goes up, the waist is certainly tight enough to prove I'm not pregnant, and the trail of skin showing from my neck straight down to the waistline is as direct a response as I could give him. I won't even think him vain for assuming this has to do with him. I'm glad I had Lucy remove the strap between my breasts. Keeping them contained isn't a problem, but they look like they're waiting to fall out.

I turn around to get a glass of wine and display the back of my dress where the two lengths of fabric from the front come together to form a single braid down my back. Let's see Urian maintain his Cerauno decorum now. I'd kill to hear his thoughts.

Jamys and I sit with Lillian; her countenance is tight, discomfort thinly veiled by refined manners. Regret ricochets through me—it was only Urian I wanted to upset, not anyone else. Jamys relaxes from his initial shock, though, settling closer to me than usual.

"Lovely as you are in the Cerauno gowns," he says, "this is a stunning alternative."

"Thank you. It's a matter of comfort." I turn my attention to his sister. "Your fortitude to wear those *beautiful*—but heavy—gowns every day is astounding."

Lillian's smile becomes a touch more natural. "It's all a matter of what one is used to."

Throughout our conversation, my gaze flickers to Urian to see that his glare hasn't softened, and my chest swells with pride. How such a brute managed to have a son and daughter who are so agreeable is beyond my comprehension. Queen Anilla's involvement in their upbringing probably saved them. But then Jamys and Lillian turn their attention toward their father as well, and I see that one of their attendants has come in to speak with the King.

His eyes widen, and his face colors a deeper shade of red. He speaks in hushed tones to the man and stands abruptly. "Elea, Gratian, I'm afraid I must cut my visit short."

Anilla's demure smile drops. "What is it?"

"A Penuman army is a day's march from Dockerly Keep. I'm leaving at once."

"How is that possible?" Now Jamys is on his feet.

I sink back into the sofa and take Lillian's hand as Rylan pushes his shoulders back, straightening into a rigid posture. "How could they have marched all the way across Ceraun to the coast without your notice?"

"I don't know," Urian says. "It shouldn't be possible, yet there they are."

"I'm going with you," Jamys says.

"No. You'll stay here with your mother and sister."

"That's absurd. I can't just—"

"It was not a suggestion." Urian's words are steel.

Mother presses her lips together as she glances between them. "Can we send aid?"

Urian looks to his attendant who nods. "It sounds as if that would be useful. Thank you."

"Of course. Arabella, would you bring a message to Lord Coyle for me? His fleet will be able to approach from the sea."

My breath catches in my throat. "Yes, of course." My skin feels too tight as I wait for her to prepare a message. If Lord Coyle's fleet sails to Ceraun, I know who will be at the head of it.

Though the flight doesn't require any physical exertion, I land at Highbluff out of breath. I blow the doors open and let myself in, which sends the staff fumbling to announce me.

"The Princess—"

"That won't be necessary." I cut the footman off as I bustle into the sitting room.

Jo and her mother talk over each other asking what's the matter, but Tomas only keeps his unyielding gaze on me.

"Mother asks that your fleet sails to Dockerly Keep. They're under attack by Penum and need assistance."

Mariana gasps. "Oh, dear. I'll get Wymond at once." She hurries out of the room as Tomas puffs out a breath and goes outside.

I follow him toward the docks. "Tomas?"

"There's a lot to do, Bell."

"You can't go with them."

He shakes his head and continues on. "I have to."

"No." I fling a wall of air in front of him.

He knocks into it and whirls on me. "What is that for?"

"You cannot go to Ceraun. King Urian knows about us, and—"

"How could he possibly—"

"I don't know, but he does. Needless to say, he isn't pleased by it."

Tomas' brows lower. "Is he calling off your betrothal?"

"No. He wants a magical heir for his kingdom, even if his son must marry a *whore* to accomplish it."

"He did not call you that." A dark fury simmers under his voice. Even without seeing my own face when that dagger flew toward him in Lambridge, I know he must mirror that expression now. I should not have told him.

"That isn't the point."

"It is now!" he bellows.

"It doesn't matter. What matters is that you cannot go to Ceraun."

"I..." I don't think I've ever seen him search for words like this. He pulls a hand down his face. "I need to go burn down whatever Penum misses."

"Tomas, away from here, from us... What if Urian tries to remove you from Jamys' way?"

His expression drops to an incredulous look. "Bell, I've trained with four magical royals who have little regard for personal safety. I can handle Urian."

"You'll be in his kingdom, surrounded by his men—"

"And my own. We'll be there to help him, whether he deserves it or not, and he should really have more important things to worry about than the lordling ensuring your inevitable disappointment with his son."

My hand covers my mouth; I don't know if I can contain the laugh he's coaxing from me. "Tomas, this is serious."

"Don't I trust you to take care of yourself?"

"Yes."

"So give me the same courtesy. Afterwards, I will remember Urian's exceptional mistake in disrespecting the Princess of Alchos."

"Didn't you just say you trust me to take care of myself?" I say.

"This is different."

"No it isn't."

He shrugs and arches an eyebrow. "Are you dressed that way to spite Urian?"

"Will you think less of me if I say yes?"

"Not at all. It rather improves my opinion of you." His eyes sparkle. "You look absolutely delicious, by the way."

"Thank you." We hold eye contact and level tones, as if this is a perfectly normal conversation, even as my heart sputters. A different kind of excitement surges through my veins, replacing the adrenaline brought on by the situation. The earthy scent of the surrounding vineyards reaches me as my senses readjust to focus on the moment.

"And if those Cerauno pricks think I've ruined you for Jamys, I will show you just how *ruined* you can be."

I run my tongue across my teeth. "You're awful."

"In comparison, you will be so bored by his lovemaking, you'll fall asleep during it."

His assertion would be depressing, but I'll never know the feeling. "Tomas, when you return—"

"The admirals have been sent for," Lord Wymond calls out as he approaches. "Here is your ship's inventory log." He hands a bundle of parchments to Tomas. "Be ready to go by sunrise."

I offer him a thin smile. "Thank you for being perpetually at the ready."

"Of course, Arabella." He continues toward the docks.

Tomas squeezes my hand. "I have to go."

"I know. Be careful." To leave him without confirming that we're going to do what we can to be together pains me, but this isn't the time. Perhaps while he's gone, I'll find a way to do it without ruining any parties involved.

He walks away, taking a piece of me with him. Soon I'll be able to kiss him goodbye regardless of who might bear witness. I have to believe that to turn away.

Chapter Thirty-Seven

Fires light up the walls and parapets of Mirador, looking festive and welcoming. How many times have I thought this to be my gilded cage? Compared to the prospect of Ceraun and Urian, this is an open range of endless freedom. I land on my balcony and go in to send word to Mother that Highbluff is preparing their fleet. Hair down, face cleaned, and undressed, I sit at the foot of my bed, but how could I possibly sleep? Tomas is readying to sail off into a battle where even our ally is his enemy.

My stomach knots.

His joking and downplaying of the situation wore off on my return home. I'm right back to being worried sick and desperate for him not to go. What is Penum trying at anyway? I pull my legs up to my chest, curling myself into a tight ball. There will be no sleep for me tonight. After enough sitting and rocking to drive me mad, I go back out onto my balcony. A spring breeze should offer me solace. Or at least a distraction.

My attention is pulled to the figure pacing about the garden below. I dive off the balcony and land behind him. "Jamys?"

He jumps and turns toward me. "Arabella!" He pulls a palm down his face. "Do you make it a habit to sneak up on people?

And"—he looks me up and down and presses his lips together—"going outside in your nightclothes?"

I cross my arms over the pale linen. "You can't possibly be uncomfortable with this. Let's be honest, this covers me up more than the dress I wore tonight."

"Well, yes, but propriety…"

"I don't care. What are you doing out here?"

"I can't rest." He rakes a hand through his hair. "I should be on my way back to Ceraun."

"I'm sorry."

He sits on a stone bench, and I join him, pressing his hand where it sits on his knee. He looks up at me with sad eyes.

"What is it?" I ask.

He pauses before responding. "Penum has been an ever-increasing problem for us. I hate to point out yet *another* unromantic reason for us to marry, but the truth is, we need you." He's marrying for kingdom and duty as much as I would be. Except I can't give up my entire life and any chance of happiness for it. "What I'd give… I'm sorry that you…"

I wrap his hand in both of mine. I don't want to soothe him with lies, but what could I say that would be both truthful and helpful?

"I promise, I will try to make you happy," he says. "I don't know if I'll succeed, but if you help protect Ceraun, I will do anything you wish."

Jamys knows as well as his father that they're planning to use me, but at least Jamys is kind about it, maybe even remorseful. I hate to take away his hope of protecting his kingdom by dissolving our betrothal, but I'll have to. "Of course I will protect Ceraun." *As an ally.* "Why haven't you asked for our assistance before?"

His shoulders rise and fall with a slow breath. "We didn't want you to think you're aligning yourself with a weak kingdom. My father would kill me for telling you that."

At least this evens the score between Urian and me. We each know secrets about each other now. "How bad has it been?"

"Ara, I can't—"

"I'll be living there soon." Or I'm supposed to. "Tell me what's going on up there."

"Please, don't tell anyone else in your family. Mine would be mortified."

"Of course."

He nods. "We've lost western cities to Penum already. I wouldn't have thought they'd get all the way across to the eastern coast, but they have. I don't know how much of Ceraun will be left without some intervention. I suppose that's why Father finally accepted help for Dockerly."

"Oh, Jamys..." I rub my temples. "What state is your military in?"

"It's dwindling. Penum is strong and ruthless. We've never successfully stood against them."

And Tomas is going to face them.

Trust him to take care of himself. Our forces are no doubt stronger than Ceraun's ever were. Trust him to take care of himself.

I jump to my feet and pace. I cannot sit still thinking about it. How will I survive weeks of this? Penum has been quietly invading Ceraun; they likely sent those imposters into Lambridge. King

Kirnon must at least know something about the disappearances out there—I wouldn't be surprised if he had something to do with them. I cannot sit here in the palace while he continues to drive his influence across the continent like a dagger through its heart.

"I'm going to go put an end to Penum's attack." My declaration even surprises me a little.

Jamys' eyes widen. "By yourself?"

"Yes." Ry, Nina, and Marcus would be helpful, but not necessary. Also, I'm not planning to ask permission, so I don't need to drag them into trouble with me.

"My father ordered me to stay here."

"He gave me no such order, not that I would feel obligated to obey as he is not my king."

He shakes his head. "You don't even know how to get there."

"I can figure it out."

He studies me a moment, and regret revisits me. I may be endearing myself to him further. "I can't let you go alone. If you go, I'm going too." Before I can offer excuses, he adds, "It's my kingdom. I need to be there for them."

What a perfect time for my boldness to catch on. I don't want to do this, but I don't feel like he's going to give me a choice. "We need to leave immediately. I want to have some distance from this place before our absence is noticed in the morning."

We breakfast near a stream as the sun rises over distant hills. Mirador will be frantic by now, having misplaced two royals. But out here, all is calm.

"Do you run away often?" Jamys asks.

"No, I'm a fairly well-behaved princess—most of the time."

An incredulous look disappears from his face as fast as it appeared. "Well, you made the choice rather quickly. And seemed to know what you needed to do to make it happen."

"It wasn't a difficult decision to make. Once that's done, of course I'm going to act quickly." *Now.* I wanted Tomas to tell me we should try to be together instead of trusting my own mind when the betrothal was presented to me. Perhaps I've learned my lesson.

"It's not always possible, though, is it?" Jamys says. "Most of our choices involve so many other people, we can't act quickly. Our steps have to be measured carefully, even once we sit on the throne. Now..." He bites his lip and stands. "Well, now, we hardly get to make any choices at all." He offers me his hand, and I take it as I rise.

"Your father can't dictate everything you do."

He frowns and turns to ready the horses. On our way again, he seems to debate with himself some time before speaking. "He can, you know."

"What?"

"My father. He *can* dictate everything I do. He's the King."

A breath puffs out of me. "Even make you marry me." It's not meant to be an affront to Jamys. Urian's audacity to insist upon our marrying despite anything I do, all to gain an heir with my power, is appalling.

"That's not why I'm marrying you." His lips are pursed slightly, but I arch an eyebrow at him. "All right, technically, yes, but now I want to marry you." His voice drops, as if wanting to marry the woman he's betrothed to is some terrible secret. It twists my heart into a knot.

Ending our betrothal was always going to be an indignity, and problematic for a kingdom that needs a powerful person to defend it, but I'm going to break Jamys' heart as well. My hood brushes my upper back as I shake my head. "I didn't mean to question your intentions." Though it would be easier if he were planning to marry me under duress. "It was more about your father. I don't think he likes me very much, so I can't imagine what it's like to have him continue to demand you marry me."

Jamys pales. "Did he say something to you?"

"A little something, yes. It's fine."

"I don't suppose you'll tell me what exactly."

"No, I won't." Primarily not to incriminate *myself*, but it's also wholly unnecessary.

"Well, I'm sorry. I know he expects everything to be a certain way, and he gets cross when that order isn't maintained. Neither his opinions nor his feelings affect mine. No matter his plans or motivations, the feelings I've developed for you are real."

A dizzying lightness sweeps through my head, and I push my voice past the lump in my throat. "Jamys, I—"

"Don't respond. I'm sorry. I don't know why I said that."

"You needn't apologize. Really, it's—"

"Honestly, don't."

Terrible as I feel not responding, it is a relief. What could I say that wouldn't either be a lie or hurtful? We should not be making this journey together. How am I to spend these days alone with him? Jamys was probably correct about me needing him for navigation. The Highbluff fleet will have to swing out around the peninsular shape of the coast, but on horseback, we can take a more direct route which should get us there a day or two before the ships. Still, it'll take nine days, and we've managed to make things uncomfortable between us on the first. We ride in silence until we stop for the night.

The horses are settled, and we eat some cheese and brown bread I took from the kitchens at the palace. I always knew those skills would prove useful. When we're done, Jamys turns to me, seemingly determined to be happy and calm now. "All right, princess-who-packs-lightly—"

"It was necessary for this trip." I take out the blankets which are the only bedding I allowed.

"Well, I have a hard time believing you'd be able to sleep on the hard ground."

"Who said anything about that?"

"You told me not to bring—"

I raise him up off the ground, and he startles. "You can lie down."

He slides his hand along the airy bed and puffs out a laugh. "I don't see how this could ever seem normal."

"You'll get used to it." Because we have this time, not forever. I levitate myself and recline on my side, head propped on my hand. "Go ahead."

Gingerly, he lies down, facing me. "This will remain, even while you sleep?"

"Yes." A thought flashes through me of how much more it can withstand than *sleep*, and guilt pools in me. It would be kinder to get it over with, but the rest of this trip would be awful if I confessed everything to him now. I wish I could forget it all until this adventure is over.

Selfish though it may be, I ask Jamys to help with that. "Will you play for me?"

His neck strains, and his eyes get glassy for a moment. "All right." He sits up and takes out the pipe to play another new tune, unlike either of the two I've heard before. It's melancholy, but affectionate, like an embrace that lingers long enough to tell a person you really care. And just like that, I feel even worse.

When it ends, I whisper, "Thank you," but it feels like an apology. If I'd known Jamys this way before anything had happened with Tomas, I could have been truly happy with him. For convenience's sake, I almost wish for it. However, I can't regret loving Tomas any more than I can regret having magic. Both are intrinsically part of me.

Jamys blinks slowly and lies back down facing me. "Goodnight, Arabella."

"Goodnight."

His hand trembles, as if he's deciding whether he should reach out to me or not. It's a little thing, and he should feel comfortable enough for it at this point. His hesitation is because I've not opened the door for it. There's a lock on that door, sky blue like the eyes I see in my dreams. My moral compass is flawed. Lying here *near* Jamys makes me feel as if I'm betraying Tomas, when really, it's been the opposite all along. Still, knowing that doesn't mean it settles into my heart. My mind is made up, and accepting a future with Tomas is so comfortable—so easy—that I could never pull out of it.

CHAPTER THIRTY-EIGHT

Sunlight warms my face, and I blink my eyes open to find myself alone. It's so peaceful here, I could almost forget the whole plan, let the kingdoms tear each other apart, go wherever the wind takes me.

If only.

Jamys approaches; his hair is darker wet. Water clings to his bare chest and stomach as well. "Good morning."

Well, I didn't decide to find a way out of our betrothal because he isn't attractive. I clear my throat. "You were up early. Didn't you sleep comfortably?" It may be impossible to sleep next to a woman who keeps changing her mind about whether she can love him.

"Very much so, thank you."

We eat a little, ready the horses, and soon, we're on our way again. Jamys asks about how our magic passes between the generations, how Mother split it instead of giving it all to her firstborn as all the rulers of Alchos had done before. The difference being that a king and keeper of elements doesn't have a choice but to pass on the sparks of his magical spirits. A queen spends more time making the babies, and hence can determine what to give them. Previous queens had followed tradition, but Mother divided it up.

A family with multiple children, each with magic, was what she wanted, tradition be damned.

"How did she do it?"

"I don't know the mechanics of it." I shrug. "It isn't something I need to worry about as I only have one element and cannot split it."

He considers this as we ride on. "But it's a conscious choice to pass it on?"

"It seems that way."

"Does that mean you could withhold it from your firstborn?"

"I don't know. Mother will have to give me more information when it's time, I suppose." Topics of our marriage and breeding are inevitable. What else do we have in common? But talking about it as if it will still happen carves out a part of me. Dragging this out is cruel. I can't keep on like this. It might be easier to tell him while we're moving. Riding would provide an adequate reason to avoid eye contact.

I'm a pathetic coward.

My gown collapses into a puddle around my feet, an art piece of fabric and crystal fit for a royal wedding. The hands which released me from the dress slide down my back—my husband's hands. He wraps his arms around me, and I press against his bare body. Warmth seeps into me. Everything I've ever wanted is realized.

I sigh and tilt my head away from the kisses tracing down my neck as fingers splay over my hips. Every touch is consuming, and I want more. I turn around and gasp when I behold the man I've just married.

"Jamys?"

He smiles as he looks over my naked body. My skin could melt right off in the heat of the embarrassed flush that runs through me. "You are beautiful."

His hands slide up my sides and to my breasts. He rubs my nipples with his thumbs, and I stiffen from head to toe. I drop my head, but a hand comes to my chin and lifts my face toward his. His mouth covers mine in an impassioned kiss. Fingers weave into my hair, the other hand finding my ass and pulling me tighter against him.

I can't breathe, which would be an effective way to get out of this—falling unconscious. Our bodies are molded together. They're one. We're one. Forever.

He lays me down reverently, but the bed might as well be stone for how comfortable I am on it. Nudity has never made me feel more exposed, but being on display is nothing compared to when his body covers mine. His warmth burns when every inch of me feels frozen. Gentle kisses on my neck might as well be claws slashing through me. He grips my hip. Aligns himself to get us closer together in the only way left.

No. No, I can't.

I jolt awake, panting and heart racing. I press a hand against my chest as it rises and falls too quickly. Despite shivering, my body is coated in a sheen of sweat. And Jamys' hand is indeed on my hip. I rub my forehead and pull my hand down my face.

It was only a dream. But it will be reality soon if I don't get this over with. I've got to end it once and for all.

Sunrise does nothing to soothe me. Guilt, discomfort, and embarrassment are as real and powerful as if that encounter had actually happened. My skin feels too tight, and a queasy ache runs from my chest through my stomach. I can't bring myself to look at or speak to Jamys. Instead, my eyes remain locked ahead of me as we ride on, but I can't appreciate the views.

I've tried to hold on to the promise I made myself not to lie to him. Withholding the truth is no longer a technicality I can hide behind, though. It'll eat me alive.

Eight days. We made it eight days together, but I've cracked now. I tried to keep us casual and friendly, to stick to safe topics, but it's impossible. Even talking about our surroundings—shimmering lakes, elk, waterfalls—all parts of the place I'm supposed to make my home but cannot, knots my gut.

Tomorrow, we'll reach Dockerly Keep, then there will be too much to do. I'll see Urian, which might make me lose my nerve, so I have to do it. We settle for the night, and I'd vomit if there was any food in me at all. How he hasn't asked me what's wrong, I don't know. Jamys is usually more attentive to me.

"Are you nervous about tomorrow?"

There it is. Tomorrow would be the logical thing to be concerned about. I am planning to take on an army by myself, after all. Still, that doesn't seem nearly as daunting as this.

"I'm not looking forward to it, but it must be done." A deep breath does nothing to calm me. "More so, I need to talk to you about something."

He pales, and his lips purse slightly.

"There's no way to say this without sounding horrible, but—"

"Then don't say it."

It's tempting. My teeth grind together, but I take one shaky breath and force my mouth to work again. "I have to."

"No, you don't." It isn't until he wraps his hand around mine that I realize I'm trembling. "You don't owe me anything, Ara. You're already going far beyond anything I could ask for by helping Dockerly right now."

"I'll always be there for you in such matters..."

His chest heaves with rapid breaths.

"But I can't—"

He clasps the sides of my face and pulls me in for a kiss. For a moment, I'm shocked by his assertiveness. Then his lips distract me, moving deftly and parting my own. His tongue brushes mine, and I reel in confusion. How is this the same person I kissed in the garden not two weeks ago? My heart pounds, but beyond the fact that it's a very good kiss, it's still wrong. Physically, it's perfect. There isn't anything I'd change... except the person.

I pull back and lean my forehead against his. "Jamys..."

"Did you not enjoy that?" His voice is low. Longing and desperation weave through it.

"That's not the problem."

"Then enjoy it." He kisses my jaw, my ear, and I shudder. "I'm going to be king, but I will kneel to you. I will worship you." His hand slides down to grip my hip, and every vivid feeling from my dream comes to the forefront. Panic slashes through me. "We can have everything, Ara."

"No, we can't." Tears spill over my eyelashes. "I've been sleeping with someone else."

He closes his eyes and clenches his jaw as his hand drops from the base of my skull to my lap.

"It started before our betrothal. I never meant to hurt you."

"Then why—*why* would you tell me?" He fixes me with a glistening stare. "Wouldn't it have been bad enough to be married to someone who supposedly doesn't know?" I suck in a sharp breath. "Isn't it worse to know I'm aware and feigning ignorance?"

"You already knew?"

His jaw ticks. "Yes."

"And still you wanted to..." My gaze slides down to his hands still on my lap. That fevered kiss. The way he gripped me. He'd have made love to me, even though he knew...

"Should it matter?" He wraps his hands around mine. "I can't say I like it, but it isn't important. We can move forward together. I meant it when I told you I *want* to marry you. It isn't an obligation to my kingdom anymore. All this time together... You're remarkable. All that you are would make me think there is no chance of you ever being interested in me, but you *have* shown interest. You've put more effort into learning about me than anyone I've ever known. Lillian is the only other person who knows about the music. We've shared so much. Didn't that mean anything to you?"

I drop my chin to my chest. "Of course it did." I was trying to open myself up to fall in love with him, but it only worked in the other direction.

"Then there doesn't need to be a problem." He strokes my cheek with his thumb. "You've had... experiences. That's fine. We'll have our own." He pulls my chin up so our eyes meet. "We've spoken of wanting a proper marriage with love and family, and I also want us to have every physical pleasure together." His fingers weave back into my hair. "Ara, I want to make you happy in every way. Give me the chance to."

Before I can untangle the jumble of emotion blocking my throat, he kisses me again, strong and impassioned, but lovingly. Gods, I've made such a mess of this. I pull back from him again with the feeling I'm about to stab him.

"That's not the problem." My heart thrashes against my ribs like it would rather be ripped out than do this to Jamys. "I'm in love with him."

He rocks back and covers his eyes—his thumb and middle finger press into his temples. I was supposed to be Ceraun's hero, but I'm a villain. If someone else hurt Jamys like this, wouldn't I hate that person? Perhaps I do hate the person who's done this right now. He stands and walks away without a word.

I always thought my element and I were the least destructive of my family and our powers. How wrong I was. He offered me a perfectly good heart, and I crushed it.

CHAPTER THIRTY-NINE

Spring in Ceraun doesn't feel much like spring at all. There's an unseasonable chill in the air—or perhaps it's me.

I wouldn't have thought I slept, but alertness comes over me with a jolt when my eyes open and Jamys is before me, preparing the horses. Reality makes my stomach turn. I can't believe I told him about Tomas. Not that I was giving him any new information. When and how he found out seem like unfair questions for me to ask. They don't matter much anyway.

He turns to see me awake then focuses his attention back on the horses as he speaks to me. "Are you still going to help Dockerly?"

"Of course." I rise and creep over to him. "Jamys, I—"

"Please. I don't want to discuss any of it."

My heart sinks, but I only nod and walk away to ready myself for the day.

Jamys leads the way, and I sulk behind him. There wasn't any good way to have that conversation, I suppose, but all I can do as we ride along is think about how poorly it went. He must be mortified after I rejected him that way. His desperation to do anything to win me over... My conscience will hold that against me forever.

The distraction is so complete, I don't realize Jamys has stopped until my horse stops behind him. I shake myself into the present and come up to his side. We are on top of a hill overlooking the city, the entire walled expanse visible from here, bordered by the coast on the east and thousands of soldiers on the west.

Penum's black and burgundy banners wave from the encampment, and multiple towers are up or in progress of being built. Dockerly is under siege.

Highbluff's fleet will arrive soon to save the city, but there would be casualties. No number of deaths would sit well with me, not to mention the potential of *who* could fall.

Jamys tenses as a cannon fires over the wall. I reach out and catch it in a flexible band of wind. It slows as the shield stretches with it, then it bounces back toward the camp, careening into a gathering of tents.

Jamys gapes at me. "From this far away?"

"I wasn't entirely certain I'd be able to, honestly."

"Now they'll know you're here." At least imminent danger is a distraction from all that's brewing between us.

"Good. Perhaps they'll leave before more people get hurt."

"Can you get us into the city?"

I don't need to be in the city; I'll be more productive over it. "I'll get you into the city, then I'll go to the top of the wall."

"You can't take on an entire army yourself."

"I never do anything by myself. I've got the air on my side."

He head tilts in an exasperated look. "That's not the same as *someone* to help you."

"You're correct—it's quite better. Are you afraid of heights?"

"No."

"Good." I lift us both, and he grabs my shoulder to stabilize himself. We stay low to the ground then near the surface of the water. Waves brush against the bottom of our translucent, moving floor.

"Could you have flown all the way here?"

I shake my head. "I've never tried to go that far. It didn't seem like a good time to try and possibly end up stuck in the middle of nowhere without horses."

We rise as we approach the waterfront fortress, and a lookout gapes at us before he gets another guard to witness our arrival. I amplify Jamys' voice to let them know who we are. Still, an archer keeps us in his aim. *How quaint.* They stare as we land alongside them on the wall.

"Prince Jamys, it is you. But how—" The one is cut off by a nudge from the other, and they both bow.

"This is Princess Arabella of Alchos." Jamys' introduction is explanation enough.

"And I must be going," I say. "You have a bit of an army at your gates." Before they can question me, I take to the sky.

From a distance, it didn't feel like so many people. Closer, I start to wonder if I *can* actually take on an entire army. Suddenly, my magic doesn't feel like enough. I hover in a cloud to conceal myself, reaching out with my power, feeling the air around the city. How far can I stretch it? Can I wrap it around the entire army? Farther and farther, I push out, until I feel all the people along the city wall and curl my magic around the edges where they stop by the shore.

This is much too large. I can't make a shield so big. What then? I can't just catch their fire bit by bit. They need to be sent away.

I take a deep breath. *If they cover too much space, constrict them.* I can fortify borders... like Jamys told me about the game.

A gale builds over the water at my beckoning, circling to gain momentum so when I pull it to shore, it whips into the army with enough force to uproot trees. Tents fly away. Men brace against it, but the wind pushes them into each other, and they slide away from the shore in a writhing heap of limbs. As if with a great broom, I sweep everyone and everything away from the sea, squeezing the army together in an ever more crowded cluster.

The wind's deafening roar is the only sound to be heard, even as the mass of people scrambles. Once I've illustrated my capabilities, and they look sufficiently uncomfortable, I descend to the wall. Standing above this host of my enemy, a storm of my own creation blowing my braided hair to my side, an intoxicating sense of power rolls through me—not magical power, but that which I can wield over man.

And I feel like the monster Penum paints me to be.

I hold out a hand and lower it. The gale dissipates. "This is your opportunity to return to your own kingdom." The air carries my voice across the army. "Ceraun is under the protection of Alchos. We do not wish to go to war with you but make no mistake—if you cross us, it will be like no war you can conceive. Retreat now, before—"

Another roar from the other side of the city, but this one isn't wind: it's water. A wave higher than the walls grows as it races toward the shore. The wall of water slams into the left flank, crushing everything in its path. I shoot across the wall to the southern end of the city.

Where is he? But it isn't Marcus I find. Siege towers spontaneously combust into pillars of flame as Nina struts toward me along the wall, Tomas on her heels.

"What are you doing here?" I demand.

They both shout at the same time. Bits of *'What the hell is wrong with you?'* mix with *'You conceited—'*

"I was handling the situation. Where is Marcus?"

Tomas plants his hands on his hips. "Taking Ry to the north end."

I roll my eyes. "Did *everyone* really need to come?"

An arrow flies toward us but burns and drops as nothing more than ash. "Yes," Nina says.

"No, you did not. This is perfectly under control."

"It's an army, Bell!" Tomas points out over it in case I'd missed that. "You cannot take down an entire army by yourself."

"Didn't you say you trusted me to take care of myself?"

"This is not taking care of yourself." The words snap out of Tomas so quickly, they could be a whip. "This is taking on too much for one person."

An outcropping of rock juts up from in front of the city wall and slowly pushes the offending army. Marcus glides toward us along the wall as thick, tangled brambles sprout up along the edges of the now-compacted army, giving them only one way to go—away.

The stone barrier presses on, the retreat chaos made human. People trample each other, trying to avoid the thorny walls at their borders. Tomas fixes me with a hard gaze but says nothing.

"I... left a note this time."

He closes his eyes as if summoning patience. Excellent. I've alienated myself from Jamys on his behalf and gotten on Tomas' bad side.

"Where is your fleet?" I ask.

"On their way. I joined Ry and the twins as they were overtaking the bigger ships, and Marcus only sped us up." His eyes darken. "Though there isn't much of a reason for the rest to come now, I suppose."

"You say that as if it's a bad thing."

He only shakes his head before we're joined by Rylan, Jamys... and Urian. Tomas' hands snap into fists, and I brush a cool breeze along his face to calm and reassure him. His jaw tightens instead.

"Thank you all," Urian says. "It's a true testament to the Queen to send all of you here to aid us."

No one corrects him, but a glance at my siblings tells me Mother did not send them after me.

"It would be our honor," Jamys says, looking at all of us except Tomas and me, "to escort you to the fortress where you can rest."

"Thank you," Rylan says. "We can stay only one night. Your hospitality is much appreciated."

Tomas' glower gives me the impression one night is too long for him. However, he doesn't argue as Rylan speaks for us.

"Of course," Urian says. "Right this way."

We follow Urian and Jamys. Nina meets my eyes, so I put a little soundproof shield before us. "Go ahead," I say.

"I can forgive you trying to subdue an army alone, but consider yourself indebted to me for having to stay in Ceraun."

CHAPTER FORTY

We're all tucked away into rooms like crystal in cupboards. Mine has a musty feel to it, which I remedy quickly with a cleansing breeze. The stale air goes out the window, and I drop onto a cushion of my own creation. It's undoubtedly more comfortable than the furniture. Everything looks so heavy and stiff.

Before I can begin cataloguing the events of the day and making sense of them, I close my eyes. After very little sleep last night and a very long day, the edges of my consciousness start to blur. I'm not asleep two minutes before my door flings open.

"Get up," Nina says. "Let's get this over with."

I bury my face in my hands. "What do you want?" I peek through my fingers to see Marcus walk to the washroom.

"I want us to dine with these people so the day can be over, and we can leave as early as possible tomorrow." Nina sniffs and shakes her head. "Before we retire for the night, I'll need you to do this"—she traces circles in the air—"to my room as well."

"What?"

"Whatever you do to make it feel livable."

Marcus returns and tells me the bath is ready.

"Can I have a *minute's* rest first?"

"You've had an hour," he says.

"It has not been an hour."

"It has," Nina says. "Go."

The air pushes me upright. "And since when do you use your power to draw baths for people?"

Marcus' lips turn down as he glowers at me. "Would you like to call for a servant who will gawk at you? They aren't quite used to magical people here."

"I suppose not. It's lucky Nina and Ry picked you up on the way. Was that only so they could sail here faster?"

"Get ready!" they say in unison.

"Fine." I stretch my back and neck. "You both look charming, by the way."

"I hate you." Nina looks down at the offending dress. It's pretty, but being Cerauno, there is so much of it. She appears uncomfortable, covered from the neck down. "I don't know how you've been doing this."

I shrug and go off to get ready. A similar dress waits for me which Nina helps me into. We go back out to find Rylan has joined our party, but Tomas hasn't. "Do I need to refresh your room as well?"

"Yes, but that can wait." Rylan stands and rolls his shoulders back. "Let's get this over with."

"What, no reprimand for running away?" That's what I'd really like to get out of the way. All three of them, plus Tomas, are furious with me, though I have no doubt the reasons vary. "Why did you really come after me?"

Nina crosses her arms. "Our idiot sister went off to fight an army by herself."

"Which was a problem because?"

"Do you discount our affection so completely?"

"Yours I do." Tomas' motivation is the only one I'm confident of. He would come for my sake, as I did his. Nina would have her own reasons.

She rolls her eyes. "Well, if you think you can show us all up by—"

"Are you joking? You can't possibly believe I did this to prove myself!"

"Of course not," Ry says. "That's never the reason, which makes it all the worse. You never have to try half as hard as any of us to achieve things. You just stroll into being the most perfect person in the family."

A hysterical chuckle pushes out of me. "You are insane. I am far from perfect, I assure you." Thank the gods Tomas isn't here; I'd flush bright red if I looked at him now. *Me? The perfect princess?* The one who sneaks off during a ball to fuck in the cellar. At a ball where *her betrothed* is. "And if you thought I was before, my running off should have cleared up that misunderstanding. I assume Mother and Father were furious?"

"Of course they were," Rylan says as Nina presses her lips together and avoids looking at anyone.

"What are you not saying?" I ask.

"Nothing." Her coy smile says otherwise, but I'm not sure I care.

"We're here now," Rylan says, "so let's get this over with. I want an early start tomorrow."

Aggravated though we may be, we do *get it over with*. Dinner is miserable. Neither Tomas nor Jamys speaking to me is a unique kind of torment. The three of us plus Urian in a room together is a thing of nightmares. We all know the awkward truth, except that Tomas doesn't know Jamys is aware. Tomas and I also haven't discussed having more between us than sex. How I managed to tell my betrothed I'm in love with Tomas before I told him still baffles me, and I am dying to tell him that I'll refuse to marry Jamys. Urian insists that Jamys return with us to Alchos for the remainder of the trials—he was meant to remain there with his mother and sister after all. Tonight, I am not of the mindset to stare Urian down as I was our last night at Mirador, but I don't have to meet his wretched eyes to guess what he wants—Jamys to stay as close to me as possible.

At least it can't be worse.

As we rise from the table to retreat to our rooms, King Urian stops me. "May I have a word with you, Princess?" His voice is gentler than I've ever heard it.

My gaze slides to Tomas, to his blanched knuckles where he grips the back of his chair. I half-expect him to throw it at Urian, but he turns and marches out of the room. I roll my shoulders back and meet Urian's eyes. "Yes, of course."

My siblings file out. Jamys stops at my side. "He'll behave this time," he whispers. "If I wasn't sure of it, I wouldn't allow him to be alone with you."

"I'm not concerned for myself."

He looks at me pleadingly.

"Don't worry, you won't rise to the throne today."

My assurance only pulls a sigh from him before he leaves.

"Thank you again for coming here," Urian says. "You saved this city."

"Not for your sake."

"No, it wouldn't be. Arabella, I am sorry for my horrendous behavior toward you. Difficult as it may be for you to believe, I am trying to protect my son and his happiness."

I almost laugh. "You care nothing for his happiness. Wasn't it you who told him about my affair?"

"He deserved to know. You obviously felt the same."

I grind my teeth together. How dare he compare our choices. He'd only have shared the information so Jamys could try to wedge himself between Tomas and me. I needed him to understand why I've been so hot and cold and why I can't marry him.

"How did you find out?"

Urian's remorseful, downcast eyes glitter when he raises them to me briefly before the mask snaps back on. "Servants see more than they let on."

The fire of my rage is doused by the statement. Of course they do, but I wouldn't think anyone in Mirador Palace would betray our trust that way.

Urian shifts the conversation. "But it's for the best that everything is out in the open, I think. The two of you can move forward on equal footing now. In fact,"—he raps his fingers on the table—"since you've travelled for days alone together, perhaps it would be prudent for you to marry now."

I rub my lips together, almost guilty for how delighted I am by his pathetic attempt. "You know well enough that such impropriety is of little concern to me." I step toward him slowly, predatorily.

"You think you're sorry for your treatment of me now, but you have no idea how sorry you'll be. I'll not be marrying Jamys here or anywhere. It is only because he is twice the man you are that I won't dissolve our betrothal in the most indelicate ways possible. But do not think for a moment that I don't see your desperate attempt to lock me in."

His face pinches into a tight scowl. "We have a contract."

"I don't care. You cannot contain me. You cannot control me. My magic and my body will never belong to you or Ceraun." I turn my back to him. On my way out, I add, "At any rate, I wouldn't be the kind of queen you'd like to have in your kingdom."

CHAPTER FORTY-ONE

First light seems to come rather quickly after endless tossing and turning. I just slipped into sleep when the knock on my door came. At least I should be able to rest on the ship. Jamys and I join Tomas and my siblings on the small ship they had brought up until we meet with the Highbluff fleet, then we board a bigger one and turn everyone back. Fortunately, they were close enough for us to make the transfer before our first night. To have added Jamys and me would have made for uncomfortable sleeping arrangements. As it was, on the way to Dockerly, the four of them couldn't have enjoyed only two small cabins.

On the Highbluff flagship, we displace the officers and have private accommodations. My own is modest, but at least there's a bed. Even my magic is too drained to be of service to me, and I want nothing more than to rest. I've just sat on the thin sheets before a knock sounds, though.

I sigh before speaking. "Come in."

The door opens, and Jamys peeks in. "I hate to bother you, but..."

"Not at all." He isn't a bother, even if anxiety seizes me when he comes in. We haven't spoken privately since I told him I'm in love with Tomas, but there is more to be said, I suppose.

"I'm sorry if being in such close quarters together is uncomfortable with where we had left everything."

Uncomfortable may be an understatement. He could mean the entire ship, though.

"May I?" He gestures to the bed, the only seating in the room, and I nod. Seated, he says, "What all of you did, the power you wield, it helped me understand Alchos, I think."

"How is that?"

"Why worship gods long gone when their power clearly lives on in you? Religion would seem pointless to people who already have godlike rulers walking among them."

I sigh. "We are not gods, nor are we worshipped as such. You know better than most I'm wholly unworthy of such devotion."

He taps his knee with his knuckles. "I didn't realize what I was up against with Tomas."

"You aren't against him in anything. I don't mean to pit the two of you against each other. There's no contest or anything to be done. I doubt Tomas even wanted me to fall in love with him at the onset, but it's happened."

"We're young, Ara. Love can come and go."

"Then perhaps the love you feel for me will fade."

He presses his lips together and slumps under my argument.

"It doesn't help, I know," I say, "but it's truly not because of you. I know I *could* love you. You're wonderful. But my heart isn't mine to give anymore."

"Perhaps given time—"

"There isn't time, Jamys. When we return to Mirador, I'm going to find a way to dissolve our betrothal. I'm so sorry, but I cannot marry you."

His chest rises and falls slowly. "We could have had everything."

Tears sting my eyes. "I know."

He leaves, and I collapse onto my back. Days ago, "we could have everything" was a hope for the future. The addition of one little word, and that idea of his became a regretted loss.

Tomas' role is clearly that of the lordling escorting the royals, as duty requires. He's not acting like the lifelong friend of said royals, let alone my lover. He's completely indifferent to me—not angry, not sad, not loving. By our final night at sea, I wonder if the entire affair was only a dream. I lie in bed—or rather hover above it, because it isn't particularly comfortable—rubbing my arms, wishing it was his hands on me. The gentle rocking of the ship soothes my frayed nerves but also pulls my mind to the fluid rocking of hips, the rhythm that rolls through our bodies like the waves, the sound of his breath near my ear like the wind in the sails.

Enough! I throw the sheets off and pull on a cloak. I can't stand this silent treatment from him anymore. Even if it doesn't result in lovemaking, I must at least get us speaking.

"Tomas!" I whisper-yell when I barge into his cabin. "This is ridiculous! You can't just—" I yank the sheets from the bed, only to find it empty. I rub my face and sigh. *Lovely.*

The deck is quiet at this hour. There are only a few sailors about, and one lone figure at the bow. Even lit only in moonlight, I recognize Tomas. He leans forward against the railing, looking out over the sea.

In my second attempt to confront him, I find myself less aggressive. I approach him slowly, the salty wind brushing my hair back from my face as I make my way to the front of the ship. "Tomas?" This time, my voice is gentle, apologetic.

He drops his head, and his shoulders rise and fall with a deep breath before he turns to me. "What are you doing out here?"

"I could ask the same of you."

The stars reflect in his eyes as he looks upon me. In the silence before he answers, I wish I could trade my magic for the ability to hear his thoughts. "What do you want, Bell?"

You. I always want you. "For you to go on and yell at me. Tell me I was a fool for disappearing off to Ceraun. Whatever else you're angry at me for."

"I have no right to be angry at you." His jaw ticks, and his throat bobs with a swallow. "As a future Lord of Alchos, I would prefer that you consult *anyone* before you run off, but I cannot presume to have any authority over your actions."

My eyes prickle. Anger, I could stand. If he were angry at me, it would mean he cares. This, though... this indifference cuts like a knife. *As a future Lord of Alchos?* As if that is all that connects us. Our titles? I pull in a shaky breath. "You know that isn't true. You can presume anything with me because you love me better than anyone else in this world." I can't believe I put it out there. To give voice to this, to make him acknowledge that we *are* in love—this isn't how I meant for it to happen, but we can make it real. We can breathe life into it instead of letting it drift around out of our grasp.

His gaze shifts back over the water. "I love you well enough to know it's long past time I walk away."

"No!" I grasp his arm and turn him to face me. "We aren't going to start another cycle of pulling away from each other. You needn't ever walk away from me. I'm not going to marry Jamys."

"Yes, you are."

"I won't. If it means renouncing my name and title, I'll do that, but I don't even know if it will come to that. I won't live a lie with another man when I love *you*!"

He winces. "A life with me isn't an option."

"Did you hear anything I said? I'd live in a cave with you over a palace with anyone else."

"I can't do that to you, Bell. I can't ruin your life that way. I'm vowed to protect you."

"Protect me from a miserable, insincere life." I drape my arms over his neck. "I can protect us from everything else."

"Arabella, please."

"Don't call me that."

He steps back, pulling out of my arms so they drop to my sides as tears flow freely down my cheeks.

"I'm sorry I got you into this mess. I will forever be your loyal servant."

My throat tightens, and I strain to swallow against it. A tremor rattles through me as if the ship's run aground. Our soul-binding lovemaking feels like it took place in an alternate reality. This one is cold and unfamiliar. "I do so appreciate your commitment to the kingdom and our family."

His jaw clenches, but he doesn't fight me. *Fight me, damnit!* That's another thing we've always been good at. He doesn't, though. He even looks different. The cool exterior he always wielded to draw me in is ice cold now, impenetrable. "Good night, Your Grace." He turns and walks away.

Are we done then? Not only ended, but will we truly be this dry in our interactions? Titles and courtesies as if we don't even know each other? If so, I'm as likely to die of thirst as I am from a broken heart.

Chapter Forty-Two

Etherlee House glows in dawn's light as we pass it. I don't know how it came to be a symbol of whatever I had with Tomas. It was only one night, but I'm not sure I can go back there anymore. Ridiculous really, as there are many more places in Mirador and Lambridge that hold intimate memories as well, but the idea of those doesn't frighten me. Etherlee is the one I can't imagine going back to. That stretch of shore where we shared our first kiss and altered the trajectory of our lives forever—or at least *my* life.

We arrive at Highbluff, where Jo appears ready to jump out of her own skin. I'm scarcely off the ship before she throws her arms around me.

"You idiot. What were you thinking?"

I squeeze her in return. "Oh, just that things were so boring around here."

"Well, I'm thrilled you survived a siege, but you are aware your parents are going to kill you now?"

"Of course." I glance away to see Rylan, Marcus, Nina, and Jamys mounting up to go to Mirador. "I must be getting to that. We'll talk soon."

She nods, and I leave Highbluff without so much as seeing Tomas. My stomach tightens, but apparently, I should be getting accustomed to this kind of relationship with him.

The five of us ride in silence. Upon arrival, a jittery ministry member informs us that the Queen and King are waiting for us. His twitching fingers and lack of eye contact makes me wonder how furious Mother appeared when she gave him this task.

Jamys goes to seek out his own mother, and the four of us face our fate.

The Queen's glare could cut steel as we file into her study. Her imperious posture and narrowed mouth give her the appearance of being battle ready as thoroughly as armor would. Her fury, I can handle. Father looks *disappointed*, though. Disappointment is always my undoing. I drop my gaze from his and take a seat.

Silence hangs over us, more torturous than anything likely to be said. It's as if we're all children again. I tap my teeth together and swirl wind around my hands. Never have I been so grateful to have the invisible element. The others can't fiddle with theirs unnoticed.

"First, Arabella disappears." Mother's voice startles me, her stern glare fixed on me. "An action as foolish and headstrong as it was dangerous. Then, the rest of you find this to be such a wonderful idea, you follow suit."

"What were you thinking?" Father's question could be asked of nearly everything I've done for the past year.

I swallow and take a breath. "Ceraun needs our protection. Penum is not hostile toward us because they know they're no match for us. Ceraun has sided with us which probably drew Penum's wrath. They must see that Ceraun will also be defended."

"As we were going to illustrate by sending the Highbluff fleet." Mother folds her hands and rubs her wrist with her thumb. "Do you think Alchos is protected in its entirety by having magic here in the capital? It isn't as if we keep the four of you posted around our borders. When do you think I ever fought an enemy?"

"Alchos' strength is renowned from generations past." I keep my voice level, but if my sanity wasn't already in question, it would be now for arguing with her. "It's known that we are impenetrable. Ceraun does not boast that reputation yet."

"Urian may be foolish enough to believe you alone, and some-day your child, will be enough to make his kingdom strong, but I thought you were smarter than that."

Mother's words make me draw back. *Not enough?* My magic is the only thing that might be enough, the only thing I'm good at. I'd have been a wretched wife, an uncouth foreign queen, unfit in every way. But at least I could have been a shield.

"That's not to diminish your abilities," Father says as if he can read my thoughts. "But a kingdom cannot depend solely on magic or one person. Alchos' strength does not come only from the powers in this family."

This makes the lot of us squirm, our collective ego probably a touch inflated. We all enjoy feeling powerful. There's no use deny-ing that. Our display in Dockerly probably didn't help matters.

"So," Mother says, "you went to Ceraun because you felt the need to defend your future kingdom?"

"Yes. Jamys felt he needed to be there and pointed out that this was why they need me." This isn't the time to tell her I've informed Jamys and his father that it won't be my future kingdom. They're angry enough without knowing I may have shattered that alliance.

"Again, do not buy into their belief that you can do it all on your own."

"But I can. I was." I don't even want that anymore but having my ability to do it questioned makes me bristle. "I had the siege perfectly in hand before the rest of them came."

Mother glances around at my siblings who are much smarter than me in keeping their heads down. "Yes, the next mistake made. Why is it that when I was already frantically dealing with the disappearance of your sister and Prince Jamys, the rest of you decided to *compound* my problems by leaving yourselves?"

Rylan clears his throat. "We were worried about Ara. We acted in haste, and I'm sorry for that."

His motivation wasn't quite so noble, but I won't accuse him of it here. We're all in enough shit already.

"I expect more," Mother says. "From all of you. Marcus' idea to have another child to be my heir looked rather tempting this week."

Don't smile. Don't smile. Don't smile.

"In three days, three of you will be trying to prove yourselves worthy of my throne. Start acting like you have some sense."

I find my voice—it's meeker than I prefer, but that's probably for the best. "Is there any news on the missing people in—"

"Oh, do you care about that now?" Mother's words crack like a whip, and I collapse into myself. "It's rather difficult to accomplish anything when I'm stretched so thin, Arabella. Tracking down runaway royals takes resources which could be otherwise utilized for another of our mounting problems. Perhaps you could keep that in mind before you jump at the next reckless opportunity you're presented with."

Eyes downcast, I nod.

"You're dismissed."

As I climb the stairs, I realize this misery is at least a trade from my other ones. The distraction from my personal problems is short lived, though. The instant I step into my rooms, the sight of the sofa where I decided I'd pursue a future with Tomas sends me reeling. I was so certain...

Tears flow again.

I collapse face first onto my bed, wishing it would consume me. My failures replay in my mind on an endless loop. What's left for me? I've been refused everything I want, and I've rejected everything that wants me. Despite the cyclical depressing thoughts, sleep claims me eventually.

Unfortunately, it's not a restful sleep. I wake even more tired than I was to begin with. I sit up and stretch forward over my legs. There is so much to deal with from the past couple of weeks.

The first item on my list is my betrothal. I've already told Jamys in no uncertain terms that I wouldn't marry him, plus I told Urian off who would be a brute to live with regardless. Securing the end to our betrothal is the priority.

I believe Tomas loves me but doesn't want to be the cause of me renouncing my life. If I find a way to end my betrothal without destroying everything, I think he'll want to be with me. However, even if he isn't an option, finding a way out of my betrothal contract is a must. Tomas' position is irrelevant.

It seems like such a long time ago that I found the betrothal agreements. Mother's was swept from my thoughts by a torrent of other surprises and problems. I find both at the bottom of my wardrobe and unroll Mother's first. *The Betrothal of Princess Elea Millicent Exos of Alchos to Prince Kirnon Lawlor of Penum.* Perhaps I can find the way she got out of it.

My head spins. The garrulous document doesn't state anything in a remotely forthcoming way. It's all formalities and meaningless rules, but I need to understand what happened with the people involved. Part of me doesn't want to speak to Mother about it. Her keeping it from us stabs at me. I'd ask Father, but what if she didn't tell him either? No, they don't have secrets from each other. Furthermore, it would have been known at the time. I wonder how much Grandmother knows about it.

The direct source will probably do me better. And if Mother got out of a betrothal, perhaps she'll sympathize with my plight to end mine.

I dress and roam the palace in search of her. She's not in her study, or the sitting room, or the throne room, or her rooms, or the parlor, or the gardens. On my way to ask if she's taken a horse out, movement on the bridge catches my eye. Mother is returning to the palace from the cave, skirts billowing behind her ethereally. I redirect back inside.

Her footfalls sound down the stairway of the west tower, and I wait at the bottom to meet her. "Mother, I need to speak with you."

"What is it?" Her words come out like a sigh, weariness aging her eyes and pale face. We have been taking a toll on her, haven't we?

"Somewhere private, if you please."

She nods and leads me to her rooms. On the way, we pass a maid, and Mother orders tea. In her sitting room, she gestures to an armchair for me and reclines on the chaise. "What do you have tucked to your side like that?"

"This is what I need to speak to you about." I place the rolled parchment on the table between us. "My betrothal agreement."

She sighs and shakes her head. "Did you steal that from my study? You could have asked to see it."

"I suppose I could have, but then I wouldn't have known about this one." I unroll it to show that two documents are rolled together. One is hers.

Her warm brown eyes lock onto it, and her entire countenance stiffens. Out of the corner of my eye, I think I see a plant retreat back toward its pot.

"Why didn't you ever tell any of us?" I ask.

"I thought this was about *your* betrothal." Her voice rasps in a low way I haven't heard from her before.

A knock on the door precedes a maid's entrance. Mother snatches the document and rolls it up as tea is set out. An uncomfortable silence fogs the room until we are alone again.

"I assume Father knows?"

"Of course your father knows. Don't be ridiculous." She looks at the tea and frowns. If she's wishing the tea were something stronger, then we are of the same mindset. Rather than taking her cup, she wraps her hands around each other, holding her wrists in her lap. "The fallout with Penum over it was... catastrophic, as you may have guessed by our current relations."

"But hadn't you chosen to marry Kirnon?"

"Not exactly." She sighs. "It had been the arrangement made by our parents, and I wasn't terribly *opposed* to it, though I wasn't excited about it either." *That sounds familiar.* "But when..." Her gaze goes distant before she squeezes her eyes closed and clears her throat. "When I came into my full power, I became queen, and even before being crowned as such, I declared I would not marry Kirnon. My father was furious, but he no longer had any control over the matter. Your father and I married immediately, and I made it law that the heir to the throne could not have his or her marriage arranged in any part but by their own choice."

"I didn't realize that was a new rule." Perhaps this is part of why Lord Altman said we are *another* generation of surprising royals.

"Yes, kings and queens already have so much of our lives decided for us. I couldn't let the seat of consort be another obligation. The entire ordeal is a painful memory I don't care to recount, and I would appreciate it if you didn't tell your brothers and sister."

I've gotten good enough at keeping secrets, and maybe doing her this favor can leverage my request. "Fine. Tell me how you got out of that betrothal, though." I can't believe I'm about to voice this to my mother. I've never blatantly gone against her wishes like this. "I need to dissolve mine."

Her chin jerks back. "What? Why?"

If there is a way out without disclosing the situation with Tomas, I'd prefer to do that. Maybe it doesn't help the issue of my hiding so much from her all this time to *keep* hiding it, however, that would redirect the conversation to Tomas and me which is still uncertain. The first thing I need us to focus on is my betrothal.

"Mother, to marry Jamys would doom me to a life of unhappiness. I've never asked for anything like this, so please know it's of dire importance to me."

"Did something happen with Jamys? Did he hurt you when you were away?"

"No. No, of course not. Jamys is wonderful."

Her shoulders relax slightly. "Good. Your safety is of the utmost importance. If it were in question, the contract would be void."

"It would?"

"Yes. Didn't you read the item you stole from me?"

"Not yet. I was distracted by yours."

"Well, it's clear as day." She hands me back one parchment only. "But you're certain there's no concern about Jamys? You know, darling, we never wanted to force you into something you didn't want. Yes, we've always thought it important for the stability of the continent, but you seemed open to it."

Because I was trying to be a good daughter and princess. "I know, and no, I don't have *concerns* about Jamys. Does the confrontation in Dockerly hold any weight toward my safety, though?"

Her eyebrows draw together. "Why do you want this so badly?"

"Please, just... Does it?"

"One incident shouldn't, though we could argue that if need be. Truly, the kingdom would need to be unstable, but if you tell me why—"

"Thank you, Mother." I jump to my feet and rush out.

CHAPTER FORTY-THREE

The kingdom would need to be unstable.

Ceraun *is* unstable—they've been losing cities and territory to Penum. Jamys was reluctant to tell me that, and Urian's suggestion to marry us right away...

They know it's enough to lose me. Urian, I'm not surprised by, but Jamys? Would he keep that from me?

My heartbeat pounds in my ears as I hurry through the palace. Without so much as knocking, I burst into his rooms. "Jamys!"

He nearly jumps out of the chair at the desk and closes a small book. "Ara, you scared the—"

"Did you know?" I throw the rolled parchment at him.

"Know what?"

"That Ceraun's weakened state could null our betrothal."

He closes his eyes, and his lips press into a thin line.

"You did. Of course you did." Air feels hard to come by suddenly. "You went along hiding it so you could lock me into your monarchy." Tears sting my eyes.

"Ara,"—he stands, but keeps his distance—"we needed you. We *do* need you. You know that."

"That's despicable, even before! But then once you knew about Tomas, you *had to* guess there was a chance I didn't want to marry you!"

"By then I loved you!" His eyes widen, and he throws his hands out with that exclamation. The burst of passion fades to sadness as he closes his eyes and rolls his lips in before continuing. "When we arrived, I hid it because we needed you to marry me. By the time I found out about you and Tomas, I *wanted* to marry you."

Tears gather in the corner of my eyes and begin to leak out. "You'd have let me go into that life without any choice in the matter."

"Would it really have been so horrible to be married to a king who worships you like a goddess?" He closes the distance between us and grasps my shoulders. "I still can, if you'll let me."

I drop my gaze to the floor but see nothing through the blur of tears. "No, Jamys. I can't."

His hands swing down off me. "When I told you how bad things were getting in Ceraun, I thought you knew it would be enough to end our betrothal. I thought you'd still want to be with me." I look up to meet his eyes which are also swimming in tears. "Yes, I knew you were sleeping with Tomas, but I thought that was all it was. It felt like we were developing something between us."

We were developing something, but it's not enough. I never wanted to turn him into a person who would tolerate an affair. He's going to be a king. But desperation makes people act unreasonably. He loves his kingdom, and I respect that. It doesn't mean we can live that way, though.

I take a breath and lay my final decision before him. "I'll do it in such a way as to minimize any embarrassment. Ceraun will still have our support and assistance."

He turns away and grips the back of the chair he vacated, head bowed. I turn to leave. The back and forth of my relationship with Jamys is nearly over. There's solace in that, even if it had to go up in flames.

"For what it's worth," Jamys says when my hand reaches the doorknob, "I'm sorry."

"So am I."

The door shuts with a foreboding feeling of finality, and I wipe away tears as I make my way to my rooms. I wouldn't have thought this would make me cry, but I also didn't think Jamys would ever hurt or deceive me. Relief should be my only feeling, however nothing is as clear as that. I'm not ready to speak to Mother about it again just yet. I need a moment to calm down.

Jamys' actions are understandable, and not any worse than what I was going to do. I had planned to marry him and live a long, *happy* life without ever telling him about my history with Tomas. It's just shocking, I suppose. He was the good one, and I thought our destruction was going to be solely my doing. As it turns out, neither of us are as perfect as people think.

In my rooms, I do not find the solitude I need. "Ry, it's not a good time."

"The next trial is in two days. When do you think you'll have time to train?"

I trudge over to a cupboard and grab a glass and a bottle of wine. It's all I can do to keep my voice slow and steady. "I do not care about the trials." Slow and steady may have taken on an undercurrent of rage.

"Are you no longer supporting me in this then?"

"You're no longer outnumbered, so it shouldn't matter."

"But it's *Nina*."

I swallow too much wine at once, the warmth stinging down my chest. "If you don't think you can take on your youngest sister by yourself, I really don't know what the point of any of this is." For as much as I've told people they can't say I'm *letting* him win, he's really making it sound much more like he couldn't possibly win without my assistance. The theory of whoever can win should rule is crumbling.

He stands with a huff. "When this started, you acted as if you supported my claim to the throne, but you've undermined me at every turn. Now, Nina has Marcus *and* Tomas helping her, and you'd abandon me to forge on by myself."

"Not everything is about you!" I rake my fingers through my hair, tugging at the roots. "Gods, Rylan, might you consider I have other things going on!"

"What can be more important than the future of the Alchosian throne?"

"The throne I have never had any interest in sitting upon? Anything can be more important to me! Yes, I care about it, but it isn't my concern."

"You aren't going to try to win it then?"

My hands clench into fists. "No. If I'm forced to show up, I'll sit quietly off to the side while you and Nina go at it." He looks skeptical, so I add, "I'll even see if I can get Tomas to withdraw his assistance to her." Seeing Tomas is the only idea that soothes my buzzing nerves. Though I'm not thrilled with how it came about, my betrothal *is* ending, and I can't wait to tell him.

"He refuses to discuss it with me," Rylan says. "You won't get anywhere with him."

A smile tugs at my lips. "I'm more persuasive than you are."

Tomas and Nina aren't here, though. I learn she's gone to High-bluff along with Marcus. Emotionally wrung out as I am, I have a horse prepared and set off. There's a comfortable rhythm to riding which helps put everything into perspective. My fallout with Jamys is sad, but it was inevitable. Everything is going the direction I want now.

As I approach the castle, I wonder what it will be like to arrive as the Lady of Highbluff—having that salty breeze to comfort a baby of our own, sailing, chasing children through vineyards. Seeing it through the eyes of a resident makes me feel lighter. I'm comfortable enough after a lifetime here with Tomas and Jo that it doesn't take much imagination to see myself calling it home.

But when I make my way to the courtyard and the only person to greet me is Marcus, my mood dampens. "Where are Tomas and Nina?"

"They don't want to be disturbed."

My face scrunches uncomfortably. "Excuse me?"

"You don't want to—trust me." He drapes an arm around my shoulders and turns me back the way I came. "Nina is in a frenzy. I'm much more pleasant company."

I slip out of his arm. "I need to speak to Tomas."

"He's not available."

"I'll wait then."

Marcus frowns. "Ara, he doesn't want to see you."

Rejection rakes through me with sharpened claws, but it's only because he thinks I'm marrying Jamys. I swallow back the wretched feeling that came with those words. "He will once I speak to him."

I start to walk toward the castle, but Marcus steps in front of me. "I mean it. I'm sorry. Under no circumstance am I supposed to let you go to him."

My eyes narrow. "You couldn't actually stop me."

"Let's not rehash that, please."

"Do not make me use magic in this." I try to get around him, but he matches my movements to block me. After several back-and-forth dodges, I swat his shoulder. "You don't understand."

"I do understand, and the answer is still no."

Finally, I duck under his arm to pass him, but he grabs me, spinning me back to face him. "Even if you're his lover, he does not wish to see you right now."

The blood drains from my face. Firstly, how does Marcus know? Secondly, *Tomas really doesn't want to see me?* Words escape me as I stare at my brother.

"That night you threw Tomas off the tower at Lambridge... You're still indebted to me for my role in calming Ceanna down, by the way. I didn't fail to notice you were both gone an awfully long time."

I run my tongue along the edges of my teeth. "And Tomas confirmed your theory?"

"Not directly."

"Did you tell Nina?"

"No. Not that any of that matters. The point is, you think I'm keeping you from him because I don't know the truth about the two of you, when in fact that is the very reason I'm keeping you from him."

A knot forms in my chest. This is rejection then. Too many thoughts rush through my mind at a time. When I reach for one, what comes out is, "Where's Jo?" Jo would know the most, and she's my dearest friend. If everything is being dashed to bits, I need her.

"She's not available."

It's the final blow to shatter me. I always feared my relationship with Tomas would damage my friendship with his sister, and now, it has. She's never been *unavailable* for me. What will I be left with if the two people I need most can't forgive my many mistakes? "All right. I'll go then."

Should my feelings about a place be able to shift so quickly?

I arrived as if I was coming home, but I leave a stranger.

Chapter Forty-Four

The crowd's roar washes over us. The air buzzes.

I close my eyes, willing it to snap me into the moment. Never have I been less prepared for anything. Not that it matters. Yesterday, I slipped into such pathetic desperation as to reconsider marrying Jamys. He was correct—there are worse fates than marrying a king who adores me. After declaring in no uncertain terms that I would not marry him, though, I'm not sure I could live with myself if I changed my mind again.

A day of emotional turmoil left me exhausted, and now it will be a challenge to muster enough energy and motivation to make it appear I'm trying. At least this will all be over soon. One less thing to deal with will be a welcome change. Mostly...

This could be the last time anyone apart from family sees me in anything other than a dress. Obnoxious though this display may be, the freedom to show what we truly are is invigorating. To be seen as powerful, rather than a delicate, curtsying flower, is an opportunity I may not get again.

Mother's speech resounds, but the words wash past me. A mass of shrubbery stands before us, split down the middle by brick walls: a maze of greenery for Nina and me and a route less pliable for Rylan. Even the ground in his path is bricked, though he could get through that easily enough.

The pendant Mother describes as representing Alchos weighs against my chest. We must protect the kingdom as we carry it into the future, and so we must traverse this labyrinth while keeping these symbols safe. They aren't sturdy. This glass globe could shatter easily, like the kingdom. Like anything worth having.

My eyelids flutter to blink back tears. People think the challenge is this trial, but it's far more difficult to keep myself from looking up at Tomas or even Jamys. Meeting the gaze of either of them would probably break me. To see Jamys' pain and know my part in causing it would be about as horrible as seeing Tomas unaffected by this situation which constantly adds cracks to my already-crushed heart.

Lost in my thoughts, the commencement of the event comes as a surprise. My brother and sister split away from me, rushing to their respective entrances.

I could simply fly over the top of the maze. It would be—as Nina would no doubt point out—utterly unfair, and it would be contrary to my purposes. Participation in the final trial would be torture. Instead, I run in and am engulfed by greenery. After several turns, I slow my pace, pretending this is a leisurely stroll to clear my mind. It's certainly more enjoyable than the last trial. I wrap myself in a bubble to muffle the sound of the crowd. Now if only I could make myself invisible.

The next turn takes me to a rough stone wall blocking my path. I turn back and try other options, but those routes go nowhere. I'm meant to get *through* the rock. A sigh escapes me as I mourn the end of my leisurely stroll. This isn't terribly complicated, though. I float up to go over the blockade. At the top, water splashes against the shield around me and dissipates. Blocking myself off from the world is coming in handy in more ways than one.

On the other side, I return to my quiet trance. The small, tightly packed leaves around me exhale life-giving air, and I trail my hand along them, my magic drawn to it. My power reaches into the hedges. The border between my magic and Ry's blurs. Plants are his domain, but they produce air. I close my eyes and sigh—reaching into the fabric of the shrubs without meaning to. Something pulls me, calls to me...

Until a shriek breaks my daze. *Nina.* I race toward the sound, but our paths don't cross. I float up over the maze to find smoke rising from a writhing mass of leaves and branches. I drop to the area to find Nina engulfed in green. Every time a burst of flames burns away an offshoot, an arm emerges from the plant only to be wrapped up again. Her yells sound more frustrated by the second.

"Nina, calm down! I'll help you." I try to pull away branches, but they're too hot to touch.

"Back off!"

The entire mass bursts into flames, and searing heat washes over me. "Gods, Nina!"

She brushes the ashy remains of the plant off herself. "Where's Rylan?"

I cough and whisk the smoke up and away from us. "He's probably already made it to the end."

"Not if I can help it." Flames flicker across her outstretched fingertips before she closes her eyes. A fireball darts away from us.

Nina's eyes remain tightly shut, her forehead wrinkled in concentration.

"Nina?"

She doesn't respond, her eyes shifting under their lids, her body rigid from head to toe. *What is she doing?* I rise above the maze again. A flame races through the maze as if it can navigate it better than us. It weaves and searches, slithering through like a snake, leaving a blaze in its wake. It speeds toward Rylan as he approaches the end and leaps over the wall to block him.

"Nina!" I shout. "Enough!"

Black plumes of smoke billow from the destroyed playing field as fire spreads from the path Nina's phantom fireball took through the maze. The crash of flames in Rylan's path sent sparks over the wall and into my side. Soon, the entire arena will be ablaze.

I drop back down to my sister. "Nina, put it out."

Her eyes finally open, practically glowing as they fix on me. She's a stranger to me—lost to her lust for power. I'm not going to get anywhere with her. The gusts I'm pulling from around the arena are only fanning the flames. I wave my arm in an arc over my head to contain the entire field in a dome. It's a huge shield. My heart races with the effort as flames lick the dome and mold against its arch.

Nina looks at me, and her jaw drops. "Do you *seek out* opportunities to prove you're better than me?"

"That's not what..." Shallow breaths don't allow me to get the thought out. This isn't about *beating her.* This is about the safety of the people in the stands. Doesn't she feel the size of the inferno? "Nina," I wheeze, "put it out."

"You don't even want this!" Heat builds at the base of the dome. I *feel it* licking around the edges as if they were my ankles. "You don't *need this!* But you won't let me have it either?"

Flames eat at the shield, hardened though it may be, picking off bits as I gasp. Our elements feel as if they belong together, even though they're struggling against each other now. Something in the air reaches out to the fire—not to extinguish it, but as if to soothe it.

My legs wobble, and I drop to my knees.

"And gods help me now if I do win!" Nina goes on with her tirade. "There won't be a soul in the kingdom who doesn't believe you could easily restrain me."

Easily? I can hardly breathe. Doesn't she feel the struggle raging around us? It's a miracle the shield is standing at all. I dig my fingers into the ground and drop my head as I try to pull in enough oxygen to respond, the pressure against the shield rising.

"You're practically *unconscious*, and I can't get past you. I'll never..." She lets out a frantic sob before she screams out. My shield is weakened from its own attempts to befriend the flames that assault it. As Nina screams, the pressure reaches excruciating levels.

Then the shield breaks.

Flames burst forth on the momentum they were pushing with. Without my shield surrounding the field, I only feel the temperature change out there, faint at this distance.

My arms give way underneath me, and I collapse onto the ground as the inferno around us roars. Smoke fills the air, choking me. Screams ring out from the crowd.

Nina gasps and drops to me. "Ara! Are you all right?" She wraps me in an embrace. "I'm sorry, darling. I'm so sorry." She swings her arm out, and flames extinguish in a radius around us, but not everywhere. The fire has gotten too big.

It takes all my remaining strength, but I get us up over the blazing field. Nina's arms fall slack as she takes in the view. Mother and Marcus work to keep flames away from the stands as people evacuate, waterspouts pushing back the blaze. Rylan sees we're out of the way and drops the ground out of most of the arena to bury and smother the inferno. It can't be done too close to the perimeter, though.

"I didn't mean to..." Nina shudders.

"Put it out." It's all I can do to whisper the words.

She reaches out with shaky hands, but the fire only recedes a little as tears streak her cheeks. "I can't."

"Those flames *are* you. Feel them, take a deep breath, and put them to sleep."

She closes her eyes and trembles, slowing her breathing.

A loud *crack* resounds. Screams ring out. Both of us snap our attention in the direction the sounds come from—fires have reached a section of the stands. Nina cries out, and some of the flames pull back. The pilings underneath smolder and crack as a torrent of water finishes the job, but the stands sway slightly. They're too unstable now.

People are still screaming, rushing down and away from the danger, when the entire thing buckles. Supports crack, but the earth juts up to hold it in place. Rylan is nearby, scanning the underside of the stands, manipulating the earth to rise where it's needed to hold everything steady. Smoke wisps up around the arena, but the flames are gone. Nina buries her face in my shoulder, and I hold her as we descend off to the side of the sunken field.

Ry storms toward us. "Nina! How could you—"

I meet his eyes and shake my head. His expression melts as we drop to the ground. Nina cries against me, and Ry kneels down with us. A cocoon of floral shrubbery grows around us, hiding us from view. In here, we're only siblings taking care of each other, as it should be.

"I'm so sorry," Nina whispers between sobs.

I rub her back. "I know."

Rylan takes her hand. "It'll be all right. I don't think anyone was badly hurt."

She tenses in my arms and jerks upright. "We need to—" Nina jumps to her feet, and our living barrier opens for her. She rushes out but freezes when Mother, Father, and Marcus approach.

Even with Ry's assistance, standing is a struggle. My legs sway, but a sweep of wind holds me steady.

"Are there injuries?" Rylan asks.

Mother's lips press together, her gaze falling on me. My heart falters. *Tomas. Where is Tomas?*

It's Father who speaks. "He wasn't near the fire. I don't know what happened..." *No. No, no, no.* "Jamys is dead."

CHAPTER FORTY-FIVE

Jamys? My hand flies up to my mouth. Of course Father wouldn't have given me attention if it had been Tomas. Jamys is my—was. Jamys *was* my... Oh, gods.

"Darling, I'm so sorry." Father wraps his arms around me, and my chest heaves against him.

"What happened?" Jamys can't be dead. It hasn't even been two days since I last saw him. Since I... fought with him and broke his heart.

"We don't know. It was loud, so I don't know if he even made a sound. His mother screamed, and when I turned, he was on the floor."

How horrible—his mother and sister were with him. I can't imagine what that must have been like for them. "Where are they now?"

"They're all still in the box. Their attendants are trying to get the Queen and Princess away from... him."

My stomach turns. Shaky as I am, I need to be there, to offer... something. After a couple deep breaths, I muster up the energy. I land on wobbly legs and lean against the rail.

Anilla's face is buried in her son's shoulder. She shudders as sobs tear through her. Lillian's lovely face is soaked in tears for the brother she admired. What a horrid thing for her, to watch as siblings nearly kill each other then lose the one she loved so well. She looks up at me, and her lip trembles.

I drop to her side and wrap my arms around her. "I'm so sorry." She nods against me.

It's unreal how quickly Jamys' appearance changed. The lips I've kissed are unnaturally pale. His skin, which had bronzed during our travels, is already taking on a gray hue. I reach out to his hand where it lays on his chest but flinch at the cold stiffness I find. *Oh, Jamys. You deserved so much more than what you got.*

A tear rolls down my cheek, and I swipe it away. The guilt for all the ways I wronged him overwhelms me. None of it matters, I suppose, but it seems worse now. Perhaps because I'm only one of the horrible things that happened to him. This man who was gentle and sweet and... gone.

Lillian squeezes my hand. "I'm sorry, too... for your loss."

My throat constricts. I'm an imposter crying here with them. They should hate me, not console me. I don't deserve any of it. Still, despite all the dread I'd built up about marrying him, his death guts me.

I look up, realizing this isn't the most private place to grieve. "We should go." I pull Lillian to her feet and gesture to a guard to aid her mother before I take one last look at Jamys. A cloak is shaken out to cover him... by a stone-faced Tomas.

Back at the palace, Lillian takes her mother to her chambers. I let them have some time alone, both because they need it and because I feel like an intruder. Rather than cry with them, I go to my own sitting room, where Lucy promptly brings me tea.

"Your Grace, I'm so sorry to hear about Prince Jamys."

"Thank you."

She leaves but is quickly replaced by Father. "How are you doing?"

"I don't know." I sniff in a shaky breath. "It isn't as if we were in love, but we were already partners in a way. We shared our situation I suppose, and we got along well. He was a good person." Tears well at my lashes again. He was good, and I wasn't. Why should he have died when it could have been me? I was the one in danger; I'm probably deserving, but *he* died. Why? How?

Father wraps me in an embrace. "There isn't anything I can say. This must be very confusing for you at this early stage of your relationship, but you had plans together, so I imagine it's very difficult."

His words invite me to sink into his warmth as much as his embrace does. I'm not sure how supportive he'd be if he knew the whole truth of the matter. He wouldn't spurn me, though it would invite some of that dreaded disappointment to color his opinion. For now, I'll let myself enjoy this pure, if blind, state of our connection.

"Darling," he says, "you should get cleaned up and rest."

I nod and wipe my eyes. "I will. I... I'm going to need to go to Ceraun with them. For the funeral."

"I'll go with you."

My instinct is to say no, except I don't suppose they'll send me alone. And who else would I want to bring? Jo would be a decent option, but will she understand my grief since she knows about Tomas? I'd really like to be able to lean on Tomas right now. At times, I've forgotten that he is so much more to me than our physical encounters. I really count on him—want him—for everything. This would be even more bizarre for him, though, and I certainly can't show up in Ceraun with him.

Even without Tomas, Urian won't be pleased to see me, but if I don't go, it would prove him right. I owe this much to Jamys to be there.

I answer Father's offer with a nod. "I'd like that. Thank you."

"I'll work out the arrangements. Shall I ring for your maid to draw a bath?"

Even pulling my power to ring the bell sounds exhausting. "Yes. Thank you."

He rises and does it. "It's been overshadowed now, but Arabella, you were extraordinary in the trial."

If it weren't for the aches and exhaustion, I wouldn't believe that had happened today. "I couldn't even contain the fire."

"It's not about whose power is the strongest. It was the intent."

I was trying to protect people. It shouldn't have to be from my own sister, but she got so lost in winning... "Nina is out, I presume?"

"Yes. It'll be you and Rylan now. But we'll delay it however long you need."

He leaves, and I sink back onto the chaise. This should simplify things—no more dealing with the power struggle if I simply allow Rylan to win at the last trial.

By the time I slink into bed, I've concluded that my biggest problems were solved today. The marriage I didn't want won't happen, and there won't be a shift in the line of succession. I don't have to live in Ceraun.

Not that I have any guarantees for alternatives. A hollowness settles into my chest at the change. I've gone from struggling between two good possibilities for love to maybe having none.

Still, there's some relief for the struggle being over which feels like I'm a coward at best, a wretch at worst. I wish I could turn my mind off. I wish it could be blank so I could rest. Alas, these thoughts toss and tangle through me until I fall asleep due to sheer mental exhaustion.

Chapter Forty-Six

This time, I do believe my siblings are worried for me. They don masks of sympathy to see us off.

Mother is coming as well. I can't remember the last time I spent any significant amount of time alone with both of my parents. It would be a novelty if it weren't for such a morose reason.

A parade of carriages takes the Cerauno royals, Jamys' coffin, and the three of us to Highbluff Castle to board our ship. The streets are lined with people quietly showing respect for the man who was to be part of their royal family, likely misdirecting their sympathies to me as well—the poor, sweet princess whose love story was cut short by tragedy.

No one knows what happened. Jamys' heart simply stopped—from the shock of the calamity, supposedly, but I wouldn't think that possible. The romantics say it was because he feared my death. It might be fitting for me to be his cause of death. I feel enough guilt for it.

Highbluff's towers seem to be watching, and the proximity to Tomas as I walk in this mournful procession down the dock makes me sick. The comfort of being in his arms like when he found me after my confrontation with Urian—that's all I want. But even that seems like a betrayal.

I spend most of the voyage wrapped in blankets, the building dread settling an icy cold deep into my bones. I worry what Urian will be like. My guess: even worse than before. Though mourning could soften him.

This was a terrible idea. How can I possibly face him?

Father offers comfort and solace. Mother brings joko. She comes into my cabin wrapped in a knit sweater and drops the pouch of white stones into my lap. My first thought is to refuse, but what else do I have to do? I levitate the board so the rocking of the ship doesn't affect it, and we begin. The only sound is the tapping of stones placed on the board. It's soothing, actually.

"You've gotten better at this," Mother says.

"Jamys tried to teach me."

"Apparently it went well."

A lump forms in my chest. We did make a decent team. If all we were ever expected to be was friends, we'd have been excellent at that. My chain of stones grows as I try to surround Mother's pieces, and my mind flitters to the trial. I couldn't contain Nina's fire. I had it surrounded, but it broke through.

"How did Nina break my shield?"

Mother sighs. "I can't pretend to understand what it feels like to have the elements set against each other. They are all interconnected, so I imagine it's complicated."

Tap. Tap. Tap.

"I felt that—their connection."

"Good. You should explore every facet of your element." Our hands keep moving in an unbroken rhythm. "I wasn't sure how the lines between them would blur when they were separated."

"How did you decide which element we'd each get?" My entire life, I never gave it any thought. Our magic seems like anything else in our blood. I'd never ask why Nina is slightly shorter than me, or why Rylan's eyes are darker. But this is something she chose.

A few taps of stones pass before she answers. "It didn't feel like much of a choice, really. Rylan made me a mother. My whole world shifted, and it seemed as if he'd continue shifting earth. You... well, you know air was never my strong suit."

"Could you tell so early I'd be the troublesome one? Figured you'd dump your least favorite power with me?"

Her lips tip up at the corners. "You *were* a bit troublesome. It was a more difficult pregnancy, but I didn't give you air because I didn't like it or you. I thought we'd be different, that you'd have different strengths. I knew you could be things I couldn't."

Different indeed. She's calm logic while I'm impulsive spirit. Mother is grace and poise to my flighty eccentricity. She does things her own way—splitting the magic, having multiple children, forming the ministry—but she knows how to make people come around to her ideas. As opposed to me, running off to Ceraun on a whim without seeking out approval.

Our differences have always appeared to me as ways I'm worse, but she makes it sound as if I could be better. If only that were true.

Though the hours drag, the days pass quickly, and before I know it, we are back on land for the final leg of our trip. The Queen and Princess keep to themselves, which I am infinitely grateful for. I can't expect to understand their devastation, but they think I share it. The family takes time to reunite and grieve alone, delaying my reunion with Urian.

Mother, Father, and I are given rooms and dine alone the first night. In the morning, we ready for the funeral. Cerauno fashion seems to have been designed for funerals. Today, I don't mind the dark, heavy fabric, or being so concealed. It feels like a continuation of being in a blanket. It's almost enough to soothe my nerves over my place in the procession.

The ominous stone cathedral looms ahead as Jamys' coffin is brought forth, followed by the King and Queen, Princess Lillian, then me. Before other family members. Before the lords and ladies of Ceraun. Keeping up this charade is a punishment I probably deserve. Though I may not be grieving properly, my discomfort with my position manifests in a bowed head and meek gait. Perhaps all negative feelings result in the same appearance.

The road is lined with a dark sea of people paying their respects to the fallen prince. Sniffles and sobs resound. At least he was well-loved by others, even if I couldn't offer that.

I don't know if Cerauno funerals are all so dreary, or if it's worse because it's a young prince, but it is truly the most depressing thing I've ever seen. There is no room for happy memories, or appreciation of the time he had. It's all grief for the loss, how terribly unfair and untimely it was, all he could have done and been if only given the years he should have had.

Father grips my hand. I pull a bubble around us and do my best to speak without moving my lips. "I suppose the purpose is for everyone to feel worse about the situation." He only squeezes my hand in response.

For people who believe death was not the end of the gods, they certainly catastrophize human expiration. Perhaps knowing the gods went willingly into death soothes our feelings about our inevitable endings. It can't be so bad if they chose it. It's worse for those left behind, particularly when funerals are like this.

We suffer through the remainder of the service, and Jamys is put into the royal mausoleum. After another morose parade back to the castle, the extended family and high-ranking aristocrats come together for a reception. It's more tears and quiet, and I no longer feel guilty for not grieving properly. If this is the appropriate way to grieve, no one should be doing it.

When Lillian is alone, I go to her with a glass of wine and a small plate of finger sandwiches. "Have you had anything at all?"

"Only a little." She takes one of the sandwiches. "Thank you."

"Would you like to go for a walk? Get some fresh air?"

"I shouldn't." Her gaze drops to the floor.

"Why not?"

She looks around. "I don't know." She eats a little more before I take it upon myself to remove her from this.

"Come on." I pull her to her feet and out to the garden. "It's too depressing in there."

"Of course it's depressing." She sniffles. "My brother is dead."

I take her by the shoulders. "Would he want you to spend all your days crying for him?"

"It's not just for him." She buries her face in her hands and sinks onto a bench that backs up to manicured rose bushes. "I'm crying for myself, too. I love Jamys, and of course I'm devastated, but now, it all passes to me—the expectation, the responsibility, the crown. I can't live up to it. He would have been a good king."

"Do you doubt your effectiveness as princess?"

"No, but that doesn't matter." Lillian twists to look at a flower and brush her fingertip along its petal.

"Of course it does. You've always had a role of great importance to Ceraun. Now, you'll have a different one."

"A very different one." She shakes her head. "You know what it's like. At least you had time to come to terms with potentially becoming the heir to your throne."

"Oh, but I'm..." I suppose it isn't a good time to say I'm choosing not to take the responsibility when she's just been forced into it herself. "There are some similarities, but of course, your circumstances are horrible."

"I wish there was a way to know what happened to him."

I kneel and wrap my hand around hers. "I know. I suspect the sadness will always be there, but you'll feel happiness again."

"I can't imagine it."

"Would you like me to show you how I lift my spirits?"

Curiosity glimmers in her wide eyes. I keep hold of her hand as I pull her to stand, slide a wedge of air under our feet, and push us up off the ground.

She shrieks and wobbles and clings to me. "Oh gods!"

"It's not so bad." We rise higher, and her chest heaves. "Relax. It's fun."

"We have *very* different ideas of fun." Despite her words, her arms loosen slightly as she takes in the view. I follow her gaze over the sprawling stone castle, the pristine grounds, the town down the hill. She starts to breathe slower. "It's beautiful up here, that's for certain."

"It is a lovely change of perspective. And, as I said, it can truly be fun. Watch."

"No, no, no!" She tries to keep hold of me as I pull my arm away. "You are just fine."

She holds completely still, as if gravity won't remember she's here if she isn't moving. I do a flip, and she gapes at me. "How can you keep us both up and do things like that at the same time?"

"You can walk and breathe and blink at the same time without thinking about it. This is natural to me."

Lillian settles down enough to enjoy herself. Smiles that look natural, if a bit tentative, reach her face. We play up over the castle, and some light and color return to her eyes. "I can't believe this is how you and your siblings always diverted yourself."

"There were times you could have joined us. Why didn't you?"

"It didn't seem like the way a princess was supposed to behave." She gasps and snaps her head toward me. "I'm sorry. I didn't mean to say you—"

"Oh, that's fine. I know I'm not the most well-behaved princess there ever was."

"Perhaps behaving is overrated. You can do everything just right, and what does it signify? It can all end in an instant."

I'd worry she's come back to thoughts of death, but if Jamys' helps her realize she should live while she can, perhaps some good can come of it. On our way back down to the garden, Lillian sighs. "Oh, no."

King Urian awaits, stiff-backed and stern-faced.

"Father—"

"Go inside, Lillian."

She bows her head and acquiesces.

I hold his stare as Lillian walks away. "King Urian, I haven't had an opportunity to offer you my—"

"Save it. I don't expect you to be forlorn about Jamys' death any more than I expected you to be happy about marrying him."

"Of course I'm saddened by his death. He was a good man."

His eyes narrow. "But not good enough for you, I suppose?"

"Too good, actually, but that has nothing to do with it. Neither of us had a choice in the matter, and none of it can come to pass now anyway."

"How lucky for you." His nose flares as he stares me down.

"You *cannot* think me so depraved as to wish him dead."

"I don't presume to know the limits of your depravity."

He's grieving. Ignore him. His opinion is of no importance. I may never have to see him again. The boldness I threw at him the last time we met would be uncalled for in the wake of Jamys' death, but I cannot let him walk all over me. "I came to pay my respects, and to let you and your family know I share in your sorrows. Whether you care to accept that or not changes nothing."

"I don't care to share anything with the likes of you."

My jaw tenses, but I manage to swallow back any hostile words. "Fortunately, we aren't likely to find ourselves in each other's company again." I offer a slight curtsy. "Goodbye, Your Majesty. Again, I'm sorry for your loss."

As I walk away, I remind myself he hasn't lost our alliance. Penum is already battering them for their relations with us, and the entire kingdom of Ceraun can't be punished for their king's vileness.

CHAPTER FORTY-SEVEN

Light glows from the edges of the curtains. I'm in no mood to start another day. The sound of my sitting room door closing reaches me, but I don't want to eat. Being home hasn't helped. If anything, it's made it all worse.

Hundreds of miles between us and a place where he's never been, allowed me to set Tomas aside in my mind. To consider what Jamys' death means for us is despicable, but now that I'm back, the pull toward him is another ache in my mangled soul.

The smell of bacon sweeps under the door, and my mouth waters. "Who's really in control here?" The air seems more autonomous by the day. Enticing me to eat is just one of the ways it's been trying to manipulate me. It's supposed to be the other way around.

I trudge out of my bedchamber to find my breakfast, acquiescing to the less-than-subtle hints. My desk beckons me as I eat. I'd like to send for Jo or Tomas. They're the people I went to when I learned of my betrothal. They're the ones I go to for everything. But they're too involved, and this is complicated. They can't be impartial. And perhaps I'm afraid to know where Tomas stands...

My entire life has changed. I'm no longer betrothed. I won't be Queen of Ceraun. From an outside perspective, it's too soon for me to think of other marriage prospects, but I had been thinking about that all along. The glimmer of hope lies in my chance to be with Tomas without blowing up lives and politics, without any regrets. But what if I was wrong? What if he doesn't want that? Our affair being only that because we *couldn't* marry was acceptable. Maybe that's the only reason it went on; we were able to have our fun, and Tomas never had to worry about me demanding a commitment because I couldn't make one. If that hadn't been the case, he may not have continued to seek me out.

The thought shrivels my heart.

Would that have been better? If we had cut everything off before it got so far? Not knowing the rush of each encounter with him sounds horrid. I'd only have been happy with my life because I never would have experienced true ecstasy.

I drop my face into my hands. None of this should be a priority.

A knock sounds before Lucy peeks in. "Good morning." I merely nod, and she comes in. "The Queen and King have requested your presence in the Queen's study this afternoon."

I rub my forehead. "The formality isn't necessary, Lucy. I'd really like for *anything* to feel ordinary."

"Right. Of course. I'm sorry." She flitters off to prepare a bath while I finish nibbling on my breakfast.

After bathing and dressing, I enjoy the familiar feeling of pins sliding into my hair. This little bit of normalcy means more when nothing is normal at all. So many days spent tossing my hair in a simple knot while traveling was fine, but these rituals calm me.

"How have things been here?" I ask. "In the wake of that trial, does everyone think we are indeed monsters now?"

"Not at all. On the contrary—people think you're gods now that they've seen such an exhibition of your powers."

She doesn't sound thrilled by the idea, or perhaps I'm projecting. I don't want people to think we're *all powerful,* but I suppose it's better than the alternative.

As I make my way through the palace, heads bob to me—not in reverence. In pity. I do feel deserving of it, just not for the reasons people think.

"Thank you for coming," Mother says with a soft smile when I enter.

"You didn't actually give me a choice." I attempt a grin and take a seat.

Father folds his hands together. "Now that we're home, are you ready to talk about it?"

"There isn't much to talk about."

They look at each other, then their gazes fall on me. "Sweetheart, did Jamys know you were trying to get out of the betrothal?" Mother told him then.

"Yes." I swipe a tear from the corner of my eye before it has a chance to fall. "Last I saw him, we fought about it."

Mother's eyes glisten. "It must be difficult to have that as your last conversation."

"There's nothing to be done about it."

"Perhaps you should all go take your holiday at Etherlee," Father says. "It would give you time to sort yourself out before the last trial."

My shoulders slump. "Do we really have to do the trial?"

"Yes." Father taps his fingers together. "It's perhaps more important now. Without the potential conflict of interest with Ceraun, many see you as a more viable potential heir."

"Arabella," Mother says, "I know you haven't been trying to win, but if you *can*, then you should. Our kingdom deserves the best. I love your brother, but his temper gets the best of him. You're levelheaded—"

An incredulous hiss escapes me.

"You are," she continues. "You don't think I see through your antics and jests? Darling, you always do the right thing. I trust you'll do so with this as well."

I wish I were obstinate enough to throw my affair at her. *Oh, was sleeping with Tomas when I was betrothed to another the* right *thing?* But their disappointment would mortify me. "How could anyone expect it of me at this point?"

"There's no rush," Father says. "Take your trip. The sea air will do you good."

Not long ago, I wished to have one last week at the shore. The story of Tomas and me could be wrapped up so nicely. It started there, and it would end there. But at my last attempt, he wouldn't even see me. Without Jamys, we have decisions to make—at least, we would, if he's stopped avoiding me. Would he agree to marry me out of guilt? I couldn't stand that. Would it change everything between us to be betrothed? Did we only work because it was exciting and forbidden? Would he still want me the way he does if I were his wife? Would he trust me? I maintained an affair for my entire betrothal with Jamys; perhaps I'm not deserving of trust. *Dead gods, take me.*

"I don't know." Tears pool against my eyelashes. "I don't know if I want to go to the shore. It's always been a light, fun trip, and it couldn't be now. So... I don't know." I rub my forehead and avoid their eyes.

"Take your time," Father says. "Let us know when you're ready."

When I'm ready to choose the crown. Ready to betray Rylan. Ready to risk my heart. What training is there for that?

By the time I arrive back at my rooms, I don't wish to leave again for weeks. The confusion and chaos in my mind build, and I don't know how to act in front of people. I'm going to explode. There's usually an excellent release for this kind of thing, but as he's at the heart of most of my turmoil...

I open my door and puff out a breath upon seeing I have company. "What are you doing here?"

"Ara, I'm worried about you." Rylan wraps his arms around me, and I drop my chin to my chest. "How are you holding up?"

"It's complicated."

"I'd imagine so." He sits on a sofa, and I drop onto the chaise. "The two of you seemed to be getting on well."

"We were. It's not as if I was in love with him, but..."

"That must make it even more strange to mourn him."

"Indeed." Rylan coming to offer me comfort, to listen, warms me. Things have been so charged between us with the trials. I just want my brother, and finally, it feels like we can be the siblings we once were.

"I can't believe they're going to make you go through with the trial," he says. "I tried to have it cancelled. I'm sorry."

Even though I just made the same attempt, Ry trying to cancel it feels different. "Did you try to have it cancelled for my sake or yours?"

"Can't it be both?"

My lips press together, but I'm not sure if they form a frown or a smile. "I suppose so."

"Of course it can. We've always been on the same team."

Yes, we've always both been on *his* team.

"You can be honest with me." His eyes are wide and earnest. "Aren't you somewhat relieved? You didn't want to be Queen of Ceraun."

"I don't know. Some things would have been easier that way." I am a terrible coward. Part of me would rather have my choices made for me than risk rejection. At the time, it felt like growth to accept a role greater than the comparatively carefree existence in Alchos I'd enjoy as a lower royal. Securing relations with Ceraun was something Alchos needed me for, and Ceraun needed me to secure their strength, even if it was only my presence that did it. I was taking responsibility for others. Except, I was still only taking what was given to me, not having to make any real choices.

"Well, yes. Queen consort might have been a happy position. Sovereign will be quite the headache, I think."

I bite the inside of my cheek. "Rylan, you needn't slither around it. Would you like to know if I'm still intending *not* to win the trial?"

His gaze drops. "It seemed inappropriate to ask."

"It is. It *really* is. Do you ever stop thinking of yourself?"

"It's not just me. I'm thinking of *you* and the kingdom."

"Do you really think I'd be so dreadful for Alchos?" I get back to my feet and pace my sitting room, and a cool breeze calms the heat rising through my neck.

"No, of course—"

"And *how* could you possibly be thinking of me?"

"It would be a massive responsibility, for one."

"And furthermore?"

"*Furthermore,* if you're thinking that, as the heir, you wouldn't end up in another arranged marriage, I can assure you Mother and Father aren't going to rush into a new betrothal for you after Jamys. I don't want you to make a rash decision based on something that won't affect you."

Underneath the tempest of my fury, I find a glimmer in his words. Even Rylan thinks the crown is mine for the taking—I just have to decide I want it.

"Well then, I appreciate your concern. I certainly wouldn't want to rearrange my entire life based on a feminine, romantic whim."

"That's not what I said."

"Isn't it?" I lean against the back of the sofa. "I assure you, I won't base my performance on my marriage preferences."

"Ara..."

"You may leave."

His jaw clenches, but he goes.

Thank you, Ry. This makes things considerably less complicated. He's right. I've been dwelling on how all of this affects me romantically, but that's not a good reason to fight for the crown. Now it isn't out of cowardice that I'm not confirming Tomas' intentions. It's to keep my own motives pure.

Whether being queen gets me Tomas or not, I will compete for Alchos. And for myself.

Chapter Forty-Eight

Lucy's eyes bulge when she enters my sitting room with breakfast. "Oh! You're up." She sets down the tray and looks me up and down. It must be surprising to find me in a tunic, leggings, and boots—ready for training instead of sulking. "If you'd have rang, I could have done your hair."

"I can manage this." I toss my braid behind my shoulder. "Thank you, Lucy. I wanted to get an early start today."

"Of course." She curtsies and presses her lips together as she looks at me inquisitively.

"What is it?"

"I'm sorry if it's improper to ask... but are you going to try to win the trial?"

A smile threatens to break through as I sit down. "I've been trying all along, of course."

"Of course." Lucy gives me a knowing grin. "Good luck then."

Alone, I sip the tea and bow my head. Does everyone think I can do this? Can I, really? There's only one way to find out.

I eat my breakfast and escape via my balcony.

The wind welcomes me back with all the playful excitement of a puppy. I stretch my arms up and back as it carries me away. A deep breath tastes like freedom. Freedom I won't have quite so much of if I'm queen. But for now, I can twirl around in midair, carefree and relaxed. Trees and meadows, villages and farms whisk by below me. It's a beautiful place, and I don't see it from this vantage point nearly enough. Alchos would be worth the work and stress and torment. I'd do anything for this kingdom. The reasons to step aside were all rather selfish. And cowardly. I'm better than that.

I *will* be better than that.

This is a delightful way to get around, but I usually take a horse for this distance. That's why I don't immediately realize where I'm going.

"Oh, no. No! Stop it right now!" I pull myself upright, try to push my feet against the direction I'm being taken, to redirect myself, but the situation is beyond my control. "This is *utterly* absurd!"

My feet land softly. I push away, but the air refuses to lift me. "Fantastic. I'm not the most powerful at all! I only have the strongest element." A sweet breeze brushes my cheek like a kiss. "Unfortunately, it's also the most *obstinate!* Let me go!" I try to rise off the floor again to no avail. "I'll jump! I know you won't let me die." I lean over the balcony—or try to. My face hits a wall of air with a thud, and I gasp and gape at... nothing visible. "How *dare* you!"

"How dare I what?"

I whirl around to face Tomas. Of course, I wouldn't be lucky enough for him to not be in his rooms. The air probably knew he was here. "I wasn't shouting at you."

"That's unusual." Despite the light tone, his eyes hold concern as he walks toward me. "How are you doing, Bell?"

"I'm fine." I was, anyway. Even out on his balcony, us being alone in his rooms is too similar to being together in mine. That last time when we'd made love and I decided to pursue a future with him plays in my mind. This proximity to him makes my throat tighten. He's my weakness. Why would the ridiculous air bring me to him when I'm trying to get ready for the trial?

"You looked to be in agony during the last trial." He scans me for injuries, and my skin prickles under his gaze. "Were you burnt?"

"No. It was how our magic was going against each other. I can't explain it. Really, though. I'm fine."

"And about Jamys?"

I close my eyes for a breath. "It's very sad."

"Yes, it is." He looks away and rubs the back of his neck. After a dragging silence, he says, "I may go back to Lambridge for a while. I hate being useless when they have so many unsolved problems."

"Is there anything you can do?"

"I don't know, but I'd rather be there trying." His eyes go distant, making him look more haunted than he should be. He wasn't at fault for any of the problems out there the way my siblings and I were.

"So would I."

Despite its warmth, his gaze sends a chill down my neck. "If you'd like, we could go together. After— Oh, but do you expect to be able to after the final trial?"

A loaded question if ever I've heard one. I run my tongue over my teeth and raise my chin. "It seems like a perfectly reasonable thing for the heir to the throne to do."

His eyebrows raise slightly. "Are you really…"

"Going to compete to the best of my ability? Of course. I have been all along." I wink, but his expression remains serious.

"Why?"

Blue eyes make me think it's because of him. Because he thinks I should, or because as heir I could choose who I marry. But that isn't really why. After all, it may not be necessary. I want to do this for the right reasons. "For Alchos."

"Good. Is there anything I can do to help?"

My face warms, and I clear my throat. "I don't really think that kind of *practicing* is what I need right now."

"That isn't what I meant, but why are you here then?"

"I was brought here against my will, which proves I need to focus. It would appear I'm losing control over my magic."

His smirk brings me back to simpler times. "Interesting. Different methods then." He leans back against the rail. "Catch." He teeters over and flips into a fall.

Oh, it lets him through. Lovely. Well, it can catch him then—only it doesn't seem to have that plan. I pull up the air below Tomas to slow him and set him on the ground gently. "How gracious of you to give me some control." I swing my legs over and jump, *very* intently controlling my decent. *That's better.*

"Did you control our landings?" Tomas asks when I reach him.

"Yes."

"Excellent. Let's continue."

I cross my arms. "Is it all going to be my preventing your attempts at suicide?"

"Honestly, Bell, I'm certain my life is at risk any time I'm around you."

Tomas notches an arrow. "I'm not sure what you could do better with more practice." The arrow flies true, but I turn it away from its intended target to pierce another in the center.

"You say that as if you're one to settle for *good enough*." I arch an eyebrow at him.

"You aren't merely good enough."

My cheeks warm, and I have to shove down the impulse to lean into his compliments. "If you were so sure of my abilities, you'd shoot at me."

"I can't do that." He notches another, and I step in front of it.

"Rylan would pardon you for killing me. I'm only in his way now."

"You're ridiculous."

I step backwards toward the target. "I thought you wanted to help."

"Bell…"

"You watched Marcus try to drown me and Nina nearly burn me alive. This is nothing."

His eyes darken. "I didn't enjoy that, and it's quite different from *me* attacking you."

"You know I can stop it."

"I don't know if *I* can do it." We're both toeing the line into something else, and I'm not ready to go there.

"A dagger then." I gesture to the one sheathed at his hip. "Certainly that's slower than an arrow, and—"

"Not much slower." His raised eyebrows give an even cockier edge to his sly smile.

"All the same." It takes all my self-control not to appear affected by that look. "Go ahead."

He stows the bow at his back and removes the dagger, his hand trembling, as if it pains him to hold it.

"You said you believe in me."

His eyes don't leave mine, and a thousand unspoken thoughts float between us. Until the dagger soars toward me, and I whip a shield up a few inches in front of me. It strikes, and for a moment, it sticks in the shield. I gasp. It pierced the shield. That can't be. As quickly as possible, I use a gust to toss it back. Hopefully, it looks like it ricocheted.

"See?" I say. "That wasn't so bad."

Tomas blinks a few times and narrows his eyes. "I won't be doing that again." I pick up the dagger and offer it to him. "No, you keep it."

"What do I need a dagger for?"

"They come in handy." He unstraps its sheath and hands it over.

"If you say so." It would be rude to point out I have far greater weapons at my disposal. And it would be embarrassing to admit I like the idea of having something of his. "What's next?" I follow him as he puts away the bow and quiver.

"This kind of training really isn't like you. You're at your best when you're having fun."

And oh, what fun we've had. In the grief of Jamys' death, our affair feels more shameful. I can't jump back into bed with Tomas like I'm glad Jamys died, giving me the freedom to do so. "Tomas…"

"That isn't the kind of fun I meant."

Faster than should be possible, I go from uneasy about the suggestion to terrified by the correction. I don't think we should be engaging in those sorts of relations at the moment, but his motivation worries me. Our relationship was guaranteed to be free of obligation from the onset. He could pull away from me now that I'm not promised to someone else.

"Good," I say. "But I don't need to take up any more of your time." Plus, he keeps having strange effects on my powers.

"You know that isn't how I feel about it."

I wouldn't dare to assume I know his feelings about anything, so the only response I give is a shrug.

"If you don't want to be around me," he says, "I understand."

"You were the one avoiding me, if you recall."

He rakes his hand through his hair. "It wasn't that I—"

"It's fine. I'm sorry I brought it up. It's just a very confusing time. There's a lot going on."

"I know."

I've never felt uncomfortable around Tomas before. We're good at anger, teasing, fun, passion, but this is miserable. We've known each other too long for this. Our friendship was too good, and when we're more, we're even better. The tightness in my chest threatens to break me. A few weeks ago, I'd have thought I'd miss his body most of all, but it's just him. Talking to him. Laughing. He's become so many things to me.

"I think what I need is a break." I wipe my palms on my leggings. "You're right about this not being the type of training that helps me. Is Jo around?"

Jo's embrace does wonders to set my nerves back into place. "I went to call on you when you returned, but they said you weren't taking visitors." She leans back and holds my shoulders at arm's length. "I tried to explain that I'm no ordinary visitor, but it did not work."

"They'll be reprimanded, I assure you."

She grins as we sink onto a chaise in her sitting room. "Well, some things have occurred since last I saw you. Your sister nearly burned down the arena."

I match her casual, matter-of-fact tone. "I recall."

"You've moved on to the final trial to potentially become queen of Alchos."

"I have."

"And Jamys…" She bites her lip.

"Yes." We slip into a sad silence for a moment.

"You seem rather calm about all of it."

Perhaps I am now. It was difficult even before Jamys' death, though. "I can't change any of it."

She nods and takes my hand, giving it a squeeze. "I thought this would make some things simpler for you. I know that's dreadful to say, but we know—"

"It's not simpler." I pull my braid around my shoulder and twist the end around my finger. "Marrying Jamys would have been simple." Not that I'd still planned on that eventuality, but I never told Jo I had greater feelings for Tomas. She had enough to deal with knowing I was sleeping with him. "Now Rylan thinks I'll try to win the crown so I can choose my own husband." As much as I hate the trials, I'd rather talk of that. Sometimes, it's rather inconvenient to be in love with the brother of my best friend.

"Will you?"

"No."

Her lips pinch into a frown. "You're not going to try to win?"

"I am going to try to win, but not for that purpose."

"Does it matter?"

"Yes. It matters to me." I twiddle my fingers. "I'll not be crowned sovereign just to avoid being betrothed against my will. They'd likely let me choose anyway. It isn't as if Ceraun has another prince I could marry. There aren't any other obvious, advantageous choices."

Jo's chin drops conspiratorially. "Really?"

"None who would benefit the crown."

"Because House Coyle is already so spectacularly loyal?"

My jaw clenches. "Precisely."

"Ara, now you could—"

"Please, stop. I'm not ready to think about it." Is she only assuming we'd marry because we have sex, or does she know of his feelings on the matter? This is all a distraction I don't need right now.

"When will you be?"

"After the trial." Because if he breaks my heart, I'll be useless, and I want to do well. Sorting out things with Tomas is a risk I can't take right now. "No matter what happens between Tomas and me, you and I shall remain."

Her brows pull together. "Of course."

The words are right, but everything else is wrong. I never wanted to cause a rift between Jo and Tomas or in our friendship. Now it feels as though it's all interwoven and I could lose them both in one swoop.

Chapter Forty-Nine

The familiar sound of a breakfast tray being set on the table rings out from the sitting room. As I make my way in, I say, "Thank you, Lucy. I— *What* are you doing?"

"Offering moral support to my sister on this most important day." Nina settles down and pats the cushion next to her. "Come now. You need your strength. You must eat."

My gaze remains trained on her as I sit. "Why do you care about this if you can't win?"

"Tomas is convinced you're going to try to win. Is that true?" Did she even hear my question?

"Why do *either of you* care?"

She shrugs. "You're the next best choice."

"That's... wonderful. I'm honored, really. Is it simply that after all these years of having a sovereign queen it would be difficult to get used to a king?"

Nina's head bobs back and forth. "I do think women are more apt for ruling. Also... as your own betrothal was rather disastrous, I would *hope* that you might help convince Mother and Father to give me some more time. As heir, you'd have more sway."

"Is that why you were determined to win? So they couldn't arrange your marriage?"

"Yes."

It's not surprising. Nina has always been the most opposed to it. I assumed she'd have chosen someone by now to get ahead of our parents. Unless she wanted to marry someone wholly inappropriate, they'd allow it. The only thing they can't allow is for her to never marry. She needs to pass her magic on, lest it die with her.

"Well, I can't make any promises, but I'll try."

"Thank you." Asking for and accepting assistance is unlike her. She shifts her legs, crossing and uncrossing her ankles.

"Have they started any negotiations that you're aware of?"

"I don't know." Her shrug is not convincing in the slightest.

"Yes, you do."

She bites her lip and stands. "I shouldn't be bothering you. It *is* a big day, and I really do wish the best for you."

"Nina, tell me."

"No, I—"

"You're my sister. You take priority."

She shakes her head. "Not today."

"Always. You can tell me anything."

Her chin drops as her eyebrows arch toward her hairline. "Sisters certainly don't tell each other everything."

Heat rushes up my neck. "I'm certain I don't know what you mean, but I didn't say *everything.* I said we *could* tell each other *any*thing. Furthermore, you seem like you need help, which is completely different than whatever you might think you know about me."

"It's actually quite related."

"What is related?" I ask.

"Your affair with Tomas."

I take a sip of tea and pull a breeze to cool my face. "Marcus told you then?" I knew he would.

"No. Tomas did."

"Tomas? What would possess him to—"

"So that I wouldn't be offended by his discontentment with our betrothal."

All the heat that had been building in my frustration is sucked out of me. Everything goes cold and still. "Your... betrothal?" My voice shakes. "The two of you?"

She nods.

I'd think my heart turned leaden, but it wouldn't ache like this if that was the case. "When was that decided?"

"That evening when the Merricks and the Coyles dined with us. You were out for a drunken stroll with Jamys when they called us in to tell us. They were stewing over Lambridge, and since Tomas is so well liked there, it seemed like a good way to make them feel more connected to our family, but it hasn't been *decided*. At the time, I was in the running to be heir to the throne, and if I'd won—"

"They wouldn't have arranged your marriage."

"Precisely."

Connections fall into place in my mind. "Was that the cause of the fire glowing outside that night?" Her sardonic smile confirms it. "And that's why Tomas wanted you to win."

"Yes. It seemed the only way to avoid our most unhappy union."

Air rushes through me too quickly. "And now you think I can simply tell Mother and Father you shouldn't marry him?"

"I *assumed* if you won, your choice of husband would be him. Quickly. Before they can finalize our betrothal."

"You assume a lot, Nina." I rise and pace the room, pulling in deep breaths through my nose, trying desperately to get more oxygen to my heart. "I don't know if he would even *want* to marry me."

An incredulous puff escapes her. "Need I remind you that *you* are the primary reason he can't stand the thought of marrying me?"

"That doesn't mean anything! Of course he couldn't marry you. He's bedded your sister, for the gods' sake! It is not the same as him being in love with me."

She blinks slowly. "Jamys is no longer an obstacle, yet you haven't broached the subject with Tomas?"

"No."

"Why not?" Her pitch skyrockets, and smoke twists off her.

"Because I need to focus today!" An idea which has now been completely ruined. *Dead gods.*

Flames flicker against Nina's shoulders, and a frustrated screech is muffled by her sealed lips. "Do I have to do everything? *Gods,* you two are absurd. He refused me asking for your support in the second trial due to this nonsense, and now, even without Jamys, you're too stubborn to deal with the situation."

"I'm not being *stubborn!* I'm terrified."

"Of what?" The volume of the conversation reaches a peak, but I can barely find my voice to respond, much less continue the shouting match.

"Of him choosing not to be with me." Voicing it makes it so much worse. I've dwelled on the possibility, but saying it out loud makes it feel real. With the idea out in the open, the first glimmers of loss and dejection grip me. "Before, we had no choice. But what if we do, and I'm not his choice?" A tear spills over my eyelashes, and I wipe it away. "*None of this* is what I need to be thinking about today."

"You'd be thinking about it anyway. You can't go into today with this open-ended."

"Better to leave it as a possibility than to go in heartbroken."

"That is not what will happen."

"Did he say as much?" Hope sparks in my chest.

"Everything was about and for *you*. You must see that."

Not enough to bet on it.

A knock on the door draws our attention. Marcus opens it and stands in the doorway. "It's time to go."

"Perfect." I scrub my hands over my face. This is as far from how I intended to go into the trial as possible. "I'm going to be a disaster."

"No you're not." Nina comes to me and rubs my arms. "You'll be brilliant. You always are. *Hence,* Tomas is obviously in love with you."

"Why does it sound like you're convincing her of that?" Marcus asks.

"Because I am." She looks at Marcus with wide, incredulous eyes. "She hasn't spoken to Tomas about any possibility of their future together now that Jamys has died."

Marcus' jaw tightens. "Are you saying you may still end up stuck with Tomas?"

"No. Of course not." She turns her attention back to me. "Because, win or lose, you'll have time to verify that Tomas does indeed wish to marry you before they have a chance to make our betrothal official. None of this should affect you during the trial."

She makes it sound so simple, like I can tuck all of this away. "How closely are your powers connected to your emotions, Nina? Because mine are so thoroughly interwoven, I can't always separate them. This will undoubtedly affect it!"

"Then speak with Tomas before you go in. You can be perfectly euphoric during the trial that way."

"There isn't any time," Marcus says.

"And no guarantee I'd be any better off!"

They both roll their eyes, looking more like twins than usual.

The last thing I wanted was to get worked up about this before the trial. This is exactly the type of distraction I don't need. I should have sealed my rooms. Nina is out of her mind to lay this on me now!

But none of our feelings on the matter are of any importance. Now it's time to find out who will sit next on Mother's throne.

Chapter Fifty

Rylan refuses to look at me. I let it focus me rather than upset me. Our fight replays in my mind—every patronizing, selfish sentiment. I tried to be the good sibling, and he hasn't the slightest gratitude for it. What kind of behavior is that for a king?

The final trial is more remote than the first two. Repairs to the arena will take some time, and being near the clash of magic has proven dangerous. Instead, we are out in the middle of nowhere with a fraction of the audience. Only the ministry and high houses attend, all the better since there was very little notice for this one.

Nina might have demonstrated that we are too dangerous to be trusted, but it's been spun quite nicely. No one had ever seen this magic in such full force, us included. Trying to use our elements against each other has brought out new ways to use them alongside greater levels of awe and adoration. Our people are more amazed by us than they've ever been.

There's no need for as much spectacle this time. Lords and ladies gather under picturesque shady trees too perfect to have shaped themselves. Spring's floral presence is fading across the kingdom as temperatures rise, but Mother and Rylan have gardened the spot well for the occasion. The rainbow of blooms on the topiaries would be a charming setting for a festive tea. Perhaps this trial won't be as destructive as the previous ones.

Attendants flutter behind the aristocrats and representatives, bringing them drinks and fans. Nina weaves through the small crowd as the four of us approach, her route taking her to Tomas, whose gaze flicks down to my hip where his dagger rests. A breath of a smile whispers across his lips.

Mother and Father lead, and Rylan and I walk side by side perfectly oblivious of each other. Our parents stop before us, and we step to their side to greet the assembly.

"Lords and ladies of Alchos, Ministry Representatives, thank you for being here today." Mother's voice doesn't require amplifying in this more intimate setting. "We are honored to have you bear witness to this historical moment."

Nina steps close to Tomas during the introduction. She whispers to him, and I see the result on Tomas' face. His jaw clenches, and he stiffens from head to toe. He tips his chin toward her ever so slightly, speaking through his teeth. Is it Nina's goal to make *everyone* miserable today?

"Our kingdom will no doubt thrive under either of our potential rulers," Mother continues. "Prince Rylan and Princess Arabella have always put the well-being of Alchos above all. I look forward to the future they will create."

Applause rises after her words—not that either of us deserve it. We've not been concerned about Alchos. Rylan has only cared for his own position, and I've let my personal circumstances drive my actions. They deserve better.

Tomas narrows his eyes at Nina in disbelief. Either I'm getting better at lip reading, or I know his too well, because I see clear as day that he says *"What?"* before turning rounded eyes toward me. My heart beats a little harder. *Not what I need right now, Nina.*

"In this challenge, creating is exactly what they will do. One at a time,"—*Oh, the desperation to keep us apart has peaked.* That solves the issue of it being destructive. My attention is pulled back to my mother, where it belongs.—"they will show us what they can *build* with their power. We've seen them on offensive and defensive tasks, but such occasions are rare and do not typically require direct interference of a ruler."

I glance sidelong at Rylan, who looks content with this task. Of course he is. What am I to create out of *air?*

Mother turns toward us and nods, so I step back and gesture for Rylan to proceed.

He rolls his shoulders back and presses a foot to the ground in front of himself. Six saplings spring up, encircling him. They grow and thicken, reaching for the sky and branching out toward each other. Rylan's hands twist and stretch, molding the trees into stunning whorls as they take on decades of maturity in minutes. Leaves sprout in a wave, like an artist swept green paint around the ring of them. Above the lush cushion of leaves, the trees reach toward each other to form six grand peaks.

A new branch reaches into the center of the ring, and Rylan steps onto it. The tree raises him to stand above the living crown he's created. "The gods saw fit to entrust my family with the powers that shaped the world." A lifetime of preparing for this role shows now. Ry looks and sounds every bit the ruler he was always meant to be. "I shall continue to shape our kingdom, ensuring it remains the strongest in the land."

Applause marks the end of Rylan's performance. The tree lowers him gently, and he doesn't look at me as we switch places. I take in his creation up close before turning back to face our audience. It is a testament to Rylan's priority: power. That's not me. It never could be, though I'm often told how powerful I am. Perhaps that's the deciding factor—having power versus wanting it.

Mine buzzes within me. I close my eyes, take a deep breath, and slide my power out along the ground as I exhale. Large stones rise up, and I pull them toward me. One comes to rest before me, levitating at a height halfway up my shin. Another floats just beyond it, that much higher. I step onto the first one as more stones move into place, rising and twisting to create a spiral staircase.

"I could build almost anything." My voice is low but carries on the wind. "Except nothing you'd see here would matter." I continue climbing as the stone staircase forms before me, one step at a time. "The most important things I build are trust and loyalty."

The bend turns toward those watching, and my eyes meet Tomas'. *I've never had a problem following you, Bell.* He wasn't talking about dancing. And I don't think he's the only person who would feel that way.

"I don't wish to rule over people. I want to raise them up, to shape our kingdom together, to—"

The stones fall away beneath me, and gasps resound as they crash against each other and the ground. Dust and dirt billow up from the pile. I'm left floating above it all, heart racing.

What is *happening* to my power?

Rylan presses his lips together, by no means hiding his satisfaction. Did he do it? Move the stones? I've always been able to withstand that, and I didn't feel any struggle.

Before I realize what's happening, the wind pulls up under Rylan. His curls ruffle in it, and he looks at me incredulously. My attempts at getting a grip on my magic fail. He rises into the air and shoots away.

Chapter Fifty-One

My hand snaps up to cover my gasp. It looks like I just threw him off into the woods, and we aren't even supposed to be confronting each other.

I look over my shoulder at my parents, the twins, Tomas, finding them all shocked and confused. I grit my teeth and release a flustered breath. *Just when I started trying...*

It's all over, but I suppose I need to retrieve my brother. I soar after him and catch up quickly.

"What do you think you're doing?" he roars.

"It's not me!"

"No one else can control the air!" A tree grows to catch him, but he sweeps past it. A hill rises to meet him, but he floats higher still. This is not the time for the air to take on a mind of its own.

"Stop this!" I shout. "This isn't accomplishing anything!"

"Who are you speaking to?"

"The *air!*" We're carried past the trees and to the edge of a cliff overlooking the sea. "I don't know why it's dragging you out to—"

A fleet of Penuman ships.

Rylan and I land and gape at the amassment of vessels blanketing the coast.

Fear spreads through me like a crack in glass, obscuring the once-clear picture I had of the world. A whisper sneaks through my trembling lips. "I didn't think Penum had a fleet."

Whatever I thought doesn't matter, though. Dark sails hang limp from the masts. The wind has died, and a warm breeze slinks around me like an embrace. *You've done that.* The air stopped them and brought us here to see.

A boulder rises behind us, Rylan's hand matching the movement and clenching, ready to throw.

"What are you doing?" A downward draft pushes against the boulder, and it wobbles but remains levitated.

"They are in our territory unannounced, approaching our coastline with enough ships to do battle."

"Perhaps they need our assistance."

He wheels on me with wide eyes. "Why would they come here? They hate us."

"They can't mean to fight us—it would be suicide. Any one of us could lay waste to that fleet in a moment."

"Suicide indeed." The boulder trembles as Ry tenses in preparation to heave it.

"Rylan, if you sink their ships, *you* are starting a war, not them. We must speak with them first. And alert Mother and Father."

His expression darkens. "A sovereign needs to be capable of making decisions."

"Rash, uninformed decisions? I don't recall that lesson."

"I'm not running back to Mother for help." The earth rumbles.

"Neither of us have to *go* anywhere." I pull the dagger Tomas gave me from its sheath. I can't leave, but I need to tell them. This is more dramatic than I'd prefer the message to look, but without ink or parchment... I wince as I slice my fingertip, and blood drips from the wound.

Waves crash against a barrier of rock newly erected from under the sea.

I press my bleeding finger to the side of the blade. The crimson ink looks ghastly, but "shore" is legible, so I wipe my finger on my tunic and squeeze my thumb against the cut. Hot air blasts to dry the message, and I throw it. *You're good at finding Tomas,* I silently tell the air.

The wall of rock rises higher still.

"I'm going to find out what they want," I say.

"Ara, you can't go by yourself."

"So come with me." Ry's eyes dart between me and the ships. "I'll keep us shielded the entire time."

"I do *not* need you to protect me."

"We're family! We protect each other."

With a resigned sigh, he rolls his shoulders back. "Let's go."

The sea churns below as I float us to the flagship. "What are you doing?" I ask.

"Being ready for any eventuality."

Hopefully, whatever he's preparing on the seafloor won't be necessary. Sailors back away as we approach, watching us wearily. I set us onto the deck like we own it. Penum will not come into our kingdom and see us cowed.

"We are the Prince and Princess of Alchos." Rylan's voice carries all the gravity of his position, even through the shield I have us wrapped in. "Who commands this fleet?"

"I do." A man steps out in full regalia, his burgundy cloak billowing behind him from the obsidian clasps at his shoulders, the black leather of his boots polished to a high sheen. "I am King Kirnon of Penum." The King himself—the one meant to marry our mother. His sharp sneer makes the hair on the back of my neck stand erect. Now, I'm even more grateful that she found her way out of that betrothal to marry her friend who has made such a loving father.

"It is unusual for a king to travel with such an escort into a foreign land." Rylan avoids threatening him for now.

"When the foreign land is protected by dark magic, one must take precautions."

Waves roil, jostling the ship, and I don't have to look at my brother to confirm that a quake shook it up under us. "We do not possess *dark* magic," I say.

"With that opinion, it is rather daring of you to venture here uninvited and unannounced." Well, Rylan didn't *open* with a threat.

"Indeed it is," Kirnon agrees. "However, if ever there was a time to have a chance against you, it is now, with the powers divided as they are and your military scattered."

I strengthen the shield around us. The troops sent to secure the border after our mess out there wouldn't have been right here anyway, but now, they're twice as far. "Was it your doing? Drawing our forces to Lambridge?"

The King grins, laughter in his eyes. "No, you did that."

"But you attempted it to begin with!" My chest heaves. Of course it was our doing; we are the ones who wreaked havoc out there, but it came of the deceptive request.

"Yes, that's true." Kirnon steps to the taffrail leisurely. "I thought you were hindering my plans, but when you created a true reason to militarize the area, it opened up my timeline considerably."

"So, you mean to war with us." Rylan keeps his voice level, even as his shoulders tense.

"I already am."

An arrow flies toward us, and I blow it away into the sea. He can't possibly think it would be so easy. "Your archer has terrible aim. The next one might hit you."

"You will have no further chances," Rylan says. "Another act of aggression will result in the destruction of this fleet."

"There are only two of you," Kirnon says with a smile. "Only *half* the power of Alchos. Less, I suppose, if your witch of a queen still wields some." We've always said Penum is jealous of our magic, but this is personal. Is this how Jamys would have spoken of me someday after I jilted him?

The nearest ship shudders and creaks, then a sea stack springs from the sea, splitting it in half. The explosive sounds of boards and beams breaking are accented by screams from the crew as the bow slides into the sea. The stern is pulled up with the land until it loses balance and goes crashing down on the other side.

Rylan's glare doesn't leave the King. "I shall be merciful and allow the rest of your ships to leave my shores. Do so immediately, and there won't be any further loss of life."

Kirnon's smile is foxlike. "If only."

Another pointless arrow makes its way toward us, only to be redirected into the arm of another Penuman sailor. I lift the archer off the ship and throw him into the sea. "I do hope he is a better swimmer than archer." Despite my confident rhetoric, a tingling runs up my back—using my magic violently again grips my heart in a vice. Kirnon can't possibly think to accomplish anything this way when Rylan can take out a ship without lifting a finger.

I raise us up off the ship. "Do not force us to destroy you."

Rylan and I are well above the ship now, and someone calls out, "Spotted!"

"Fire," the King responds.

Two booms announce cannonballs being shot into the air. I block the one heading toward us, hurling it through the deck of another ship. Another sails past us, and I drop it into the sea. I had been joking about the archer's aim, but this shot really was— I look in the direction it was headed to see Nina and Marcus at the cliff's edge.

Chapter Fifty-Two

Angering the twins is a dangerous idea.

People think we are godlike already. Nina and Marcus at the cliff's edge, fury raging, could be a painting of wrathful gods: flawless beauty, exquisite finery, and power beyond imagination.

A wave pushes away from the cliff, growing in speed and size as it approaches the fleet. It not only crashes into the first ship, it curls around it, pummeling it as it sucks it down into the depths. Another ship erupts in flames. The screams are horrid. Again, a ship is raised from the sea and destroyed. My siblings will lay waste to thousands this way.

"Rylan, stop!" I fling domes over ships as quickly as possible. Another wave sets upon a ship but splatters out against my shield.

"Ara, what are you doing?" Rylan stretches his arm toward another ship, but I push it away on a gale. The outcropping of rock merely sends it jostling in the waves.

"We cannot kill them all!"

Nina and Marcus ride out to us on a swell of seawater. "And why not?" Marcus calls out.

I lower us to them. "If we do, we are the monsters they fear us to be."

"It is our duty to protect our kingdom," Nina says.

"They haven't attacked Alchos, only us."

"Then clearly, they don't fear us as much as they should." Fire dances in her eyes.

"We should send them away," I say.

"Giving them another opportunity to attack us?" Rylan crosses his arms. "Next time could be in the capital. Our people could be caught in the middle of it."

A cannon fires at us. I throw wind at the projectile, but it continues toward us. *I missed?*

"Look out!"

With no room to spare, we dive out of the way. Underwater, I stare at my hands in disbelief. I pull bubbles from around me, surrounding my head in air and gulping it down. The air in the water calls out to me. I feel it as if it were an extension of myself. So how did I miss? I never miss.

I swallow back my nerves and kick to the surface. The others are already huddled together, and Nina is the first to address me. "Why didn't you shield us from it? That's *what you do!*"

"It was too fast."

"Nothing is too fast for you." Marcus' brows furrow.

A ship speeds toward us. "They can't be serious." Ry looks toward one of his new rocky hills, and the top rips off with a deafening roar. It soars toward its target, or rather, us.

"Rylan!" I scream out as I throw a shield around us. The boulder shatters against it, sending a shockwave straight through to my bones.

This ship still approaches us. A towering wave launches us out of the way together, and we all go tumbling under the water again. We rise gasping for air.

"What is wrong with you?" Nina is the first to criticize again.

Rylan's chest heaves, and his jaw quivers. "I don't know how that happened. It was as if the ship wasn't where it was supposed to be."

"Your *aim* wasn't where it was supposed to be! You nearly killed us!" Nina rolls a fireball in her hands and flings it at the passing ship, except when it should hit the ship, the ship is farther along and safe. The fireball steams as it falls into the water, and Nina's jaw drops.

"Do you see what I mean?" Rylan splashes her out of her shock.

A breath shudders out of me. "How are they doing that?"

"Is that why you didn't block the cannonball?" Marcus asks.

"Yes. I threw my power out at it, but I missed."

"I'm still holding us up here, though." Yes, the water is holding us at the surface without any effort on our end. "Could they have found a way to thwart your powers?"

"Don't assume it's only *ours*." Nina holds up a flaming hand. "Note we still *have* magic."

"It figures that Kirnon had some way to fight us," I say. "He wouldn't come here without a viable weapon against us."

"Let's go finish our conversation with him then." Rylan looks at Marcus and me. "Can you two bring us to his ship from below?"

"Wait." I look up at the cliff where people are arriving. Mother, Father, and Tomas are at the forefront, a crowd gathering behind them. When it was only the inexplicable presence of the Penuman fleet, I wanted Mother and Father to be here, but now, it's too dangerous. Even the four of us are struggling to hold our own, and I wish there wasn't anyone else here to worry about. I squeeze my eyes closed, focusing my power on creating a wall to protect them. A cyclone forms as I pull as much air as possible to create a strong shield.

"All right. Let's go." My eyes remain on Tomas as I wrap us in a bubble. *Please stay safe, my love.* "Go ahead, Marcus." We sink below the waves and push through the sea.

"He'd have beaten us here," Nina says, understanding my hesitation, "if we hadn't glided out on an impromptu river."

"This isn't the time." I look through our shield and the turquoise waters at the hulls of so many ships that have come for us.

"You terrified him with that message, you know." Nina's timing is determined to be terrible.

My heart wrenches for all the stress Tomas and I are putting on each other. He's got to be frantic, but I can't be distracted by him right now. "Well, it worked. It got you here."

"Yes, thank you for dragging us into what has already nearly killed us multiple times."

"Enough," Rylan says. "Save your aggression for Kirnon."

"And if he can manipulate our powers?" Marcus asks.

Is it our powers? It seems like space itself is being contorted—nothing where it seems, our perception betraying us. Mine is working just fine to keep us dry and breathing, and Marcus doesn't seem to have a problem directing us under this fluid battlefield.

"Then we kill him." Rylan looks resolute. Calm. Perhaps he would be a good king. I feel as though I'm going to be sick.

I reach out to feel the shield at the cliff. *Still there. Good.* I can focus on the task at hand if I know they're safe.

"That one," Ry says, pointing to the bottom of the largest ship in the fleet.

"How are we doing this?" Marcus asks.

"Nina," I say, "if I can get you a dry spot, can you burn through it?"

"Of course."

I open the bubble against the hull, pushing it out to give us space. Nina sloshes over in her drenched gown and presses her hands to it. Smoke sizzles from the contact. The wood dries, blackens, and crumbles away in smoldering ash. She expands her hands out until we have a hole large enough to climb through.

"Well done." Ry is the first through.

I'm last. I dissolve the waterproof barrier behind me, and the sea starts pouring in around barrels. Perhaps this will distract them from us. We pass through the cargo hold and start up the stairs. Two decks up, a sound catches our attention.

"I assure you they are not dead," a voice says from the other side of a closed door.

We slow and creep close enough to hear while remaining hidden around a corner. My siblings pack together, leaning against each other, and I pull a current of air from under the door to drive the sounds to me.

"They are gone." Kirnon sounds agitated. Poor thing.

"They'll be back." This unknown voice is silky and polished. "They've seen a glimpse of our defenses. People used to having ultimate power do not walk away from something that may take it away."

We glance between each other, silent conversations that probably wouldn't be any more coherent if they were out loud passing in familiar looks. I know most of them to mean profanities.

"You maintain your end of the bargain. Keep the devils occupied, guarantee my safety, and they're yours."

"Don't fret." The confidence in that voice chills my bones. "I'll keep you protected, as promised."

A door shuts, and one set of steps march up the stairs. Nina peeks around to watch.

I wrap us in a soundproof shield. "We need to get that man."

"We also need the King," Rylan says. "There are four of us. Two of us can take Kirnon. Two can get this person."

"I want the King," Nina says. "He went up."

"With me then." Rylan and Nina continue up the stairs—gone before I can think it through.

"Come, Marcus. We're shielded." I slide a barrier under the door, just like I did on Rylan's birthday. Then, it was to surprise him—fun and laughs. So much has changed between us since then, and now I use these tricks against true enemies who would see our family destroyed. Mother said the end of her betrothal to Kirnon was catastrophic, but this seems an extreme reaction.

I open the door slowly and step through, holding my breath. My brothers' insistence on mastering swords doesn't seem so ridiculous at the moment. Having a blade to hold before me would be a comfort. The empty sheath at my hip gives me a sense of longing—both that dagger and its true owner would give me some of the confidence I'd like to have right now. I'm glad Tomas isn't here to face whatever dangers we might find, though.

The cabin is dusty and stale, but empty. A small window illuminates floating dust motes while leaving the space shrouded in shadows. There doesn't appear to be any way out.

"How could he have left?" Marcus asks.

"I don't know."

He walks the perimeter of the room to see if there is anything we've missed.

A large desk is covered in dusty tomes. I open one, but the language is unfamiliar to me, the letters like nothing I've seen before.

"I suppose royals assume they can pop into any place they please."

I gasp as my attention pops up to the man with the silky voice. Marcus stiffens on the opposite side of the room. This man appeared right between us. His long, black robe is simple, covering him from the neck down. Only papery hands with long fingers stick out from the wide sleeves. His face is as smooth as his voice, with eyes that appear to glow in the dim lighting.

"Who are you?" Marcus asks.

"My names are long forgotten." His gaze shifts between us. "So much forgotten." He seems to shake himself out of a reverie. "You may call me Aevus."

"How did you do that?" I ask.

"What?"

"Appear out of nowhere." Marcus sidesteps along the wall, keeping his distance from the man while trying to reunite with me.

"I did no such thing." Aevus' smile sends a chill up my spine. "Reality is an ever-fluctuating thing. I'd say I don't have time to explain it, but I have all the time in the world. It fluctuates as well, you see."

"Time..." The false investigators in Lambridge spoke of time pulling. "You were in Lambridge. You manipulated time there."

"Yes, and Kirnon thinks he's quite clever to know how to trace it." So, it was Kirnon's men looking for information there.

Marcus continues around the room, step by slow step. "He's clever enough to keep you working for him."

"I do not answer to any mortal. Our interests align currently, so we've formed a partnership of convenience." *Any mortal?* As if he isn't?

"How convenient," I say, "to come across someone who also wants us destroyed."

His pale eyes rake down me like I'm a dessert he can't wait to devour. "You aren't my goal, though my intentions could change. In the meantime, you make delightful bait."

His words succeed in making me feel insignificant. "Are you after our mother? That would be Kirnon's dirty work to a T." No matter how much his gaze makes my skin crawl, I'd rather keep his focus on me. Numbers might be our only advantage. I wrap Marcus in a soundproof shield to better keep the attention off him.

"If I cared about your magic's former home, I'd simply turn the Queen's clock back."

My face must betray my bewilderment, because his eyes glitter at the change in me. Her clock. The ticking of time has taken her magic and given it to us. If it went backwards… The idea that my magic could be taken from me leaves me feeling hollow. This isn't about me, though. My own power can't be my focus, as it clearly isn't his. "What did you do in Lambridge to draw Kirnon's attention? They were looking for multiple people—an old woman who was around when the boy disappeared, a man who visited the brothel—"

"It shouldn't surprise me that my words aren't the kind of distractions to draw *your* attention." In a blink, he goes from halfway across the small room to our noses nearly touching. I gasp but steel myself to minimize my reaction. "What is it about you?" He raises his hand to brush my cheek, his fingertip a feather on my face before I swat him away.

"Do not touch me." Marcus' silenced fury catches my attention from my periphery, but I hold him in place. My eyes never leave the unearthly pale ones before me. "What did you do in Lambridge?"

"Mystical, but not particularly clever." Aevus frowns and backs away slightly.

My head and heart are spinning too much for me to guess what I should have been able to deduce.

"All of the *people* Kirnon was looking for were one—me." He steps back and shrinks into the form of an old woman. *Dark magic.* In another blink he becomes an average looking man with a dark beard. This isn't possible, but didn't the fake investigators say she could change form? There was so much going on that night, I'd forgotten. Seeing the change back to his original state brings it to the forefront of my mind. This might not even be his natural form. He could look like anyone. "I am the best thing that happened to those people. Who wouldn't want a new chance at life? A fresh start without a shattered knee, without the ailments of old age, or the sad life of a whore."

Richard was nearly right. It wasn't a witch who took those people—it was whatever this person is. He shape-shifts and plays with time as if it's a toy. Kirnon didn't come in a foolish, suicidal attempt at all. This is more than we can hope to conquer.

"They helped me find something of mine, so I gave them new life. To be raised from infancy again, loved and cared for, is a gift."

The babies in Brasport. Two boys and a girl, the same as our missing people from Lambridge. I'm such an idiot not to have seen it. Not that such magic could have ever occurred to me. "You turned back time for them? Could..."

His eyes sparkle. He looks so much younger than his words suggest he is. Logical if he can manipulate time and his form. "Do you have a request for me?"

It's not a request. He wouldn't do anything for me, but the question comes out anyway. I just want to know if it's possible. "Can you bring someone back from the dead?"

"In the right circumstances." He drums long fingers on his arm. "Not after any significant time has passed." His glare takes a cruel edge. "Nor when the cause of death is magic."

My heart jumps up to my throat. "You killed Jamys?"

"Not at all."

As if I'd take his word for it. He may have murdered Jamys. There was no evidence of how he died... But Jamys is a lost cause.

If I can learn anything about the situation with our people in Lambridge, this may still prove useful. "What did the people help you with before you rewound their lives?" Apparently, he has no issue with me knowing these secrets we've chased for months. If surprising me is enjoyable, I'll let him keep doing it until I understand everything.

"No, this is where my stories end for you, Princess."

Or not. "Fine. I don't need to know why you're attacking us to destroy you over it."

"I've not attacked you."

"You manipulated our powers." I push Marcus' hands up to ready him. At least that still works.

"Not at all." The man arches an eyebrow. "Perhaps you're losing your abilities."

My eyes narrow at Aevus' barb. My abilities brought me here to stop him, and that's exactly what I'm going to do.

I dissolve the shield around Marcus, who sneers as he says, "Let's test that, shall we?" His hands flick out in front of him, but no water splashes anywhere. Has this man stopped Marcus from—

Pain sears through my lungs. I cry out, but it comes out as a gurgling wince. I pull air into the bottom of my lungs, and water comes pushing out in coughs.

"Ara!" Marcus rushes to grasp me as I double over. The pain subsides, and I heave breaths. "What did you do?" Marcus demands of Aevus who is now leaning casually across the far wall.

"No, what did *you* do?"

He springs to his feet. "I did that to *you!* Not her!"

"But what if I was never here?" He vanishes.

Marcus drops back down to me. "Are you all right?" He lays his hand on my back, and an odd prickling sensation spreads through my chest.

"What are you doing?"

"Making sure all the water is out of your lungs."

I look at him wide-eyed.

"I'm so sorry. It was aimed at *him*, but then where he seemed to be, you were instead. I don't understand how it happened, but I am so, so sorry."

I allow myself one more deep breath before I rise to my feet, Marcus supporting me as I regain my composure. "Well, at least this mess is improving your ability to apologize."

He shakes his head incredulously. "Are you sure you're well?"

"Yes, but if this man can make us believe we're attacking someone else when we are in fact attacking each other, our strategy needs to change."

"What can we do?"

Chapter Fifty-Three

"Do *not* engage," I say as we race up the stairs—a task made more difficult by the jerking of the ship. "We get Nina and Rylan, and we get a safe distance away."

"I *remember*, Ara."

"Can you blame me for being concerned about your ability to *think* before you attack?" Phantom pain puddles in the bottom of my lungs like a shadow.

Marcus doesn't bother with excuses as we reach the trembling deck. Nina dives out of the way of a boulder. The sea floor juts up in sharp crags, and Rylan lets out an infuriated roar. His tunic is all but gone, the remaining scraps burnt at the edges. I lift them both up off the ship, levitating Marcus and myself to meet them. Nina's jaw clenches as she glares at me, but her heaving shoulders tell me she needs a break. Rylan plants his hands on his hips, resigned to my interruption.

"This isn't working," I say when we are high enough to be safe.

Nina rolls her eyes. "Your true power lies in observation."

"Nothing and no one are where they appear to be." Rylan pushes his ruffled hair back from his face.

"Kirnon has some kind of sorcerer who manipulates time and reality." My words do not result in questions of my sanity, so I continue. "Anything requiring precision will fail. So, we clear the entire area. Use large scale forces." They all look at me, and a weight settles over me. It's a weight I can manage. "If we work together, we are unstoppable."

Ry presses his lips together and turns to Nina. "You have all the fire magic, right?"

"Yes."

My eyes snap wider, but I don't have time to ask.

"Good," he says. "Nina and I can attack from underneath them. Can the two of you hit them from above?"

Marcus and I nod.

Ry looks at Nina again. "Let me show you a different source of fire." Nina's face scrunches in a confused look as one of the crags in the middle of the fleet rises higher. "Ara, drop us there."

"Be careful." I wrap them in a hefty shield and push them to their destination. When they land, a tunnel opens, and they disappear into it before it seals behind them. I hope he knows what he's doing.

"Ah, the two middle children left unattended." Marcus' eyes gleam.

"Are you ready to make trouble?"

"Absolutely." He stretches his arms out to the sides, like a falcon spreading its wings in the moment before it dives at its prey. His hands ball into fists and come together before him.

This vantage point offers a spectacular and terrifying view as the sea churns on either side of the watery battlefield. Towering waves build and crash in, pushing ships into each other and toward the center. The groaning of lumber sounds like the ships are crying. I pull a gale down along the shield at the cliff face to keep them back, but— *Dead gods, take me.* Tomas is climbing down.

I bring Marcus with me. My powers are stretched thin enough. Tomas clings to the rock face as the wind tears down around him. I shield him from above and pull him up and away from his horrifying descent. "What are you doing?" I demand as we all converge.

"You sent me a message *in your blood!* Did you think I'd stay behind your damned wall?"

"How did you get past it?"

Marcus interrupts. "Is there perhaps another time you might do this?"

There are so many things I could say to Tomas, but Marcus is right. This isn't the time.

"Is Kirnon here?" Tomas asks.

"Yes," we say together.

"Put me on his ship."

I gape at him. "Absolutely not." My winds push ships away from our coastline, and Marcus' currents push in from the sides. The fleet is bunched together—battered and breaking, some sinking. They crash into each other and the outcroppings of rocks Rylan had raised. The King's flagship at the center pushes up against the crag Rylan and Nina entered.

"What the hell am I supposed to be able to do from up here?"

Before I can tell Tomas that I'd be *more than happy* to return him to the other side of the barrier, because all I *want* him to do is remain safe, the rocks Ry and Nina disappeared into begin to quake. All the ships reverberate. With the sound of a thousand falling trees, the peak collapses in on itself. Smoke and steam rise out of it, then it explodes.

I turn away to guard my eyes from the sudden flash of light. Tomas shields me with his body, and when I turn back to peek past him, flaming rocks the size of horses are flying through the air, pummeling ships. Fires blaze, but the crackling of wood doesn't drown out the screams. I draw back in horror into Tomas' chest. His arms tight around me provide the clarity I've been needing all day.

"Nina is *in* that!" Marcus wails.

"Rylan will keep her safe." Tomas' voice is flat, distant.

The masts of the flagship crack and drop into the deck, collapsing the ship in on itself. Fires on it extinguish as it sinks into the raging sea. I suppose we've won—Kirnon and his magic wielder are no more. Still, the onslaught of molten earth rages on.

"I've got to stop this."

"We don't have to stop anything." Marcus whirls on me. "They came here and started this. They are a danger even to *us*. Elimination is the only option."

Tomas releases me to stand my own ground while I address my brother. Not that we're standing on the ground, but... "Kirnon started this, and that *wizard* was the danger. They are on their way to the bottom of the sea. The rest do not need to suffer the same fate. Put out the fires, Marcus."

He clenches his jaw, but water rains down on one ship after another, turning fires into steam and smoke. I push a couple of ships from the outskirts away from the destruction and move people onto them. Survivors are going to be few and far between with this volcano continuing to fire, though.

"Tomas, would you *please* wait for me on land? I need all my concentration."

He sighs. "Please be careful."

I remove my love and my brother to the top of the cliff and fly higher, directly above the volcano. The heat is enough to melt the flesh from my bones. I take a deep breath and pull a cold wind to build a bubble around it. Each strike of flaming earth cuts to my nerves, and I grit my teeth against the pain. I continue my chore of removing people to safety; it won't help them much if I drop them into the sea, though. My strength diminishes with each hit against my shield, and it shudders as I struggle to catch my breath.

Rylan and Nina's powers combine into this horrifying spectacle, and I don't know if mine are enough to hold it back.

Ships aren't being hit anymore, so I give up the rescue. Men are arranging their own evacuations, and the shield pushing against this gash in the earth takes all my effort. The pressure building against it takes my breath away, but I've almost got it capped.

It looks like a window straight into hell.

I picture my containment of Rylan's growth through the ground and Nina's fire in a bubble during her training. My magic can do this. It can calm the other powers and end this battle.

I make one last push and feel myself falling before I lose my grip on consciousness.

CHAPTER FIFTY-FOUR

The familiar rocking of a slow horseback ride makes me want to continue sleeping. Warmth and the secure hold around me could keep me content. But there are other things I need to know. Did everyone make it? What happened? Who is holding me now? No, I know the answer to the last one. I'd know him anywhere.

I take a deep breath and blink my eyes open. Sky blue eyes meet mine, and Tomas pulls me in a little tighter. "How are you feeling?"

"Tired. Confused."

"Sleep then. The rest will keep."

I shake my head, which feels much like nuzzling against him. "Did Rylan and Nina get out?" I stretch my neck to see behind him. We're in a narrow path through the woods. There are more riders a distance away behind us and a good deal ahead of us. I almost ask why they're so far, then I feel it—a gently breathing shield around us. Magic has gifted us some privacy yet again.

"Yes. They are alive and well."

"How am I alive?" I was so high up when I dropped. And over a molten inferno.

Tomas tenses. "You didn't fall long. It *felt* eternal, but the wind caught you and carried you to me."

"My petulant element does seem to prefer you to all others."

"It does its best to keep us both alive." His eyes glisten. "I'd have died too. If you had fallen into…"

I wipe my thumb across his cheek where a tear rolls down. The sight is enough to make my heart rattle. "Tomas…"

He lets out a shaky breath. "I thought I'd lost you."

"You haven't."

"I could have, and you'd have died with the absurd belief that you aren't everything I want in this entire world."

My throat tightens.

"Bell, I thought you knew." Everything that went unspoken the last time we made love comes rushing back to me. It wasn't all in my imagination. That adoration I felt from him was real. It *is* real.

"I thought so, but there was so much uncertainty, all the back and forth."

He transfers the reins to the hand near my thigh and uses his free one to brush hair away from my face. "The words don't feel like enough, but I love you. I've been so hopelessly in love with you, I thought it might kill me. And I wouldn't have minded death, for I'd lived a better life than anyone could dream of just to have held you, heard your laugh. I've felt your power, and it has nothing to do with magic. It's you."

My face crumples, and I pull his in to hide it. There, with the steady rocking and thumping of hoofbeats, my lips endeavor to express what words can hardly say. Then I pull away from our kiss to say them. "I love you, Tomas. I can't imagine a life without you."

"Then don't. Marry me."

A smile pulls my cheeks so hard, my eyes water—or perhaps they're tears of joy. "Aren't you meant to ask that?"

"If I form it as a question, it will likely take on the tone of begging, but if that is what you want from me…"

"No." A breathy laugh spills out of me. "I don't care how you say it. I've wanted to hear those words from you too long to worry about technicalities."

"I should have said it that night at Etherlee. I knew it from the moment we kissed."

The image of water rushing in over us flashes through my mind. "Well, that moment was rather ruined anyway."

"That moment was perfect."

There is so much more I need to know, but this is enough for now. To never again have to pretend I'm not in love with him, to know we will never let anything come between us… that's all I need.

The rest of the ride is quiet. I'm wrung out in every way possible, and nothing feels terribly urgent anymore now that Tomas and I know where we stand.

Within the palace gates, stable hands put horses away. My siblings and the Coyles walk inside, but Jo's neck is craned back to watch us return. She smiles at me before her mother pulls her along. We come to a stop, and my attention shifts as Father takes my hand to help me down. He wraps me in an embrace, mumbling worried whispers into my hair.

"I'm fine, truly."

Another layer of pressure wraps around me from the side. "Arabella." Mother sighs. "You gave us a terrible fright."

They both release me, and I blush under their loving scrutiny. "There's no harm done to me, but Kirnon—"

"We'll discuss all that," Mother says. "Let us freshen up, and we'll all meet in the lounge."

I look down at my disheveled, damp, blood-stained tunic and leggings. A bath would be heavenly.

Mother clears her throat. "To avoid speaking out of turn and making things uncomfortable, I'd like to confirm..." She glances at Tomas and back to me. "Do I have a betrothal to announce?"

Tomas steps forward and bows. "If it pleases Your Grace, your blessing of our marriage would mean the world to us." Hearing him speak of us as a singular unit makes my stomach flutter. When he didn't pose it as a question to me, I teased him. However, stating it as a matter of fact to my parents is so perfectly fortifying I could jump into his arms again now. We shall be one. Forever.

"Excellent." Mother's smile is as warm as I've ever seen it. "Alchos could not ask for a better king."

My jaw drops. "What?"

"You'll be queen someday, dear. That makes your husband—"

"But how am I the heir? The trial was interrupted at best. At worst, I lost."

"You completed a trial far graver than anything I could have arranged. You faced danger to yourself and our kingdom with selfless bravery. You sought out support rather than trying to manage on your own and showed compassion to our enemies. You displayed everything we need in a ruler."

Tears well up, and my head and shoulders drop forward. It doesn't feel real. In a song or a story, this would be a more glamorous moment. Instead, I'm rundown and ragged as I become the heir of Alchos and the happiest bride-to-be.

Steamy water soothes my body, but relaxation allows my mind to wander to places I don't want to go. Lucy asks questions about the day's events, and I answer absentmindedly. *Queen Arabella and King Tomas.* My eyes sting, but *why?* This was what I wanted.

Lucy finishes combing out the filthy mess of my hair. "Well, thank the gods the King is dead."

"He's what?" The words startle me out of my reverie.

"Down with his ship."

Oh, Kirnon. Not my husband, the future King of Alchos. *Oh, gods.* The thought is overwhelming. "Yes. Of course. I'm sorry, I'm having a difficult time processing it all. Is that floral dress back from the seamstress?"

"I believe it was being pressed. Would you like me to get it?"

"Yes please."

"Certainly. I'll be back shortly."

"Take your time." Time alone is the very reason I sent her for a dress I knew wasn't here. Alone, I get out of the bath and wrap a thick dressing gown around myself. I pull warm air through my hair as I step into my sitting room for a sip of wine. Upon entering the room, I'm taken aback by Tomas' presence. He seems to already have found a place to clean up and change.

"You can't be here." It's true, though seeing him has the immediate effect of making me smile.

"Because you aren't dressed?"

"Precisely."

His gaze scrapes down me, as if he can see through the dressing gown. "You're far more dressed than I'd prefer." He closes the distance between us with a few strides.

"My maid will be back any minute."

"I believe she is supposed to keep your secrets." His arms slink around my waist, and mine drape behind his neck on impulse. "And soon you'll be my wife. Then it won't matter." He kisses me slowly, intimately, and my core melts. This is everything I want, yet...

"Tomas." I swallow back the dread of my next words, but they must be spoken. "It hasn't been announced yet. Are you certain you wish to marry me? Now that I'm heir to the throne?"

He draws back. "Are you joking? Why wouldn't I want to marry you?"

"Because I won't be able to give you my entire heart." His brow furrows, and I hate myself for being the cause of his consternation. "As queen, I must put the kingdom above all. I'll belong to the people, not just you, no matter how much I love you. It will be a terrible burden for you, and it must be more than you expected when you first started to love me."

His expression softens as he combs his fingers into my damp hair to settle his hand at the base of my skull. "Bell, my love—" Heat blooms in my cheeks, and he smirks. "Do you like me calling you that?"

"Of course."

"Well, my love, I would take on any burden to be with you, however I don't consider this to be one. I love Alchos as well, and it will be an honor to serve as consort. Furthermore, I know how dedicated you will be. You'll make sure everyone is taken care of, and it will be my pleasure to ensure that *you* are taken care of."

Tears sting my eyes again, but the only overwhelming feeling is how much I love this man. "Thank you." It's a scarcely audible whisper, but I hope he knows how deeply grateful I am.

His kiss is tender and sweet. Being certain his attachment to me isn't only physical makes me want him more than ever. I press myself against him, kissing him desperately, when a gasp and the sound of the door shutting splits us apart.

"Oh my." I cover a giggle I can't contain. "I told you!"

His smirk paints his face with amusement and adoration. "You ignored your own rules."

I go to the door to find Lucy standing in the hall, dutifully staring at nothing on the opposite wall. "I can manage this myself," I say as I take the dress from her. "I've been terribly demanding of you. You should go have a cup of tea."

"Thank you, Your Grace."

She walks away, and I reenter my rooms to shake my head at Tomas. "You have to help me into this now."

"Putting a dress *on* you is in direct contrast to my intentions."

I hang up the dress before it turns into a wrinkled pile on the floor. "And what are your intentions?" I ask with my back to him.

The air buzzes between us as he comes up behind me. His arms encircle me, and hands trace down my chest, opening the dressing gown on their journey down my body. The trail seared down me in the wake of his touch ends just short of the ache building for him. He pulls the dressing gown past my shoulders, letting it drop around my feet. My heartbeat pounds up my neck and through my ears as the sounds of his boots dropping to the floor and the rustling of his shirt brushing off him make me squirm. The warmth of his bare chest presses against my back, and I drop my head against him with a soft moan.

"Please don't make me wait any longer."

He spins me around so we are chest to chest. "Yes, my queen."

"Not yet."

"You've *always* been my queen."

Chapter Fifty-Five

"What happened here?" I brush my fingers over a fresh pink scar on his shoulder. Even if every bit of his body weren't imprinted in my memory, this injury the size of my hand could never go unnoticed.

Tomas shakes his head, sinking farther into the pillow. "Helping Nina had its risks."

"She did this?"

"Don't go trying to avenge me. It was mostly accidental."

I roll my eyes. "When did it happen?"

"When she came to Highbluff to train."

I prop my head up on my hand, and Tomas' gaze flickers to my bare chest for a second. "Was that why you wouldn't see me that day? Marcus made it sound like you wanted nothing to do with me."

He shakes his head. "Marcus' communication skills are lacking."

"I couldn't even see Jo! I thought you both hated me."

"She was tending to this." He tips his chin toward the healing burn. "And fighting with Nina."

I rest my head on him again. "I can't believe you didn't tell me about the possible betrothal."

"It would have been fairly hypocritical to ask you to help Nina after I disapproved of your plan to help Rylan. Furthermore, that marriage never would have come to pass. I'd have found a way out of it." He wraps his arms tighter around me.

"Why weren't you this adamant about fighting my betrothal?"

Fingertips slide over the bumps of my spine. "We'd only had one night. We hadn't talked about it at all. For you, it could have simply been a night of passion." His hand stops rubbing my back, and his fingertips press into me. "I... wasn't brave enough to suggest we were more than that, not as unsure as I was of your thoughts."

I kiss his chest and look up at him. "I can't really fault you for that, since I had the same problem."

The idea that either of us could have married other people is so ridiculous now. Nothing could have kept us apart. But we do have to take brief interludes from each other.

It's an exercise in self-control to drag myself away from Tomas. I want nothing more than to remain here, wrapped in his arms, but this is what we're agreeing to—there will always be a job to be done. He doesn't complain as I stand, but still I feel the need to make an excuse. "We're keeping everyone waiting."

"It's only our families, and you did have a rather close brush with death today. I don't think they'll be impatient."

Only our families, as if our families aren't the two most powerful in the kingdom. His lightheartedness draws a small smile from me. He'll keep things in perspective for me. "Fine, but what shall your excuse be?" I go to my vanity and sit on the velvet-cushioned stool as Tomas flings his legs over the side of the bed.

"I had a tiring day as well," he says as he pulls trousers on.

My hand clenches into a fist for a breath before I relax it to grasp my hairbrush. "How did you get past my shield?" I do my best to sound carefree as I pull the brush through my hair, as if this is a typical chat and not something that terrified me on several levels.

"I cut through it."

I freeze. "What?"

Ever so gently, he takes the brush from my hand and takes over the task. "The dagger. It pierced a shield once, so I tried it again."

"You knew the dagger did that?"

"Yes. You're a terrible liar." He continues brushing my hair, a small way to make good on his promise to take care of me.

"I don't know if I should be concerned about that dagger or you having some power we are unaware of."

"Your magic has thwarted your commands in favor of your subconscious needs before." He shrugs. "We can further examine the dagger if you wish, but perhaps you could refrain from putting me behind a wall again?"

My shoulders and chin drop. "I needed to know you were safe." The soothing feel of my hair being brushed stops.

He turns me toward him and kneels before me. "I'll not stand by and watch as you take on the world. I'm going to be by your side."

I press my lips together. "But you're my greatest weakness. I only lose control of my power with you."

The moment the words leave me, I worry I've offended him, but one side of his mouth tips up in a smirk. "You're usually so intelligent."

I cross my arms with a huff. Obviously, acknowledging our love will not stop him from teasing me ruthlessly. "Perhaps you thwart my power *and* make me stupid."

"I'm not capable of either." He kisses me softly, but I keep my frown in place, which amuses him. "I make you stronger, you ridiculous woman. Or have you forgotten that it was with me that you came into your full power?"

I open my mouth, but my retort is lost before I can form it.

"Hurry up." Tomas pulls his shirt on. "We are keeping everyone waiting."

Someday, it will be commonplace for us to get ready together, but right now it's a delight. Just like how I've come to appreciate all the ways Tomas and I need each other for more than physical pleasure, the idea of all our routines happening together feels both exciting and peaceful.

He leaves ahead of me in an attempt to mask the reason for our tardiness, and I take one last look at my reflection before making my way down. It's hard to imagine that the girl in the mirror can rule a kingdom, but others see it. Perhaps I'll come to as well.

When my feet reach the floor at the bottom of the stairs, I'm nearly startled back up into the air. Grandmother's demure smile gives away nothing, but I hope Tomas took a different way down. There are some things I don't need my grandmother to know.

"Arabella, dear, it seems I must corner you if I'm ever to have an audience, and you aren't even queen yet."

"I'm terribly sorry. I've been so very busy with all the madness going on."

"Of course you have." She loops her arm through mine, and we make our way to the lounge. "And avoiding me between it all."

"I have not been *avoiding* you."

"Sweetheart, I've been in this world too long not to recognize such things." Her hand is warm when we stop at the door, and she wraps it around mine. "You didn't want my advice on becoming a queen consort, and I won't presume to give you any about being sovereign, though I've given your mother and grandfather enough. It's probably of more importance now that you're coming into a position you never expected." She squeezes my hand. "Don't suppose that since Rylan was born first he was *meant* to rule. We are all born the same—helpless, noisy little things. Despite birth being the primary, if not sole, condition to be crowned, I do not believe anyone is truly born to rule. We are born to grow into whomsoever we are meant to be, and you, dear, have grown into a young woman who will do great things."

My eyes prickle, but she guides me in before I can respond. Though Mother selected a casual location, this discussion will be anything but. In the lounge sit my parents, grandparents, and siblings, alongside the four Coyles. Where Tomas' presence used to put me on edge, he now brings me comfort. Security is a satisfying new feeling.

Jo comes to greet me with an embrace. "That was terrifying. How are you feeling?"

"I'm well." I would swear my expression gives nothing away, but Jo sighs and rolls her eyes. She knows me too well. And now we're to be sisters. We walk arm in arm to sit with our families.

Mother clears her throat. "Thank you all for being here. Today was trying for all of us, but there are points on which we all need to be clear. Firstly, though the trial was not completed in the way we planned, a trial was certainly had. Arabella displayed everything and more we could ask for and will be crowned heir."

My eyes meet Rylan's. I don't think he's breathing, but he dips his chin toward me. Mother must have told him already. Of course, she'd have to. I'm surprised I didn't feel the palace tremor. Or perhaps if the timing was right, I wouldn't have noticed...

"Out of delicacy and sympathy for our allies in Ceraun, we will not make this next announcement public yet, but..." She turns toward Wymond and Mariana. "Fortunately, our plans hadn't been finalized. It turns out, that was impossible."

Nina masks her delight with a perfectly indifferent expression.

"Tomas and Arabella have received my blessing for their nuptials."

My heart swells as Tomas smiles at me from across the low table, his attention drawn away by his mother when she takes his hand and offers him her own smile. "That sounds like a perfect arrangement," she says.

Congratulations are sprinkled from around the group, and Jo kisses my cheek before hugging me tightly.

"Alchos will have much to celebrate," Mother says. "However, there is also the matter of Penum. Marcus told us of the magic wielded in Lambridge and during today's battle. Kirnon will use anything he can. He will not give up his crusade against us."

My head jerks back. "What? Kirnon and his sorcerer were defeated."

Mother looks at me wide-eyed. "Whatever did you speak of during the ride back?"

Tomas flushes slightly and shifts under his own mother's glare.

"The King's ship got away," Father says. "It wasn't where it appeared to be. It was farther back in the fleet."

All the relief I'd let myself feel is washed away. I'm heir to a kingdom at war. A war I already know I can't fight well in.

"If I hadn't stopped the volcano…"

"No, darling," Father says. "It was too far away. You did not let them go, but you did save the lives of those more innocent."

Mother heaves a breath. "Though they proved formidable, so did we. We are no easy target for them, and they will be cautious in acting against us. They saw your full power—the power shown by all four of you was greater than anything ever seen. You protect us with that legacy as much as with your ability to act in any future conflict. I am so proud of all of you."

The sentiment doesn't pull the dread from my bones.

Apparently, it doesn't for Rylan either. "We cannot sit here and wait for them to rally against us again."

"We won't," Mother says. "Plans for how to proceed will involve more than those in this room."

"The plans should include me going to Penum."

"No." Mother wraps one hand around the other wrist.

"We need to understand their magic." Rylan stands and paces the room. "We cannot prepare without more information."

"And you'll simply go gather information?" Mother knows him too well for that.

"If I can neutralize the threat, all the better."

Her jaw tightens, but it's Father who speaks. "Rylan, this must be handled delicately."

"I can handle it delicately!" Rylan fires out before Father is properly finished. "Though I'll never sit on the throne, this is still my kingdom. As a part of this family, I have a responsibility to Alchos, and Penum is a direct threat to us all. I'm not needed here, so I will go there."

My throat tightens. He doesn't want to be here now that I've taken his place. Guilt threatens to overtake me, but Jo's hand tightens around mine. I have support from so many people I love. It will help, I know, but I don't want my brother to hate me.

"We'll discuss it another time," Mother says. "For now, let us celebrate our victory and all the happy news for our family."

CHAPTER FIFTY-SIX

Dinner passes in a mostly happy blur, certainly much happier than the last time my betrothal was agreed upon. I don't think I spoke during that one. My focus remained steadfastly on keeping a pleasant expression on my face with Jamys and his family around. This time, I can chat with Jo and Tomas' mother without having to feign my excitement to join our families. Nina's glee is obviously selfish, but at least she's happy. Rylan is the only damper on the mood. He's not doing or saying anything to mar the occasion, but his silence grates on the edges of my merriment.

Jo and I walk out together as the Coyles prepare to leave. "Do you know," I say, "when we last spoke, I was so afraid our friendship wouldn't survive if Tomas and I didn't end up together. Of course, I'm glad we're to be married, but the idea that *anything* could come between us is still depressing."

"Well, it seemed the only way you wouldn't be with Tomas was if you broke his heart. I love you, but he's my brother. It would kill me to see that happen to him."

My lips twist to the side. "I was certain it was my heart primed to be broken."

"No, I knew that couldn't happen."

"You might have shared that with me."

"You only ever shared your physical exploits with me," she whispers. "Which was *the last thing* I wanted to know."

I can't help the grin that spreads across my face. "I wish I could tell you more. There are some very fun details..."

"Goodnight, Ara." She hugs me, and I laugh into her. "You're impossible."

"Your brother likes it."

"Because he's also impossible. You're perfect together."

We are, aren't we? "Goodnight, Jo."

She and her parents get into a carriage, and I look around for Tomas. He rounds the corner of the stable with Rylan as his family makes their way toward the gates, leaving him to catch up. Mother takes my arm to lead me back in. "Leave them be, darling. You need your rest."

I nod and go along with her. Out here, it would be impossible to say goodnight to Tomas without winding myself up in desire anyway. I'll see him tomorrow. But inside, I ascend a different tower than the one with my bed. The bridge takes me to the cave, and I float just outside it to watch the Coyles shrink into the distance. My mind wanders over the events of the past day and visions of the future. I'm not sure how long I've been up here, but it seems like I should have seen Tomas leave by now.

"I hope you're happier than the last time you did this."

Oh. That's why. I turn to see my betrothed leaning casually against the railing. "A little."

He smiles at my jest and moves to wrap me in an embrace. I breathe him in, feeling the weight of my responsibilities drift off. Until I remember why he was still here.

"How is Ry?"

"He'll be fine. Disappointed, of course. He might hate me."

I pull back to look at him. "He's not so protective of me to be the *'you better not hurt her'* brother."

"I don't doubt he'd kill me if I did, but that's not his primary concern. I was meant to be his friend, and now, I belong to you over him."

If it were Jo, I suppose I'd feel the same way. He lost a lot today. "Is he really going to go to Penum?"

Tomas' chest rises and falls against me in a sigh. "He wants to."

I shake my head. "Better to die than live with his younger sister as queen?"

"No, Rylan loves himself far too much to willingly walk into death." He rubs my back in slow circles. "I should go."

His kiss melts away any hint of uncertainty and reminds me of another victory I've had today. "Tomas Coyle, that is at least the third time today you've initiated contact with me."

A laugh bubbles through his chest. "You'll be sick of it soon enough. It will be the great challenge of my life to keep my hands off you in public."

I drag my fingertips around his neck to his throat. "It shall be my goal to make that as difficult as possible."

In some ways, we've been together a year, but with our change in circumstances, Tomas and I have a new relationship. We have enough to catch up on to fill the three-day journey to Brasport. He's the one with meaningful connections to the people displaced by the time artificer, but I want to be there to explain to Tosha why we must take two babies from her.

Delaying the announcement about the result of the trials took some convincing, but it was well worth it. This time alone has been invaluable. It took days to clear up every hesitation between us, all the misread motivations. Being overly cautious has been a reoccurring problem for us. As we arrive in Brasport, I'm beyond relieved we can be open with each other from now on.

Lord and Lady Kinrade are gracious hosts again, and we shoulder the sympathies for Jamys' death as gracefully as possible. Tomas' rage over Jamys' misrepresentation was only softened by the fact that Jamys already suffered a fate worse than he deserved. Though the claim that he was killed by magic seems nonsense. If Aevus had been there, why go after Jamys?

Thankfully, there hasn't been much room for negative feelings with us having unrestricted access to each other.

"Are you certain you can't stay longer? You must be exhausted from travel." Cara is especially disappointed that we're leaving after only one night, but I'm sure her staff will prefer us not to extend their uncomfortable task of pretending we don't share a bed. I'm not sure how long I have to "mourn" Jamys before we can be in public together.

"We can't delay reuniting these families," I say. "And we have obligations back in Mirador."

"Yes, of course." She knocks on Tosha's door and steps back. "She's going to be heartbroken."

This is the sad part of the matter, but it's unavoidable.

Tosha opens the door and her eyes light up. "Your Grace, welcome back! It is such a pleasure to see you."

"And you as well." We step into her home, and I gesture to Tomas. "This is Lord Tomas Coyle of Highbluff."

"An honor, my lord." Tosha curtsies.

"The honor is mine," he says. "Princess Arabella has told me of what a wonderful job you're doing with these mysterious infants." I can accept him calling me by my full name in public now, knowing I'll always be Bell to him in private.

Tosha blushes pink. "She is too kind."

Alas, that opinion of me is about to change. I walk over to the babies and smile down at them. "Tosha, I have some bittersweet news for you. We've found the families of the baby boys."

She pales, and her jaw drops. Her eyes flicker between me and the babies she's been loving.

"One of these boys has a grieving mother who has been beside herself over his loss."

Tosha wipes a tear from her eye. She knows that feeling all too well and can't begrudge another woman getting her child back. "And the others?"

"The other boy has a family as well." No need to explain it's his daughter who will be taking him. "When we bring them back, the families will tell us which is which."

"But the girl," Tomas says, "has no family. To be raised with you as her mother would be a blessing for her."

I can't imagine how it feels for him to look upon the face of this woman he knew, now a swaddled babe. We didn't delve into *how well* he knew Emblen—it really doesn't matter—but my curiosity rekindles with them in the same room.

Tosha lifts both boys and hugs them to her chest. As she rocks them and whispers to them, Tomas wraps an arm around me. "She'll have a good life here," I say, looking down at Emblen reborn as Tessa.

"Yes. A much better life." He strokes my arm with his thumb. "I almost wish I had come with you to begin with. Perhaps I'd have recognized them, and we'd have sorted it sooner."

"It only feels that way because you know now. You couldn't have guessed before."

He nods, but the burden remains in his eyes. Tomas takes on so much responsibility for everyone he encounters. He'll make a phenomenal king.

"There, there." Cara takes the boy called Dollin into her arms. "Their families will be forever grateful for the care you've given them."

Tosha nods and kisses Gavan before passing him to me. "What are their real names?"

"George and Parick," Tomas says.

"If it's at all possible for me to ever receive word of how they're doing, I would love that."

"I'm sure that can be arranged." I squeeze her hand, and she looks down at her last baby.

"At least I know now she'll never be taken away. Right?"

I nod. "Of course."

"Everyone wins then." She sniffles over a sad smile. "Three complete families."

Almost. I look down at the baby in my arms. If this is George, his brother died in the fire, but at least their mother will get one child back.

"Gods, please stop that." Tomas snatches Gavan out of the air from where he sits across from me in the carriage. We use their Brasport names, as we don't know who is who yet.

"I've thrown you off a tower; you've *jumped* off a balcony because you knew I could catch you. Holding a baby up in the air really isn't anything to worry about."

But worry he has; hence, we took a carriage from Brasport to Lambridge so the little ones could sit in our laps. "I know, but they aren't even ours."

Ours. Someday, there will be babies who are. The sight of him sitting here being protective over these two as we bounce along the road is enough to make me want to slip onto his lap and expedite that. A smile rises unbidden to my lips. "So, you'll approve of me cradling our own children in the air?"

"If you must."

"Well, only having one at a time would make this easier. Perhaps it won't be necessary."

He cocks an eyebrow at me. "As if you only use magic when it's necessary."

I brush a breeze around his neck to prove his point, and his eyes flash with a promise to return the touch and more. Fortunately, we'll be alone again soon. The carriage comes to a stop, and Tomas hands me both boys so he can step out. He makes his way to the house while an attendant helps me out—unnecessary though it may be.

Breda's gaze meet mine from where she speaks to Tomas by the door, and her face pales. Words appear to gush from her mouth as her eyes plead with him. There's no need to pull the air to hear her. She doesn't want to see me ever again—my presence will always be a reminder of her son's death.

I pad toward them, but she doesn't look at me again. She keeps her gaze down as she says, "I mean no disrespect, Your Grace—"

"There is none. No need to worry about my feelings."

"I can't keep reliving my losses." She sniffles and wipes her eye.

"That's not why we're here," Tomas says.

"You said you need to talk to me about George."

"Yes, because we're bringing him back to you." Tomas gestures toward me, and I step to his side. His hand warms the small of my back.

"Strange magic was involved in George's disappearance," I say. "The clock of his life was reversed."

She looks down at the babies, one cradled in each of my arms. Her eyes focus in on Gavan's face, and her jaw drops. "Holy gods." Her chest heaves as she takes him from me with trembling hands. "George. My baby." Tears pour down her cheeks as she hugs him tightly and sobs openly.

Tomas takes hold of her elbow lest she collapse and leads her inside.

In Breda's state, I'm not sure how much she comprehends about the situation. Even if she weren't overcome with emotion, it's a difficult thing for any of us to understand. Still, we explain as best we can, little Parick curled up in my arms all the while.

You will be quite the surprise for your family. I imagine Richard will enjoy teaching his grandfather how to walk and run and play. We'll have repaired as much as we can, then it's on to our new lives as the future Queen and King of Alchos.

Chapter Fifty-Seven

Breathe in. Breathe out. It's all I focus on as Lucy weaves my hair into an elaborate style. The braids have braids within them, and I'm certain my hair has multiplied during the process, because there appears to be more of it than usual. Perhaps it's the sheer number of pins that give that illusion.

"There," Lucy says as she places a final one then steps back to admire her work.

"It's perfect," Mother says from her spot on the chaise next to Nina.

I step behind the dressing screen, and Lucy follows, cradling the gown with tender care. Stepping into it somehow makes the entire thing feel real. She lifts it up, and I slide my arms into the sheer sleeves. I've often found tightly drawn gowns confining, but as Lucy pulls the lacings, it feels like an embrace, as if the dress could keep me together and upright. When she's finished, I run my hands down over the golden boning and straps crisscrossing the bodice and lay the gold chains across my chest so they're spread just right.

Mother gasps when I return to her view. "Oh, Arabella. You already look like a queen."

"It suits you." Nina looks genuinely happy. Who would have thought it possible?

"Thank you."

"Are you ready?" Mother asks.

"I suppose so."

Mother can't presume *why* Kirnon has taken to such aggression against us, but a personal vendetta from her not marrying him can't be ruled out. Everything seems to be in a holding pattern, waiting to learn more or waiting for something else to happen seems to be the way of things. But this is one less thing everyone will need to wait for.

"I know what will help you relax," Nina says. "Grand Mama is having Etherlee prepared for us. We're leaving in two days."

I shake my head. "We cannot take our week at the shore with everything going on."

"Don't tell me you're going to become a bore now that you're the heir."

I roll my eyes at my sister.

"You all need it," Mother says. "You should go."

"Are you certain?"

"Yes, darling. The kingdom's problems will keep, and you aren't queen yet. Enjoy the time. You'll be bored to tears when you have to be my shadow afterwards."

Not long ago, I thought this year's week at the shore would be the finale of my love affair with Tomas. Then I was certain I'd never be able to step foot in the Valnora estate again without plunging into misery. Instead, it'll barely be the beginning of my life's romance—a joy I couldn't have hoped to experience in the midst of our mayhem. Perhaps Nina and Mother are right. The idea makes me feel better already.

The three of us make our way down to the palace's main level, and Father lights up when we appear at the top of the stairs. "Arabella, you are a vision."

I embrace him and glance at my brothers over his shoulder. Marcus looks content. This wasn't his initial goal, but enough has worked out in everyone's favor, I suppose. Rylan avoids looking at me. We'll see how long that lasts.

Tomas keeps a reserved smile, but his eyes sparkle as they look me over. I offer him my hand, and he lays a tender kiss on my knuckles then loops my arm through his. We bring up the rear of the family procession to the stage in front of the palace.

I look up at him with satisfaction wrapping around me—I don't have to hide any of our looks, touches, or words. At least not around our families. Soon enough it'll be widely known. "You are about to be betrothed to the Heir of Alchos."

"Are you going to ask me if I've changed my mind again?"

I smirk. "No, it's much too late for that. You are quite stuck."

"It's my own fault. I had my chance."

"Indeed. Would you like to mourn the lost opportunity for a week at Etherlee?"

His eyes light up. "Are we still doing that?"

"Apparently."

"Well, since this invitation to the shore *isn't* written in blood, it sounds delightful."

We stop short of where my family is gathered, and I turn to look at Tomas one last time before our lives change forever. He takes my shoulders softly. "You're going to do great things, Bell."

"*We* are going to do great things."

He gives me a light kiss. "Congratulations, my love." He walks away to join his family in a nearby place of honor in the audience as I nod and turn to my family.

"Right then," Mother says. "It's time."

She leads us up the steps and takes center stage with Father. The twins stand side-by-side off to Father's right, Rylan and I to Mother's left. The roar of the crowd washes over us. A sea of people who look to us for protection, guidance, peace. They'll look to me, and I will not fail them. I glance down to see the Coyles front and center, beaming. I blink back tears, but this time, they're joyful ones.

Despite Grandmother's assertion, Mother addresses our kingdom with the regality of someone born for her role. They think I was, too. I'll have a lot to learn from her—the way she can enrapture thousands, the balance of showing love while maintaining authority. To be but an echo of the queen she is would be an accomplishment.

"It is with great pleasure that we present to you the future of our kingdom." My heart picks up at Mother's words. "The heir to the throne and next ruler of Alchos is Arabella, Princess of Air."

The excitement would be palpable even without my particular sensitivity to the air. The volume is enough to shake the trees as I step forward. To cheers and applause, I lower to my knees for the second-to-last time in my life. Queens only kneel to be crowned, then never again.

Mother steps forward, holding out the ethereal diadem. Metal twists and swirls as if blowing in the wind, and a perfectly clear diamond reflects light in rainbows in the front. "Do you, Arabella of House Exos, pledge yourself to the kingdom of Alchos, to keep her safe, just, and prosperous?"

"I do."

The crown settles onto my head, and I think of the cushion of air I had gifted Rylan. I don't want one—the weight of it should be felt.

"Rise, Princess Arabella, future Queen of Alchos."

The applause rises with me. Mother takes my hand. "All hail Princess Arabella."

"All hail Princess Arabella." It echoes against the palace and the buildings lining the promenade.

Then every man, woman, and child present bows before the two of us. My own sister drops to a graceful, low curtsy while my brothers, Father, and Tomas each take a knee, heads bent in deference.

"They bow to you," Mother says quietly, "in the faith that you will raise them up. Never forget your power comes from them."

I squeeze her hand. "I won't forget, and I won't let them down."

"I know, darling."

My family rises, starting a wave of people following suit before us. Bursts of dazzling light explode in the sky, drawing the crowd's attention upward. I glance at Nina, who winks in return.

For months, I've focused on endings. The end of the trials. The end of my betrothal. But for all those endings, there are new beginnings. This excitement has been a prologue. As I watch the colorful display in the sky, I know my story starts now.

EPILOGUE

Lillian turned the corner and rose to her toes to walk through the hallway that housed the King's study. Avoiding him was nothing new, though his foul mood in the wake of Jamys' passing amplified her motivation to not attract his attention. If he'd been sorrowful, this time might have united their family. But Urian didn't comprehend emotions as inane as *sadness*. The King's only feeling was bitter rage at the loss of an heir who would have added magic to his line. And disappointment that he was left with his daughter.

Hence, she kept the heels of her shoes from hitting the floor. This slowed her pace enough that an attendant strode past her and into her father's study before she passed it. Now she was still close when he received whatever message was being delivered and—

"Those gods damned idiots!"

The King's roar was like a bowstring to propel her faster. She might have been a successful ballerina for the way she could prance about on her toes. Her dance was cut short when she slipped into an alcove to listen for the reason behind this outburst. It would do her well to know before she was potentially part of any conversation about it. Not that she was generally expected to add much to conversations.

"They're putting that fucking whore on the throne?!" At least his temperament allowed her to hear from a good distance. The unfortunate messenger's response was not loud enough to reach her, but her father's end was enough to piece together what had happened.

Nina had already been eliminated from Alchos' competition for the throne, so Arabella must have won.

"Jamys would have been the King of Alchos!" Urian's words were punctuated by loud steps on the stone floor. The Princess could picture him spinning the dagger between his fingers as he always did when he was agitated. The blade had never seen a physical fight, only his internal wars.

Whether the King was angry about this turn of events due to the missed opportunity to install Jamys there as consort, or because he hated Arabella as he implied, was left to be determined. It would have been nice to think he wouldn't have had his son marry a woman he thought a whore, but the magic in her blood would certainly forgive all flaws.

That these flaws were machinations of the King's mind was also easy enough to assume. Lillian continued to her apartments, replaying her interactions with the Princess in her mind. Arabella had been nothing but kind and amiable to her. Jamys was besotted with her in a way Lillian never thought she'd see. He'd even played music for her. That secret had been tightly held by him for as long as Lillian could remember, and if he was close enough to her to...

A tear tumbled over her eyelashes, and she swiped it away.

Jamys was an exceptional brother, and Arabella would have been a lovely sister. Of course, Lillian could see why her father would have issues with the next Queen of Alchos. The way she dressed was certainly... Well, it made Lillian blush to think of it. The dress Ara had worn the night they found out about the siege in Dockerly—that displayed her long leg, the smooth skin of her back, and nearly exposed her breasts—would be enough to earn her the label of whore from Urian. Lillian's reaction to it was more akin to jealousy. Of Arabella, of course. That she had such freedom and confidence.

Lillian got to her apartment and collapsed onto the chaise. Had her corsets gotten tighter since they returned to Ceraun? Breathing was more difficult after the time spent in Alchos, since Jamys died and she became the heir to her kingdom.

"I wanted to prepare you, but there's no time," Anilla said as she and Lillian walked to the sitting room. "Your father was talking my ear off."

Lillian wondered what he gained from that as he doubtlessly wouldn't care about any response her mother might have.

"Princess Arabella won the trials in Alchos."

Lillian nodded. "Yes, I heard."

"Well, your father's fury over the loss of Jamys' betrothal has been reignited." Anilla's lips pursed then. Where Lillian was disappointed in her father's lack of care over Jamys' death, her mother was enraged. "Unfortunately, that means his sights are set on you again."

"It's not as if I can marry Arabella."

Her mother puffed out a laugh, and her expression softened. Lillian's heart twisted at the thought of how infrequent Anilla's smiles were now. "Consort may be out of his grasp, but there are still other magical heirs to be made."

Lillian's shoulders sank back as they entered the sitting room. This idea of her father's wasn't new. It was as old as it was ridiculous. Why would he only want *one* magical grandchild when he had two children to produce them? As if it were that easy.

Urian came in as the ladies sat on a sofa. "Lillian, we've learned that Elea has crowned Arabella as her heir." He dropped into the seat across from them, his eyes never leaving his daughter.

"That's probably causing quite a bit of excitement in Alchos." It was the most neutral thing Lillian could think to say. All three kingdoms in the continent had female heirs now which must feel like a fork scraping a plate to her father.

"Indeed. And you could have been her sister."

Lillian wasn't bold enough to say Arabella could have been his daughter. That shade of purple wouldn't look good on his face. "It is tragic," she said instead.

"Quite," Urian said with all the stoicism of someone who only knew the technical definition of the word tragedy. "However, our connections to that family needn't be lost."

A shallow breath was all she could take in this gown, so it would have to do to fortify her. "Rylan's betrothal is still out of the Queen's and King's hands."

"Yes, because they are idiot romantics."

Anilla sighed. "Urian."

"It doesn't mean the girl couldn't seduce him," her father said as if she wasn't present. It was almost comforting for how familiar it was.

"Darling, I don't foresee Prince Rylan choosing to marry into our court."

Now her mother was the only one who could come to Lillian's defense in such matters. Last time, Jamys was there to talk their father out of sending Lillian along for the Exos royal tour. The pragmatic reasoning that Jamys would lose time with Arabella to be his sister's keeper was something Urian could accept. Their betrothal was a delicate blossom that could have easily been destroyed by Ceraun's strife. Not that it mattered in the end. Still, without such justification, her father would have shoved her to the sides of either Prince Rylan or Prince Marcus in a heartbeat. Such a plan seemed to be returning to the forefront of his mind.

"Rylan wanted to be king." Urian took the wineglass offered by a servant. "He could still be a king."

"It would have to be initiated by him," her mother said, "and I don't think he will."

Rylan rather frightened Lillian, but there was no reason to voice that. Urian wouldn't care if he married off his daughter to a man whose ground-rattling temper made her cower. He'd probably consider that a point in Rylan's favor. It was a blessing that Anilla was right, and Rylan would not choose Lillian of his own free will. The only way to secure a marriage with an Alchosian royal would be through a contract. Why else would any of those powerful, outspoken, beautiful people want to stick themselves with the cloistered, quiet girl she was?

"He should be looking for a replacement for his crown," the King said. "If this doesn't strike him as a prime opportunity, he's a conceited fool thinking Ceraun isn't grand enough for him."

"And he may be,"—Anilla's voice was soft—"however, that will be his loss."

"There's Marcus then," Urian said.

Another too-shallow sigh pressed Lillian's ribs into her corset. Marcus wasn't intimidating the way Rylan was. The Prince of Earth radiated raw power in a way that always felt it was on the brink of bursting. Marcus, on the other hand, always appeared to be in control. Even when he was about to drown in the first trial, he was focused and composed. His expulsion from the competition after that was a mystery to Lillian. Her own father would have applauded the use of threatening self-destruction to manipulate someone.

However, nothing about Marcus' soothing calm or quiet confidence or piercing dark eyes mattered. He probably hated her, because his twin did. The many reasons being with Marcus would be horribly awkward made her shudder. These, too, were reasons her father would not take into consideration.

"If you wish to ask Elea and Gratian about it," Lillian said, "of course I'll do whatever is required of me."

It wouldn't matter. The Exoses had more say in their lives, and Marcus would certainly turn down such an offer. The sting down her middle was still her corset, not preemptive hurt from the expected rejection.

"Of course you will," Urian said in a way that made it seem her unnecessary agreement offended him.

She didn't need to agree to anything. Her opinions were not relevant.

Lillian knew as well as her father did that she would do whatever they asked of her. Like a good princess.

Tensions between kingdoms rage on as Marcus attempts to calm the waters.

Dive in to the next installment of the Elements of Royalty series for more tempestuous twists and another steamy romance.

Find *Prince of Water* at https://nataliewritesthebooks.com/

Acknowledgements

Thank you, reader! I hope the time you spent in this world brought you smiles, laughter, swoons, and (sorry) maybe tears. *Princess of Air* would not exist or have finally been published if it weren't for the amazing team I've been fortunate enough to surround myself with.

Nicole Bailey, obviously I wouldn't even exist without you, much less write and publish books. Thank you isn't enough, but thank you... for all of it.

My agent, Jessica Reino, who loves on my books just as hard as she champions them. Thank you for crowning me "the queen of breaking readers' hearts" for this one.

Milly at Gray Plume Editing for an incredibly thoughtful edit that dragged the words out of me because apparently readers can't just read my mind.

Alexa at The Fiction Fix for a thorough line edit and proofread.

Huge shout out to Stefanie and the Seventhstar team for the beautiful cover and custom crown.

Megan and Robin, since you aren't chickens in this book, I will name you here. Thank you for being the first readers. Eating popcorn while you freaked out over stuff (and somehow chose the wrong guy again, Megan) was very entertaining.

Libby and Shanna thank you for being my bee and honey. (And sometimes my ass.) Your unwavering support means the world to me.

Gabby, you are the cheer captain, but you still belong with me.

Thank you to everyone in my family who bought this book to support me but DID NOT READ IT BECAUSE YOU BETTER NOT HAVE.

About the Author

Natalie has a bookcase with a ladder and is on a texting level relationship with her local indie bookstore owner, so her life had peaked. But then she quit drinking coffee and alcohol so she can still be miserable enough to write books.

Natalie's journey through genres is a dance of witty banter and captivating narratives. Her young adult dystopian series, *Falling & Uprising*, is a TikTok star. Her repertoire spans from the intricate realms of science fiction and fantasy, where her name is synonymous with imaginative escapism, to the heartfelt and humorous lanes of contemporary romantic comedy, set to debut in 2025 under the pseudonym Natalie Acosta.

Join her newsletter or follow her on social media for updates on her cats. And her books maybe... if that's what you're into.

https://www.nataliecammarattabooks.com/contact